Before the Coming Dawn

Other Books by Steven

Under a Waning Moon, Book 1 of As the Starlings Fly

Also read about Steven's role in uncovering the story behind the top-secret crash of the plane en route to Area 51 in *Silent Heroes of the Cold War Declassified.*

Before the Coming Dawn

AS THE STARLINGS FLY BOOK 2

Steven L Ririe

Groundswell Books

Copyright © 2025 Steven L Ririe

All rights reserved, including the right to reproduce this book, or portions thereof, in any form. No part of this book may be used or reproduced in any manner whatsoever without written permission from the publisher, except in the case of brief quotations embodied in critical articles and reviews. The views expressed herein are the responsibility of the author and do not necessarily represent the position of the publisher. For information or permission, visit StevenLRirie.com.

Cover design by Miblart
Author photo by Rick Fowler Photography
Interior print design and layout by Marny K. Parkin
Ebook design and layout by Marny K. Parkin

Published by Groundswell Books

·Groundswell·
Books

ISBN Paperback 979-8-9925832-3-6
ISBN Hardback 979-8-9925832-4-3
ISBN eBook 979-8-9925832-5-0

To the inspiration we all receive from above. Much of what lies within these pages comes from that insight. Often, I woke in the early hours of the morning with strong impressions about even the smallest details of the story. The twists and turns revealed themselves along with the wisdom garnered along the way. I had only to place my fingers on the keyboard and bring the story to life.

Acknowledgments

My profound thanks to Eschler Editing, Michele Preisendorf, and others who lent their talents in polishing my words and preserving the message I wish to convey.

A Note from the Author

If you find yourself in New Harmony, Indiana, and look north, you won't see a large mountain. The only Mount Erebus in Indiana is the one found in this story. In Greek mythology, Erebus is a place of darkness in the underworld on the way to Hades. Similarly, if you could go back to just before the American Civil War, a time many people believe mirrors the divided world we live in today, and scan the sky for Starlings, you wouldn't see any. It wasn't until 1890 that sixty European Starlings were intentionally brought to America and released in Central Park, in New York City.

Both the mountain and the Starlings are fictional. Together, they make up an allegory, and Mount Erebus and the Starlings, as found in these pages, are but metaphors. There are many additional metaphors, and I hope you enjoy sorting out their meanings.

Part 1

Rise of the Monster

Chapter 1

Perched on the ridge south of the gorge, the beast peered off into the distance at the valley below. His keen eyesight surveyed the town beyond the pastures and fields, the faint sound of a bell ringing and the procession of humans moving to the east end of town igniting his curiosity.

What is this?

Hungry to know, he sprang from the ridge, then followed the creek out of the gorge as it bent around fields and swung toward where the humans gathered. He moved swiftly through the vegetation, then crept slowly, crouching when exposed. The crowd entered what appeared to be a grove of trees on the outskirts. Here, the creek ran alongside the tree line, allowing him to approach undetected.

He'd intended only to keep an eye on the town, anticipating retaliation for something he had no part in doing. But the strange gathering of humans triggered a memory, something he recognized but lacked the words to explain. He hoped to reclaim a connection to his humanity by watching. He drew close enough to hear them breathing. Then, concealed by the brush that skirted the creek, he watched without fear of being seen while scanning the crowd.

Where were the humans who'd murdered the boy—those who would cause Jonathan harm with their deceit? He observed those who gathered, one by one, waiting for their heads to turn, looking for familiar faces.

Too many, too closely gathered.

Jonathan sniffed the open air. A good breeze found him downwind. He drew in another breath and held it, searching for a scent. *Yes*, he thought. *They're here.*

As he followed the scent, he noticed a young woman, her expression of grief unmistakable.

She sorrows.

Then he saw the pinewood box and looked once more at the woman's anguished expression.

He finally knew what this was—a burial. The young woman must belong to the murdered boy. This was his funeral.

Jonathan felt empathy. He looked hard at the grief-stricken woman and the young man comforting her. Nearby, others mourned the dead and newly departed. Jonathan's eyes drifted through the crowd until he saw them. Behind the grieving woman stood two men, their expressions blank.

There you are. Liars. Murderers.

He tasted the breeze again.

Yes, now I see you.

He'd found what he'd come for, which was enough for now. He would return later, preferring to hunt in the dark. A gentle breeze stirred the leaves, allowing him to retreat undetected, and he was gone.

Chapter 2

From the top of the steps of the town hall, the mayor looked across the street to where sheep attended to the trimming and fertilizing of the town park. He organized his thoughts while rubbing his belly, akin to scratching his head.

"Place it here," he said, tapping his foot. "I want everyone to see me."

Weston Riley, the youngest and most recent council member, listened carefully to his instructions.

"While you are at it," continued the mayor, "have Sheriff Weasley block the street on either side."

"Pardon me, sir."

"What is it, Weston?"

"It's not related to this, but . . ." Weston hesitated.

"Go on and be brief about it. I'm a busy man!"

"Yes, sir."

"Well?"

"It's just that . . . Should Hyrum, Ernie, Jonas, and I be worried? I mean—"

"Why wouldn't you be?" the mayor interrupted. "You heard Bronson Parrish. His grievances included the entire council, and, if I remember right, that's all of you. So, just imagine I lose the election. You, as well as the rest, will be finished. Ruined. No more town council as far as you're concerned. I suggest you make sure my campaign posters are on every corner."

Weston tripped over his words. "I certainly will, sir, but what I meant to say was, should we be worried about the monster? The voices speak of being torn apart, and the Wallaces and Christian, well—"

The mayor interrupted again. "Shear's boy?"

"Yes, sir. Him. We were schoolmates. I knew him well."

"There have always been monsters, Weston. No different now. Your immediate concern should be the election. Worry about that."

"Yes, that is a concern, sir. I agree. Perhaps I should make other plans just in case?"

"No!" barked the mayor. "Stop worrying." He smirked.

"But you just said, sir . . ."

"Listen here, Weston. I know what I just said. Don't I always manage things to our benefit?" The mayor placed a hand on Weston's shoulder. "Just do as I say. Start with this." The mayor resumed tapping his foot. "Fetch the podium and put it here."

"Of course, sir," said Weston. "I'm on it."

"And get my damned posters up! Should have been up the moment Bronson announced his intention to unseat me." The mayor's nerves were frayed. He watched as Weston beat a hasty retreat, nearly tumbling down the steps. He then hooked his thumbs in his suspenders, took a deep breath, turned around, and walked inside.

"Beatrice!" he shouted, then sighed, realizing there would be no answer. He had yet to understand why Martha let her go without discussing it with him. He passed her office and peeked inside, where paperwork flooded the desk, campaign posters filled one corner, and her chair sat empty. Growling to himself, he retreated to his office.

Sunlight streamed in from the window, warming his back as he sat alone, relishing the rare moment of quiet. Finally, overcome with weariness, he laid his head on his desk. He needed the boost coffee provided but was too lazy to make himself a cup. Without Beatrice, there was no coffee to keep his eyes from drooping. And so he commenced snoring, unaware that his fatigue was not all that called him to slumber.

The voices whispered to him in verse, spinning webs inside his head, capturing his thoughts.

Sunlight grants sufficient harvest.
Nonetheless, stoke the fires of doubt.
We'll fan the flames of dreaded hunger
Until their fear comes gushing out.

Strip from them precious sovereignty.
Corral them into forced dependency.
Mold their fears, and you will see,
Submission is their tendency.

Execution is not murder.
Your will is law and common need.
Give into Ares for your power.
Make your enemies kneel and bleed.

Oh, glorious day! Oh, glorious day!
What a glorious day for you.
Our warning is but a courtesy.
You know what you must do.

The mayor's eyes snapped open, scanning for the unseen presence. His initial panic turned into steely resolve. Their alliance made him powerful.

And so he reasoned with himself. *I no longer need to deal with my problems in the dark of night, hiding my intentions. I am the law, justified by any means. I set the sun free and staved off starvation. I am the savior of New Harmony, incapable of murder, vindicated by the necessity for the common good. I am the law, and there is no guilt in execution.*

His conscience numb, he addressed the unseen presence openly. "It was you who brought the monster," he stated as if he'd recently discovered the knowledge. "The monster *is* useful, useful indeed. It is clear to me now. You could have made the ground quake or sent a plague. Either would've been beneficial, but the monster is the courtesy sent to grant me the continued fortune I deserve. From crisis, control, and by means of control, power. Great power."

Deep within the mayor's brain came a whispering so quiet it might have been lost in the background, jumbled with thought. But he heard it.
Yesss.

Chapter 3

Marco left home early the following day, his medical bag in hand. Instead of walking to his office, however, he headed to the oldest neighborhood in the center of town and the dark-green house with white shutters, where he knocked and waited.

"Around back!" came a voice from within, one he didn't recognize. Marco stepped off the front porch and made his way to the rear of the house. The back door stood slightly ajar. "Come in!" someone said from inside.

Just inside stood Lamont LeFevre, staring at Marco.

"You're Mr. LeFevre."

"Yeah, and you are Shear's boy, the doctor. What about it?"

"Forgive me, sir. I'm looking for Mr. Parrish. Have I the wrong house?"

"Nearly so, but not quite. Bronson's here. Follow me. And, Doc, from now on, whenever ya extend us the pleasure of yer company, never come from the street. Enter from the back door and don't be seen. Applies to my house as well."

"You live next door, Mr. LeFevre?"

"Yep, only one house. That'd be mine."

"I'll try and remember, sir." Marco followed LeFevre through the house. They entered the front parlor, where Bronson sat with a broad smile, his scruffy, gray Irish wolfhound, Old Coot, curled at his feet.

"Come in, Marco. Come in. Never mind LeFev. Might you diagnose his paranoia now that you are a doctor—or so I've heard? I must have done a swell job as your teacher. Goodness gracious, you've done well."

"Yes, sir. I was your student for two years."

"I was thinking three, but all right."

"Only two, Mr. Bronson." Turning to LeFevre, Marco said, "And I'll come through the back door from now on."

Bronson dismissed the notion. "No need for that."

"There most certainly is," LeFevre insisted. "I keep tellin' ya we're dealin' with killers. Precautions are in order."

"Hmm, I agree," said Bronson. "Even so, perhaps you're slightly overdoing it?"

"Hell no!" LeFevre said adamantly. He turned and looked at Marco. "Now on, back door. Understood?"

Marco nodded.

"Enough of that," said Bronson. "What can I do for you, Marco? I'm assuming this isn't a social visit." Coot jumped on the couch and onto Bronson's lap, his wet nose nudging him for a good scratching.

"I wish this were a social call," said Marco.

"Well then, please sit. You as well, LeFevre. You're making me nervous."

Marco quickly obliged, sinking into the well-worn couch, a puff of down floating into the air. He turned to see LeFevre sitting on the floor. "Mr. LeFevre, have I taken your seat? There's room here on the couch."

Bronson and LeFevre both attempted to answer, but Bronson won the draw. "The comfort of my couch corrodes his rugged manhood. He prefers the floor. Don't you, LeFev?"

"Sharin' a couch with you is what corrodes my manhood."

Bronson reacted with a quick smile, then returned his attention to Marco. "Truly sorry about your brother."

LeFevre nodded. "Condolences."

"Much appreciated, both of you," said Marco.

"To the point of your visit," said Bronson. "What brings you?"

"A favor, Mr. Parrish."

"A favor? What sort of favor and for whom?"

"Emmy. She asked a favor of me."

"Emily Hampshire, I presume. And what favor is that?"

"To kill the monster, the one that killed my brother."

"And you said what, exactly?" asked Bronson.

LeFevre grinned. He liked where this conversation was headed.

"I told her I would and intend on doing just that."

"Hmm." Bronson sighed and scratched Coot behind the ears.

"Hell yeah, he did," said LeFevre. "Killed his brother. We'd do the same."

"Maybe," said Bronson. "But we're talking about a monster, not a man. Why not allow the sheriff to handle it? With any luck, the creature will do us all a favor."

"Killed his brother," LeFevre stressed. "He's gotta do what he promised."

Marco agreed. "I'm going to kill it, Mr. Bronson."

"So why are you here?" Bronson stopped scratching, and Coot whined.

"Well, I figure you'll help me, perhaps both of you."

"Marco," said Bronson. "I know it was your brother, but what you're asking . . ."

"Mr. Parrish," Marco interrupted. "Since the sun returned, the town thinks the mayor is some sort of deity. But if we, you and me, and Mr. LeFevre, kill the monster, people will see the mayor isn't the only one who can protect New Harmony. People fear Mayor Owen. They need a reason to believe they can shake off that fear. Once they see past it, you're sure to win the election, but not unless people see the mayor for what he is—limited in what he can do for them and what he can do to them."

"He's right," LeFevre interjected. "That's what I keep tellin' ya. Yer bound to win, but first—"

"But not with the monster scaring people—that it?" asked Bronson.

Marco leaned forward. "Do you believe the mayor made the sun appear?"

"No, I don't," said Bronson.

"But the town does, and that's the problem. And now people believe only he can save them. Do you follow me?"

Bronson slowly nodded. "I suppose I am."

"Anyone can kill the monster except the mayor," said LeFevre. "Doesn't have to be you, me, or the doc here, only that the mayor can't get the credit."

"Exactly, Mr. LeFevre," agreed Marco. "And, gentleman, I'm not a hunter, per se. Squirrels and weasels, perhaps, but a monster? No. So I've come for your help. Help me organize some men. And if we kill it, by my reasoning, the town will stop obsessing and get back to normal. The election may reflect that. So we need to eliminate the monster, and then you, Mr. Parrish, must win the election so New Harmony can rid itself of the mayor and sheriff."

"Careful, lad," said Bronson.

"Careful nothin'!" said LeFevre. "Boy's right. The town fears the mayor but even more so the monster, for now at least. First we get rid of the monster, and then we rid ourselves of the mayor." Turning his attention to Marco, LeFevre said, "One stipulation and ya got yourself a deal."

"What is it, Mr. LeFevre?"

"I get to put its head over my fireplace."

Marco agreed without hesitation. "Deal."

Bronson's brow furrowed. "No, no. No deal!" he said. "You're not hunting the monster alone, just the two of you. Besides, what are you suggesting, LeFev? What exactly? If you two fail or die in your attempt to kill the monster, do you intend for me to kill the mayor?"

"Win the damned election and don't worry yourself," said LeFevre, who then added, "but if'n ya don't win, I say, 'ballot or ball, the fifty-caliber variety. You choose.' The man's a murderer, and you know it. The town lives under his tyranny, and it's time we do somethin' 'bout it."

LeFevre stood, turning his attention to Marco. "And you, young'un, be here before sunup. And bring your rifle."

Marco stood, launching another puff of feathers into the air. "I'll be here!"

"Now, both of you, listen to me!" said Bronson. "I'm going with you. You can't face the monster alone."

LeFevre scoffed. "I've hunted grizzly bears west of the Rockies all by my lonesome. I'm not scared. Besides, I've got the doc here. Just do your part concerning the mayor. Let us busy ourselves with Wallace's beast."

Chapter 4

Bong, bong, bong. The school bell sounded shortly before noon. Repeating sets of three rings meant a call to action, mobilizing the volunteer fire department. With the threat of a monster, everyone, excluding children, felt the need to respond. People poured out of their places of work and homes as they came to see what emergency had caused the bell to ring. Quickly, the word spread that the mayor was about to make a statement.

As people arrived, they found Main Street blocked by horses and wagons. At the top of the steps stood the sheriff, barking orders from behind a podium. It wasn't long before the area in front of the town hall, Main Street, and the park across the street overflowed with people. Those who lived on the periphery, the many farmers on the outskirts, came on horses and wagons. Still, no one saw the mayor.

The mayor was late, or so the people thought. They became more agitated as the minutes ticked by. Then, packed together under the hot sun, they murmured to each other as tension rippled through the crowd.

Unbeknownst to them, the mayor watched from the comfort of his office nearby, his face obscured by the glare on the poured-glass window. He pulled a bourbon to his lips, letting it hang there before taking a sip and inhaling the vapor, which carried hints of charred oak and vanilla.

The anxious crowd, extending in all directions, gave him such pleasure. He could not suppress a smile. They waited for him. He saw the worry on their faces, knowing that as their savior, he would have them hanging on his every word.

It's my name they speak of, me they long for. I will keep them waiting a little longer.

The mayor heard a sweet melody in his head. *Oh, glorious day! Oh, glorious day!* Though alone in his office, he said aloud, "It's time!"

The crowd hushed as Robert Owen exited the building, stepped up to the podium, and looked around. In the park across the street, he spied Bronson Parrish. A smile brandished his lips. This was perfect.

"Quiet now!" yelled the sheriff, who looked over his shoulder at the mayor, perched at the podium, ready to speak.

"Good people of New Harmony," the mayor addressed the crowd, "accept my sincere apologies for bringing you out of your homes on this ever-so-sunny afternoon. But do you see the sun shining?" He lifted his hands as if absorbing the rays, then yelled, "I'm to understand the crops are growing again, as I promised!"

Some clapped, and some cheered. The mayor shot a glance at Bronson, and his chest puffed out.

He continued. "We may yet have a bumper harvest. However, we are not out of danger—not entirely. Of course, a scant harvest is always a concern, even during a typical growing season. But now, we must also face the uncertainty of a monster lurking about our borders. It is that threat I now address. As some of you know, I traveled to the capital to meet with our governor. I informed him of our need. For a moment, I believed that military assistance in dealing with the monster was assured. However, it became apparent during our conversation that such aid is impossible. It appears the state militia is stretched thin, says my friend Governor Willard, who has confided in me that he grows weak in health. There may soon be a need for a new governor, but let's not speak of my greater ambitions to serve the people of Indiana now. Instead, let me say I assured him that we, the people of New Harmony, are not weak in resolve or spirit. We shall overcome whatever challenges we face. I've promised my friend that we will not seek his assistance further. Though unable to help, Governor Willard sends his regards.

"That said, the council and I are devising a plan. First, let me extend my condolences to Shears." The crowd responded positively. All heads bowed in reverence, the gentlemen removing their hats and several ladies their bonnets, some taking handkerchiefs from their handbags.

"The loss of his son was a loss to us all. And therefore, we are resolved that no more innocent blood will be shed. And with our leadership, myself and the council as now presently constituted, we are confident we can keep you safe. The sheriff learned a lot from his encounter with the monster. With that knowledge, we are considering a way forward, a plan."

"What plan?" hollered Old Man Taylor. A murmur rippled through the crowd.

"Mayor!" yelled Norman McNeil. "How will you keep us safe?" At this, the crowd quieted, waiting for a response.

"Mr. McNeil, I'll discuss our plans soon, rest assured. Until such time, as a matter of business, the election fast approaches. Only eight days remain. I could initiate an executive order to postpone such due to the current emergency. However, I've decided not to. I'm certain that'll come as welcome news to Mr. Parrish."

The mayor smiled at Bronson and continued. "Each of you should now have a ballot. If not, it means you haven't checked your post office box.

On the morning of the election, you can drop your ballot in the locked box just inside the door of the town hall. Neither I nor the council will have a key. As in prior elections, that responsibility falls upon the sheriff, who alone will guard the ballot box.

"Per the charter, ballots received after Friday at 7:00 p.m. are invalid. No change there. The sheriff, I, Mr. Parrish, the council, and selected observers will open the box and count the ballots together.

"Putting that aside, may I remind you of more urgent matters? We still face starvation if the weather deems us unworthy or being torn apart by a beast that has already proven savage to our community.

Therefore, I urge that we stay the course and, as quickly as possible, put this election behind us. Now, remember! We are New Harmony, sons and daughters of pioneers and people of great faith and sacrifice. We follow in their footsteps. However, this is our time. Right now! We shall do it together, so follow me now. Follow me!"

A feeling akin to worship rippled through the crowd, their voices ringing loudly, chanting, "We are New Harmony!" And as the sound rose skyward, the mayor felt powerful. He continued. "I'd invite Mr. Parrish to share his brilliant plan to deal with the monster, but, sarcasm aside, I doubt he has one."

Bronson remained quiet, unprepared to challenge the mayor, at least not at that moment. Notwithstanding the mayor had not himself presented a plan.

Gratified by Bronson's silence, the mayor resumed his speech "How to deal with the monster—isn't that the question we're all asking ourselves?"

People hushed as he stepped back from the podium and waited, letting the question sink in. Once he had everyone's attention, he grabbed the podium in a powerful gesture and called, "We are New Harmony, and we are united! We will emerge victorious!"

Swept up in the excitement, the crowd erupted in cheers, hungry for more. The mayor winked at Abigail, whose smile curled up to the corners of her eyes.

"Now, I must caution everyone," he said, "and spread the word. There is no going north! The pass through the gorge is officially closed. It's far too dangerous, and nobody wants to see anyone else hurt. So leave the beast to the sheriff and me."

"It's all fine and good, Mayor," yelled Norman McNeil from the far side of the street. "But we don't know how safe we are. Based on the howling we heard the other night, the beast seems close. It could've been right here, in the town center!" The crowd stirred, remembering how loudly Wallace's beast had roared, nearly waking the whole town.

Boyd Kensington shouted, "Prohibiting us from traveling north may not be enough!" His argument incited others to protest the mayor's lack of action.

"Calm down! Now calm down!" urged the mayor.

The sheriff stepped forward, a scowl on his face, a hand on his sidearm. "Quiet!"

"Yes, please. Patience! We are near completing our plan," said the mayor. "For now, stay in your homes. And if you must venture out, don't go alone. For your safety, there is no going north while the council and I devise a plan. I repeat: the gorge is closed. So long as I am mayor, I assure you all will be safe. I promised the sun would shine, and did it not? Have you forgotten? Trust me. I will keep you safe!"

On cue, folks applauded, some even whistling. The mayor stepped back from the podium, waving and smiling. He looked at the sheriff and nodded. Taking careful note of any who might show disdain, they scanned the faces staring back at them. The number of people not thrilled with the mayor's plans was not insignificant, Bronson among them. What was significant was the intimidation. It was enough to keep quiet any who opposed him—just what the mayor counted on.

Chapter 5

Having left at sunrise, Marco and LeFevre approached the gorge. Behind them, off in the distance, they heard the school bell and knew people gathered at the town hall. And while the mayor duped the townspeople with his cunning, they arrived at their destiny.

"Mr. LeFevre?"

"Yeah, Doc?"

"I'm wondering, if we find the beast, how will we sneak up and kill it without being murdered?"

LeFevre peered over his shoulder and whispered, "Don't rattle your teeth."

Marco cocked his head to one side. "Huh?"

"Quietly," LeFevre added, still whispering. "We go quietly. And keep our nerves."

"That's the hard part," said Marco. "I'd feel more comfortable if we had a dozen or so men with us."

"Comfort ain't got nothin' to do with it, Doc. Bravery means you're willin' to accept whatever, even death, despite your fear. Ya do it cause some things are more important than you or me. There ain't nothin' more important to a coward than himself. That simple. Whatever we encounter beyond the gorge, we face it. The fact you ain't turned tail and ran says a lot."

"I keep my promises, Mr. LeFevre. If my *word* has no value, neither do I."

"Your promises mean more to ya than yourself. That's good ta know, Doc," said LeFevre. "If'n we find ourselves at the pearly gates, you and I will die knowin' we did our best." Lefevre patted the birchwood stock of his rifle, his finger finding the nicks and scrapes and the memories they conjured. "Now clear your head, boy. We've work to do."

"I'm ready," said Marco. "Whatever the outcome, whether death or glory."

"Yeah, Doc. Death or glory."

Just short of the gorge, they stopped, dismounted, and tied their horses to the branches alongside the road. "Don't tie 'em too tight, Doc, in case we don't return."

"All right."

Rather than applying a clove-hitch knot, Marco wrapped the reins around a dead branch twice as LeFevre watched. "That'll do, Doc. With Providence's blessing, we'll be back."

They then saw to the priming of their rifles. LeFevre finished first and watched as Marco tamped down the lead ball.

"Listen, Doc," said LeFevre. "First thing, if ya gotta reload, take a knee. Shoot standin' and try not shootin' over me. Till we got somethin' to shoot at, we gotta be quiet. We ain't in no hurry neither. Nice and slow. Nice and slow."

"Like our lives depend on it," said Marco.

"Yeah, like that."

Slowly, they walked side by side, the breeze at their backs. At this rate, it would take all day just to get through the gorge. They looked suspiciously at every bush and clump of trees, pointing their weapons as they went, knowing the attack could come at any moment. Neither dared speak, grateful for the sound of the stream muffling their footsteps crunching against the gravel.

There was something they failed to realize, however, something they couldn't conceal. It wouldn't matter how slowly or quietly Marco and LeFevre inched along. The breeze that flowed steadily through the gorge carried the sweet smell of their sweat, ensuring that the beast, a monster more terrifying than either could imagine, awaited.

Chapter 6

Not known for her compassion, Mrs. Owen had, nevertheless, shown a morsel of kindness by allowing Emily a day of mourning before returning to her classroom duties. Mrs. Owen did stress, however, that there would be no pay. Emily felt grateful all the same. Unfortunately, her students were less pleased with her leave of absence. Even one day with the tyrannical Mrs. Owen made them anxious for Emily's return.

Monday morning came quickly, with Emily due back at school. She walked somberly, missing Christian at every step. Then she waited quietly in her classroom for the day to begin. Finally, the bell rang, and her students came pouring in. No sooner had they taken their seats when several hands shot into the air.

"Oh, Miss Hampshire? Miss Hampshire?" Isaac, a youngster in the back, nearly jumped out of his seat.

Miss Hampshire, thought Emily, *never to be Mrs. Salvatori*.

For a moment, Emily lost her train of thought. Then she quickly steadied herself and addressed the young boy. "Forgive me, Isaac. What is it?"

"The monster—it can't hurt us, can it? It wouldn't come into town, would it?"

Other students lowered their hands, obviously intending to ask the same question. Emily didn't wish to frighten her students, but she didn't feel it appropriate to lie to them either. She struggled with how to answer.

"I don't know," she said honestly. "But there are many in town suited to protect us. And you children are our main concern."

Her thoughts turned to Marco and how she may have inadvertently sent him into danger. She excused herself and stepped into the hallway, not wanting her students to see the fear on her face.

What was I thinking? Had I thought only of revenge before considering the consequences?

She had to stop Marco, but hours remained before the final bell. She returned to her room and began devising a plan for leaving early when the bell rang inexplicably. Bong, bong, bong.

Ms. Woolhauser suddenly appeared at her classroom door, a sense of urgency in her voice. "Miss Hampshire, release the children immediately. Some of their parents are already outside. The mayor is about to speak." Ms. Woolhauser clapped her hands at the students. "Move along! You mustn't linger about, you older children. Hurry home without delay!"

Frightened, the children only stared. Never had they been sent home so unexpectedly. Emily forced a smile. "Hurry home, where you'll be safe. Stay inside and follow your parents' instructions. Tonight, read from Frederick Marryat's *Poor Jack*. We'll discuss it tomorrow morning. Now hurry along."

She moved against the crowd toward the center of town. Ahead lay Marco's office. She tried to open the door, but it was locked. She peered through the window, and when she saw no movement, she hurried across the street to the barbershop. There, Tommaso swept the floor, preparing to close and follow the crowd to see what had caused the bell to ring. His shoulders drooped, and he hardly acknowledged Emily when she entered.

"Mr. Salvatori!"

"Emmy?" He barely glanced up.

"Yes, Mr. Salvatori. It's me. Please tell me you've seen Marco."

"This morning, we leave together. Why?"

Emily's breathing grew shallow. "I may have done something I'll regret."

"What?"

She peered out the window and then back at him, lost for words, eyes cast downward.

Tommaso asked again, "What's wrong?"

Emily took a deep breath, steadying herself. "I asked Marco, at the burial . . . I . . ." She paused, not wanting to admit what she'd done.

"You ask him what?"

"A thing I shouldn't have."

"You tell me. It's all right."

"I shouldn't have asked him to kill the monster. I don't want him hurt or worse. Please tell me where he is so I can stop him."

"At his office. Try there."

"He's not there. I went there first. Could he have headed to the town hall?"

Tommaso's face reflected his concern. "No. The bell rings; I wait for him. He comes here first, always. Go to the stable. If Marco left, he took Rosso, our horse. If Warren's there, he'll know where to look."

"I'll go see! Thank you, Mr. Salvatori. Emily crossed Main Street a block south and headed toward the stable. The closer she got, the more fervently she prayed. *Please, God, let his horse be there.*

She rushed through the open doors amid the smells of manure and hay and went directly to where Tommaso kept the horse. But for the fresh straw scattered on the floor, the stall stood empty.

It can't be. Rosso must be here somewhere.

She hurried out back to the livery yard, where four horses stood in the sunshine. Rosso was not among them.

She came back in and slumped onto the wooden bench used for shoeing, feelings of despair overwhelming her, the spacious interior of the barn amplifying her loneliness.

A sudden scraping noise came from an open stall near the rear doors. Rising to her feet, she called, "Warren? Is that you?"

Christian's best friend looked over the worn, wooden slats dividing the stalls, pitchfork in hand. "Emmy? What are ya doin' here? The bell rang. You should be halfway to the town hall by now."

"I haven't time for that! Tell me, have you seen Marco?"

Warren looked at her with a dazed expression. "What's wrong?"

"Marco, where is he? Tell me, please."

"Can't be certain. Rosso was missing when I arrived this morning. Marco must have left early."

"Where?"

Warren shrugged.

Emily began pacing back and forth while biting her lip.

"What's goin' on, Emmy? You must tell me."

Chapter 7

As the afternoon sun crossed into the western sky, it hid on the far side of Mount Erebus. Little twilight remained, and both men felt a sense of urgency. LeFevre stretched his back while Marco swung his powder horn and ammo pouch to rest in front of him, just in case. He watched as LeFevre crept along, bowie knife strapped to his hip and beaver-skin pouch slung from his shoulder. Finally, they stopped at the river. LeFevre dug around in his pouch and pulled out two hard-boiled eggs and two apples.

"Gettin' late, Doc," LeFevre whispered. "Eat. Keep up your strength." He handed one of each to Marco. The apple was sour green, and Marco worried it would add to the acid in his stomach. He pocketed it to eat on the way home—he hoped. Marco then considered the egg but lacked an appetite. He slipped it into his ammo pouch.

"Getting' off the road here," LeFevre whispered, "walk along the river, real quiet-like."

They scooted on their backsides down an embankment and traversed the brush alongside the rushing water.

LeFevre tossed his apple core into the stream. Marco watched as the current carried it away.

Mr. LeFevre's right. I'd better eat. Marco reached into his bag and retrieved the egg. He peeled it, then bit into it. Powdery yolk blew out his mouth, too dry from nerves to swallow. He bent down, scooped up a handful of water, and drank. The egg went down more easily, but his stomach churned.

Near dusk, the gorge widened. Farther ahead, it opened into a meadow surrounded by woods.

"We're getting' close," said LeFevre. "Keep yer eyes open."

"Not too late?" asked Marco. "Sun'll be down in less than an hour."

"Come this far. Ain't no goin' back, Doc."

They moved methodically up the river when Marco began to fall behind, his nerves slowing him down. He forced himself to quicken his pace until he was close enough to see LeFevre stop. Marco inched his way closer, then waited. Suddenly, LeFevre motioned for Marco to get down. Marco knelt, the cold water from the creek soaking through his pants. He watched as LeFevre looked up and down the river, scanning the bushes. Marco's heart pounded in his ears. He willed it to slow, fearing the monster would hear it beating.

They both listened for any sounds above the churning of the water. Without warning, a critter scampered into the brush along the dry creek bed parallel to the water. They both jumped and swung their rifles around, peering into the bushes, their hearts beating against their chests.

A moment later, the stillness returned, leaving only the noise of the water bubbling at their feet. "Feel yer toes?" LeFevre asked.

"No, too numb. Do you feel yours?"

"Yeah."

"Huh, then why'd you ask me if I—"

"Shh." LeFevre looked back and whispered, "We're being watched." He raised his gun. Marco did likewise. "Come alongside me where ya can't shoot me. Remember, one shot, maybe. Steel your nerves and let it come for us."

Marco nodded.

LeFevre focused on a clump of bushes up ahead near where a tree had fallen in the creek. Something moved. The light had faded to shadows when he motioned for Marco to stay back.

One step at a time in the chilly water, gun raised, LeFevre slowly approached the log. A fawn sprung from its hiding place and quickly scampered away, darting into the brush around a bend in the river. Marco sighed in relief and turned to LeFevre only to see something huge come at the man, and then LeFevre disappeared to the sound of branches breaking and screams of pain.

Marco held up his rifle, afraid to shoot into the bush, fearing to hit LeFevre. He saw something move, too large to be human. He pointed the muzzle skyward, pulled the trigger, and squinted at the blinding flash that followed. The rifle kicked, and a fiery lead ball shot from the muzzle. Something moved off into the bushes, obscured in the dim light. Marco ran to where he heard the screams, but he couldn't see LeFevre in the twilight. He frantically climbed a grassy embankment, stumbling through the brush until he stood on the road.

He knelt, his cold fingers fumbling to reload. A lead ball slipped from his fingers and rolled into the grass, too dark to retrieve. He'd just pulled another from his ammo pouch when he heard something crash through the brush.

Out of the brush the monster leaped, hurtling into the young human and sending him tumbling. The beast was on top of him instantly, pressing down hard, trapping his prey against the ground.

Why does this human hunt me? I'm not safe anymore!

Keeping the boy pinned under his considerable weight, he stared into the fading light, snarling, his dark eyes looking for more men with guns.

Where are the others? You woke me, said men were coming. This one's but a boy!

A gravelly voice scratched its way into his thoughts. "Would you rather have us allow them to sneak up on you while you sleep in your putrid cave?"

"Where's your gratitude, beast?" said another grating voice.

The gravelly voice came again. "Yes. Where is your gratitude? We've delivered you a meal. It is time you eat."

Then he heard the low, raspy voice he most feared. "We hear your stomach growling and see you salivating. How can we see? Simple. We hold your fate. We are the inevitable. Your life is our yarn, as this human's life is yours to do with as you will. Sever it. Take your kill and eat!"

The monster stared hard at the boy struggling helplessly under his weight.

"Why did you kill my brother? Why?" the boy cried.

The beast's eyes widened.

Then, suddenly, there came another scream, one only the beast could hear. It was the cry of a woman, familiar yet distant in memory. "Don't, Jonathan! If you do this, there is no turning back, no redemption!"

The beast watched as tears pooled in the human's eyes.

"You killed my brother!"

The beast issued a guttural growl and shook his head back and forth, still angry. Then, slowly, his anger turned to pity, and he stopped thrashing about. Only then did he recognize the young man.

I know you from the burial of the murdered boy. Your brother? And now you believe I killed him.

Pinning Marco to the ground was a monster beyond description. In the faint light, Marco could see steam rising from the fur that covered the creature's head and shoulders. It's sharp teeth glistened in the moonlight, and the eyes of death bore down on him.

So this was how it ended. Marco squeezed his eyes shut and braced for the horror about to unfold. But the monster hesitated. The final crush of the windpipe didn't come. Instead, a terrifying moment passed before the wild breathing of the creature slowed and the crushing weight lifted off Marco's chest, allowing him to breathe more easily. He slowly opened his eyes, and for the briefest of moments, thought he detected intelligence in the black eyes staring back at him.

Marco could hardly comprehend what happened next. The monster sniffed him, then slowly backed away, shaking its head from side to side, its eyes never leaving Marco. Finally, with claws retracted, no longer threatening to tear him apart, the monster stood like a man, towering over him. Then, as quickly as the beast appeared, it disappeared into the night, leaving only the sound of the creek and the chirping of crickets.

Marco lay in the dirt in shock, his chest heaving as he slowly regained his wits. Stumbling to his feet, he called to LeFevre in little more than a whisper. "Where are you?" When he heard nothing, he called more loudly. "Mr. LeFevre!"

From somewhere behind him came a weak voice. "Over here!"

Turning around, Marco exclaimed, "You're alive!" He limped about, looking for LeFevre. "Are you hurt?"

"Over here!"

Marco finally spotted LeFevre trying to free himself from the thick vegetation. "I'm coming!" He broke through the hawthorn and gray dogwood and quickly aided in freeing LeFevre from the branches. "You look hurt. Let me help you." Marco examined him for injuries. "Where does it hurt?"

"Where doesn't it?" LeFevre gingerly tapped his right side. "Here, Doc. Mighta broke my arm and a rib or two."

"Hard to know, Mr. LeFevre, not until I can examine you in a proper light."

Marco carefully lifted his arm and noted that the humerus bone hadn't broken through the skin. "No protrusion, so that's good. More likely it's fractured, Mr. LeFevre." Marco tore his shirt and used the strips of cloth to secure the arm. Looking around, he peered into the dark. "Stay here."

A moment later, he returned with a stick and tied it to LeFevre's arm with the strips of cloth. "This will do for now," he said. "I can hardly believe we're alive. What was that?"

Lefevre groaned. "Coulda been anythin'. I never saw it. What about you?"

"Never mind that. First things first. I must get you out of here. It requires that I leave you to retrieve our horses. Stay here."

"You're not leavin' me. No, sir. Not with that thing out there."

"All right, then. Can you walk?"

"If ya help me. Nothin' wrong with my legs."

Marco draped LeFevre's good arm over his shoulder, and they slowly made their way back through the gorge. Soon, the rock walls narrowed, plunging them into almost total darkness.

"I know we set out early, Mr. LeFevre, but it's apparent we should have brought a lantern."

LeFevre groaned. "I'd prefer not to speak if that's all right with you."

"All right, Mr. LeFevre."

Carefully stepping so as not to trip, they wound their way through the dark, cold gorge. LeFevre began to shiver from shock, the chill of the wind, or both. Only then did they see a distant light piercing the dark and hear horses approaching.

Marco stopped to listen. "Someone's coming."

"Bronson?"

"No telling."

A lantern swung from a horseman's hand, the shadows on the rocky ridges on either side of them shifting in the light. A moment later, the lantern illuminated the face of Warren Sowell, their horses trotting behind him.

Marco felt a surge of gratitude. "Warren!" he hollered. "So glad to see you, friend."

"Likewise!" said Warren. "Yes, likewise!"

Chapter 8

Finished his speech, the mayor turned to see the sheriff herding the council inside, as per his orders. Meanwhile, the mayor stayed outside, receiving accolades and congratulations with the practiced grace of a seasoned politician.

"Pardon me, but I must excuse myself," he finally said. "I'm late for a council meeting." He shook a few more hands and then made his way to the front door.

An anxious Martha waited for him inside and shooed away the stragglers. "They're waiting, Robert."

"Good."

Together, they entered the chamber room, where the council members sat. Sheriff Weasley guarded the door. The mood in the room was pleasant. The mayor stood at the front, chest puffed, thumbs hooked in his suspenders. Martha took her usual seat.

As the mayor stared into the faces of the council, he could not help but think, *What a difference a crisis can make. Such lovely things!*

But the most pleasurable part for the mayor had been seeing Bronson Parrish in the crowd. *I hope Mr. Parrish saw how the people swooned over me. How foolish he must feel.* He nodded to the sheriff, who closed the door.

Martha pounded the gavel and announced, "Mayor has the floor!"

Robert looked into the eyes of each council member and grinned. "I suppose you're all rather confused, aren't you?"

There was no need to ask. The mayor could see it in their faces. "My sincere apologies. I suppose the time is now. I've things I must tell you, things you need to know, things I couldn't share until now. But I suppose the time has come. So take note—"

"Pardon me, Mayor," an anxious Jonas Becker interrupted, "but have you a plan? You do, don't you?"

The mayor's grin disappeared as curious eyes stared back at him.

"Don't interrupt me, Jonas. Of course, I have a plan."

In a show of support, Hyrum Blaylock piped up. "Of course, the mayor has a plan."

"Stop interrupting me, all of you, and listen."

The sheriff stepped forward, his brows drawn in a scowl.

The mayor shot him a look and shook his head, causing the sheriff to step back.

"Did you see how the people supported me? Do you believe that happened by coincidence?" Blank faces stared back at him. "Of course not. It's all part of a plan. And what's more, my plan *is* working. However . . ."

The mayor paused to accentuate the seriousness of what he was about to say. Then, when the room was deathly silent, he spoke in a little more than a whisper. "None of what I tell you leaves this room. Is that understood? That includes wives." He looked at Jonas and Hyrum. They solemnly nodded that they understood. Then, all watched as the mayor and sheriff exchanged glances, knowing precisely what was at stake. Everyone in the room knew the consequences of disloyalty.

"All right, then," said the mayor. "The time is at hand. I've been to the top of Erebus. Sheriff Weasley can attest."

A gasp filled the room, followed by curious looks.

He continued. "I didn't go on my account. Rather, I was summoned. I cannot say what I saw, but something is up there. Abigail Williams refers to them as guardians. I wouldn't refer to them as such, but they are our benefactors. And with their help, we cannot fail. But we also cannot let others know our secret, or it will be our undoing, our ruin. So, for now, all that is required is that no one goes up the mountain, and no one, I mean no one, ever attempts to harm the monster. Consider the vile beast protected. Consider it an arrangement that ensures our success—a deal, if you will."

With eyes wide and jaws dropped, the council members stared.

It was Weston Riley who drummed up the nerve to speak. "A deal? Is that what you said?"

The mayor sighed. "Those floppy things on either side of your head are ears, aren't they?"

"Well, yes, sir, of course. It's just that—"

"It's just what, Weston?!"

"It's that . . . I've heard it said that witches or something else, either good or, dare I say evil, reside on the mountain. Can you tell us which it is?"

"I cannot, Weston, but I don't believe they are evil, as one might assume. However, I suspect they are of very, very ancient origin and very powerful. I assure you I did my best to question them. And they clarified that they were not witches, even offering me proof, after which I made a deal to save the town. Do you suppose I've power over the sun, or that I can somehow save the crops? The very thought is ridiculous! But not with the arrangement I made to save New Harmony. It is within their power, and with the deal—yes, Weston, the *deal*, the very same I made with them—that they are, as Ms. Abigail Williams attests, our guardians."

An uncomfortable silence filled the room. Even Martha, the mayor's wife, appeared surprised and confused. The council members gawked at the mayor.

As before, Weston ventured to ask what they all wanted to know. "They, sir? So there is more than one of whatever they are?"

"Yes, Weston."

"But why spare Wallace's monster? It killed Christian Salvatori. We were schoolmates."

By this time, Martha had regained her senses and spoke in support of her husband. "You've all heard what your mayor has to say. Be grateful. My husband saved the harvest, and don't any of you forget it! He always does what must be done, as unwelcome or difficult as it may be. If he says the beast is off-limits, not to be hunted or hurt, that's it. I don't want to hear anything more!"

"But what about the election, sir?" asked Hyrum. "What's the use of saving the town if you lose?"

"It's been taken care of," said the mayor. "But listen to me. If I go to ruin, so do you. Any Judas Iscariot among you, it will be he who faces crucifixion. Do I make myself clear?"

The mayor looked at Sheriff Weasley, who in turn looked threateningly at each council member, conveying the necessity of their silence.

"Mayor, no Judas here. Not me," said Hyrum.

"Wouldn't dare," agreed Ernie.

Jonas quickly added his pledge of loyalty. "Not a word."

Weston came out of his stupor, seeing everyone staring at him. "Yeah, of course," he finally answered. "Never."

Round-bellied and with patches of moisture under his arms, Jonas stood. "I've supper waiting. Are we done here?"

The mayor nodded. "Long as there's food in your mouth, you'll never talk, will you, Jonas?"

Jonas laughed nervously, his belly jiggling despite the mayor's comment not being intended as a joke.

"Don't worry, any of you. I'll keep you all fed, and you, Jonas."

"Thank you, Mayor, sir."

The mayor nodded to the sheriff, who stepped aside and opened the door. "We're done here."

The council members quickly exited, along with Martha, leaving the sheriff and mayor alone.

"Have you any thoughts?"

The sheriff shrugged, thought momentarily, and asked, "What about Bronson? What do ya want me to do?"

"Nothing."

"But, sir. What about the election?"

"Taken care of, Weasley, but keep your ears open. Make sure no one talks."

"And Bronson, are you certain?"

"So long as he accepts defeat without a fuss, he's no threat."

"I don't know, Mayor. I don't care for the teacher."

Weasley, there's always plenty to worry about, and there will be more trouble after the election. One must remain in control. It never ends!"

"And the monster—couldn't that ruin everything?"

"I thought so Weasley, but no. The monster has already been useful, and I suspect it will be more so in ways I'm just now beginning to understand. Have patience, Weasley. A beautiful thing, the monster. You will see."

Chapter 9

Jonathan lay curled in the grassy meadow under the glow of the late summer moon. An easterly breeze blew softly, but his soul was in turmoil. He recalled the face of the human, the one who'd shot at him, the human he'd pinned to the ground.

He thinks I killed his brother. Will he come after me again?

His thoughts went back to when he'd stared through the branches and witnessed the murder.

"Scratch him up good," the murderer had said. "Make it look like the monster's responsible."

They're not wrong, he thought. *I am a monster. Who could believe otherwise?*

Jonathan's eyes narrowed as he remembered the pudgy man who'd appeared to give the orders and the tall, skinny one who'd done the dirty work. His lips curled as he ground his molars and snapped his canine and incisor teeth.

I will taste blood, after all. I will rip the meat from their bones. I will—

"Jonathan," came the sweet, familiar voice. "Jonathan." The innocent supplication in the sound of her cry triggered a memory. Suddenly, he felt as if he'd tumbled into a dream. Thunder boomed, and all around him was darkness. He relived the moment as a human riding a horse on a road that wound through thick woods, the way strangely familiar. He rode as fast as he could, worried and anxious—frantic, even.

I must hurry. Someone needs me!

He struggled to remember. *Where are they? Who must I reach?*

Suddenly, he felt the warmth of an invisible hand upon his cheek. It didn't matter that it was only a memory; it felt real.

A woman. I must reach a woman! Yes, she is in distress, and I must hurry! But who is she?

"Jonathan." Again, the familiar intonation released within him a swell of emotions he could not fully comprehend.

Who are you? I don't remember. Why can't I? Please, I beg you. Tell me!

He did remember one thing—the memory of what he'd felt for this woman, whoever she was. And at that moment, he experienced the most prized of human emotions—love.

And so he proclaimed his love in his heart and head, though he scarcely remembered her. The fact that he loved her was enough, at least for now.

Chapter 10

"Where are they, Coot?" Bronson worried aloud as his faithful pet sniffed the ground at his feet. "Should have been back by now." He looked impatiently out his back window. It was midnight, and everything was quiet. Not even the elm that shaded the back porch moved.

They shouldn't have gone. Pure foolishness. I fear they're dying somewhere out there, and for what? As he kept vigil at the window, he listened to Coot lapping at the water in his dish. Straining against the dark, he saw two figures emerge from the darkness, one leaning against the other. Quickly, he ran and opened the back door, allowing Marco and LeFevre to stumble inside.

Marco asked, "Where can I put him?"

LeFevre groaned, lacking the strength to look up. "Put me anywhere. Just set me down."

"Over here," Bronson led them to a bedroom where he readied the sheets.

"No," said Marco. "Broken ribs. He won't be able to lie down for some time. You have a soft chair?"

"In here." Bronson led them through the house and into the parlor.

There, the two helped LeFevre settle into Bronson's favorite chair, the more padded one with cotton and down.

"He'll be sleeping here," Marco said.

Bronson tossed Marco a pillow the young doctor stuffed behind LeFevre's head. "I need to examine your arm. This may hurt. It appears you've dislocated your shoulder."

"Hold on, Doc. Bronson?"

"What is it, LeFev?"

"Sip of whiskey, if ya don't mind. The doc here's 'bout to make me less comfortable."

Bronson left and returned with a small cup of Irish brew in one hand and the bottle in the other. LeFevre forced it down his gullet in a single gulp. "Another, please, if you don't mind."

Marco had begun examining LeFevre's injuries when LeFevre held up a finger. In a raspy voice, he said, "Give it a minute, Doc. My throat's burning." They all waited until LeFevre nodded. "All right. I can feel the effects. Do your worst, Doc."

Tears rolled down LeFevre's cheeks as Marco pushed and pulled.

"Mr. Parrish?"

"Yes, Marco."

"Water, soap, and a towel, please. And do you have clean linen? I need to wrap his ribs."

With his good arm, LeFevre held up an empty cup. "And more of this while you're at it."

Bronson went back and forth, bringing this and that for nearly an hour, until LeFevre emptied the whiskey bottle. Then, finally, they all sat back and relaxed.

They remained quiet until LeFevre broke the silence. With a pained face, he shook his head. Unsolicited, he answered the unspoken question. "No, Bronson."

"No, what?"

"No, we didn't kill it."

"Mr. LeFevre is right, Mr. Parrish," said Marco. "We're fortunate to be alive."

LeFevre started to cough but suppressed it. He knew enough not to cough with fractured ribs, but after a minute or two, he couldn't suppress the urge and groaned at the resulting pain.

Bronson turned his attention to Marco. "What about you? You hurt?"

"Minor scratches, light concussion. I got the wind knocked out of me pretty damned good. Mr. LeFevre, here, he got the worst of it."

LeFevre dropped the empty cup onto the wooden floor, and with his good hand grabbed Marco's arm and drew him close. "Doc," he said. "The vultures—they should be pickin' our bones right now. It felt like bein' trampled, caught in a stampede. Then I heard your rifle. Must a hit it, or scared it, or somethin'."

"No, sir. I did none of those. As you heard, I fired my rifle. I hoped to scare it off you. My aim was such that I dared not risk hitting you, but it didn't retreat as I hoped. After it took you, it came for me, knocking me to the ground and holding me there. I stared into its eyes, empty and cold as death, while it breathed hot in my face. I'll never forget it. Then there was something I can't explain, something I saw. Though we couldn't understand one another, it somehow felt like we did. And then it left for no reason, or none I'm aware of. Just left me lying there, and it was gone."

"You don't suppose you frightened it when you shot at it?"

"No, Mr. Parrish. I can assure you it was not frightened at all."

"Killed your brother yet left you two alive? What sense can there be in that?"

"None," agreed Marco. "But it is what happened."

Bronson leaned forward and cleared his throat. "Marco, I hesitate to put forward this question . . ."

"What is it, Mr. Parrish?"

"Just a thought."

"And that is?"

"Well, it's about your brother . . ."

Marco appeared confused. "What about him?"

"Did you examine him the night it happened?"

"Of course I did."

"Your brother's injuries, what you saw . . . were they . . ." Bronson hesitated, uncertain how to proceed.

Thankfully, Marco understood. "Mr. Bronson, if you are asking whether Christian's injuries are what I would expect if the monster killed him, then I must consider it for a moment."

"That is what I'm asking, yes."

Bronson and LeFevre waited as Marco thought.

Finally. He took a deep breath and shook his head. "No, his injuries were not what I would expect after my encounter with the beast. Christian's skull was fractured but at the back of the head. And if I recall, there were scrapes on his face and chest but not his arms." Marco held his arms and hands so Bronson and LeFevre could see his scrapes and bruises.

Marco continued. "As you see, my brother's abrasions were not what I would expect from defensive wounds. And why a broken neck? Come to think of it, there were no claw or teeth marks, nothing to indicate an animal had anything to do with his death. You were right to inquire, Mr. Parrish. It certainly does raise questions."

Any tact on LeFevre's part had washed away with the whiskey. He had something to add to the conversation and lacked the good sense to choose his words carefully. "I saw the carcass of old man Taylor's bull, clawed and torn, guts ripped out, blood everywhere—a gruesome sight. There were cuts and slashes, not scrapes and bruises, and chunks of meat and ribs torn out, chewed on, and left in the dirt."

"That's enough," said Bronson.

"No, wait, Mr. Parrish. I want to know what Mr. LeFevre is getting at."

"It's simple, Doc. If that thing we saw in the gorge killed your brother, you'd know it."

The conversation left Marco stunned. Shoulders slumped, he stared at the floor.

"I'm sorry, Marco," said Bronson. "I can only imagine what you're feeling. What is certain is that there is nothing left for us to solve tonight. Go home. Take rest. I'll look after LeFev. But before you go, keep what happened in the gorge to yourself. So far as anyone knows, neither of you went north, especially intending to hunt Wallace's monster."

Marco and LeFevre both stared, confusion written on their faces.

"What for?" asked LeFevre.

"While you were away, the mayor ordered the gorge closed. No going north, and no hunting the monster. I should add that he threatened everyone—or at least anyone who even thinks of hunting the monster."

"What's the sense in that?" LeFevre groaned. "And why hasn't the sheriff formed a posse?"

"Mayor doesn't want anyone else hurt, or so he says. The sheriff will incarcerate anyone entering the gorge, supposedly for their own good, so keep it to yourselves."

"Look at me," said LeFevre. "How am I to explain all these bandages?"

"You won't have to," said Bronson. "You're staying with me until you're better."

Chapter 11

Marco slowly opened the back door and crept inside, trying not to wake his father. Fumbling around in the dark, he located the table before quietly setting down his rifle and gear. A faint light emerged from the sitting room, along with voices.

Emmy? What's she doing here at this hour?

Swollen, puffy eyes fixed on Marco as he entered the sitting room. Emily rushed toward him and embraced him before slowly letting go, tears streaming down her face. He didn't care that he was tired, sore, and beaten. He'd somehow survived an encounter with the monster and was now surrounded by those he loved most. Marco looked at his father, now also on his feet. Tommaso's expression of relief and joy matched his own.

Emily held his hands in hers. "Thank goodness you're alive." Then she gasped. You're hurt!" She let go, stepped back, and looked at his bruised face. Leaning forward, she touched the bruising on his forehead and then felt his arms and hands, seeing the wounds there.

"I'm fine, Emmy. Mr. LeFevre fared worse." He slumped onto the couch, so tired he could hardly stand. Emily quickly sat down beside him while Tommaso stood watching, waiting for Marco's strength to return enough for him to tell them where he'd been and what happened.

Finally, Emily asked, "Did you go north? Marco, I'm so sorry! I should never have asked you to risk your life. I had no right." The room went quiet as she and Tommaso waited for Marco to answer.

His eyes fell to the floor, and he became emotional, overcome with shame. "No, Emmy. It is I who should be sorry."

"For what?" Emily stared intently, waiting for an answer.

"For having disappointed you. I failed. The beast lives."

More tears filled Emily's eyes as she gently lifted his chin, turning his face toward hers. "I don't care about that. I should never have asked that of you. It is I who am sorry. Will you forgive me?"

"Nothing to forgive. I went for no other reason than for Christian to rest in peace. But now I'm not so certain my anger isn't misplaced."

Tommaso appeared confused. "Why, son?"

"I'm left questioning, Papa."

"Questioning? What questions?"

Tommaso and Emily both stared at him.

"I'm left questioning whether the monster is a killer. If it were, I wouldn't be here. It had to know I wanted to kill it. I even shot at it, yet I am essentially unhurt, sitting here safe, with you, at home. But why? I stared into its eyes, resigned to my fate—never seeing either of you again—when it did something I could never have imagined."

Silence filled the room as Tommaso and Emily waited to hear the rest of what happened.

Emily finally asked, "What was it?"

"Mercy? Yes, that's it. I was shown mercy."

Tommaso stood. "You're home, safe. That's all that matters. It's late, and poor Emily's been here all night. Have you the strength to see her home, son?"

"Of course, Papa."

Tommaso excused himself, but before leaving the room, he turned to face Marco. "You did what you had to, and I'm proud. Now don't you ever do it again! It's in God's hands now, so let it be. And, you, young lady," Tommaso smiled at Emily, "you're family. Always."

"Good night, Mr. Salvatori, and thank you for staying up with me and keeping me company."

A glow in the east announced the coming of a new day. Crickets chirped a soothing melody for the sleeping birds tucked away in their nests, soon to awaken with the rising sun. Marco and Emily walked in silence, side by side, past houses with curtains drawn over darkened windows. The stillness of the early morning assured them they were alone, perhaps for the first time.

Emily whispered so faintly as to be nearly indiscernible. "I lost your brother, and somehow the thought of losing you . . . I don't know whether I could bear it."

"But you didn't, Emmy. I'm here."

For a moment, Marco allowed himself to feel the warmth of her words, smell the fragrance of her presence, and lose himself in the hazel of her eyes. Then, just as quickly, he reminded himself that she'd chosen Christian and was not and would never be his. He hated that his feelings for her betrayed his love for his brother.

Upon arriving at her home, Marco turned and faced her. He opened his mouth, but words failed him. The words his heart wanted to impart, his head would not allow. So there was nothing more he could say or do to comfort her. There was a line he could never cross. So, instead, he steeled his resolve to keep his distance, the yearning in his eyes undetected in the half-light.

Emily left his side, passed through the gate in the picket fence, and stepped onto the front porch. She turned and looked at him with tentative affection. "Thank you for walking me home."

"You're welcome, Emmy. Good night."

Chapter 12

As the end of the school day drew near, Constance's class grew restless. She clapped her hands to get their attention. "Now listen here. Close your books, quiet down, and remember that tomorrow's Friday, election day. That means no school."

A cheer erupted, flowing into the corridor and embarrassing Constance at how little control she had over her students. "Now, children, it's nearly time I ring the bell. While I'm away, I want you to remain quietly in your seats. You may leave when you hear me ring the bell. Understood?"

"Yes, Miss Madison," came the chorus of students eager for the end of the school day.

Constance excused herself and hurried outside, not wanting to be late to pull the rope. She watched several young mothers gather in the schoolyard, waiting for their children.

It all seemed so familiar—the classroom full of children, the voices that echoed in the hallway—and she might have been at her old school in Bloomington were it not for the foreign faces. A sense of being far from home accompanied her wherever she went.

She peered anxiously over her shoulder at the clock. It was time. She reached up, grabbed the rope, and pulled hard. Bong!

Children emptied the classrooms, the sound of footsteps and chatter ringing through the corridor as they filed out the main door, hurrying past her without a word. No "Bye, Miss Madison" or "See you Monday, Miss Madison."

Back to being invisible.

Constance sat on the steps and watched the children set off for home. She remembered doing the same. She could close her eyes and recall every step from her school in Bloomington to her front porch—turning left at the large hedge, heading over the north canal bridge, and taking a right at the white country house with the unpainted window frames. Some days, while walking home, she'd tell herself there wouldn't be the screaming or violence, but there was always the smell of alcohol. What she couldn't remember was ever hurrying home. She never had a reason to. What should have taken five minutes or less nearly always lasted an hour or more, sometimes a good deal past sundown.

Even now, while staying at the Owen ranch, there was likewise no reason to hurry. She felt as if she were homeless, even if she'd never understood the meaning of a real home.

Before walking south down Main Street toward the ranch, she sat on a bench in the schoolyard. There, alone, she let her mind wander.

What am I doing here? Mrs. Owen seemed kind back when we first met, offering me a position and a place to stay, but I'm a stranger here, nothing more.

She sat motionless, her head cradled in her hands, when she felt someone sit down next to her.

"How are you, Miss Madison?" Emily scooted close.

"Oh, Miss Hampshire, I'm . . . not sure, honestly."

"Takes someone brave, especially for a woman, to do what you've done. I've never lived anywhere besides New Harmony. It surely can't be easy."

"It's not. It feels like I'm somehow infected with the plague and I'm the only one unaware of it."

"That's not the case. It's not you." Emily assured her while taking her hand with a sympathetic smile. "You've come to New Harmony at a precarious time. People are worried, even frightened."

"Yes, I've heard and should be less concerned with my troubles, especially in your regard. Please believe me when I tell you how sorry I am. You've suffered the loss of your fiancé. I can't even imagine."

"Thank you, Miss Madison. Thank you for saying that. May I call you Constance?"

"Yes, please. I would prefer it."

"Likewise, call me Emily or Emmy, like everyone else." Emily let out a sigh. "Have you time to talk, like we said we would?'

"Time? I've nowhere to be and nowhere to go."

Emily smiled. "Very well. Where to start?" She paused and studied Constance's face for a moment before continuing. "There are things in New Harmony that aren't exactly as they seem, things that make some of us nervous, and with good reason. We're all frightened of saying the wrong things, so we're all shut like clams, but you're not to blame. May I offer some advice?"

Constance nodded. "Yes, please, go on."

"When I was a child, my father taught me to swim in the river. He cautioned me to stay clear of the undercurrent. You can't see it, but knowing the river, you must stay clear. Visible or not, it's there and dangerous. With the Owens, there's always an undercurrent. I don't know how else to say it. But be careful not to get sucked in and swept away."

Constance appeared bewildered. "I'm afraid you must be more direct with me. I'm sorry, I don't understand."

"All right, more direct." Emily drew in a deep breath, calmed herself, and began again. "No doubt Mrs. Owen already recruited you to report on what happens at the school." She could see the truth of it in Constance's face. "If you believe her and choose to stand on her rug, eventually, she'll pull it out from under you. Does that help?"

Constance shook her head. "Not exactly."

"Please try and understand. Some people got too close, too involved with the Owens, never to be seen or heard from again. Is that direct enough?"

Constance found it difficult to believe. Even though the woman she met in Bloomington differed from the woman in New Harmony, Mrs. Owen didn't appear dangerous. "Really?" was all she could say. Then she noticed the stern look on Emily's face. "You are serious, aren't you?"

"I am."

"But she's elderly, and her husband is mayor. They can't be all that bad, can they?"

What seemed to Emily a defense of the Owens unnerved her, though she knew Constance couldn't possibly understand. She lacked a history with Mrs. Owen, and Emily couldn't bring herself to dredge up the old memories of losing her parents.

"I've shared too much. Constance, you cannot repeat what I just told you. Just be careful is all I'm saying."

"You needn't worry. The Owens treat me as if I'm beneath them. I'm a guest at their ranch and have yet to be invited into their home. And yes, she already told me my success as a teacher required that I keep her informed. I'm to share with her all things 'inappropriate.'"

Emily sighed. "Exactly as I expected. But please be careful. They're not to be trusted. We need to find you another place to stay. I'll help. Until then, come for dinner on Sunday. We'd love to have you."

"Are you certain? You're not just—"

"I'm positive. I mentioned you to my auntie, who asked why I've neglected to invite you for supper."

"You live with your aunt?"

"And my uncle, yes."

"And your parents? Is it rude that I ask?"

"No," Emily assured her, wondering if Constance noticed how she winced as she answered.

"I'm sorry, Emmy. It's not my place. I shouldn't have—"

"Swept away," said Emily.

"Excuse me?"

"Yes, both of them, with the undercurrent."

"Seriously?" Constance could hardly believe it. "The Owens?"

Emily nodded. "But I risk everything in telling you, so please . . ."

"You have my word," said Constance, her voice trembling. "Should I even be there, at the Owens? I can't go back to Bloomington. There's no way. I just can't. What do I do?"

"Just come for supper Sunday. We'll find a suitable place for you to live. And, of course, be careful. Stay clear of them as much as possible."

"Oh, I will."

Emily smiled. "I must hurry home," she said. "My auntie will be worried. It's all she does anymore: worry about me. I'll tell her to expect you for dinner Sunday."

"Yes, Sunday."

Chapter 13

The much-anticipated day of election arrived. Mrs. Owen unlocked the town hall doors at precisely 6:00 a.m. sharp, allowing people to drop off their ballots before tending to their fields, chores, and other business. Just as the mayor had said, inside the building, in the corner, sat a locked ballot box constructed of pinewood. On top was a small slit, barely large enough to allow a completed ballot to be inserted and locked securely away until counting the votes later that evening. There wasn't a moment during the day when Mrs. Owen or the sheriff didn't greet people at the front door. She insisted Sheriff Weasley stay close until after Bronson made his appearance, which he did early in the day.

After Bronson's departure, the sheriff stuck around until, upon seeing her son, Mrs. Owen said, "Sheriff, I'd like a moment of privacy with my son."

"Yes, ma'am." The sheriff took his leave, passing Eugene Owen climbing the steps with a ballot in his hand.

Eugene was short, like his father, but not rounded like a prize gourd in the Posey County Fair. His sturdy frame and rough hands were those of a man who labored to put food on the family table. Besides his height, like his father, he'd experienced youthful baldness—a family trait passed down from generation to generation. Eugene had lost much of his hair before age thirty but made up for it with a bushy gentleman's mustache. The quality for which he was best known and revered was his integrity. His mother disagreed. As far as she was concerned, he bordered on disrespect in the worst possible way by dishonoring his parents, which, she reminded him often, was breaking a commandment.

Eugene tipped his hat as he climbed the steps. "Good morning, Mother."

"I can only imagine which name you've written on your ballot."

Eugene shrugged off her concern. "It's one ballot, Mother. I'm but one person."

"He who votes against his self-interest is a fool, but, regardless, we haven't seen you in months. I've begun wondering if I had a son or a grandson."

Eugene stared at her, perplexed. "You haven't a clue as to why?"

"Fine, I understand you're upset, but it would be nice to see Alexander. We're his grandparents, for heaven's sake."

"Would be nice if you and Father allowed me to raise my son without interfering."

Martha looked at him sternly. "Your father's only watching out for our family. That damned Stewart boy beat him up. You cannot deny that. I saw his black eye. What your father did was noble, and if you can't recognize that—"

"Noble? That's what you call it? I arranged for our boys to meet and apologize. But the Stewarts moved. I suspect they fled in the middle of the night, in fear. I'd like to know where they are. Please tell me, Mother. Where are they? And where are the others who've just disappeared? The Stewarts aren't the only ones."

"Now just you wait a minute!" said Martha, becoming more ruffled with each accusation.

"Oh, Mother, what about Ms. Hampshire? Ruth—remember her? You hired her daughter, your new teacher. I remember the sheriff asking me if I'd seen her, the teacher's mother, though it was some time ago, but I still remember. Sheriff said he had to keep her quiet—his words, not mine. Someone found her dead the following day. How you can turn a blind eye, I will never unders—"

"Shut your mouth!" Martha looked about nervously to make sure no one overheard. "Lower your voice. Your insinuations are appalling!"

"They're not insinuations. Far from it."

Martha glared. "You don't get it. Families of affluence must be stronger than everyone else. And we are a family, like it or not, and we are stronger. Every person in this wretched town would trade places with an Owen. And they'll scheme, plan, and plunder to steal what is rightfully ours. It would be one thing if any of them were worth a damn, but it's another . . ."

Martha caught herself just as Old Man Taylor and his wife, Amelia, started up the steps. She smiled warmly at them. "How are the Taylors this sunny morning? Isn't the sunshine wonderful?"

"It is," Amelia answered cheerfully. "So grateful to have your husband watching over us." Her husband smiled but said nothing.

Martha embraced the compliment, hoping her son noticed. "He does such a splendid job, doesn't he? I wouldn't trust anyone else to keep our town safe. I hope you won't either. Please go inside. The ballot box is to your left."

After a few more pleasantries, the Taylors were about to excuse themselves when Martha noticed Eugene coming out of the building, his ballot no longer in hand.

As he hurried past her, she flashed him a hostile glare, and then, just as quickly, turned amicable. She shook hands with the Taylors and wished them well as they went in to cast their votes. "Eugene, wait!" She descended the steps, calling after him. "It's none of my business how you regard your father. My grandson, on the other hand, is my business. Your father did what he felt he had to for us, for you."

As soon as she caught up with him, she grabbed his arm and turned him around. "You've rejected us, your family, but you've no right to make that choice for our grandson. I can assure you I will not have it!"

"What does that mean?" Eugene's eyes narrowed on his mother. "What are you trying to say?"

"Just that, well . . . It's well known, son. The mental illness in Nellie's family is no secret. It's only a matter of time before she's declared an unfit mother. Convincing people would be a simple matter."

"Yes, I can imagine how everyone would agree with you, Mother! Who would dare disagree? But I'll ask you again to keep my family's concerns to yourself. My wife is more fit as a mother than . . ."

"Fair enough. But what about *our* family, *our* grandson?"

"Nellie and I decide what is right for Alexander, not you. Nor am I interested in what either of you have to say about it."

Martha put her hands to her chest as if the victim of a great injustice. "Dear, dear," she cried. "Everything was fine until you and Nellie married. She soured you on your father and me. Having your wife declared unfit would be the last thing I'd ever want. It's just that I could." Martha paused before adding, "Believe me, I don't want to."

Eugene's face turned crimson red. "You'd do that?"

Martha could tell she'd crossed a line. "It's just that I could. That's all. I didn't mean anything by it."

"Well, I've heard enough." Without another word, Eugene turned and walked away, never glancing back.

Minutes before seven o'clock that evening, the ballots were collected and locked securely in the election box. All that remained was the tally. Martha never stayed for the latter since there was little doubt about the outcome. It would be as it always was.

On the other hand, the sheriff stood guard outside the town hall at the top of the steps, waiting for the hour to expire. He was responsible for ensuring the integrity of the election by observing the final count and announcing the result to the public. When the clock struck the hour, the appointed observers assembled, waiting just inside the hallway as usual. Among them was Bronson Parrish.

Upon hearing seven strikes of the clock, the sheriff entered the building and began clearing the hallway. "That's it, everyone! Need y'all to leave!" He started pushing people toward the front door while the official observers remained inside. "You, too, folks. Out!"

Bronson protested. "We're here for the counting, Sheriff. We're not going anywhere."

The sheriff opened the door and tilted his head. "Mayor's orders. Out!"

Bronson held out his arm, preventing the election observers from leaving. "What is this? What are you doing?"

"Following orders, teacher. Now out!"

Bronson stared at the door to the mayor's office. It was closed. "Is he in there?"

"None of your concern, teacher. Now leave!"

Several of the observers pushed past Bronson and headed to the front door, not interested in locking horns with the sheriff. Bronson moved quickly toward the mayor's office, but the sheriff was already in front of the door, blocking him. "Appears I gotta do this my way." He grabbed Bronson by the arm and forcibly led him toward the front door.

As he did so, Bronson hollered, "I know you're in there! What are you up to, Mayor? You've no right to do whatever it is you're doing!"

Once Bronson and the official election observers stood outside, Bronson noticed several leaving. "Wait here, please. What they're doing is illegal. We can protest if we do so together."

To his surprise, Abigail Williams agreed. "Yes! He's right. Come back. Our mayor is a reasonable man. So let us reason with him and put this election behind us." Abigail persuaded them to return and wait patiently outside the door. While they waited, Abigail turned her attention to Bronson. "I'm sorry, Mr. Parrish."

"I don't follow, Ms. Williams. Sorry for what?"

"I know you believe you may somehow be the next mayor. Whatever you may have convinced yourself of, however, it is not to be. I offer you my condolences."

"Is that so?"

"Yes, Mr. Parrish."

"And you know this how?"

Abigail grinned. "I have it on good authority."

"I imagine you do. And what authority is that?"

"The Guardians, Mr. Parrish. They have your fate, mine, and everyone else's in their hands. They tell me."

"Ms. Williams, you may be right, and I intend to find out this very evening. I believe we are due a better explanation for this breach of legality than simply complying with orders."

"On that, Mr. Parrish, we agree."

A few minutes later, the mayor exited the building and handed the election box key to the sheriff. He then turned and warmly greeted those assembled, even addressing Bronson personally. "Good evening, everyone. You as well, Mr. Parrish. Beautiful evening, isn't it?"

"We are obligated to observe the counting this evening, and we're determined to do so—now," said Bronson. "And yet the sheriff—"

"And you will, Mr. Parrish. First thing in the morning, I assure you." Turning his back to Bronson, he began locking the front door.

"Stop this!" Bronson protested. "What you are doing is unlawful. The counting must be completed this evening."

"And where does it say that, Mr. Parrish? As your mayor, and for the moment, the executor of the town charter, I am unaware of this. Do you know something I don't?"

"It has always been that way."

"I understand, Mr. Parrish. But there are other concerns."

"Mayor, my only concern is that this sets a dangerous precedent."

"Dangerous times, Mr. Parrish. We don't want anyone out past sunset, not with a monster lurking about, do we? Do you care about the people, Mr. Parrish? Care about their safety? You wish to be mayor, so, of course, you do." The mayor smiled.

Abigail interrupted. "Mr. Parrish has grounds. It is highly unusual. But since you, Mayor, are the only elected official here and have our best interests at heart, we should do as you say and wait till morning."

"You would all do well to listen to Abigail and trust me. There's nothing sordid here. Because these are unusual times, we must make unusual concessions to ensure the common good while keeping everyone out of harm's way. Now go on home. I'll see each of you in the morning."

They started to leave, but Bronson stood his ground. "No. We do it now, or else how may we be assured of the integrity of the election? Please tell me. When did that become unimportant?"

"Oh, Mr. Parrish. You do understand that you are the problem here, don't you? I believe we're all growing tired of your obstructions and veiled accusations. So tomorrow morning, no later than seven o'clock, we will meet here and do the counting in the safety of daylight. Don't be late. The counting will start on time."

Once again, satisfied with the explanation, the observers started to leave.

"Wait!"

"What now, Mr. Parrish?" The mayor no longer hid his impatience.

"What keeps you and Sheriff Weasley from returning much later and tampering with the ballots?"

The suggestion of impropriety caused a ripple of tension among the observers. The sheriff approached Bronson. "Can't speak to the mayor like that. Who do ya think you are?"

The mayor grinned so all could see. "Now, now, Sheriff, it's all right. Hand the key to the box to Mr. Parrish. That should settle things. And now, you'll have to excuse me. My dear wife, Martha, happens to be waiting for me, and I can't be late." The observers watched as the mayor hurried down the steps, climbed aboard his fancy carriage, and drove away.

The sheriff stared at Bronson and the others. "You heard him. We're done here!"

"Yeah, we heard," said Bronson. "I'm curious, however, who's to say the mayor hasn't already removed the ballots? You had us leave, and he was in there alone. The ballots may be sitting on his desk right now."

The sheriff appeared confused. "What good would that do?"

"Figure it out," said Bronson. Unblinking, he stared into the sheriff's eyes. "The mayor's plenty smart enough to know how to tamper with the ballots."

The sheriff rested his hand on the gun strapped at his side. "Who ya accusin'? Now ya listen to me. Your mouth's gonna get ya in a lot of trouble here. You're the problem with this town. So either ya leave now, or there's a bed waitin' for ya behind bars. Either way, we're done here." This time, all but Bronson quickly left. He stood alone, facing the sheriff.

Annoyed, the sheriff sighed and shook his head. "What now?"

"The key, Sheriff."

"Hmm." He held it between his fingers, twirling it around, then dropped it at Bronson's feet. "Now, see ya in the mornin', teacher. Oh, just a minute. I must've forgotten. Lost your position, didn't ya? Ya ain't even a teacher no more."

As candles and lanterns blinked out and down pillows were fluffed for the night, the lull of the spell flowing down from Mount Erebus played so softly upon weary minds that eyelids grew heavy, no longer resisting. A deep quiet settled over New Harmony as everyone drifted into somnolence. That is, nearly everyone. A stray dog barked in the distance before it, too, fell silent. The buzzing of cicadas calling for their mates slowed to a trickle. Even the breeze fluttering the leaves couldn't resist the lullaby.

A faint flicker of light appeared in the back window of the town hall. Shortly thereafter, smoke poured into the night from the stovepipe above the roof, a crime shrouded in darkness taking place. Yet someone else, whom the spell had intentionally overlooked, watched from the cherry grove as a dark figure crept out through the back door and disappeared into the night.

Chapter 14

With the school closed, Constance Madison had nowhere to be and nowhere to go. She finished rinsing her dishes in the room beside the barn, with its cold stone walls and musty-smelling earthen floor. This was not the lavish kitchen in which the Owen's meals were prepared. Even their food cellar was more spacious and clean. That cellar had only one key, which Mrs. Owen herself held on to. Although Constance was not on the Owen payroll and could have been considered a guest, Mrs. Owen afforded her no extra courtesies. And so Constance prepared her food and ate where the workers took their meals.

Once she placed her last dish in the wooden crate that functioned as a cabinet, she grabbed her book and went outside. Finding a warm spot in the late-afternoon sun, she turned the pages, looking for where she had left off. Before finishing a single paragraph, however, she stopped reading. She wasn't in the mood. Her conversation with Emily left her far too uncomfortable to allow herself a moment of relaxation. Instead, she nervously contemplated her situation.

I can't stay here. With the undercurrent Emily described, it may not be safe.

She closed her book and remembered the unread letters on the dresser in her bedroom. There were two, each with the same return address. As homesick as she was, they remained unopened for plenty of reasons. But with her mounting worries, she figured she could use the distraction.

She climbed the stairs at the back of the stable and locked herself in her room. Finding her mother's letters where she had left them, she took one, opened it, and started reading. Once finished, she reluctantly opened the second. Her eyes filled with tears; caught between anger and sorrow, she tossed the crumpled letters into the waste basket.

I don't need your criticism, Mother, or to be told I'll surely fail.

She stood and peered through the small window above the dresser to the livery yard below, where four horses—one liver chestnut, one gray, one spotted black and white, and one black as ink—lazily grazed. Her eyes followed the fence lining the path that divided into two paths, one leading to the ranch house, the other continuing to the main road. And even farther east, somewhere under the shimmery blue sky, lay Bloomington. Her eyes sharpened, and her jaw tightened.

I'm never going home. Never!

Falling back onto her bed, she curled into a ball, wrapping her arms around herself. Here in cruel and cursed New Harmony, she'd been haunted by voices and was now threatened by a beast. She was alone, but who could she trust? Mrs. Owen? The mayor? Emily?

She put her pillow, wet from tears, over her head and found her way to dreaming. As she slept, the dark of night crept in until it filled her room. How much time passed, she couldn't tell, only that something had startled her awake. It was the hour nocturnal predators—owls, bats, and wolves—hunted, but all were still. Nonetheless, something had awoken her.

Alarmed, she sat up and peered into the dark, listening. The crescent moon peeped through the open window, bathing her room in a silvery light. Then she heard it again, the sound that woke her. Tap, tap, tapping on the glass, though her window was on the second floor.

What comes knocking at my window? Is someone trying to get my attention?

She pattered to the window in her bare feet and peered out but saw nothing—at least nothing that explained what she heard. Outside in the moonglow stood the livery yard, the ranch house, and nothing more.

Had she imagined things or awoken in a dream?

It was then she heard the voices that haunted New Harmony, voices that spoke to her in a manner she couldn't explain. Though they could be pleasant and soothing for some, Constance found them unsettling.

"Open the window quietly," the voice in her head told her. "Do it now."

She did as instructed and lifted the windowpane, a cool breeze brushing her fingertips as she bent forward to look out.

"Don't be seen!" warned another voice. "Stay hidden."

She felt a ripple of fear and moved back into the shadows while continuing to stare out the window. In the distance, she saw the mayor walking up the dirt path from the main road. His feet dragged, and his shoulders slumped. What was he doing out at this late hour?

He stopped and looked about as if trying to find something. Constance froze. Something had his attention.

Instead of turning toward the house, he continued until he came to the livery yard next to the stable. Constance retreated farther into her room but not so far that she couldn't see him. She watched in silence, hidden in the dark.

Then she heard squawking, loud and deliberate. Constance stretched to see while trying to piece together the meaning. Below her, though it was nearly invisible in the dark, she could see a large blackbird sitting on the wooden fence. It cawed into the night, and two birds of similar color and size flew out of the darkness, landing on the fence on either side of it. The mayor slowly made his way to where the birds waited. They seemed unintimidated by the mayor—much the opposite.

Why weren't they flying away? The mayor should be rather imposing to them.

As she pondered their strange behavior, she thought she heard the mayor mumbling to himself. She listened intently as the strange scene unfolded.

"Saw to it myself," said the mayor. "I didn't require your assistance after all, and there will be no surprise come morning."

The blackbirds cawed, sounding, if that were possible, somewhat irritated.

"I'm just—" The mayor hesitated as the birds fussed. He interrupted their cackling. "It seems it's all up to me, regardless. However, I meant no disrespect." Clearly listless and tired, the mayor stumbled over his words.

Constance struggled to comprehend what was happening. *What is this? He listens to their squawking as if he understands them, and the birds respond in kind.*

Then she heard the mayor speak as if defending himself. "I've done hard things, things other men would regret, even hurtful things. But, on the other hand, I'm perfectly capable of something as minor as cheating in an election. And I never suggested I brought the sun out of hiding or that I don't need our arrangement. I know perfectly well my debt."

Again, as if agitated, the birds flapped their wings, making a great ruckus. The mayor stood quietly before answering, his tone more conciliatory. "I understand. Yes, you require sustenance, as you say. I've devised a plan. It won't be immediate, but soon enough."

The blackbirds calmed and cawed into the night while the mayor listened, growing more agitated.

"What?" he interrupted their cawing. "Someone nearly killed the monster? But I strictly forbade it. Tell me. Who was it?"

The strangeness of the scene and the harshness of his words heightened her fear. She slunk farther into the room's dark interior and listened as the blackbirds' clamor grew louder and the mayor addressed them more forcefully.

"If you can't tell me, what will I do? I must know."

Again, the cawing and tension mounted. Constance's heart beat uncontrollably.

"Of course I'm aware! If the monster dies, our arrangement terminates. What need do you have to remind or threaten me?"

The sounds of screeching and wings beating filled the air, then suddenly stopped. Then, at that exact moment, the gentle breeze blowing from the east ceased, and all went silent.

Constance ducked down and waited, scared to be seen or to make a sound. Time slowed, and what might have been only a few minutes felt like an eternity, enough so that she assumed the mayor might have retreated to the house. She steeled her nerves and leaned forward again, hoping to see what happened while remaining hidden. What she saw shocked her to her core and made her tremble. As she peered out her window, the three blackbirds turned and looked directly at her.

The large one cawed, and the mayor turned his head and looked directly at the open window above the stable.

Chapter 15

In the crisp air of a new day dawning, a small crowd gathered at the steps of the town hall.

"Nice seeing you ladies on this bright morn!" the mayor said as he climbed the steps. Abigail, Susannah, and Elizabeth returned the greeting. They were among the first to arrive, beating the sizable crowd now gathered for the seven o'clock ballot tally. Word of the delay in counting had spread, and people wanted to know the outcome. Many sensed that the race might be closer than expected. A herd of old farmers meandered about, unshaven and mumbling to each other. Sitting alone on the steps was Bronson Parrish. He looked to see one of the farmers smile and nod at him.

Susannah seemed delighted to be there, her red lipstick painted on her snow-white face and her eyes fluttering with curiosity. In contrast, the mayor's demeanor lacked curiosity, appearing as if this were any other day. The counting seemed as eventful for him as plucking a sliver from the pad of his foot.

"Could have done this last night, Mayor," Bronson grumbled. But I suppose that would've kept things honest."

"Casting aspersions already, Mr. Parrish? Nothing amiss with this election. Any suggestion to the contrary is irresponsible for a man who wishes to be mayor. I can assure you that any malfeasance resides in your imagination only. People here understand that safety comes first. Otherwise, we would have counted last night."

Bronson replied, "What about the safety of our democracy?"

"Exactly, Mr. Parrish. Questioning an election threatens our democracy, so I urge caution."

As usual, the sheriff shadowed the mayor, interjecting his share of snide comments. "Who's threatin' democracy when ya got the only key?"

"The key doesn't mean a thing," said Bronson as he followed the crowd into the building to the election box.

"Give it here," said the mayor, holding his hand out. Bronson fumbled in his pocket, then handed him the key.

The mayor unlocked the box and spilled the contents onto a table. The crowd drew closer, some on their toes, peering over heads and shoulders.

"Are we ready?" asked the mayor. The anxious crowd hushed as the mayor stepped back and motioned for the sheriff to do the same. "Mr. Parrish, do us the honors." Again, the mayor smiled at the people, his smile too confident for Bronson's liking. It could only mean one thing.

Bronson stepped forward with no choice but to play the mayor's little game. He picked up each ballot, one by one, read what was marked, and then held it up so everyone could see. Next, he sorted them into two piles, one for himself and the other for the mayor. The observers watched every movement, whereas the mayor hardly showed interest. It soon became apparent that one pile grew faster than the other. Finally, when only a few ballots remained, the mayor attempted to shut it down. "I believe we've seen enough!"

"I'd like to finish," insisted Bronson.

"If it were any closer, I'd agree, but it's not. We're done here." The mayor motioned for the sheriff, who busied himself with lighting the potbelly stove.

Bronson interrupted. "We're done when we're done. Everyone who casts a ballot deserves to have it counted. I believe the town would like to know the final numbers." Bronson looked to the people gathered around the table for support.

Events like these were fodder for the gossip mill, and Abigail was determined to learn the juicy details. "Yes. I'd like to know," she said. Susannah Boyer and Elizabeth Howe nodded in agreement, as did many others. Abigail continued. "People are curious, Mayor. They'll want to know who won and by how many votes."

The mayor shook his head. "At this point, what difference does it make? Can you not see which pile is larger and to whom that pile belongs?"

"I'd still like to know the number," Bronson said bravely. "I'd be more interested in knowing the total number of all the ballots. It seems a great deal more voted than expected, more than there are men in New Harmony—and not by a few!"

The sheriff scowled at Bronson, and the mayor sighed. "There's always one. Conspiratorial. Everyone out to get you, Mr. Parrish? That it?"

"Not in the least."

"Well, you can always try again in another four years."

"It won't matter—four, eight, twelve, or sixteen—will it, Robert?"

"Mr. Parrish, I believe you've addressed me inappropriately. Care to try again?"

"No, Robert."

The mayor gave Bronson a stern look as the sheriff gathered the ballots and stuffed them into the potbelly stove. The fire inside burned hot as the paper caught fire, matching the mayor's temper.

"Now's not the time for your conspiracy theories. We've real problems in New Harmony, Mr. Parrish. Time for you to gracefully accept defeat. I warn you not to spew your ridiculous accusations. Run along, or the sheriff here will provide a place for you to stay for a very long time!"

The sheriff stepped forward, his face within inches of Bronson's. "Ya heard the mayor. Spewin' yer filth, yer foolish accusations . . . If I had my way, I'd—"

"Back off, Weasley! You don't frighten me," said Bronson. "Enough people know what happened here. If I go missing, everyone will know why. I will never leave in the middle of the night. You all heard me, didn't you?" He looked at those gathered, the tension growing by the minute. Bronson scanned the room until his eyes fell upon Abigail Williams, who stared at him, wide-eyed. "And you, Ms. Williams!"

"Me?"

"Yes, you! You and the other two—Ms. Boyer and Ms. Howe. Tell everyone exactly what you just witnessed. Tell everyone I will never flee. Only one thing can make me disappear. You tell them!"

"Now, now," said the mayor. "No one just goes missing."

The sheriff scowled. "Wouldn't be so sure, Mayor."

"Leave Mr. Parrish be," said the mayor. "Losing is never easy, though I wouldn't know personally. Nevertheless, we must set the example, gracious in victory as in defeat."

The mayor and sheriff watched as Bronson turned and walked out. Then the mayor craned his neck and whispered in the sheriff's ear. "Best keep an eye on him. He's trouble!"

Chapter 16

The smells of sage, damp grass, and pollen permeated the opening of the den as the sunlight illuminated the entrance. He heard the stream trickling in the meadow and a woodpecker tapping at a tree. These things Jonathan came to love, though they were not enough to convey the hope he yearned for. His encounter with the hunters filled him with worry that they or others would eventually come for him again. He no longer felt safe.

Triggered by his apparent insecurity, the old, familiar voice of torment echoed in his head. "Yes, monster. Unfortunately, for you, they will know where you are, where they can find you."

Why won't you leave me be? I don't want to hear you. Leave me to my misery.

"Are you certain that is what you want?" said another, more high-pitched voice.

I am certain.

A voice as wretched as the others answered, "Then tell us who will warn you when they come? What if they hunt while you slumber?"

I will live with the consequences. After all, it is my fault they come. I was careless.

All three voices answered together as if only one spoke. "Yes, you were. We told you to take the kill. They wanted you dead, after all. You'd be sleeping in peace right now. Or gathering berries or whatever else you do."

Then the more ancient one spoke, the one he feared the most, the one who called herself the Inevitable. "But now, since you've disregarded the laws of nature, pretending you are not a beast, the humans will hunt you. They will come for you, for it is in their nature to do so, and they won't deny their nature as you deny yours."

Jonathan crawled out of his bed and peered through the branches and leaves over the opening of his cave. He couldn't deny the meadow no longer felt safe.

The humans believe I'm a threat, but I'm no murderer. I know two humans who are killers, the ones who murdered the boy, and I have their scent.

The beast contemplated the warning from the voices, and although he didn't trust them, neither could he deny their reasoning.

And so he concluded, *I may not be able to deny my nature much longer.*

"Yesss," answered the voices, now more animated and sinister. "Start with them. Make them pay, the two humans who falsely accused you. Their blood will taste sweet!"

I must be careful. I . . .

"Go on," the voices urged.

I'm a beast, not clever like humans, and, therefore, any killing on my part can only bring more harm upon me.

"Unless . . ."

Unless what?

"Unless we help you. Of course."

Help me? How?

The thought sent Jonathan's mind spinning and his eyes rolling back into his head. Like a vat of hot tar splattering onto his conscience, a flash of memory invaded his mind. He heard a woman's pleas for help. *Jonathan!* It was the same voice that, from time to time, called to him from the beyond. Now her ear-piercing screams rose from a fiery blaze. *Jonathan! Jonathan! Jonathan!*

Somehow, he knew he was responsible for the blaze, condemned to be a monster because of it. Frightened, he retreated into the inky blackness of his den, curled into a fetal position, and covered his head with his arms and paws.

Have I killed? These memories convict me! Am I a killer, and have I been so all along? Is that why I'm running from lawful men who would put me down into the ground?

There was only silence as he drowned in his self-imposed condemnation.

Showing me this, is this what you mean by helping me?

He stayed hidden throughout the day and waited for the cover of night, when the shadow of the world would hide him in the darkness. He was a prisoner, and the voices from the mountain kept guard, warning, scolding, and watching. From now on, he would check his snares only by moonlight.

In the seclusion of the den, Jonathan could no longer hold back the oppressive darkness in his mind, the darkness that told him he was a killer. He stared at his hands, extending his claws, hard as iron, sharp as knives.

I am what I am. I do not need to run.

Once the daylight surrendered to the dark, Jonathan stepped out into the open. He held something in his grasp. He brought it to his snout and sniffed it long and hard, capturing the scent.

It's time. It's time I tend to unfinished business.

Chapter 17

Once again, it was Emily's responsibility to ring the morning bell. Since it had drizzled the night before, she skirted the puddles along her way, arriving early. She was surprised to see Constance had yet to arrive. It didn't matter if Constance was assigned the morning bell or not. She always came before any of the other teachers. Emily looked south down Main Street, past the church and lumberyard, where men loaded a wagon with sheets of lumber. Farther down the street, she saw Constance hurrying toward her, not even raising her white skirt as she hurried through the puddles.

Emily quickly greeted her. "Good morning." Constance didn't answer. Her breathing was labored, and she stared blankly at Emily. "Don't worry," Emily assured her. "You're not late. It's my turn to ring the bell." Emily looked at the creases of worry in Constance's forehead as the woman gasped for air. "What's wrong? I assure you, Constance, what we discussed must be a worry, but it will be fine."

"I don't care about that!"

Constance's abruptness left Emily unsure how to respond. "Well then, what's frightened you so?"

"Last night . . ."

"What about it?" Emily heard the fear in her friend's voice and saw her eyes dart about as if afraid. Emily took her hand to comfort her.

"Last night, Mayor Owen . . . he . . ." Another pause.

"Constance, you must tell me. What did you see? What about Mr. Owen? You might want to start from the beginning."

Constance swallowed hard and drew in a breath. "Yes, the mayor. He . . ."

Emily nodded reassuringly. "Go on."

"I woke last night. Rather, something disturbed my sleep. What it was, I can't be certain. But it told me to open my window, so I did and looked out. They have me staying in the room above the stable. I saw the mayor walking toward the house from the road, not riding a horse or in a carriage as one would suppose. And it was late, far too late to be out walking."

"And what troubled you?"

Constance tried to remember, to re-create exactly what she saw. Emily watched as Constance covered her face with her hands. She noted how young this new teacher was, how innocent and unable to hide her emotions. Emily waited until her new friend continued.

"So, he walked to the ranch house, and something changed his mind because he turned and walked over to the livery yard, to the fence there, not far from where I watched and listened. As I told you, my window is above the stable, where I could see and hear clearly."

"That's when something told you to open the window?" asked Emily.

"No! Something woke me just before, as if it wanted me to see the mayor walking around late at night. I'm sorry. I must not be explaining well enough."

"No. You are doing fine. Please go on. Tell me what you saw."

"It's more what I heard. I heard Mr. Owen saying strange things about cheating and hurting people as though he were confessing, and—" Constance paused. She turned to look behind her as if to make sure no one listened to their conversation. Then, confirming they were still alone, she whispered, "I believe he's lost his mind."

Constance then told Emily everything she had heard and seen. Then, realizing their time was up, she fell silent.

"Listen to me, Constance. After school, come home with me. My friend Marco can accompany us, and we'll pick up your things. We must be cautious. Watch yourself. You can't appear to know anything. Can you do that?"

"Yes, I'll try."

"Do your best."

As they made their way into the schoolhouse, Emily held Contance's hand. "We'll find another place for you to stay. But, in the meantime, stay with me. Don't go back there alone. Whatever you do, don't go back there!"

Chapter 18

LeFevre removed his shirt and carefully sat on the couch closest to the parlor stove. He called out to Bronson, "You say Doc's comin' to change my bandages?"

Bronson set a bowl of water on the kitchen floor. As Coot drank his fill, Bronson went into the parlor. "Have some patience. I told you as much. He's coming."

"That's good. I haven't bathed in a week. I'm startin' to smell as poorly as you."

"Worse," said Bronson.

"Maybe. So, how ya think he did it?"

"Who, Robert?"

"Yeah, the mayor. What? You and he on a first-name basis?"

"From now on we are. And to answer your question, any number of ways. Robert was in the building alone before he came out with the key."

"So?"

"It's simple," said Bronson. Before he could explain, Coot bounded into the parlor, wagging his tail, and jumped on the couch beside Bronson, laying his head on his owner's lap.

"All right. How did Robert, as ya now refer to him, do it?"

"One way is he could have emptied the box and eliminated any unwanted ballots while alone in the building. Or he could have stuffed it with extra ballots. Who knows if he had more printed? There were a lot of ballots to count, more than I've ever seen."

"What if there were two boxes? How would anyone know?"

"Or two keys," said Bronson. "I could've been holding a dummy key the entire time. He could have switched keys after I handed mine back to him. It doesn't really matter how. There's still no proof. He knew there wouldn't be any and that he'd get away with it. He knew all along."

"Weren't you watchin' him?" asked LeFevre. "The man reeks of corruption. His stench would send swine running off a cliff."

"Believe me, LeFev. I was paying attention, but he may have done me a favor. I may be alive today because I lost."

"Ya didn't lose. People know it. If not, they sense it. They're only afraid."

Coot rolled over so Bronson could rub his belly. "At least I can say I wasn't."

"Wasn't what?"

"Afraid. We're not afraid, are we, Coot?" Bronson scratched Coot behind the ears, and the dog let out a satisfying groan. "Come what may, LeFev. I had to try and change things, and I've done that. I can live with it."

Clutching his broken ribs, LeFevre leaned forward. "There's a matter left undone before ya see me livin' with it."

"Now, LeFevre, sometimes you must let things be."

"Maybe you, but not me."

"I hesitate to ask what you have in mind."

"I told ya before, Bronson: ballot or ball."

"I know you say that, LeFev, but no. Our souls are worth more than that."

"Ya see, that's how they get ya, why they always win. They ain't got no rules, all while we cling to principle."

"LeFev, it's all right. We are men of principle and will remain so."

"But then they win!"

Just then, they heard the back door.

"Your doctor's here," said Bronson. "We'll continue this conversation later."

LeFevre shrugged. "No need. I'll get the doc to help me. He ain't afraid. He and I, we faced worse than Robert."

Bronson shook his head. "Shhh!"

Marco closed the door behind him, his medical bag in hand. He called out, "Mr. LeFevre!"

His voice still weak, LeFevre answered, "In the parlor, Doc."

Marco walked through the kitchen and into the front sitting room, where Bronson sat with Coot curled in his usual place. In the corner, next to the parlor stove, sat LeFevre, still wrapped in the same white linen now turning sour and in desperate need of changing.

Marco approached. "Let's have a look at it. How are you feeling?"

"Kinda like bein' ripped apart by a hellish monster, Doc, left to die."

Ignoring the Frenchman, Marco reached into his medical bag.

Bronson chuckled. "He's a cantankerous old goat, Marco, but that's good. Means he's getting back to normal."

Then, suddenly, there came an unexpected knock at the back door, and Coot barked loudly and raced to see who it was.

Bronson went to the kitchen and peered through the curtains. "Who is it?"

A woman's voice answered. "Emily Hampshire."

"Come in! Come in!"

Emily opened the door and entered the kitchen. "Is Marco here?"

"Follow me. You too, Coot. Come on, boy." Emily and Coot followed Bronson into the sitting room.

LeFevre, only partially dressed, covered himself. Emily didn't seem to notice. "Marco, I need your help."

Marco looked up at Emily, leaving LeFevre to attend to his injuries. "What is it?"

"I spoke with Constance this very morning. Something's wrong."

Marco appeared confused. "Constance who?"

"The new teacher." She turned to Bronson. "Sorry, Mr. Parrish. Mrs. Owen hired Constance to replace you."

Bronson shrugged it off. "No need for sorry. What happened?"

Marco led her to the couch. "Sit down, Emmy. Tell us what happened."

"I saw her this morning. She was terrified. She said she saw the mayor walking home late—well past midnight, I assume."

Bronson suddenly became interested. "Did she mention what time?"

"By late, I believe she meant early morning, perhaps two or three."

"Of course it was."

Bronson and LeFevre exchanged glances.

"So what frightened her?" asked Marco, ignoring LeFevre's medical concerns.

Not one to be ignored, LeFevre cleared his throat. "I'd like to hear as well, Doc, just not half naked in the presence of a lady."

"Oh yes. Sorry." Marco resumed wrapping the bandages. "I'm listening, Emmy. Please go on."

Emily continued. "Constance said he behaved oddly, like a lunatic, talking to himself, saying things about hurting people and cheating. Then, she mentioned something akin to conversing with birds. Blackbirds!"

"What?" LeFevre burst out laughing, then quickly sobered. The others stared at him curiously. "Look! I've been drunk plenty before and never talked to birds. Seems odd, doesn't it, a bit comical?"

"Sounds ridiculous, I know, but it's no laughing matter. It frightened her good." Emily appeared fidgety and anxious.

Bronson asked, "Did she mention anything else?"

"Not that I remember, other than him admitting to hurting people and confessing things. But we ran out of time. We were going to talk after school, and I went to see her as soon as I dismissed my class, but when I walked by her classroom, she wasn't there. Mrs. Owen was filling in, so I kept walking."

Bronson leaned forward. "Now, Emily. This is important. Did the mayor see her? Did he know she overheard?"

"From what I gathered, it's possible. But what concerns me most is that I saw the parson across the street while searching for her. I asked him whether he'd seen her leave. He said he had, about an hour earlier. Constance asked him to pray for her mother. Worse, the sheriff waited for her and told her to hurry. She left with the sheriff in a carriage for what could only be out of concern for her mother."

Bronson thought for a moment. "She left with the sheriff. The question then becomes whether the news of her mother was real or a ruse."

Emily's concern deepened. "A ruse? For what purpose?"

Marco spoke quietly, more to himself than the others. "To have her leave with the sheriff, like my brother."

Emily paced back and forth, thinking. "And Mrs. Owen was there, orchestrating it all."

LeFevre piped in. "The old spittoon's a liar. She would have told the girl anythin' to get her to leave with the sheriff."

"Quiet, everyone." Bronson motioned for everyone to remain still. They didn't have to wait long before they heard it.

Emily declared. "The bell. That's not good."

Marco set fresh bandages next to LeFevre and stood. "It's an emergency. Everyone, stay here. I'll go see."

Without being asked, Emily crossed the room and wrapped the last of LeFevre's bandages while Marco grabbed his medical bag and headed for the back door. "Be right back!"

Chapter 19

Marco approached the town center by trudging through the hedge alongside the neighbor's fenced garden and following the back alleyway parallel to the canal. Once he was far enough from Bronson's house to avoid suspicion, he joined the people pouring from their homes. A mother yelled to her children to get back inside and lock the doors. Several men carried long rifles, gripped by fear over what was happening in New Harmony. A monster was in their midst, and horrible things had to have occurred for the emergency bell to ring.

Several men from the volunteer fire brigade ran past with buckets and shovels—their mantra, "Save the town at all costs," on their lips. The bell didn't ring three times unless immediate action was called for. At least, that's how it once was. However, since the eclipse, such an emergency was wholly expected, and Marco took a cue from the men and started to run, medical bag still in hand. He scanned the horizon for smoke but saw none. What Marco did see was anxious townsfolk everywhere, something he'd never experienced.

The town was in a panic, which could only be more problematic than helpful.

The closer he got to the center of town, the harder his heart pounded, and the darker his thoughts became until he also felt a suffocating fear. He staggered as worry and hesitation filled his mind, brought on by a crippling insecurity.

Why am I so afraid? I feel like I might not survive the day.

A doctor and a man of reason, Marco's good senses rejected the dark thoughts. Nevertheless, he sensed his control over his emotions slipping. What frightened him most was that his fear was not of his doing, but something or someone other than himself supplanted his emotions.

Determined to remain objective, he stopped, closed his eyes, and counted to ten, breathing slowly.

I must keep my wits about me. I control my fears. I can remain calm. I determine my thoughts and my feelings.

He counted while eerie words infiltrated his positive thinking in a tone of dread and warning. A rhythmic, poetic verse crept ever so covertly into his mind, stirring fear. He was almost swept up in what was happening, but then the words revealed themselves, and he realized there was an intruder. Once recognized, he listened objectively, without fear, thwarting the designs of whomever or whatever invaded his thoughts.

> *Jaws dripping, blood-stained claws*
> *Grind your bones to dust.*
> *Death's knocking at your door.*
> *Only the mayor can you trust.*
>
> *The monster grows hungrier.*
> *More hungry day by day.*
> *The time for action is now at hand.*
> *You're the monster's prey.*
>
> *It's coming for you. Run and hide.*
> *Cover your mouth; make no fuss.*
> *Death's knocking at your door.*
> *Only the mayor can you trust.*

Appalled, Marco found it difficult to believe the words. *What is this? Trust the mayor? Who or what could orchestrate such an attack but for the mayor's benefit? What connection do the voices have to him? And how many are listening? Everyone? Do they realize these thoughts are not their own?*

Determined to find the answers, Marco continued walking, turning the corner at Main Street. The closer he got, the more congested the crowd became and the more people packed in behind him. The street was blocked off on either side in front of the town center so people could stand in the street. Finally, he found a place in the park across from the town hall where he could watch and listen without bumping into anyone.

When it appeared the entirety of New Harmony was assembled, the sheriff approached the podium. The sun beat down on him as he ran his fingers through his sweat-dampened hair and shielded his eyes with his hand. One rarely saw the sheriff without his hat. The crowd's fear and the hot scent of nervous perspiration permeated the air. The sheriff waited to address those gathered. As he waited, the door behind him opened, and the mayor, Mrs. Owen, and the rest of the council filed out of the building, the crowd growing more restless by the minute.

"Quiet down!" ordered the sheriff. "Our mayor has somethin' to say! He has an announcement, so listen, everyone!"

The mayor patted him on the back, signaling him to step aside. From a distance, Marco watched as the mayor acquired the podium with a solemn expression and a forced smile, as one who carried a heavy burden. Then, with head hung low and eyes cast downward, the mayor slowly lifted his chin and gazed out into the crowd. "It is a sad day," he announced. "Yes, a sad day, indeed."

The people fell silent, so silent one could hear the gentle breeze rustling the leaves of the old oak in the park. They hung on his every word.

The mayor pulled up his heavy wool trousers, wiped his forehead with his sleeve, and then continued. "A terrible tragedy has come to my attention, and it grieves me so to say there's been another awful, bloody attack."

Several women gasped. Abigail fanned herself to keep from fainting.

After a dramatic pause, the mayor said, "Indeed, the attack was horrible. It occurred east of here, on the road to Bloomington, earlier this afternoon."

A commotion erupted as bewilderment gripped the townspeople.

"Who was it?" a man demanded. Others wanted to know.

The level of fear intensified until the mayor raised his hand, and the crowd again quieted. "It was a young woman, the newest member of our community, a Ms. . . ."

There followed an uncomfortable silence as Martha Owen leaned forward and whispered in her husband's ear. The mayor listened before continuing. "Ms. Constance Madison is who. She was our guest at the ranch and a new teacher at the New Harmony school. I'm saddened to report Ms. Madison did not survive. As for the attack, I won't relate the details as they are far too gruesome to mention."

Gasps filled the crowd, followed by another pause from the mayor before his demeanor turned angry. "The monster is a vicious beast. These attacks are evidence of that. But we, your town council, and I, as your mayor, have formed a plan."

The mayor retrieved a small piece of paper and his reading glasses from his suit pocket. Setting his glasses atop his nose and hooking them around his ears, he unfolded the paper and read, "Effective immediately, there will be a curfew at sundown."

He held the paper in his teeth, pulled up his trousers again, then read on. "For those with locks, make sure to engage them. For those without, I recommend you barricade your doors, close your windows and curtains, and do all you can to secure yourselves inside."

His advice caused an uproar, and Vernon Davis, who stood near the front, blurted out, "Mayor! Why not form a posse? We have sufficient numbers and guns. I'll be first to volunteer."

Others shouted, "Hear! Hear! I, too, volunteer!"

"I'll go myself. Don't need no posse," yelled Moses Carver, who rarely spoke. The crowd cheered as the overwhelming support of an armed response became apparent.

Hiding his alarm, the mayor glared at those making the fuss. He peered over his spectacles, searching for the last man who threatened to hunt the monster, Moses Carver from the deep South. The mayor didn't care for his pigment or to have his kind living in New Harmony.

Marco watched as the mayor whispered to the sheriff. For the rest of the speech, the sheriff stayed by the mayor's side.

"Now listen here, everyone! We've attempted to kill the monster. That's what got Shear's boy killed. And it came to my attention only recently that several armed men took it upon themselves, without my knowledge, to try that very thing. Unfortunately, they failed. Is it any wonder the beast sought revenge? The teacher might still be alive had they not taken the matter into their hands."

Marco was stunned. His knees went weak as the blood drained from his head, leaving him feeling dizzy. *It can't be. How could the mayor know? It's impossible! But if he knows, does he also know who's responsible? Is that what the sheriff is doing, looking for me? Worse, am I the cause of Constance's death?*

Marco wanted to warn LeFevre and run as far as possible. Instinctively, he took several deep breaths, counting until his heartbeat slowed. He again thought of leaving but decided to see what more he could find out, what more he needed to report to his friends waiting at Bronson's house. He crouched down, hiding from the sheriff while peeking through the crowd as the mayor continued speaking.

The mayor still stood at the podium, reading his paper. "Effective immediately, we will begin offering an appeasement. Tomorrow, Hyrum will have an empty—"

Hearing the crowd's murmur, the mayor paused and peered over his spectacles. "I suspect you're all wondering what this appeasement is, so allow me to explain. The Bible tells us to love our enemies. I believe few would disagree. No doubt even Parson Burroughs would be the first to suggest it. We can also agree the monster is our common enemy, so how can we show love? Now, it doesn't escape me how strange a thing this is to say. Show love to a monster? Preposterous. But is it? Well, the council and I, trusting the wisdom found in the sacred book—and who can argue with the sacred book?—have determined the following."

Once again, the mayor began to read. "Tomorrow, Hyrum will have an empty wagon in the park across the street. Everyone must bring an offering between three and six in the afternoon. Such offerings may include bottled preserves, such as fruit and meat. And, of course, spirits. Nothing appeases a beast more than whiskey or wine."

He looked down at Abigail, standing near the front. To her delight, he singled her out. "Mrs. Williams."

"Yes, Mayor?"

"You make the most delicious shepherd's pie. How about you bring a few?"

Abigail blushed radish red. "If it will help, Mayor."

"Yes, very much so," said the mayor with a wide grin. "And we shall call our contributions appeasement offerings.

Norman McNeil, near the front, raised his hand.

"Yes, Mr. McNeil. Have you a question?"

"I do, Mayor, sir. I hope it all works out for us, and it's all fine and dandy, but who'll dare deliver the wagon to Wallace's monster?"

Before the mayor could answer, Phillip Wallace yelled, "It's not my monster, so stop referring to it as such. Not just you, Norman, but all of you. Nearly killed my boy and me. And I don't for a minute believe this appeasement business will work!"

The sheriff looked at the mayor. The mayor shook his head and put a hand on the sheriff's shoulder, again whispering in his ear. The sheriff went back to staring, gargoyle-like, into the crowd.

The mayor cleared his throat and again wiped the sweat from his forehead. "You are undoubtedly correct, Mr. Wallace. The monster doesn't belong to you or anyone else. And you have every right to question the appeasement. But may I ask, do you believe it is a fearsome beast?"

The crowd's attention turned to Phillip, waiting with bated breath. "I do!"

"And do you believe the monster is so fierce it is capable of tearing a man to pieces?"

"I know it! Without question, Mayor."

"Then, if we do as I believe you are suggesting and pursue the monster with guns, may I hold you responsible for the lives of friends or neighbors who might die in the attempt? Or might you be willing to try an alternative—that is, to appease the beast?"

"If those are the only two options, then I suppose appeasing the beast is worth a try, but who to deliver the appeasement? I'd rather not be responsible for them either."

"Nor would I," said the mayor. "And that's why the council and I will deliver the appeasement."

A gasp rose from the crowd, and the attention turned to the council members standing behind the mayor. They appeared just as shocked as everyone else.

"Yes, I, your mayor, and our brave council will deliver it through the gorge and leave it for the monster. Furthermore, there is one more thing we must do. He folded the paper and put it back in his vest pocket. "I needn't read it. I will simply tell you. I've instructed the sheriff to collect every firearm to ensure no one puts us in further danger from the monster. You have until tomorrow at six in the evening to deliver them to the sheriff's office. We'll tag them so you can retrieve them once this danger passes. As of tomorrow at six, anyone not complying will be arrested. Sheriff sees you with a firearm after six tomorrow, the penalty will be severe, more than you are willing to risk, I can assure you. No exceptions. Is that clear?"

The confiscation of their guns did not sit well with many, and arguments broke out.

"Ya ain't gonna take my gun!" yelled Vernon Davis. "I live closest to the gorge. Me and mine are most at risk. How will I defend my family?"

Boyd Kensington shook his head and hollered, "We'll all be defenseless!"

"Yeah, I wouldn't advise it, Mayor," shouted Phillip Wallace. "We was face to face with the creature, and it's from hell—the pit of!"

Moses Carver hollered, "If'n Phil Wallace is sayin' what he's sayin', ain't nobody takin' my gun!"

Marco had heard enough and was about to sneak away undetected when he heard a loud boom. He looked back toward the podium from which the sound originated. There, the sheriff held his rifle, barrel raised to the sky. The crowd quieted.

"Mr. Wallace?"

"Yes, Mayor."

"If I recall, you were out hunting the day of the attack, were you not?"

"Yes, Mayor."

"And you had a rifle with you, is that correct?"

"I did, sir, but—"

Before Phillip could say more, the mayor cut him short. "Did having a gun help you, Mr. Wallace?"

"Well, it would if—"

Again, the mayor cut him short. "Just answer the question, Mr. Wallace. Yes or no will do. Did it help you?"

"No."

"No," repeated the mayor. "Now, have any of you heard anything I've been saying? How about you, Mr. Davis? You do live closest to the gorge. Have you been listening?"

Vernon answered, "Yes, sir."

"Mr. Davis, you may consider my plan foolish. However, one of the benefits of reading is learning about people such as Mr. Isaac van Amburgh. Have you heard of him?"

Vernon shook his head, not saying a word, wondering with the rest just who this Mr. Isaac van Amburgh was.

"Well, if you had, you'd know that Mr. van Amburgh is a famous New Yorker, even performing before Queen Victoria. Can anyone imagine what he is renowned for? Hmm? Can you?"

Again, another shake of the head.

"Then let me tell you. Mr. van Amburgh performed with lions—not just one but many. He even introduced a lamb into the lion's cage, not for the audience to witness the gruesome sight of the lions tearing it apart; on the contrary, the lions ignored the lamb every time he did it. But here's the most interesting part. He would take the largest cat, open its mouth, and insert his head."

The people of New Harmony stared slack-jawed and wide-eyed, soliciting a wide grin from the mayor, so he continued. "Here's the part I want you to understand most of all. Mr. van Amburgh never entered the cage with a firearm or a worry. But how do you think he accomplished it? Mr. Wallace, how do you suppose he did it?"

Phillip Wallace lowered his head and said, "I imagine he fed them."

"That's right. It's what he did. They ate from his hand and were appeased—tamed. If we feed the monster, it'll have no cause to harm us. We will be as safe as the lamb in Mr. van Amburgh's lion cage. Peace through appeasement. Everyone knows that violence begets violence. It's in the Bible somewhere, for hell's sake! Look it up. Besides, you'll get your guns back when the monster moves on. Until then, not another word. Now, one final matter."

The mayor looked over his shoulder. "Weston?" Weston Riley stepped forward and stood next to the mayor. "The sheriff is going to deputize Weston here. I'm assigning him to oversee the appeasement offerings. Hyrum will bring a wagon from the general store, and Weston will receive your offerings. You'll find the wagon across the street tomorrow. Bring something substantial. Those with guns can drop them off at the sheriff's office. You trusted me once, and the sun broke free of the clouds and the crops grew. Trust me again; let's be good citizens and act for the common good."

The mayor turned on his heels and marched off, the sheriff and council following as they went back into the building. Anxious to warn LeFevre and form a plan that didn't involve surrendering his firearm, Marco stayed hidden in the crowd as everyone departed for their homes.

Chapter 20

As people left, the council members followed Mrs. Owen through the front doors, down the hallway, and into the chamber room. Before the mayor and sheriff entered, Jonas made his feelings regarding the tragic death of the young teacher known. He wiped his eyes with his apron, which he wore daily at the bakery, and wept. "Ms. Madison, the poor girl. I don't know how to deliver the news to my daughter Daisy."

Just then, the mayor entered quietly, followed by the sheriff, who surveyed the room to ensure everyone was present before closing the door.

Not noticing, Jonas continued speaking uninterrupted. "My Daisy was one of Ms. Madison's students. She spoke of her nonstop."

"I don't have children, mind you," said Ernie, "and if I did, I suppose I would be broken up by it myself. But why the tears, Jonas? She was here but for a short time."

"That's enough, Ernie," said Hyrum. "Jonas laments for his daughter's sake. I believe my son and his daughter share her as their teacher. It's all very tragic."

"It is tragic, Ernie!" said Jonas. "And I can barely speak for the mere horror of it."

"Is it really, Jonas?" asked the mayor, now seated comfortably, arms resting on the shelf of his belly. The council members stared at him, startled by his insensitivity.

Sniffling, Jonas looked at the mayor. "Is . . . is it what?"

"Tragic, Jonas. Is it tragic?"

"Why wouldn't it be?"

All right, fine," said the mayor, who stood and faced the council. "Yes, yes, it is a tragedy. But before you all grab your hankies, did any of you even know her? I know, Jonas, your daughter . . . but besides that?"

The group responded with stunned silence.

"Oh, stop it! Must I remind you of all the good news?" The mayor flashed a toothy grin. "All of you were rightfully worried about the election only a few days ago, and you should have been. Your livelihood and future were in jeopardy. The distraction of the monster only served to secure our victory. It was *us* the people trusted to keep them safe from the beast. And keep them safe we will. Mr. Parrish fell short. For all I know, we have the monster to thank for it. And unless you are ignorantly blind, you must see that we are in charge. The entirety of the town will do precisely as we say. Here, allow me to illustrate."

He focused on Ernie. "How many taverns are there in New Harmony?"

"One, ours," said Ernie.

"That's right. And a town the size of New Harmony usually has how many? Go on, venture a guess."

"I suppose I've never really given it much—"

"More than one," interrupted the mayor.

Next, he looked to Hyrum. "How about you? How many general stores are there here in New Harmony, do you suppose? Can you give me a number?"

The mayor knew Hyrum had the answer, but it amused him as he watched Hyrum look about nervously before saying, "Only one?"

"Yes, Hyrum. Of course, only one! And then there's the New Harmony bakery. How many competitors do you have, Jonas?"

With puffy eyes, Jonas stared back at the mayor.

"Never mind, you haven't finished blubbering about the teacher, so I'll answer for you. None, Jonas. And Weston here, he receives all the towns' contracts. There's no bidding, no threat to his business or any of your businesses. But had I lost the election—all of that would've been gone for all of you, simple as that. Bronson would've replaced each of you. So forgive me for whatever means I employ on your behalf.

Now, I pose one last question. Is it reasonable for me to expect loyalty? No. No. Wait! Let me rephrase it for you. Can I *demand* your loyalty? Answer me!"

A mixture of fear brought on by their dependency stirred within, and each vowed complete loyalty.

"You're right," said Ernie. "We owe you everything."

Hyrum wasted no time in saying, "Thank you, sir. I'm most grateful."

A sniffling Jonas said, "What you're all saying here . . . I agree."

A more introverted Weston nodded, which was enough for the mayor.

"Good," he said. "We've work to do."

It was Jonas who raised his hand, much like a schoolboy. And although he was the more nervous of the members, always biting his fingernails and such, he asked the question on all their minds. "Mayor, sir?"

"Yes, Jonas?"

"As you brought to the attention of everyone—"

"Mm, hmm? Go on, though I already know what you'll ask."

"Yes, well . . ." He looked around at the others staring at him, then back at the mayor. "Just that, sir . . . as for delivering the food, or the appeasement, as you call it, to the monster, are we . . . ?"

"Get it out. Say it!" urged the mayor, appearing to enjoy Jonas's squirming.

"Mayor, sir. I'm not as concerned for my safety as I am for that of my wife and children. I have responsibilities. If something were to happen to me . . ."

The others in the room turned and stared at the mayor. There was no pretending their safety wasn't on their minds.

"Stop worrying, all of you. Have I ever put you in harm's way?"

One by one, each affirmed it. Jonas assured him most of all. "No, sir! Nor did I intend to suggest otherwise."

"And nor will I. It's all part of my plan. Tomorrow night, on schedule, we will deliver the appeasement offering. We'll do so during curfew when our comings and goings go unnoticed. Besides, I'm going with you, so rest assured you won't be in danger."

The council members breathed a sigh of relief, the sheriff even more so since he had already encountered the beast, which was enough for him.

Having been silent during the meeting, Martha now insisted on being the one to conclude it. When she spoke, the council listened, fearing her almost as much as they feared her husband. At times, she could be far less subtle. Martha wagged her finger at each of them, the sweet smell of her floral perfume turning foul as she stared them down unflinchingly. "You'd best trust my husband. The town's weight rests on his shoulders, yet he has time to manage your welfare while you casually enjoy your prosperity, never considering the price he pays. And he's never let a single one of you down. You men have made an oath, and I have no problem holding you to it. Is that understood?"

Each said, "Yes, ma'am" or a variation of the same while nodding their understanding.

Satisfied with their responses, Martha asked, "Will that be all, dear?"

"That will do," said the mayor.

The sheriff opened the door and stood, making eye contact with each man as they left. He noted the sweat beading on their foreheads and how they avoided his gaze, their discomfort adding to his pleasure.

"Skinny has the carriage out back. Wait for me there, dear," said the mayor. "I have a matter to discuss with the sheriff."

"All right, darling," Martha said and left.

Once the mayor and sheriff were alone, the mayor spoke plainly. "You realize, don't you, that I have only you in my complete confidence. I share things with you that I keep even from my wife. She is a sturdy woman, but she is a woman."

"Yeah, of course."

"Sheriff?"

"Yeah, Mayor."

"I do take care of you, don't I?"

The sheriff scratched his head. "Yeah, I've no complaints."

"Well, I've asked a lot of you. I've asked things that would keep a lesser man up at night. But you are not a weak man. I can count on you."

"I sleep well enough, sir."

The mayor rested a hand on the sheriff's shoulder. "You enjoy your work, don't you?"

The sheriff nodded, and a smile crept over his face.

The mayor smiled back. "No need to answer. I know you do. Regardless, I want you to know that what we're doing, all the dirty work we're tasked with, is for the best, for the common good. And since I've higher aspirations than simply being mayor of New Harmony, your pathway to prosperity is assured. Your bank account will reflect my continued appreciation. But, like all payments, it stays between us, all of it."

"Goes without sayin', sir."

"Yes, Weasley, it does, without saying . . . a word."

Part 2

Enemies on the Pyre

Chapter 21

Emily stood peering out the kitchen window at the back of the house, waiting, when suddenly she hollered, "He's coming!" Bronson and LeFevre, sitting in the front parlor, quieted and listened. "I see him. He's running toward us!" Emily added. "Something must have happened!"

She opened the door just as Marco bounded up the back steps and came inside. Emily wasted no time in questioning him. "Why the urgency? Has something happened?"

Panting, he raised a finger, catching his breath as she waited. Finally, Marco spoke. "May I have some water, please?"

She hurried to the kitchen, poured a cup from the pitcher, and handed it to him. She then took his medical bag and set it on the table as he drank.

"They're waiting in the parlor," she said. "We're anxious to hear what happened."

"And I'll tell you. Come."

She followed him into the sitting room, where the others waited. Only then did Emily realize that what she'd mistaken for distress was sadness, his eyes full of concern.

"Emmy?" he said.

"Yes, Marco, what happened?"

"The new teacher, she . . ."

"Constance?"

"Yes, her. Regretfully, there was an attack."

"Constance was attacked? By whom? Please tell me it wasn't the Owens."

"No, at least not as reported."

"Well then, what? Is she all right?"

"No, I'm afraid not. She did not survive."

"What?" The news brought Emily to tears. Her voice trembled. "She was at school this very morning, but she left. What caused her to do that? We don't leave our students in the middle of the day. Ever!"

"No, we don't," agreed Bronson, only recently the headmaster. "Sit! Both of you." Emily sat next to LeFevre, while Marco fetched a chair from the kitchen. "Now tell us, Marco, what happened?"

Wincing at the discomfort of his broken ribs, LeFevre leaned forward. "And leave nothin' unsaid, Doc."

Bronson nodded. "Yes, start at the beginning."

"When I arrived at the town hall, it appeared the entirety of New Harmony gathered, less you three. The mayor came out of the building, appearing genuinely distraught. At least he said as much. He then reported the attack, saying the teacher had been ambushed on the road to Bloomington."

Confused, Emily said, "I saw Constance only this morning before the first bell. We spoke briefly but intended to speak further at the end of the day once we dismissed our students. I looked for her, but she was nowhere to be found. The parson said he'd seen her leave and that Constance was worried about her mother. She must have had distressing news. What other explanation is there?"

"I suppose she was rushing home, then," said Bronson. "Explains why she left as she did."

"It stands to reason," said Emily. "Her family, they're all from Bloomington. But who attacked her, and why?" Face puffy and swollen, Emily mumbled mainly to herself. "Hmm," she said as an unmistakable thought leaped into her head. "I have my suspicions. I certainly do."

"As do I," said Bronson. "If you're thinking the mayor, that's worth considering."

Before Emily could answer, Marco leaned back in his chair, rubbed his forehead, and said, "The mayor bears no guilt, not according to him. Instead, he laid the blame on Wallace's monster. Worse, it's partially my fault, or so he says. But, of course, I share that blame with you, Mr. LeFevre."

LeFevre's brows raised. "Repeat that last part, Doc. Thought I heard ya say the mayor blames us."

"You heard correctly, Mr. LeFev. Although I doubt the mayor knows our identities, he is somehow aware of our attempt to hunt down and kill the beast. And now, apparently, it's forbidden for whatever reason."

"What's forbidden?" LeFevre asked.

"Hunting the beast. What's more, we are responsible for the teacher's death."

"Says who?"

"The mayor, of course."

LeFevre looked in shock at Bronson. "Ya hear that? Ya suppose the mayor's cider turned hard and now he's drunken to lunacy?"

"Hmm, perhaps," agreed Bronson. "But I suspect there's more to it than that."

Turning his attention to Marco, Bronson asked, "Did the mayor give any indication as to how you and LeFev here would be responsible? Neither of you were anywhere near Constance."

"To answer your question, Mr. Parrish, what I gathered is that someone agitated the monster in an attempt to kill it. That's why. According to the mayor, it attacked the teacher for no other reason than revenge—revenge for being hunted. But how could he know unless he supposes himself capable of divination, possessing intuitive knowledge of a monster's thoughts? As absurd as it is, I admit to hiding among the crowd after hearing the allegation." Marco turned to LeFevre. "Do you suppose anyone could have seen us leaving or returning? As careful as we were, there are never assurances of not being seen."

"Don't ya worry, Doc. The old sack is lying," said LeFevre. "He'd have the sheriff sniffin' our butts like ol' Coot here if he even suspected. We'd be locked up in the jail for even the suspicion."

"It's not all he's lying about," said Bronson. "It doesn't seem reasonable for the young teacher to encounter the monster on the eastern road to Bloomington."

"Monster's north of the gorge," said Marco.

"Agreed," said Bronson. "How far north remains to be seen, though it did wander into town."

"Witnessed by many," Marco added.

"Emily?"

"Yes, Mr. Bronson."

"The new teacher, Constance, you said she was alarmed by what she saw—the birds and the mayor."

Emily nodded. "Yes."

"You said she feared he might have seen her listening. You said that as well, am I right?"

"That's right."

"And she heard a confession, something not intended for her ears. Then, today, she left with the sheriff, leaving Mrs. Owen to attend her class. That what the parson said?"

"Parson Burroughs saw her leave with the sheriff just before noon," said Emily, wiping away her tears. "And I saw Mrs. Owen filling in for her, teaching her students at the end of the day."

"I see," said Bronson. "From that we can assume she did see him coming home under cover of night—coincidentally, the night he locked up the ballots. So he must have realized she . . ."

Marco interrupted, his voice angry. "She left with the sheriff in broad daylight, just like my brother. If they are responsible, they're hardly covering their tracks!"

"Aww, Doc. Prey, not the hunter, covers its tracks," said LeFevre. "They ain't worried."

Bronson agreed, adding, "Tracks or no tracks, who'd dare lay such an accusation, risking arrest or worse?"

"Risk disappearing," said Emily.

LeFevre shouted, "Enough! It's time for action. No more sittin' here like toads on a hollow log sufferin' the glare of those high on their pedestals lookin' down on us."

Bronson held up his hands. "Now calm yourself, LeFev, and that goes for the rest of you. We're on a perilous path, and none of you bargained for any part of it. Don't you see? We are all in danger, especially you, Emily. What if they forced that teacher to tell them about your conversation? They may already know Constance told you what she saw. So listen to me, all of you. I started this. I challenged the royal family, and I don't want any of you hurt on my account. What I'm saying to you, what I want you to understand, is that we're done. There will be no more talk about any of this from any of you. Please, go home. Leave it be. There is no winning, no resolution. I started this, and I will be the one who ends it."

As painful as it was to admit, Marco understood Bronson's concerns. But it didn't mean he had to agree. For now, there was no time to argue. "The hour grows late," he said, "and we need to get home. The mayor's initiated a curfew starting at sundown. Anyone on the street after that will be arrested, and the mayor promises a severe penalty, though he left us to imagine what it could be. Moreover, we must relinquish our weapons, rifles, and such tomorrow afternoon at the town center."

LeFevre screamed, "What!" again, becoming irate. "Let 'em try. Gonna get me a trophy over my fireplace yet. And as for you, Bronson, I'm in this fight with ya, shattered ribs or not! I'm good for a brawl. And don't ya dare presume ya do it alone!"

Marco stood, his feet planted firmly on the ground. "Don't you count me out either, Mr. Parrish. There may be no winning, but tyranny cannot go unanswered. I'll bleed before I see it." He turned his attention to Emily. "But you promise me you'll stay out of this. None of us can bear to see you hurt, Emmy, least of all."

Emily stood, facing them all. "No," she said emphatically. "This was my fight long before any of yours. Must I remind you who took my parents and the man I was to marry? I'm not willing to let you risk everything while I do nothing. I'm no toad, Mr. LeFevre. I won't sit on the hollow log and watch all of you risk everything. I can't, and I won't!"

Marco squeezed her hand. "Emmy, these men, they're dangerous. They're . . ." His eyes pleaded for her to listen.

"I know better than anyone, Marco. But my life is of no more value than any of yours. And as for you, Mr. Bronson . . ."

"Yes, Emily?"

"This is not your decision to make. We each make our own. We face the Owens and the sheriff together."

"Hold on," said Bronson, again raising his hands. "We're assuming a lot. What if Wallace's monster *is* responsible? There's a chance Christian and the new teacher were attacked, and not by the mayor or sheriff. I doubt it, but where's the proof?"

Marco shook his head. "The monster didn't kill my brother. I know it."

Though they all harbored doubts, they stared intently at Marco, surprised by the conviction in his voice.

A moment of silence passed between them before LeFevre spoke. "What the hell ya talkin' 'bout, Doc? The monster's a vicious killer!"

Marco continued shaking his head. "And I'm telling you it's not. The monster wasn't there to kill us, or we wouldn't be here. It so easily could have, and why not? We were there to kill it. I even shot at it and might have hit it, yet here we are. Explain that to me."

"Nah," said LeFevre dismissingly. "All a misunderstandin'. Is that it?"

"Yes, Mr. LeFevre. That's what I'm saying."

"Well, I've shattered ribs that say otherwise. And that ain't no tomata soup in my chamber pot. No, just because we're alive don't mean the monster was tryin' to be neighborly."

"We can debate forever," said Marco. "Nightfall's coming, and there's a curfew. We've no time left. And there's no sense getting arrested for being out past dark."

"Marco's right," said Bronson. "Emily, Marco will see you home safely, but hurry. You haven't much time."

"Wait!" said Marco. "I nearly forgot. There is the issue of appeasement."

Curious faces stared at Marco.

"Appeasement?" asked Bronson.

"Yes, an appeasement, an offering. It's part of the mayor's plan, which he now imposes."

"And this plan of his, what does it entail?"

"What I gather, Mr. Bronson, is that it's an offering to the monster, a goodwill gesture, I suppose. Mayor says we need to appease the beast."

"For what reason, and with what are we to appease the beast?"

"Items of food or drink. The mayor intends to offer it to the beast to ingratiate ourselves to it, to curry favor, as it were. We must drop off a donation of food—preserves, beverages, wine, and whiskey—at the town hall tomorrow. The sheriff will collect our guns there as well."

LeFevre nearly tumbled off the couch and onto the floor. "We're to render the monster harmless by servin' it food and wine? And the mayor wants us disarmed? So that's his plan?" He nearly burst out laughing.

"That's the plan. I heard it said myself."

"How can that be?" asked LeFevre. He noticed the stern look on Marcus's face, and suddenly it wasn't as humorous as he first supposed. "Has sanity—has it blown away with the wind? Are we prisoners in a lunatic asylum? Is that where we find ourselves now?"

"LeFev, no more discussion. Please," said Bronson. "There's no time left. We all agreed on finding a course of action, but not this evening. We must meet again. And, Emily, you're correct in saying it's not my decision. And although I cannot lie, I must admit to fearing the responsibility of the outcome, and I'd rather you sit on the hollow log, yet fairness demands otherwise. Therefore, I welcome your involvement, only with careful consideration moving forward. Is that agreed?"

"Agreed," said Emily.

"Then we will meet again, but, unfortunately, not here. It's no longer safe."

"I'm only next door. Can't meet there either," said LeFevre.

Emily thought a moment before suggesting a place they could come and go unnoticed. "Let's meet at my parents' house. It's fallen into disrepair enough to avoid suspicion."

Everyone agreed it was the perfect place.

"We'll have to use the curfew to our advantage to hide our comings and goings. It's a risk we'll have to take. So it means we must use extreme caution not to be seen," said Bronson. "Tomorrow night?"

They all nodded.

"Very well, Marco. Please see Emily home."

Marco followed Emily into the kitchen and through the back door. "Tomorrow night, after curfew," he said as he and Emily slipped out into the fading light.

Chapter 22

In the darkness of his cave, the beast sniffed the item left by the tall, thin murderer, the one guilty of the final blow. He recognized it as something he might have worn in his previous life, though his head was far too large for it to suit his needs now. He closed his eyes and inhaled the strong scents of felt and leather and something else. He sniffed again and focused on a singular scent hidden under the more apparent smells.

There it is.

He held his breath. His black eyes opened and glistened in the dim light. The scent he looked for—sweet, pungent sweat—filled him with purpose and brought him out of his cave and into the night.

He traversed the meadow on four limbs, his front paws pushing against gravity and the dirt road while his hind legs met their rapid pace in perfect synchronicity, thrusting and pushing him forward at remarkable speeds. He weaved through the gorge with near-perfect clarity of vision until the sheer rocky cliffs on either side eventually opened into the distant valley. There, where the gorge opened, something lay in the road. He stopped, stared, leaped over it, and then turned back for a better look. Someone had constructed a wooden barrier, a slatted fence. Nailed to it was a board with letters painted on it. He looked curiously at the writing.

There are words here. I'd forgotten about written language, but this is familiar.

Puzzling over the letters, he spelled them out in his head: *C-L-O-S-E-D*. The letters tumbled about in his brain until . . .

Recognition suddenly dawned, and he felt the urge to smile, and he would have were he able. It was then he felt another human emotion—hope.

It spells closed. The road's closed. I may not have to abandon my home in search of another.

He looked down into the valley thinking to leave well enough alone and return to his den. He prepared to leap back over the barrier but hesitated. Instead, he slowly turned around and stared for a time at the glistening lights of the town.

I can't leave. I've unfinished business.

The beast left the road and traversed the mountain's base, maneuvering over boulders, brush, and rocks to the ridge that jutted out from Erebus. Under a canopy of twinkling stars, he watched and waited for the lights in the town to disappear. As soon as the humans slept, the hunt would begin.

I could not have hoped for better. The moon serves me tonight! His umber fur was indistinguishable in the palette of colors surrounding him in the silvery light. It was difficult for human eyes to see him from a distance in the daylight, but in the dark, it was impossible. In no time, he crept through the town.

I must be cautious lest I encounter a human who would alert others to my presence.

The beast leaped cautiously over fences, ducked under low-hanging branches, and skirted the hedges surrounding the human dwellings. He darted across streets only when necessary. He tasted the breeze, his nose high in the air, searching for the scent, the one hidden in the item left by the murderer. Finally, he turned the corner of a house where a small dog sat on the porch. One look at the monster and the dog slunk away, whimpering, its tail between its legs—fortunate, since the monster preferred not to have to stop its beating heart.

There are no humans. Are they all sleeping? There are usually one or two I must avoid after sundown, but not tonight. Why?

He contemplated, then thought no more of it since it was to his advantage. The crescent moon glistened as the beast peered through heart-shaped redbuds and leafy foliage. Suddenly, he caught a scent—not the one he'd come for but familiar nonetheless. In shadows, he rose on his hind legs, his snout scanning the night air. His head turned in the direction from whence the smell came. Quickly, he crossed the street, turned a corner, and stopped. Again, he reared up and stood tall. In front of him stood a house bathed in a warm glow. Inside, a human slept unaware.

I can smell you. Yes, I recognize you. You hunted me, convinced I murdered your brother, yet I let you live. Even now, you sleep. So sleep well, and don't make that mistake again!

Chapter 23

Emily lifted her cornflower-blue dress nearly to her white cotton drawers, enough for her to run as she hurried down the street toward the school. Since Constance's class would be without a teacher, Mrs. Owen was sure to be there waiting.

The morning bell must ring on time.

Emily sighed in relief as the school came into view. Annette St. Clair sat outside and waved when she saw Emily. Emily stopped running and let go of her dress.

Upon entering the yard and after greeting several children, Emily called to Annette, "Oh my, so glad to see you safe. Did you sleep well enough?"

"Not so much, but be warned. Mrs. Owen is inside talking to Ms. Woolhauser right now."

Emily came up alongside Annette and looked past her through the propped-open front door. "I prefer to wait outside with you if you don't mind."

"Why would I mind? I'm waiting outside for the same reason. Mrs. Owen gives me nightmares."

Emily sat beside her on the steps. "Hmm, well, you are certainly not alone."

"I suppose not." With that, Annette stood, looked at the clock, and said, "Unfortunately, it appears our reprieve is over." She reached for the rope.

As if on cue, Mrs. Owen charged out of the school. "Don't ring that bell!"

Emily looked at her, confused. *Mrs. Owen considers not ringing the bell on time a carnal sin. Yet here she is, instructing us to break her most stringent rule.*

Emily watched Annette's discomfort as she, too, struggled to understand. "Oh! But I was just about to . . ."

"Yes, Mrs. St. Clair. Since I am not blind, I can see that. And that is why I've come to inform you in person. There is no school today or tomorrow. Not until further notice."

Ms. Woolhauser exited the school. She did not appear pleased with this recent development but remained quiet as Mrs. Owen continued her instructions. "Send the students straight home and stay here for any stragglers who arrive late. The children are our primary concern. For now, home is the only safe place. Go home as soon as you finish here."

"Mrs. Owen?"

"Yes, Mrs. St. Clair? What is it?"

"What happened to Constance?"

"Did you not hear my husband? He explained it very well."

"I did, ma'am. But I was wondering why she left her class early."

"I can tell you that she was at the ranch, bags packed, and said she was going back to Bloomington. Her only complaint was that not one of you made her feel welcome. I asked her to finish the day, and she agreed. But by midday, she had abandoned her assignment, so I came here to fill in. Unfortunately, she didn't have the courtesy to wait until after school. I was very disappointed with her at first, but now it seems hardly important after what happened. How sad that you did not make her feel welcome. But do not worry as we will all try harder next time. However, I'd consider how I treat the next teacher if I were you."

"I'm sorry. I could have done better by her," said Annette.

"How sweet that you, Mrs. St. Clair, now recognize it, but you all could have."

Behind Mrs. Owen, Ms. Woolhauser rolled her eyes. Emily pretended not to notice.

"This is all very unfortunate," said Emily. "Constance and I intended to dine together. We were—"

"Excuse me, Miss Hampshire, but wait until I finish." After hushing the teachers, Mrs. Owen continued. "Terrible thing that happened. But we need to move on. The council and I are unsure when it will be safe for the children to return to school, which gives me time to find Constance's replacement. With prayer and good fortune, the appeasement will satisfy the beast and things will return to normal. And so I remind you to bring your donation at the appointed hour. You must; it is the law."

While Mrs. Owen waited for each to show compliance, Ms. Woolhauser drew attention to the children, some with parents, waiting in the yard. Others continued to arrive from every direction. "Perhaps we shouldn't keep them waiting. We should do as you say, Mrs. Owen, and send them on their way."

Mrs. Owen looked at Emily. "I trust you to tell them properly, with genuine concern, that we are closing the school for their protection. And you might as well inform them there will be no Sunday services. The church is closed as well. And you, Ms. Woolhauser . . ."

"Yes?"

"Lock the doors, and then you and Mrs. St. Clair, here, and you, Miss Hampshire, can go, but be careful when you bring your offerings, and don't come alone; it's not entirely safe. The Wallace monster attacks no matter the hour. We see that with what happened to Ms. Madison, so I urge caution. Once the appeasement offerings secure our safety, we can reopen the school and church."

Mrs. Owen turned and walked briskly to her carriage. With some effort, she pulled herself up onto the seat. Releasing the brake, she whipped her horse. Everyone in the yard, including the teachers, watched as the sound of hooves and the rattling of the carriage faded down the street.

Once Mrs. Owen was gone, Ms. Woolhauser mocked, "Why, here, Mr. Monster. Thank you for killing Ms. Madison. Have some peaches, will you? I may have strawberry preserves on freshly baked bread if that interests you. How about a back rub? Soak your feet? Now, please, no more killing."

"I don't believe appeasement is the point of any of this," said Emily. "But we must be careful. Who knows who will report us if they hear us speaking sour words."

"That's right. Annette," said Ms. Woolhauser, "please, no more confiding in Mrs. Owen."

Annette wore an equal portion of disgust. "You needn't worry, Ms. Woolhauser. I've learned my lesson."

"That's good," said Ms. Woolhauser. "We must all walk on eggshells, all of us, and be careful."

Chapter 24

Nearly two months after graduating from medical school and returning to New Harmony, Marco had leased an office space on Main Street. He'd swept the floor, patched walls with paste and plaster, and applied a fresh coat of white paint, which added a smell of newness. But few knew Dr. Salvatori's office was open for business. Marco commissioned signage from Weston Riley for gold lettering on the front window and a signboard to hang above his front door. He still waited for Weston to get around to it, but there was little hurry. Weston was a council member, busy with all the changes since news of Wallace's monster had left the businesses on Main Street practically empty.

Alone in his office, Marco sat on a chair next to an old carpentry table left by the prior tenant. It now served a dual purpose—examination table and desk. He'd initially worried about the noise from the adjacent lumber and supply store when leasing the office from the Owens, but even it had gone silent, leaving him alone with his thoughts. A little farther down the street stood his father's barbershop. He wanted to find an office space closer to his father and a landlord other than the mayor, but that was rare in New Harmony.

In the quiet, he could hear what people said as they passed his window. They spoke of only one thing—the monster and anything related to it. He listened to speculation about the gruesome attacks, the appeasement offering, the curfew, and even the surrendering of guns. Later that afternoon, many carried bottles under their arms, cloth sacks full of food, and the occasional firearm, all in compliance with the mayor's orders. Marco waited while shadows grew long, intent on leaving just enough time after closing to lock up and hustle to the sheriff's office to surrender his guns. His flint rifle leaned against the wall next to the door so he wouldn't forget. A bottle of wine he had brought that morning sat on the desk next to his father's pistol. For Marco, the bottle of wine was a gesture of gratitude for the monster not having killed him, for allowing him to live.

Drink up, beast. I owe you more than this, though I find it difficult to imagine you a winebibber!

He picked up the bottle with his left hand, feeling the smooth, brown glass. With the other, he reached for his father's Colt revolver. He liked the feel of the weight in his hand. How long ago his father purchased it, he didn't know. Though made in America, the relic had been brought across the Atlantic from the old country. And as far as Marco knew, though it remained functional, it had never dispatched a single ball. He set the bottle down and scooted a chair under a support crossbeam above him, then stood on the chair and hid his father's pistol in the rafters. Then he grabbed his keys and tucked the bottle of wine under his arm. Before leaving, he stared at the rifle near the door.

What if they suspect me of going after the monster? Perhaps it is best to claim I haven't a gun.

After hiding the long gun alongside the pistol, he locked the door and headed toward the town center. When he arrived, Weston stood in the New Harmony park beside a wagon, accepting donations. A line had formed, people waiting to drop off their offerings. Since the mayor had complimented Abigail on her shepherd's pie, it was no surprise to see her waiting in line with a plate full of the stuff.

"Next!" said Weston, and everyone moved forward. Eventually, Marco's turn arrived. When he handed Weston the bottle of wine, Weston cocked his head to one side and asked, "That it?"

"We haven't much, Weston. And with Hyrum closing the store early due to the monster, it's just my pa and me, and I'm still waiting for my signage. So perhaps you haven't had time either."

"I haven't. I've been busy," Weston admitted. "But you'll get it eventually. Right now, I'm just following orders."

Weston took the bottle and set it in an open crate. "Take your guns over there." He pointed across the street to the sheriff's office, where the sheriff stood next to a table laden with firearms.

"I would if I had one."

Weston tilted his head toward the sheriff. "Tell him. Make certain he removes you from the list. And, Marco?"

"Hmm?"

"I'm sorry about Christian." Without waiting for a response, Weston looked past Marco to the person in line behind him. "Next!"

Marco slipped away, trying to be as inconspicuous as possible, hoping the sheriff wouldn't notice him. It was then he heard the sheriff yell, "You! Over here!"

For a moment, it felt as though his heart stopped. But knowing how foolish it would be to ignore the sheriff, Marco crossed the street to face the man. The sheriff eyed Marco as he approached. "Hello, Sheriff."

"Where are your firearms? And don't say you haven't any. I know better."

"But I haven't any." Marco patted his pockets and shrugged his shoulders.

"What about your brother? Little doubt he had one."

To hear the sheriff mention Christian infuriated Marco. He answered more brazenly than intended. "If my brother had one, he's no longer here to use it."

"Don't matter. Every gun's gotta be accounted for, even his. I'm placin' ya on my list, so have it ready when I come by. Now run along!"

Noting the pistol at the sheriff's side, Marco obliged. He crossed the street a second time and headed home. But before he did, he looked back at Weston, who still placed items in a crate inside the wagon bed, a gun strapped to his belt.

What might they need a gun for—fear of a monster or of us?

Marco had turned down Main when he noticed light coming from his father's barbershop. As he passed the window, he saw his father brushing off his barber chair with a broom. He pushed open the door, the bell ringing as he stuck his head in.

"Are you ready to leave, Papa?"

"Depends. You deliver our offerin'?"

"Yes, Papa. I'm coming from there."

Tommaso removed his apron, folded it, and drew down the wick of his lantern until the flame went out. "I am ready."

As they walked together, bound for home, Marco said, "The sheriff insists we surrender Christian's gun. He assumes he had one, and I'd rather our home not be searched. Do you know where it is?"

Tommaso shrugged. "His room? Christian wasn't armed when . . ." Tommaso went silent, unable to say more.

"Papa, I understand. It's all too painful to think about. He didn't stand a chance, did he?"

"No, son. No chance. So, you find it there."

"I just haven't been in his room since—"

"Hmm," said Tommaso. "I haven't either."

Chapter 25

The sun disappeared behind the western fields of grain, the resulting dusk smothering New Harmony in uncertainty and fear, the streets barren, the doors locked, the curtains drawn. An eerie silence replaced the usual chirping of crickets and hooting of owls. Instead, the gathering darkness unleashed visions of a monster lurking in their dreams, along with all sorts of horrid imaginings.

After locking the door, Tommaso lit a candle and entered the kitchen as Marco searched Christian's bedroom.

He rummaged through Christian's clothes and belongings, looking for his long gun. "It's here somewhere, Papa," he called out. He searched through dresser drawers and behind clothes hanging on hooks or folded on the bed.

Meanwhile, Tommaso filled the kitchen with the smell of crushed garlic, olives, and tomato sauce. He called over his shoulder, "You'll find the Colt in my room, in the drawer. Don't want the sheriff in there."

"I've already hidden it where the sheriff won't find it."

"You not worried 'bout the sheriff?"

Marco halted in his search. "I'm always worried, but I don't intend for us to be completely unarmed. When the sheriff comes, Papa, don't say anything. Let me talk. No one knows what we have."

Marco dropped to his knees, looking under Christian's bed. There, wrapped in his brother's overcoat, was the rifle. He pulled it out and set it on the bed. "I found it!" Looking up, Marco noticed an envelope in a partially open dresser drawer among his brother's undergarments. He withdrew the letter and read. "My Dear Christian."

It was their mother's handwriting.

The smell of pasta added to the other scents that wafted into Christian's bedroom from the kitchen, yet Marco hardly noticed.

"Supper!" Tommaso announced. He waited for a reply. When no such came, he set the iron skillet and wooden spoon on the hearth and walked into the room where Marco sat staring at the letter held tightly in his hands. Tommaso sat beside him.

"Ah, the letter," said Tommaso. "Your mother, she wrote that for Christian."

"Hmm, I see," said Marco. "Did um . . ."

"She did. There is one for you."

"Then why haven't you given it to me?"

"Your mother says, 'Tommaso, you know when to give it to them.' I was waitin.'"

"May I see it?"

He patted Marco's knee, then left the room only to return a moment later with an envelope. He handed it to Marco without saying a word and headed back to the kitchen, quietly closing the door behind him.

Alone in his room, Marco opened the envelope and read.

My Dear Marco,

Some days are good, while others aren't. Today is good. I'm watching you study in your room. I can see you through the open door as I lay in bed. I know I will not be with you soon. I'm overcome with sorrow for it. There are some things I wish to say but dare not—these things I hold in my heart. I am weighed down with concern for you, even more than for your brother. I want nothing more than to be here to help you see what I see in you. When I talk to Christian, he always looks deep into my eyes. When we speak, you always look off into the distance. I know you'll one day follow your dreams and leave this place. But remember, son, home isn't a house. Home is wherever your family resides. Don't fly far, little bird, too far from home. Your papa and brother will need you close.

What I now write, these words, they pain me. But I feel compelled to leave them with you no matter how hard they are for me to write.

It is that I know your secret. Don't be troubled; mothers know. I see it in your eyes when she comes to the house. I see your pain and feel your love for your brother, Papa, me, and another. There are mysteries in life that are just that—mysteries. The human heart is the greatest of those. But I promise you, love will find you if you stay good like the boy your papa and I raised. Such a thing as love may not come as planned. Some things can't be planned at all. Some things are in God's hands and His alone. But someone out there will fill your heart and heal it. How? That is another mystery, but it is true that you invite love by showing love, and don't ever fear it. Be the excellent man your papa and I raised. Never lose that boy who's my son. And when God places the right woman in your path, don't allow unfulfilled expectations to rob you of happiness. However, it's not as easy as words when it comes to a life lived day by day.

So remember, I will love you no matter where death takes me. I will always be your mother, watch over you, and always miss you. Our hearts belong to each other. Remember to be brave in life, always come home, and keep your heart open for God's blessing. I will always love you.

As he read his mother's words, her voice spoke to him naturally, in tune with the treasured memories of their time together. However, two words jumped out at him, words his mother wrote long ago meant for him now. In his head, he heard her voice. *Be brave.*

"I will, Mama," he said quietly, placing the letter in his medical bag and buckling it shut.

Chapter 26

As darkness from the east turned the daylight to dusk, the sheriff began herding townsfolk into their homes with the threat of curfew ticking ever closer.

"Move along!" he ordered. "Curfew is for yer safety!" He lit the lantern on the curb in front of the town hall as several ranchers and farmers complained about relinquishing their firearms. Abigail stood close by, listening, with Susannah and Elizabeth at her side.

"We're on the outskirts," said Boyd Kensington. "Ain't safe out there, not without weapons. Ain't fair, neither."

Old Man Taylor added his protest to the growing list of the disgruntled. "He's got a point, Sheriff, and you know it. We're closest to the monster with the gorge not far from our homes."

Abigail stared at the farmers accusingly. "They're probably the ones who went after the monster, Sheriff. I wouldn't be surprised if it's their fault the teacher got killed. Besides, what do they need their guns for?"

Boyd snapped at her. "Shut up, ya old hen! Yer bein' ridiculous."

The other farmers raised their voices in protest, but Abigail merely smirked, Susannah and Elizabeth joining her. She shook her head. "No cure for the ignorant, Sheriff. Sorry to say."

"Enough, Abigail," he said. "I'll handle this." Then, turning back to the farmers, he rested his hand on the pistol strapped to his side. "The outskirts, huh? If you want to sleep in town, I can arrange a bed for ya—behind bars. Now, it's the law we're talkin' 'bout here. Whether ya like it or not, I don't rightly care. It's the law, so ya do it!"

He waved them off with a hand. "Sun's nearly down, and you're on the outskirts. Best get goin.'" The sheriff stared them down as they slowly walked away unarmed. "Hurry!" he yelled after them, "lest the monster gets ya!" They heard the women laughing from behind them as they went.

As the sheriff dismissed the farmers, Skinny pulled up beside the mayor in a wagon.

"What took you so long?" asked the mayor. Skinny was about to answer when the mayor said, "Never mind! Load the guns in my wagon and deliver them to the ranch. That pile of food over there—put it in my cellar." He pointed to his share stacked at the bottom of the steps. "Do hurry!"

Skinny nodded, and the wagon moved forward with a cluck of the tongue and a whip of the reins.

The mayor called out, "Weston, how much longer?" Before Weston could answer, the mayor yelled at Hyrum. "Are you ready? Is the load tied down?"

Hyrum stopped what he was doing. "Almost. Waiting on Weston."

Weston heard and stopped hammering to look up at the mayor. "Last crate, sir. That pile there?" Weston pointed to an equally large stack of food off to one side. "You said not to crate."

"That's right. Only crate the bottles with plenty of straw, like I told you. Bumpy road ahead."

Weston nodded. A few more strikes of the hammer, and he set it down. "That's it, sir."

"Good." The mayor called to Ernie and Jonas. "Stop eating, Jonas. You and Ernie help Weston haul these crates to Hyrum so he can finish tying the load. Move it!"

Just then, the sheriff approached the mayor. "Skinny's loadin' the guns. What else is there, sir?"

"Half the food and drink is already loaded for delivery of the appeasement. The other half, that over there . . ." The mayor pointed at the pile.

"Oh, what wouldn't fit on the wagon?"

"Yes, Weasley, that pile. Divide it among yourselves. I've already separated what is Martha's and mine. Consider the rest a donation to the council and you, Weasley, in equal shares. Before we leave, instruct the council to hide their portions. Even with the curfew, tell them to hurry back and be careful no one notices. We don't have much time and a long journey ahead. Oh, and have them wear something warm."

Nearly an hour later, Jonas was the last of the council to return.

"Gather around," ordered the mayor. They all hurried to where the mayor waited. "Weston, I need you to stay back. As the deputy sheriff, you're in charge when Weasley's away. While we're gone, you enforce the curfew. Understand?"

"Yes, sir."

"And, Weston, don't worry whether you can or cannot arrest someone. It's an order; you are the law, so do it. We'll sort it out upon our return."

"I will, sir. I'll keep everyone locked up in their homes or the jail."

"That's what I want to hear. Weasley, toss Weston the keys."

The sheriff dropped the key to his office into Weston's hand. "That'll get ya in the front door. The key to the jail is in the top drawer. Don't worry 'bout how many ya put in there. It's small, but more will fit than ya think. Long as ya don't concern yourself with their comfort."

"All right, then," said the mayor. "Each of you has a share of the food and drink, but keep it between us. Consider it a benefit for your pledge to loyalty. Understood?"

Each renewed his pledge.

"Saddle up, and, believe me, you're all going to earn your shares tonight."

Chapter 27

A knock came at the back door. Marjorie shook Albert awake. "Go see who it is and send 'em away!"

Albert agreed. "Shouldn't be anyone out at this hour, past curfew."

Dressed only in his nightshirt, Albert peeked out the window and promptly opened the door. In her nightgown, Marjorie was already in the kitchen, standing behind Albert. The usually courteous woman was in a flutter. "Marco, ya shouldn't be here. We can all get in big trouble."

"I'm sorry, Mrs. Hampshire. I presume Emmy didn't tell you I was coming?"

Before Marjorie answered, Emily's door opened, and they all turned to look as she entered the kitchen and said, "It's my fault, Auntie. It's all my fault. I should have said something."

Marco appeared at a loss of words. Lucky for him, Emily did the talking.

Marjorie's eyes widened at the sight of Emily dressed all in black. Only then did she notice Marco wore black as well. "What's this? Albert! Do somethin'!"

Emily pleaded, "Auntie, please. I couldn't tell you because I dare not involve you."

"In what? Emmy, you are our responsibility. Albert!"

Albert wore a look of grave concern. "What do ya want me to do?"

"Stop 'em is what I want you to do!"

Emily saw the worry on their faces and groaned. "I'm so sorry," she said, "but we must be somewhere important and can't risk anyone seeing us. That would bring more trouble. So we must venture out under the cover of night. We've no other choice."

"Oh no, no, no, dear. Trouble from breaking curfew is the least of your worries. It's not safe out there. The mayor said as much, and we must trust—"

"Auntie, would you excuse Albert and me?"

"What for? There's nothing to discuss. Whatever you're up to, you can't! Albert, say somethin'."

Brushing past Marjorie, Albert said, "Let me talk to her, dear. It'll be all right."

Emily looked at Marco. "Please wait here with Auntie. Give us a moment?"

Marco nodded and looked down, avoiding Marjorie's gaze.

Emily took Albert by the hand, led him to her room, and closed the door. She looked into his worried eyes and to where deep wrinkles formed on his forehead. Not letting go of his hand, she asked, "Can you trust me?"

"My concern has nothing to do with trust, my dear. It's that your aunt Margie is right. It's much too dangerous. Whatever you're up to doesn't matter, not when it comes to your safety."

In his face, she saw the undying affection from the years of raising her and providing for her while picking up the pieces of her shattered life after losing her parents. Emily hated seeing him this way, frightened of losing her. Besides, she was better acquainted with losing someone than causing others to worry about losing her.

"Uncle, I can't tell you much, and you must trust me enough not to ask, but . . . I can't knowingly put you and Auntie in danger. Believe me. I haven't a choice."

"You always have a choice. I taught you better."

"Perhaps, but if the choice is doing nothing and allowing innocent people to be hurt, or worse, what choice is there?"

"But what could you possibly do, and for what? If you're thinking for one minute of going after the monster . . . I know you're justified in wanting revenge, but look at you. You're a—"

"A woman?"

"Yes, and a young woman at that. Have you shot a gun? Besides, they're all confiscated. Wait! What am I even saying? You can't be thinking of going after the monster, not after what happened to Marco."

"I can assure you that's not what we're doing."

"Then why can't you just trust the mayor? Stay safe. Is that so much to ask?"

"I'm not going after the monster. At least not that one."

"Then what? You're not making any sense."

The more Albert tried convincing her not to leave, the more Emily recalled the many nights she lay awake, remembering the darkness of the tool closet, waiting for her father to return.

I promised myself that one day I would confront the men who robbed me of my parents. But how can I make Auntie and Albert understand while keeping them safe?

When Emily became lost in thought, Albert took hold of her arms and gently shook her to get her attention. "Please don't do this," he begged. His voice cracked, and he could no longer hold back his emotions.

Emily's eyes filled with tears, as did his. "Papa?"

Albert froze. She'd never called him that. "I'm here, Emmy, daughter."

"Most of my life, that's what you've been—my father. I can call you that now, can't I?"

"Yes, Emmy. Yes, of course. I'd be honored. But that doesn't mean I can let you leave tonight."

"Papa, you've given me more than I could have ever hoped for. But I'm a grown woman now. And I know you took me in and loved me as much as any father could love a daughter, but now I'm asking, as your daughter, to trust me whatever the outcome. Even if it ends poorly, it's my choice, and it's time you let me go."

"But it's a hard thing you're asking!" Albert cried. "How can you even ask it?"

"It's equally hard for me. But if I don't return, I need you and Auntie to deny you ever saw us leave tonight. Marco was never here, and you woke in the morning believing I'd already left for the day. Make sure Auntie says no differently. And, Papa, you're right. You taught me I always have a choice. My choice is this: I'd rather die than live knowing I was a coward when it mattered. I hope you'll be proud of me one day."

Albert looked at her solemnly, still wiping away tears. "I already am. What worries me is that my brother, your father, said almost the very same thing before he went missing. It's what worries me, but I am proud. I am."

Albert hugged her tightly, wanting to keep her close, never to let go. A moment full of fear, grief, and love passed between them before he released her.

They walked out to where Marco and Marjorie anxiously waited.

"Margie," said Albert, "they're going to leave." Marjorie started to protest, but he looked at her through his lingering tears and said more forcefully, "Marco, protect her with your life. Emmy, if you're going to go, do it before I change my mind."

Emily heard Marjorie crying as they stepped out into the night, the lock on the door engaging behind them.

Chapter 28

The hour was late, and few windows glowed with candlelight as Hyrum climbed aboard the wagon loaded with crates and perishables. He nodded to Ernie and Jonas to his right, both on horseback. Even in the dim light of the street lantern in front of the town hall, he could see the worry on their faces. Behind him, the mayor and sheriff mounted their horses. They spoke to one another, though Hyrum couldn't decipher what they said. He noticed that no one had a lantern except for him. He placed it unlit on the seat beside him, to be used only in an emergency. Next to the lantern sat his rifle, primed, also for emergency only. As he waited for the order to move out, he draped his winter coat over his lap and glanced at Weston, who stood on the town hall steps. He stared at his friend, feeling like a sailor embarking on a perilous voyage on the high seas, perhaps never to be seen again.

Tired from the long day, his mind wandered. *If I had my druthers*, he thought, *Weston, you'd be sitting here in this wagon, and I'd be standing there on the steps, watching you leave. The gorge is the last place I'd be heading.*

"Hyrum!" Startled from his thoughts, Hyrum jumped as the mayor rode up alongside the wagon and shouted his name. "Hyrum!"

"Oh, yes, sir!"

"It's time. Let's get a move on. And stay alert!"

With that, Hyrum released the brake and urged the horses forward. As the wagon moved, his stomach lurched with it. He tried assuring himself that all would be well as they slowly made their way north through town. A dog barked, and eyes peered through slits in otherwise drawn curtains until, finally, New Harmony was but a few twinkling lights in the distance behind them. It was then that Hyrum felt the night close in around him. Up ahead, where Mount Erebus loomed large above the valley, darkness swallowed the stars as the steady noise of the wagon and clomping of hooves threatened to lull him to sleep. Only the cold on his face and the terrifying prospect of encountering a monster kept him awake. He peered into the black void, his hand on his rifle.

Only a sliver of moon hung in the sky. Hyrum watched as they passed Boyd Kensington's cornfield on the left and Old Man Taylor's pasture on the right. Farther ahead was the turnoff to the gorge—a place of dread, especially past midnight.

As the minutes ticked away, Hyrum became more anxious. He whispered to himself, "This is not safe! There is far too little light, only enough to cast a gloom."

They rode a bit farther until, finally, Hyrum recognized the crossroad up ahead. He gripped the reins and prepared to pull hard to the left, toward the gorge when suddenly, out of the darkness, he saw something in the corner of his eye. He jumped.

"What the . . . ?" To his relief, it was only the mayor riding up alongside him again.

"Stay right!" yelled the mayor over the noise of the wagon and horses.

"What?"

"Turn right!"

"Here?"

The mayor pointed with a finger. Hyrum pulled hard on the reins and turned the wagon away from the gorge. Confused, he watched as the mayor slowed his horse and returned to where the sheriff rode behind Hyrum. He slowed the wagon as crates and cargo rattled over the seldom-traveled, bumpy road and wondered, *Where is the mayor taking us? This road leads nowhere.*

Now, rather than passing north through the gorge, they wound their way around the base of Mount Erebus, continuing for over a mile, until they came to where the road ended.

The mayor climbed off his horse and ordered Hyrum, "Bring the lantern." To the others, he said, "The rest of you come and gather!"

Hyrum set the brake, lit the lantern, and jumped down as Jonas and Ernie led their horses to where the sheriff and mayor waited. Only the sheriff stayed perched on his horse.

Once they were all together, the mayor spoke. "We're going up the mountain. The trail is over there." Hyrum turned around and held up the lantern so it illuminated a trailhead overgrown with weeds and bushes. They all stared curiously at the trail, then back at the mayor. Why, everyone knew this trail was once a functional road when the old fort served the U.S. Calvary during the Indian Wars. But now, years of decay and erosion had left it damaged, suitable for foot traffic only.

"Pardon me, sir," Hyrum protested, "but the road is impassable by wagon. Are we to carry the crates and whatever else?"

"I said nothing about leaving the wagon or crates behind. We will deliver them up there."

"Please, sir," Hyrum pleaded. "It is not only unsafe but impossible. The way is too narrow, and the cliffs are far too dangerous, even if the road were worthy of attempt. It would be madness."

Worried faces stared at the mayor.

"Yes, Hyrum. Yes, yes, we all agree. It is far too dangerous to attempt by wagon with the road as it is now. That's why we will deliver the offering on the road—as it *was*."

"But, sir! The trail is as it is . . ."

"Hyrum! That's enough. I need you all to listen carefully. Some things in this world are comprehendible, while others are not. Tonight, you will become acquainted with the latter. I need you to pay attention, to keep your nerves and stay calm. And since nothing I say now will make any sense, you must trust me. But I assure you, before the night ends, it will. And things will change when we get up there near the ridge."

"Excuse me, sir," Ernie interrupted, his voice trembling, "This doesn't sound safe. Pardon my asking, but what do you mean things will change?"

"Stop worrying, all of you. Just don't do anything foolish. Things are going to change. In your mind, you must expect it!"

Hyrum watched as Ernie began to tremble. He turned his head to Ernie and whispered, "You all right, Ern?"

Ernie shook his head.

"Mayor?" asked Hyrum. "Not to belabor the point, but perhaps it will help calm our nerves if you tell us what to expect. How will things change, as you say?"

The mayor sighed and drew in a deep breath. "Fine. I'll explain as best I can," he said. "Yes, things will change, not be as they seem, like how light can play tricks."

"Play tricks?" asked Ernie. "How?"

"Well," said the mayor. "You've seen a mirage, haven't you? It's not water. The light fools you. Or sound—you've heard your voice echo before, like in the gorge?"

"We've all heard it," Hyrum agreed.

"That's right, Hyrum. We do not ask ourselves who might be repeating what we say. We understand that sound plays tricks. Now, here at the ridge, it is time that fools us. It wobbles like a handsaw. Do you understand?"

When he received only blank stares, he tried again. "I can't explain further. Some things just need to be experienced. I only ask that you keep calm and follow my instructions. Can you do that?"

"It would help if we knew why we are doing this, Mayor," said Ernie.

"I already told you," said the mayor sternly. "I entered a contract, a deal to save our town. Without it, many would have gone hungry. They, the ones up there, have power over the heavens and cause the sun to shine. Remember? Tonight, you will meet our benefactors, for whom the offering is intended. But I warn you, don't underestimate them. They are not our enemies, but I would not trifle with them either."

"I knew it," said Ernie. "They're witches, aren't they?"

"No," said the mayor. "We're in Indiana, not Massachusetts, and they are not witches, though I initially believed the same. They are entirely something else, something never witnessed."

"Then what are they?" asked Hyrum.

"I'm uncertain," admitted the mayor. "I questioned them, as much as my nerves allowed, but they answered vaguely. They spoke of ancient things, Rome and Greece, as if I understood when I did not. They refer to themselves as sisters, so that's what I call them."

It was Jonas's turn to ask questions. "Are they dangerous?"

"Very much so," said the mayor. "But to our good fortune, they hold our interests. They saved our town from hunger, and with this alliance, we can do much more. Consider Governor Willard, who is weak in health. Indiana will soon need a new governor. With our arrangement, I will be the next governor. And each of you will benefit, that's for certain. But that's not all of it! What about the president? If Lincoln and his party don't abandon their notion of the emancipation of slaves, denying the very nature of man and God, they'll destroy the union. And who will be left to save it? These sisters, the ones you'll soon be acquainted with, who have the power to block the sun and make it shine. I saved New Harmony with their help, and with that help, I'll soon save the union. And each of you has a part to play and will be rewarded. So, shall we?"

Sensing the conversation had ended, Hyrum jumped on the wagon as the others mounted their horses. *This better be worth it!* Hyrum thought as he released the brake.

Before ordering them to head out, the mayor gave one last instruction to Hyrum. "The lantern," he called back. "Leave it here. We don't want the townspeople to see that light as we ascend the mountain. Besides, we won't be needing it." Though it made little sense, Hyrum extinguished his lantern, and all went dark.

"Follow me!" shouted the mayor. They traveled only briefly before coming to the trailhead. There was no going any farther, and so they waited. Suddenly, a beam of moonlight shone upon the trail, which magically repaired itself. Then, the horses began following the light as if guided by what, Hyrum couldn't say. All that was required was to hold on as they moved upward, the going slow but steady. Hyrum listened to the rhythm of hooves and the creaking of the wagon.

Hours later, near the ridge that led to the summit, they saw a mist. Hyrum pulled back on the reins, but the horses kept going. Soon, the mist grew so thick it formed a wall across the road ahead. The horses neighed, and his stomach lurched again. He couldn't escape the thought that before them lay a portal to hell. But there was no stopping now. They passed through the murky gate under the power of some unseen, malevolent force. As the wagon entered the beyond, Hyrum felt a chill, and the air filled with a smell that reminded him of a trash fire. His bones rattled as the cold wind penetrated his clothing and stung his cheeks. He quickly pushed his arms through the sleeves of his coat and buttoned it.

He'd expected brisk winds at this elevation but nothing like this. And although the mayor had encouraged each man to bring a coat, only Hyrum heeded the warning. With stiff fingers tucked in his armpits, he balanced himself on the wagon bench, rocking back and forth.

Lost in the fog, unable to see clearly, he rubbed his eyes and squinted at the road before him. The trail leveled out as they arrived on the ridge. Hyrum looked hard into the mist, listening for movement. He heard an animal snarling, branches snapping, and leaves rustling. His heart beat wildly as everything around him shifted, stretched, and wobbled like a handsaw—time playing tricks, the mayor had warned. And then time snapped back to linear, just as the mayor said it would. Hyrum's fears whipped about him in the whistling wind, making him feel dizzy. He was watching the shadows churning in the mist when the horses suddenly stopped.

Chapter 29

Careful not to be seen, Marco and Emily made their way through town. Ears sharp and eyes peeled, they watched for movement in the windows before quietly moving past them. The candlelight behind Beulah's curtains flickered as someone moved. They crawled behind her hedges and waited. Once the window went dark, they slowly crept away, keeping up their guard until they reached the edge of town. In the distance, they could see the rendezvous spot. The road swung right before cutting through Mr. Carver's cornfield. Emily was listening to the creek running through the pasture when Marco suddenly froze. She reflexively did the same.

"Did you hear that?" he whispered.

Emily shivered. "No. What did you hear?"

"Something's in the cornfield. I'm not certain, but each time we stop, it goes quiet. I'd say we're being followed."

She drew close and gripped his hand. "What do you suppose it is?"

"Can't be certain, but we'd better hurry."

They had quickened their pace when suddenly, a dark figure loomed in front of them, blocking the road a little ways from where they stood. They stopped and stared, trying to decipher whether what they saw was real or imaginary. Both jumped back when it moved, and Marco slowly positioned himself between Emily and the thing.

"It's the beast! It's here!" he whispered.

"Are we in danger? You said it meant you no harm."

"Perhaps it changed its mind. But there's no sense in running. Don't move."

No sooner had he spoken than the monster moved, stopped, then moved some more, but only a little. It slowly closed the distance until they could see more clearly what confronted them. Emily's eyes widened, and her heart raced, her mind barely grasping what now stood only a few yards in front of them.

Raising her trembling hands to her mouth, she exclaimed, "Oh my!"

CHAPTER 30

Without any prompting, the horses stopped. The mayor dismounted and tied Buck to a tree, then motioned for the others to do the same. Hyrum set the brake and jumped down. The disorienting feeling had subsided enough for the men to stand without losing their balance, though Hyrum's stomach remained queasy. The fog shifted around them while the mayor appeared unimpressed, clearly having experienced this before.

Ernie called out to the mayor. "Sir, there's someone or something in the fog. I see shapes. I don't believe we're wanted here."

Jonas backed into the mayor and started to whimper. "Mayor, sir. Can we just leave the wagon and go?"

The sheriff stood with his back to the fog, waiting, when he suddenly tumbled forward as if pushed from behind. He scrambled to his feet. "Ernie's right, sir. We're not wanted here!"

"Stay calm," urged the mayor. "Keep your wits about you."

The sheriff began tucking in his shirt when the mayor noticed his sidearm. "Quickly! All of you, I forgot to tell you to leave your guns behind. Set them down now!" Seeing their hesitation, he ordered them again. "Do as I say! You're safer without them."

The sheriff glared at the mayor as if to question his sanity.

"You heard me. Do it before it's too late!" Quickly, they lay their guns on the ground and looked nervously at the mayor. "You can get them after we're dismissed."

Confused, cold, and unarmed, they waited, defenseless.

Hyrum asked, "Who will dismiss us? Who are they?"

"You'll know soon enough. Stay here, and no sudden moves," said the mayor. He walked to where the structure of the old lookout post mainly remained intact, though unkempt. Then, before he could knock, the door opened. He stepped inside.

"Not a good sign," whispered Jonas. The others nodded, including the sheriff.

From inside, they heard a hiss. The sheriff walked closer so he could listen.

"Sustenance?" said a loud cackling voice from within.

The mayor's voice followed. "As promised. Outside, though it required several others to deliver."

"We saw you coming."

The mayor soon exited, rejoining the council. All eyes were on the doorway, the men filled with an unsettling apprehension. From the dark interior of the fort issued a frail, rotting human form. One of the sisters, Hyrum thought. After her came two others, equally disgusting and smelling of death. Each was so ancient that the appointed time for their souls to have departed this world had passed centuries ago, yet, due to a tear in the fabric of time or some black, unimaginable magic, their dark, crimson blood still coursed through their withered veins. Skeletal thin, in decaying layers of tattered linen and tired thread, they moved cautiously, always watching, always calculating. Wide-eyed, the council stared at the creatures, the sisters returning their stares. Their black eyes penetrated the consciousness, causing a nervous shock, the kind one felt when encountering a viper underfoot.

The beings moved slowly toward them and stopped, the sheriff and council staggering backward. Ernie stared at his gun, then looked up to see the mayor shaking his head.

"Here's our appeasement as required." The mayor motioned for the council to unload the offerings. Once on the ground, they pulled at the nails with crowbars. Ernie discarded the last wooden plank from the containers while the others set down their crowbars and cautiously stepped back.

The mayor gave the creatures a wide berth. Shrouded in darkness, the more aged of the three glided forward, the fog parting as she approached. She surveyed the large spread. Pausing at the shepherd's pies, she stuck in a bony finger and stabbed a chunk of potato. She stared at it with a black eye, then pushed it through her thin lips. Her pointy jaw slowly masticated, her withered tongue churning the pie before she swallowed hard. Finally, she raised her hands to the sky and waited.

"My compliments," she said, her voice raspy and gruff. "Pleased. Not disappointed," she hissed while craning her neck to look back at the mayor. The old hag lowered her hands, and her sisters rushed forward, gorging themselves on the food and guzzling the bottles of spirits.

The mayor continued staring, his disgust evident on his face, while the oldest and apparent leader opened her mouth, her tongue weaving irksome words. "I'm waiting . . . yes, yes, I'm waiting!"

Composing himself, the mayor said, "We give thanks for granting us sunshine. Though damaged, our crops are responding, and our harvest will suffice as our needs for the winter are mostly secure. However, there is a matter of some urgency."

"Go on," said the more ancient one. "Listening . . ."

"It's . . . the monster."

"Yes, Robert. What about it?"

"We can't have real havoc. Do you understand? The fear in town is palpable, thank you. But any more—"

"You want the monster gone?" The ancient hag cut him off.

Hyrum, Ernie, and Jonas reflexively nodded. "Yes!"

"No, no," said the mayor in contradiction. He turned and scolded them. "Be quiet!" To the hooded creatures, he said, "The monster is useful so long as—"

Sinister smiles crossed the lips of all three sisters, who looked up from their feasting. "Appears you have not explained the necessity of the monster to your companions." They turned their attention to the men standing nearby.

"Would you care if I explained, Robert?" asked the most ancient of the three.

"No. I would prefer you explain it."

"Very well." She glided in an unearthly manner toward the council members, who shook as she came to a stop. "Hear me!" she demanded. "I am Atropos. My sisters are Clotho and Lachesis. We are the weavers of fate. The fabric is priceless indeed—life. Our loom spins the yarn. But, without crisis, there can be no fear. And suppose there is no fear. Then there is no control, and our loom spins only air. You are the benefactors of the fear we weave. Our looms spin the yarn, not nothingness, but luxurious yarn, and I hold the shears."

Atropos, the more ancient, asked, "Now, Robert, do you suppose they understand?"

"I suppose they do, but isn't that beside the point? We only ask that the monster stay where it is. We can't have it wandering into town, killing people. We have our families to concern ourselves with."

The mayor held his breath, shifting nervously as the council leaned forward, hoping to hear what the creatures would say.

Atropos spoke chilling words. "I can only promise," she said, "that if harm comes to the beast, you will assume the debt, and that owed will be more than any of you can afford. So . . ."

The mayor insisted, "Don't worry. We all agree. But . . ."

"Your companions don't seem as certain."

"Oh yes. They are, indeed. They know what they stand to gain and what they stand to lose."

"You are certain?"

The mayor looked at each member of the council and nodded. "I'm certain!"

Chapter 31

Standing in the street and blending with the night, Jonathan peered at the house with the scent he remembered. The murdered boy must have lived here with his brother, the one who'd hunted Jonathan, the one he'd spared. Hidden among the shadows, he watched and waited, holding the object in his mouth.

I can drop it here, he thought. *The young man will find it in the morning.*

He had leaped over the white picket fence and onto the front porch when he heard a faint creaking. Quickly and quietly, he jumped back over the fence and watched through the wooden slats as a man left the house through the back door.

It's him!

Keeping his distance, he followed the young man until another joined him—a young woman. *It's her!* he realized. She had been with the young man at the burial of the murdered boy. He watched as they ventured out together.

They move as if wishing not to be seen, but why? Can they smell me?

While following, he widened the distance between them. The road they traveled turned away from town. Through the cornfield he crept, peering over the stalks, keeping pace with the two, stopping when they stopped so as not to be detected.

I'll drop it in front of them, he thought. He maneuvered through the field, trying hard to be quiet until he was well ahead of the couple. Then he emerged from the corn and crept onto the road. Looking back, he could see they'd stopped moving.

What now? They must know I'm here. What if they turn and run?

Suddenly, the man and woman were closing the distance between him and them.

They'll soon be upon me. Should I drop it and hide? But what if they walk past without seeing it?

Before Jonathan could decide, they were nearly upon him. But then they stopped again. The man reached back, making sure the woman stood behind him. Jonathan waited before slowly moving closer, wanting only to drop the thing held in his teeth.

"Please don't hurt us!" the man pleaded. "We're not armed, nor do we wish you any harm."

Jonathan paused. The man slowly backed away, gently nudging the woman behind him. Jonathan drew in a breath. His stomach growled with hunger pangs. So quickly could he stop their hearts, put an end to their lives, and quench his primal cravings. Instead, he shook his head violently. With eyes shut tight, teeth gritted, and every muscle clenched, he suppressed his beastly impulses, pushing them away. He howled as he thought, *I am Jonathan, not an animal!*

The man and woman froze with fear, unaware of the struggle of the soul in considering their fate. Jonathan's black eyes opened on them, holding their attention. *I didn't kill your brother*, he thought. *I'm not a monster!* He savagely shook his head, the motion causing the two humans to draw back in fear. Jonathan stepped back, lowering his head in a display of submission. In response, they paused and watched.

It was then that Jonathan dropped the thing he held between his teeth. It was what he had come for, his purpose for following the man. He stepped back and quickly sprang away from the road, disappearing into the dark.

Leaving the two behind, he followed the creek that swept around the town and soon found himself on the road leading north toward the gorge. There, he picked up another scent hidden among the smells of manure, wheat, and barley. It made his heart race. *The murderers! I can smell them!*

He looked back at the town and then toward the gorge, his nose in the air.

They're headed to the meadow. It's perfect. I'll meet them there.

Jonathan hurried north but stopped at the crossroad. So familiar to him was the road that continued left to the gorge and his meadow beyond. But now he saw a rarely traveled route leading east, a road he hadn't noticed. He again sniffed the night air and slowly looked east.

Where are they going if not to the meadow?

He followed the scent, hugging the base of the mountain as the road wound through patches of river birch and elm, down a ravine, and over the hill. Then, finally, it came to where the road ended and a trail began.

Jonathan's nostrils flared. What he smelled made his stomach growl, and saliva dripped from the corners of his mouth. He craned his neck and peered upward. *Hmm*, he thought. *A way up the mountain. How fortunate.*

Eagerly, he leaped onto the trail, clawing at the dirt as he climbed. Suddenly, ahead of him, he saw a spot of moonlight. The unnatural behavior of the light gave him pause, and he stopped. Something didn't feel right. He'd been led too easily for this not to be a trap.

But Jonathan had reached the point where it didn't matter. It was resolution he sought, a way out of his limbo. He intended to find answers at the end of the trail at the top of the mountain. He wished to rid himself of the voices he heard, the beast he'd become, and be Jonathan the human again. So he obediently followed the moonbeam leading him up the trail.

The path was wide and easily traversed until he came to what appeared to be the final switchback before the ridge. Then the path began to change in the faint light. Small rocks tumbled down the mountain. Dirt billowed in places and disappeared in others. He looked toward the peak, obscured in clouds. On the path directly before him rose a barrier of fog, through which he cautiously moved until he reached the other side. Standing upright and bathed in the sparkling fog, Jonathan stared at his paws and how they flickered.

He patted his chest and felt his face. Confused, he looked back at the thick, swirling wall of viperous mist. He felt strange, as if caught somewhere between body and spirit. Cautiously, he moved like a ghost, still following the scent of the murderers.

How far he walked the ridge, he couldn't say. Judging distance in the mist was impossible. Then, amidst the sound of rustling leaves and the beating of wings from birds he couldn't see, he heard voices. Jonathan crept closer, cautious not to bump into anything, when the image of a man appeared in the mist.

He knew this man. Jonathan tasted the air. *Oh yeah. The man without a hat. Found you*, he thought, a deep sense of satisfaction settling in his breast.

Unsure whether he dreamed or the man actually stood before him. He reached out with a paw, claws retracted, and pushed the figure. Then he quickly withdrew into the fog as he watched the man topple. It was the murderer! The beast's claws extended, and his lips curled back to reveal his sharp teeth.

"Don't!" said a voice inside Jonathan's head. He could hear men talking and knew the murderer was within his grasp. He could see him through the fog, and his blood boiled with revenge.

Why not? I can kill them now!

"Because . . ." said another voice, deep and scratchy.

Because why?

"Because you want to end your curse, don't you? You want to know how to pay your debt?"

Jonathan moved forward, low to the ground, ready to pounce. *If you don't want him dead, tell me how to pay my debt or he dies this instant!*

"The curse for murder cannot be undone by the same," said the trio of voices. "Not while revenge is the motive!"

No more lies! Tell me! How do I rid myself of this wretched curse—and you?

"This won't work, monster. It will only condemn you further," hissed a shallow voice.

Jonathan stepped closer to the man without a hat. *Not an answer! Please tell me how to unravel this curse when you urge me to taste blood yet protect this man. Why? And why did you lead me here to see this?*

"Our reasons are not your concern," said the trio. "What concerns you is how to become human."

Yes! Jonathan stopped and listened. *Tell me! I've already damned my soul. I don't care anymore, so whatever plans you have for him end now unless you tell me.*

The more ancient, deep-throated voice answered. "It's simple, monster. You must make a sacrifice as courageous as the cowardly act that cursed you. Though, judging by your intentions at this moment, you may not be capable. Besides, would we allow you to hurt this man for one moment and thwart our plans? Think we didn't bring you here? See how easily we dismiss you!"

The conversation ended, and the sound of laughter filled his head. He staggered away from the man. Suddenly, he felt a jolt, and it was as if he'd been lifted and thrown down the mountain, miraculously tumbling without hitting a rock or ridge. His arms flailed wildly, grasping at anything and everything, despair, hope, and flashes of memory circling him. He existed somewhere between heaven and hell. He saw glimpses of a silvery moon, stars, earth, trees, rocky cliffs, and then oblivion.

When all went silent, he woke at the crossroad, curled in a fetal position. It was here, only hours earlier, that he'd diverged from the road that led to the gorge to follow the scent up the mountain. He closed his eyes and waited for the dizziness to subside and his heartbeat to slow to normal. On the mountain, he'd heard more than he could immediately comprehend. Now he craved the comfort of his cave and the straw of his bed. He'd succeeded in delivering the hat, but after learning what evil cursed him, he felt the futility of hoping to be human even more keenly. How could he atone for the evil thing he'd done when he couldn't even remember what he'd done? With a heavy heart, he slowly made his way back to the meadow and his cave.

Chapter 32

Emily watched Bronson turn the hat in his hands, inspecting it closely. Who could it belong to? A lantern burned dimly in the corner, its soft light casting shadows on the rain-soaked walls. Black streaks ran down to floorboards littered with bird droppings. The light got lost in the rafters above their heads, where birds cooed from hidden corners.

"The monster left this for you?" Bronson looked curiously at Marco and Emily.

"Yes," said Marco. Emily nodded.

"That's it? Nothing more?"

"It was terrifying," said Emily.

Bronson nodded. "I can imagine."

LeFevre winced as he shifted his weight, arms wrapped around his fractured ribs. "Did plenty to me, damnable beast. Hobbled the entire way here."

"You and I were trying to kill it, Mr. LeFevre," said Marco. "Enough to give it cause to kill us, but it didn't."

LeFevre, unwilling to grant the beast any grace, said, "So the monster's ready for vows at the Abbey of Saint-Étienne, that it?"

"I told him not to come," said Bronson, "broken ribs, but the stubborn Frenchman insisted."

Marco leaned forward. The dim light of the lantern gently caressed his face as he spoke. "From the moment I left my house, I sensed someone or something followed me. After we met up, Emmy and I, it became more obvious. We heard noises behind us. Each time we stopped, so did the noises."

"That's when we saw it," Emily interjected, "standing in front of us, and there was no escaping it."

"But it simply dropped the hat and disappeared," said Marco. "Though I doubt it's headed to the abbey."

Bronson poked his finger through a tear in the brim. "Who do you suppose it belongs to?"

Marco reached out, wanting to hold it. "Whoever murdered my brother is my guess."

Handing the hat to Marco, Bronson said, "We may never know who that belongs to. But what if the beast is a reasoning creature? We must now consider that since it wanted you to have the hat, it stands to reason that maybe it isn't the killer we suspected."

"Or have been told," said Emily.

Bronson scratched his head. "Could it be aware it's being used to cover misdeeds and thus left the hat?"

"Used by who?" asked Emily.

"I believe we all know that answer," said Marco. "The men who claim it killed my brother."

"And Constance," said Emily.

"I don't know what's worse, a monster in the woods or monsters pretending to be men," admitted Bronson. "Either way, we must be very, very careful."

Emily looked around at the worried faces in the flickering light. "Indeed," she said. "We must all be careful."

"Emily, here, take this." Bronson reached into his pocket and pulled out several official-looking documents. "These are for you." He handed her the papers.

LeFevre reached under his shirt and presented Marco with similar documents. "These are yours, Doc, for the time being."

Emily asked, "What are they?" She strained to read in the faint light.

"Bank notes for my savings and the deed to my house," said Bronson to Emily.

"Ya got mine there, Doc," said LeFevre. "Ain't no pockets in coffins, but I intend to go down fightin'."

"No one is going to die!" said Marco. "There's no reason for this." He tried handing it to them, as did Emily.

"Just hold on to them," said Bronson. "LeFev and I have no family. It makes sense that we take the risks."

"That's right. No livin' relatives," said LeFevre. "Never married. Too prickly to be trapped by a woman, or so I've been told."

"Yeah," said Bronson. "Put them in your pockets. Take them with you."

"Take them where?" asked Emily. "Where would you have us keep them?"

"Far from here," said Bronson. "We're dealing with tyrants, killers. What if the mayor learns of your involvement? Neither you nor your families will be safe. You must insist they leave town immediately and quietly, yourselves included, and this," Bronson stressed, "is non-negotiable."

Emily held the bank notes and deed to her chest. "Thank you," she said, "and I pray I can give these back. Meanwhile, Marco can keep them safe by leaving, but I'm staying."

"Oh no," said Marco. "Emily leaves, and I stay. She can take my father with her."

"Both of you are leaving," said Bronson. "You're young. LeFev and I agree this is our fight."

Marco stood. "Was your brother butchered? I'm sorry and don't mean to be rude or ungrateful. Mr. LeFevre, when we went after the monster, was I a coward?"

"No, Doc."

Emily then said, "And I've plenty of reasons myself. I thought we talked about this. I've waited my entire life to see justice served for my father and mother. I have a role to play. The parson said as much. I can't help that I'm determined to see those responsible pay for their crimes. I don't care if I die. I'm willing to risk anything to see justice served!"

"Ain't nobody dyin' here," said LeFevre, "least of all you youngsters. Listen, if fillin' an empty grave is between the mayor and me, I'm stayin' aboveground. I'm gonna see Paris, fields yellow with sunflowers, and cellars with the dancin' ladies. I'll see my home again with these earthly eyes. Ya can count on it. Till then, Doc, you keep my deed and money safe, but I'll be askin' for 'em back once the mayor—"

"That's enough, LeFev," said Bronson, "they heard. For now, let's keep quiet, all of us. Make no inquiries. Allow LeFev and me to handle this for the time being. Emily, you and Marco are both stubborn, but I'm putting you in charge. Marco will listen to you out of concern for your safety. So you're in charge of ensuring everyone is safe, you and yours. If things go wrong, get everyone out of New Harmony."

"But, Mr. Parrish, I can do more. I can do that and still—"

"Emmy, listen to me," said Bronson. "It's an important thing keeping people safe. And it won't be easy. You'll have to convince them to leave, and you're better suited to do that than any of us here. Besides, you don't have to save the whole town. Just save as many as you can if you need to."

Emily sighed. "All right, Mr. Parrish."

Next, Bronson turned to Marco. "As for you, Doc—"

"I already have something I need to do, Mr. Parrish."

"What?" asked Bronson. Both he and LeFevre looked at Marco.

"I'm climbing the mountain, see what's up there. It's poisoning our town, whatever it is, and if I can stop it . . ."

"Careful, Marco," said Bronson. "I'll go with you, but first, I have someone I need to see."

"Who?" asked LeFevre.

"Eugene Owen is who."

"Mr. Parrish, be careful," said Marco. "Eugene's a fine man, but he's an Owen."

Bronson nodded. "I suppose we should all heed that advice."

Chapter 33

Sunday morning, Emily arrived at the church alone. Albert and Marjorie encouraged her to follow the mayor's orders and stay home, saying they would pray and read the Bible together, but Emily was determined to worship as she saw fit. Upon entering the church, she sat in her usual place and waited for the parson to start the service. He appeared exhausted, as if he hadn't slept in days, and Emily wondered if he was ill. Hannah entered the chapel from the office, bringing her husband a glass of water.

"Thank you," he told her. Emily watched as she nodded politely, then sat down.

At the pulpit, the parson thumbed through his Bible. Having already greeted everyone at the front door, he wasted no time in reading from the book of Revelation. "And there was war in heaven. Michael and—"

Suddenly, the church doors swung open, and Parson Burroughs looked up. Abigail, Susannah, and Elizabeth stood at the back of the chapel, arms crossed, waiting to be noticed. The doors behind them slammed shut, and everyone craned their necks to see. Without excusing themselves, the three gossips took one of the many empty pews.

The parson slid his round glasses up his nose and steadied his aged hands on the Bible. "As I was saying, war broke out in heaven." He paused, searching the page until he found his place. "'Michael and his angels fought against the dragon; and the dragon fought and his angels and prevailed not; neither was their place found anymore in heaven. And the great dragon was cast out, that old serpent, called the Devil, and Satan, which deceiveth the whole world: he was cast out into the earth, and his angels were cast out with him. Woe to the inhabiters of the earth and of the sea! For the devil is come down unto you, having great wrath, because he knoweth that he hath but a short time.'"

The parson peered over the well-worn pages of his Bible. Then, with gentle hands, he closed the book, folded his glasses, and tucked them into a pocket underneath his black robe.

He sighed and looked kindly upon his congregation. "What we're experiencing," he said, "is nothing new. The war in heaven started at the beginning of time and will rage in the hearts of men until the very end. And what is the war being fought over?"

Emily watched as the parson looked out at the blank faces. Upon noticing her, he smiled. "Yes," he said, "the war that broke out in heaven now rages here, and to what end? The soul," he said. "The struggle is for the souls of all who have been born and are yet to be. Look around at the empty seats. Half our neighbors and friends fear leaving their homes and breaking the laws of man. Isolating ourselves makes us weak. We must encourage them to join us; strength is found in fellowship. Whether they fear hunger or the beast, it is the same. Placing confidence in the flesh, or in men, subjects us to the weaknesses of men, weaknesses such as pride, lust for power, and selfishness."

A commotion rose in the congregation. The three latecomers spoke loudly among themselves, purposely causing a disturbance while ignoring the shushes.

The parson waited for them to quiet when Abigail spoke. "Excuse me, Parson Burroughs," she said, "but who can deny that the mayor caused the sun to shine? We all saw it. But isn't he a man, and hasn't trusting him been to our benefit? Who here can deny that?"

The parson lowered his head, listening—or did he pray for guidance as Emily supposed? After a pause, he spoke. "Who can deny it, or who dares deny it? Which are you asking?"

"Are you suggesting it is only out of fear we concede that the mayor saved the harvest?"

"Yes, Abigail," said the parson. "That's what I'm suggesting. Fear, not faith, is the deciding factor here: fear that the clouds will return and block the sun, fear of starvation without the harvest, fear of the beast. Fear untempered by faith separates us from God. Faith brings us back."

"It's all so . . . ugh." Abigail rolled her eyes. "Never without fancy words, are you, Parson? Why, everything you say sounds perfect. However, the guardian voices tell me otherwise. They told me to come here, or I wouldn't have bothered. They wanted me to witness this abomination, these fairy tales you spout. They reminded me of the good your prayers did when my late husband . . . Tell them, Parson, what happened to Norbert even after all your prayers."

She turned to the congregation. "And who here didn't pray for sunshine? And then what? Nothing is what! If not for our mayor, you'd all go hungry come fall!"

"Abigail Williams!" cried Parson Burroughs. When she fell silent, he said in a softer tone, "My heart still hurts for you. I know your loss was difficult. I feel for you, Abigail. I do. But it was your husband's time. The hour is appointed for each of us, though it is understandable that those left behind may feel cheated, regardless of the year, month, day, or hour of their departure. It's for us to place our faith in seeing them again. Only the Savior offers any hope of reunion."

"More pretty words, words meant to be of comfort, but the nights are long, and the tears . . ."

She spoke of tears, but Emily saw little sorrow in her manner. "Your words," Abigail cried, "are empty. Mine, my words, are the words of warning. The guardian spirits who would rather we not starve or be torn apart by the monster are the ones who brought me here."

Emily had heard enough. She stood and turned toward Abigail. Behind her, she heard the parson say, "Please, sit down, Emily. It's all right. Let her say her piece."

"Go ahead, Emily Hampshire. Listen to your parson. Do what he says and you'll wind up like your fiancé!"

"His name is Christian!" said Emily. "You measure only *your* pain. And yes, a monster murdered my Christian, a monster like you!"

"Now, please. We're in a house of worship," said the parson.

But Abigail wasn't finished. "Your words, little lady," she said, "are not as pretty as Parson Burroughs's but are just as worthless." Abigail peered at the few parishioners and continued. "Consider yourselves warned. You've heard the guardian voices, and you're breaking the law just by being here. Parson Burroughs doesn't care so long as you drop a coin in the basket. He has failed you all as he failed me. He cannot stop starvation or mutilation, just as he couldn't control the fever that took my husband from me. And look at him. He appears sickly as well. He can't even heal himself!"

Looking as if a weight pressed upon his shoulders, the parson said, "I can't allow you to go on speaking such blasphemy, not here, not in God's house. I beseech you, Abigail, by the tender mercies of God, to stop! Only then are you welcome to stay, but only to listen. Besides, I haven't finished my sermon. So please stay and hear what I have to say. You may derive comfort through understanding, and I can see there is much you don't understand."

Abigail quietly took a seat, as did her cohorts. A hush settled over the congregation as a baby cried, everyone listening as its mother rocked it, singing soothing lullabies until it calmed.

Once all was peaceful, the parson continued. "The war that started in heaven is upon us. Voices compete for our attention. The voices that divide us and cause us to fear one another are not from heaven. The still, small voice within each of us doesn't shout at or frighten us. It tells us not to fear. And like a hen gathering her chicks under her wings, we find refuge from the battle in the hushed words that enter our hearts."

Abigail stood and screamed, "More pretty words!" Startled awake, the baby wailed. In the ensuing commotion, Emily watched as Abigail's eyes rolled back in her head. Then, in the chaos of the moment, she began to speak.

"I hear them now," she said. "The guardian voices, they call to me, and our voices join as one voice, a voice of warning. Those not listening and who remain unafraid will suffer for their deafness. I, therefore, give you a sign. Parson William R. Burroughs will die at the hands of the monster. This is what the guardian voices tell me. And this so you may know in whom you must place your trust."

She had not finished when she turned and walked out the doors, Elizabeth and Susannah in her wake, the doors slamming behind them. Heads turned to the parson, who remained steadfast. He smiled warmly and spoke calmly. "Be at peace," he said. "Be watchful, wise, and have faith. Safety is found in the light, even the light that shines in the dark of night."

Colorful light shone through the large stained-glass window and rested on the congregation. Peter reached up to where the Savior stood firmly on the water.

As the parson offered a prayer, the church doors burst open, and the sheriff charged in. "Time ya get on home!" he shouted. "The church is closed. Mayor's orders! The rules are for your good. Now get!"

Abigail, Susannah, and Elizabeth stood just outside, grinning as the parishioners filed past them. "For your own good," Abigail assured them.

Chapter 34

With only a few stragglers left in the tavern, Ernie hollered, "Barrel's dry. Go on home!"

"You say barrel's dry when it ain't," said Boyd Kensington. "It's not even six o'clock."

"Did ya forget curfew, Boyd? We're closing early."

Though disgruntled, Boyd left without further protest. With empty mugs in each hand, Ernie stepped over a spill on the floor. Then, setting the empties down on one of five long wooden tables, he retrieved a mop and began sopping it up. No one said goodbye on their way out.

Typically, Ernie did his best business after sundown. He'd initially feared the curfew would hamper his usual patrons from frequenting his tavern. Fortunately for him, the opposite proved to be true. Anxiety and stress brought in the regulars, along with a few others who rarely indulged themselves at his drinking hole.

Since Ernie was a council member, conversations usually went silent when he walked by. He heard the usual scuttlebutt—monster this, guardians that, some still holding to their belief in sirens. And although most agreed the curfew made little sense, they feared admitting it publicly. Monsters, voices, and curfew were subjects of discussion after a pint settled in the gut. That's when Ernie heard forbidden things he couldn't repeat.

Only days earlier, Old Man Taylor said, "Had Bronson been elected, he would have killed the monster. But, unfortunately, appeasers and pansies are what we grow here in New Harmony, or else Bronson would be mayor and the monster would be gone."

The mayor wasn't spared in their drunken considerations, and tipsy accusations flew about unimpeded. Since Ernie didn't consider it good business to tattle on paying customers, these conversations flowed as freely as the alcohol.

He often wondered if the mayor appointed him to the council so he could report such lurid conversations. When the mayor asked what people said, Ernie's response remained the same: "Beer tongue and cow dung ain't no different. I don't care for either." So far, the mayor hadn't questioned further. Had Ernie not learned to ignore "beer talk," he'd have been forced to close his doors years ago.

The day after the trip up the mountain was particularly hard for Ernie, not knowing how to make sense of it. He felt like he had a rattlesnake wrapped around his leg. He knew things he'd rather not, and his head pounded. The curfew fast approached. He took a swig from a near-empty mug, too preoccupied with wiping down a table to notice one straggler.

"Hey, Ern."

Startled, Ernie looked over his shoulder to see Weston sitting in the corner, hands wrapped around a mug. "You better stop your drinkin' if you're gonna enforce curfew."

"Too late for that!" said Weston as he slumped over his drink. "Besides, mayor didn't tell us to lock ourselves up, did he? No! Curfew don't apply to us, and I didn't turn in my gun. Did you? No. My job is catchin' violators and drinking as much as I want."

Ernie crossed the room and poured Weston another frothy, dark lager. "All right, Weston. Last one. If you've somethin' to say, best say it or keep it to yourself."

Weston stared at the dark beer. "Have I something to say? It's the other way around, Ern. The way I figure, you've something to tell me. Come now. What happened up there?"

Ernie stood and wiped down the last table. "You don't want to know, Weston. I'll do ya that favor."

"Whether I wanna or not, I'm asking all the same."

"Then you'll have to ask the mayor or sheriff. I don't even know what I saw."

"I'm on the council, Ern! I'm the deputy, for hell's sake, and I can't know?" Weston's feelings were hurt, and Ernie knew that the more the alcohol kicked in, the worse he would feel. Ernie rinsed his rag, wrung it out, and hung it on a hook. Then he walked over, sat back down, and looked across the table at Weston.

"Why?"

"Why what?" asked Weston.

"Why do you want to know?"

"Cause I never know anything, Ern. I never know a damned thing."

"Aw, let it go. My head hurts even more now. Do ya really have to know?"

"Ern, have you figured out why I'm on the council? I'm the only one whose business the mayor holds no interest in."

"No, Weston. Why?"

"I'll tell you why."

"All right, then. Go on and tell me."

"My papa left when I was nine, blaming my ma for things I don't understand. He said he was gonna shame her and shame her good. I heard him say it. That's before he left and never came back. The mayor came by occasionally after that but always at night. Mama called him Robert. Who does that? No one is who! And she told me never to tell anyone about his visits."

"Where's your mama now?"

"The mayor had her committed somewhere in Pennsylvania and told me it was for her good. If she were closer, I could've visited, but . . ."

"Could've?"

"Yeah," said Weston. "Could've. She died soon after. My pa disappeared before that, just like the Stewarts. Remember them?"

"Of course," said Ernie as the lines on his forehead grew long. "So what is it you're sayin', Weston?"

"I'm saying . . . Did you know the sheriff and I went to their house?"

"Whose house?"

"I just told you, the Stewarts. You just said you remembered them."

"Of course, I remember them. Listen, Weston," Ernie stood, backing away, "I think you've had too much drink. Barrel's empty for you, my friend. No more. You're inebriated, and you need to stop talking."

"Sheriff and I took everything, buried it about a mile away. Then the sheriff threatened me to keep my mouth shut."

"You went with the sheriff to the Stewarts's place?"

"Yeah."

"What did ya bury?"

"Everything," answered Weston.

"Why?"

"Yeah, why? Like, why did my father leave like he did? Disappeared. Ah yes—disappeared.

"That's enough," said Ernie. "I can't hear anymore. And you can never repeat what you just said. Promise me, Weston!"

"Promise you what?"

"Oh my, you've had much too much to drink."

"No, I know," said Weston, staring at his empty mug. "I can never say a thing. Can I have another?"

"Barrel's dry. Now listen here. Are ya listenin'? I hope you are, 'cause we all pledged our loyalty to the mayor for damned good reason. Look at all this, all we have. Consider everything we owe the mayor, and we're gonna owe him a lot more. Trust me, he'll be the next governor, and after that . . . Frankly, I don't give a damn what happened to the Stewarts or anyone else. I have to look after my own."

Weston didn't appear to be listening, and the beer continued talking for him. "Yeah, yeah, but the Stewarts? I saw dark spots in the dirt in front of their house. They had a boy, and some say—"

"Quiet, Weston."

"Why?" Weston slurred. "Ain't nobody in here, Ern. And ya haven't answered my question." Tears welled in Weston's eyes, and he asked, "Do you believe 'em?"

"Believe what?"

"Believe what they say about the Stewarts?"

"I'm not answerin', and you've had too much to drink. I'm gonna keep this between us for now, but if I hear another word, I'm goin' straight to the sheriff. I'm not risking anything for you."

"Nobody risks anything, do they?"

"Just keep your mouth shut," said Ernie before noticing Weston was snoring, his head lying on the table, his mug tipped over.

Chapter 35

Emily walked cautiously beneath a canopy of majestic pine like those pictured in her adventure books. *What is this place?* she wondered. *Heaven? Christian, are you here?*

The deeper she ventured into the woods, the less light reached the forest floor. "Christian, if you're here, say something!" Her voice echoed back, disorienting her and nearly causing her to lose her balance. Then, suddenly, something caught her eye. It moved in her peripheral vision, and she turned, only to see nothing. Did the quivering leaves tickle her senses? "Is that you, Christian? I beg you to answer."

Without warning, an unexpected dust devil spun toward her, catching her white dress and auburn hair in a whirlwind. She spun around. Through the tree trunks, branches, and pine needles, a flock of blackbirds swooped down and flew around her, spinning her even faster. And with the twirling, she became further disoriented and tumbled to the ground. Then, just as quickly, the birds flew away and the wind died.

Steadying herself, she waited for her head to stop spinning. Suddenly, a beam of light broke through the canopy, illuminating a pure, unsullied white doe that pranced through the woods. As she peered at the ethereal creature, it looked back at her, unmoving. They shared a moment, staring at one another, when Emily inexplicably felt its heartbeat pounding in her chest. "Christian? Is it you I feel?"

It stepped gracefully away from her, turned its head, and looked back. Then, once again, it took an effortless step forward, stopped, and looked back. Emily matched its movements, following and pausing. Each time it moved forward, it looked back at Emily. *It wants me to follow,* she realized.

"I'm coming," she said. "It's what you want, isn't it?"

It leaped away from her and into a ravine, stopping once more to look back, waiting. Emily walked more briskly, her hands out, feeling the bark of trees as she moved past them. Without her realizing it, the woods had grown darker. She began to worry. Had she gone too far? She looked around for the path she'd followed, but there was no trail, nothing for her to follow either forward or backward. She was lost, and the woods seemed to close in around her. She turned back to follow the white doe, hoping it would take her back to where she could find her way home. But it was gone.

"Christian!" she called in desperation. "I don't like this. I'm scared!"

"Emmy!" came a male voice from within the dense forest.

"I hear you! Where are you?" She stopped to listen, but all was silent. Then, behind her, set against the pine trees, she noticed a stand of aspens. The fall wind had already stolen their leaves. A dark figure with black hair wandered through them. She moved toward him. "Christian?"

"Emmy . . ." Her name echoed around her.

She ran toward the aspens. The closer she got, the more confident she felt that it was Christian waiting for her. Then she saw his perfect face, just as she remembered it. *There he is*, she thought, his presence shimmering in the air. She moved dreamily between the trees, doing all in her power to reach him. "You're alive!"

She heard his voice, soft and reassuring, just as she remembered it. "Follow me."

"Everyone thinks you're dead, but here you are!"

He offered no response, just a look of sweet sadness.

"Come with me, Emmy. Auntie and Albert are waiting for you at home. I'll take you there." He took her hand and led her through the aspens and onto a dirt road, the forest fading to nothingness behind them. Now there were pastures of alfalfa and other grains on either side. In the distance, she saw her childhood home with Sleepy-Girl grazing in the yard, and she could hear Tippy barking.

"I'm home! I'm really home! There it is!" she cried. "Do you see it?" Overcome with emotion, she wiped at her tears as she stared at her childhood home as it once was.

She heard Christian say, "Yes, Emmy. I see it."

They walked until they came to a small stand of poplar trees alongside a stream that gave drink to the horses in the adjacent pasture. At the stream, they removed their shoes and stockings and sat in the tall grass, letting their bare feet dangle in the cool water.

Emily looked around, recognizing the place. "We've been here before, you and me. We've done this before." As the aura of her surroundings settled in, the memories surfaced. "This is where you proposed to me. I remember." She looked at him excitedly. Then she noticed the sadness in his eyes and the wilted flowers in his hand. An overwhelming sense of remorse passed through her, and she stared into his eyes. "Christian, I'm so sorry. When you asked me to marry you, I should never have hurt you. I was terrified of losing you, frightened by my feelings. Please, please forgive me!" She wrapped her arms around him and sobbed.

He dropped the flowers and drew her close, his hands around her waist. She pressed herself against him, her arms around his shoulders. She felt the warmth of his body and the strength in his shoulders, and she relished the pressure with which he held her. Their lips found each other, and she refused to let go.

Suddenly, she sensed there was something different about him. She let go and moved back but only a short distance. *Christian's face*, she thought. *I want to see his face.*

She raised her eyes to meet his gaze and gasped. It wasn't Christian who stared back at her.

"Marco?"

Emily woke, her pillow wet with tears. She sat up, her chest pounding. What just happened? With eyes closed, she waited for her breathing to calm and her heart to slow. Then she flipped her pillow over and laid her head on it. To her surprise, she found herself wanting to return to her dream.

Chapter 36

Bronson knocked politely on the door, then stepped back. He knew Eugene and his wife, Nellie, had reason to be sore. As far as they knew, Bronson had instigated their son Alexander's beating. He questioned what sort of reception he would receive. The door opened just enough to see a woman's face peering out.

"Mr. Parrish," said the woman. She opened the door wider. "May I help you?" Nellie Owen stood in the doorframe with a warm smile. Though her natural features were striking, she lacked the pampered beauty of Bloomington's well-to-do women with their powders and perfumes.

Her demeanor was naturally polite and obliging. Men passing her in the street often tipped their hats and returned her smiles. Her pretty, blue eyes and long, blonde, wavy hair were enough to cause Bronson to tip his hat.

"Excuse the intrusion, Mrs. Owen. May I inquire as to whether your husband is at home?"

"Have you business with my husband, Mr. Parrish?"

"Not exactly, ma'am. I require only a moment of his time. I seek his advice. I assure you that I hold your husband in high esteem, and my visit here is nothing short of amicable."

"I apologize, Mr. Parrish. My husband isn't home. But not to worry—he's due back any moment. He ran next door to help our neighbor. Would you like to wait inside?"

"Thank you for your kindness, ma'am."

This might work after all, thought Bronson, though he still had his reservations. *Eugene is a member of the royal family. On the occasions we have spoken, Eugene seemed to be masquerading as a commoner. Or maybe it wasn't an act. Perhaps the sins of the parents aren't always those of their offspring. I'm betting on it. At wager is my life!*

"Mr. Parrish?"

"Oh, pardon me."

Nellie Owen remained at the door, inviting him in. "You may wait inside if you wish."

"Oh yes, ma'am. I would very much like that," Bronson said. He followed her inside, closing the door behind him.

They sat in the sitting room and quietly waited until, finally, Nellie excused herself and retreated farther into the house. A few minutes later, Alexander wandered in, head hung low, and greeted his old teacher. "Hello, Mr. Parrish."

They heard a voice from the kitchen. "Alex, did you say hello to Mr. Parrish?"

"Yeah, Ma. We're talking now."

"Be polite," she warned.

"Your mother put you up to this, did she?" Bronson smiled.

"Yes, sir."

"You have a good mother."

"Yes, sir. Mother said what happened with Matt Stewart got you in trouble with Grandmother. I'm sorry, Mr. Bronson. You were a good teacher."

"Thank you, Alexander. I appreciate that," said Bronson, and he thought, *These are good people. I may yet live.*

Alexander excused himself and ran out of the room.

Bronson heard Nellie calling out the back door. "Eugene, Mr. Parrish is here to see you."

Just then, footsteps sounded on the front porch. The door squeaked open, and Eugene walked in. "Hello, Mr. Parrish."

Bronson quickly stood and shook his hand.

Wasting no time, Eugene asked, "What can I do for you, sir? I figured you'd end up here. I expected it earlier, to tell you the truth."

"Did you?"

"Let's just say it made sense to me that you'd show up here. But I can't help you. I'm sorry."

"Wait!" said Bronson. "I know we're not well acquainted, Eugene, but I know enough about you, enough to know you can't possibly approve of what your father is doing."

"As I figured. My father—that's what this is about?"

Bronson nodded. "Yes. I was hoping—"

"Pardon me," Eugene interrupted. "I know my father is not a perfect man. So much of what he's done, I disapprove of, as you are well aware."

"Did you know he tampered with the ballots?"

"I did," Eugene admitted.

"How? How did you know?"

"I saw him do it."

"You what? You saw him manipulating the votes and did nothing to stop him?"

"First, you don't stop my father. On the latter account, I should rephrase. I didn't see him do anything. I saw him leave his office past midnight while the ballots were locked until morning. But I'm sorry to say it; he is my father."

In bewilderment, Bronson asked, "Why were you watching if not to stop him?"

Eugene looked down, wringing his hands. "It's a fair question, Mr. Parrish, but one I can't answer. Let's just say I knew he would. I figured he'd done it before, but I had to see it for myself. I'm sorry it had to be you he ran against, but either way, I can't help you. I have a family to consider."

Bronson wouldn't let him off the hook. "If you came forward, people would listen. Maybe we could restore a little decency here."

"I do what I can, Mr. Parrish, help where I can. I've warned people, written letters telling them to be careful, but just because he's my father doesn't mean he doesn't threaten me. I'm no different from you, and I'd appreciate it if we kept this conversation to ourselves. My life is on thin ice when it comes to my father. No telling what he'll do."

"So I understand. Do you know people have been hurt? I've reason to believe someone other than the monster killed Shear's boy and that teacher. I'm not at liberty to tell you how I know, but I'm certain of it." Bronson waited for a response. He noticed Eugene contemplating. Just as it appeared Eugene was softening, Alexander walked into the room and sat beside his father. Bronson saw the expression on Eugene's face change and knew he would receive no help. He indeed feared what his father might do to his family.

"I'm so very sorry," Eugene said as he motioned toward the door. "I'll see you out."

He followed Bronson out of the house and onto the front lawn.

"I understand, Eugene. We won't speak of this further, and it stays between us."

"Please, Mr. Parrish, not a word. I wish circumstances were different, but . . ."

"If, by chance, you reconsider," said Bronson, "please don't hesitate. Tell me immediately. We haven't much time." Bronson turned to leave.

"Mr. Parrish!" Eugene called out. Bronson stopped and turned around. "I won't stand in your way, either. I can promise you that."

Chapter 37

Bam! Bam! Bam! Coot barked as Bronson peeked out the front window. "You have company. Someone's banging on your door, LeFev."

"Can ya see 'em?"

"No, only Weston Riley. He's in the street, perched on a wagon."

"They can knock to their heart's content. Ain't nobody there, so . . ."

Bronson kept vigil at the window. A moment later, they heard it again. Bam! Bam! Bam!

Bronson held Coot, keeping him quiet. Then, finally, he peeked out as best he could, remaining behind the curtains.

"I can't see, but it sounds like the sheriff. He's hollering to Weston."

"Where's Weston?" asked LeFevre.

"I told you; he's sitting on a wagon in the street."

LeFevre got up to look. Bam! Bam! Bam! Only this time, it was much louder. Coot broke free and ran barking to the front door.

Bronson announced, "He's here!"

"Who's here?"

"The sheriff! Quiet!"

LeFevre quickly limped to the back room as Bronson went to answer the door. "Good afternoon, Sheriff."

"Ya forget to turn in your gun? Go get it." The sheriff stood in the doorway, trying to peer around Bronson and into the house.

"Did you consider I may not own one? Cross your mind, did it?"

"No, teacher, it didn't. But if what you're sayin' is true, you won't mind me searchin' the house. And don't be thinkin' you're bein' picked on either. Everyone who didn't turn one in, we're searchin'. Not just you."

"And if I refuse?"

"Oh, I'd enjoy that. I'd get to arrest ya. It's official." He moved uninvited past Bronson as Coot barked and growled. "Control your animal, Bronson, and show me where ya keep your gun."

"Like I told you, I don't own one, so you may leave."

"Not quite." The sheriff looked around, poking his head into the front parlor, the kitchen, and eventually the bedrooms. Finally, in one bedroom, a surprise greeted him. "Hello there, Mr. LeFevre."

"How do ya do, Sherrif? What an awkward coincidence seein' ya here. What brings ya? Here for tea?"

"I was just at your house. No doubt ya heard me knockin'. Now I can get ya both off my list." The sheriff walked through the house to the front door. He called out to Weston. "Get in here!"

Weston climbed down from the wagon and hustled over.

"I'll stay here and finish up with the teacher," the sheriff instructed. "Take Mr. LeFevre to his house. Make sure he ain't got no guns." He walked back inside and ordered LeFevre out the door. "You go with Weston. He's waitin'." As LeFevre stood, the sheriff looked suspiciously at his bandaged arm. "Hmm, I wonder how that happened. Been north of the gorge lately?"

LeFevre walked out the front door as the sheriff searched Bronson's house. Taking his time, he went through everything. He looked under pots and in drawers, patted down the linens in Bronson's armoire, and tapped the walls and floorboards, convinced he'd find a gun somewhere. If nothing else, he'd enjoy taking Bronson into custody just for questioning.

The sheriff was in the back room when Weston returned with LeFevre. "Plenty of guns next door, Sheriff."

"Load 'em in the wagon. Almost done here." LeFevre limped in and sat down next to Bronson in the sitting room. Bronson held Coot by the collar.

"Find anything, Sheriff?" asked Bronson, confident he wouldn't find a gun, and since LeFevre hadn't objected to the search or seizure, he hoped the sheriff wouldn't have cause for arrest.

The sheriff walked out of the room and into the front parlor with something in his hand. "Well, look here. I found my hat!"

Chapter 38

The door to Marco's office swung open, and Emily hurried inside. Panicked, she cried, "Marco, they've been arrested!"

"Who?"

"Surely they can't get away with this!"

"Please, come sit." Marco took her hand and led her to a chair. "Now, tell me who's been arrested."

"Mr. Parrish and Mr. LeFevre. Weston said the sheriff arrested them. He's holding them for questioning at the sheriff's office."

"Did he say what happened? Why they're being questioned?"

Emily stood and began pacing back and forth. "Only that they were on some sort of list. Weston said he and the sheriff were going door to door, searching for guns."

"I happen to know they wouldn't have found any at Mr. Parrish's house. I can't say the same for Mr. LeFevre."

"Well, so what if they find Mr. LeFevre's guns? Is that grounds for arrest?"

"I don't believe so. It's obvious we're missing something," said Marco. "Unless . . ."

"Unless what?" Emily stopped pacing to listen.

"The other night, didn't Mr. Parrish say he would contact Eugene Owen? He even said it could go badly. That's what I remember."

Emily nodded. "Yes. That's my recollection."

"That still leaves us nowhere."

"Hmm," thought Emily.

"What?"

"What if we demand their release?"

"That won't work, not with the sheriff."

"Can we break them out?"

"That'd be impossible, suicide even."

"What, then?"

Marco shook his head. "I don't know. When has the town ever stood for suppressing the enforcement of such draconian laws? Under normal circumstances, arrest without cause would be unheard of. But with everything happening, people are frightened, and I blame the voices—the purveyors of fear, the conjurors of a spell of some sort. I swear by it. People believe everything the mayor says partly because of what the voices tell them. There is an unholy alliance. And the voices, I believe, originate from Mount Erebus. That's why I must climb the mountain, see what's up there, see if I can sever the connection between the voices and the people."

"Hmm, I'm not so sure," said Emily. "I'm not convinced it's the right course of action. According to the parson, whatever is up there is evil. There's no telling what resistance you'll find. And if you recall, Mr. Parrish put me in charge of keeping everyone safe, and I say no, at least not by yourself."

"What choice have I? You said it yourself, Emmy. We can't just do nothing while Mr. Parrish and Mr. LeFevre sit in jail. No, it's time to see what's up there. To accomplish anything, we must start by breaking the spell." Marco stood on a chair and reached up to the crossbeam, sliding his fingers across it until he felt something hard and brought it down. He slipped his father's revolver into the back of his belt and stepped down. "I'm going alone, and you're staying here."

"You have a gun?"

"Yeah, and not only this one."

"Then I'm coming with you."

"No, Emmy. You're in charge of getting people to safety, remember? Start with our parents and my father. If I don't return, get them as far away from here as possible. But be careful. The mayor may be on to us."

"Marco, please. I can't sit idly by and wait like before, wondering if you're hurt or worse!"

"If you remember, I returned once. God willing, I'll do so again. But if something were to happen to both of us, who would keep our families safe?"

"I'm not happy about this, Marco. I wish you'd reconsider."

"Why don't we ride out together? You can wait for me at your childhood home. It's far enough that no one will notice. And you'll be the first to see me upon my return. And if something happens—"

Emily nodded. "I know."

"Then it's agreed," said Marco. "We leave this afternoon before sunset and curfew. There's less risk than sneaking out after dark."

"That means we leave immediately. The sun sets in a little under an hour."

Marco peered out the window to see the sun hovering above the western horizon. "There is not enough time to even inform our loved ones, is there?"

"No, unless you ask Warren to do it for us."

"If he hasn't already left for home," said Marco. "It's getting late."

"Then let's hope he's still there."

Chapter 39

The stable seemed empty when Emily and Marco arrived. Marco immediately began checking the stalls. Seeing no one, he called out. "Warren?"

"I'm out here!" At the back door, Marco's best friend, Warren Sowell, appeared, pushing a wheelbarrow laden with fresh straw. Setting it down, Warren brushed sweat and manure from his forehead and greeted them warmly. "Pleasant end of the day seein' the both of you," he said. "To what do I owe this visit? And please don't tell me you're up to no good."

Emily smiled warmly. "Hello, Warren."

Warren removed his hat and dipped his head. "Miss Hampshire." Putting his hat back on, he took hold of a pitchfork and began filling a stall with fresh straw. "I must get the horses in their stables before I leave, and there's not much time. So, what can I do for ya?"

"We're here for my horse," said Marco. "Need to borrow Mr. LeFevre's as well. He won't mind."

Warren tossed the pitchfork into the bales of hay. "You mean Rooster?"

"Mr. LeFevre's horse is named Rooster?" asked Emily. "Who names a horse Rooster?"

"Mr. LeFevre is who," said Warren. "Although his horse is red, so . . ."

"Hmm," said Emily.

Marco saddled Rosso, his father's horse, while Warren saddled and bridled Rooster, then helped Emily mount.

"None of my business, whatever you're doing. Just that if you're out late, watch out for Weston. He's out every night, enforcing the curfew.

Not sure what he'll do if he spots you two, so mind yourselves and be back before dark. Give yourselves plenty of time, and there's not much of it before sundown."

"We won't be back till morning," said Marco. "In the meantime, would you inform my father I won't be home tonight? Tell him not to worry, but first, go to Emmy's. The Hampshires have greater cause to worry. Can you do that?"

"Will do. But what will I tell them? They'll have questions, and the both of you off together for the night might give a false impression."

Emily and Marco looked at each other, hoping the other already had an excuse prepared.

"Warren's right, Emmy," said Marco. "How about I leave with Warren? We'll go up the mountain together while you stay here. You can wait for me with my father, like before."

"Wait!" said Warren. "What's this about goin' up the mountain? It's forbidden! But, of course, you already know that."

"We haven't time to explain," said Emily, "other than it being in the best interest of everyone."

Hearing that, Warren turned to Marco. "Tell me you are not taking Emmy up there."

"She's not going with me. So, you see, there's no impropriety."

"I know both of you. I never suggested there was. But I couldn't accompany you up the mountain even if I wanted to. I've got a mail run to Bloomington before sunrise and can't be out all night. I'll inform your parents as long as Emmy doesn't go with you up the mountain. I'll figure out what I can tell them. Just hurry, and don't be seen out past dark."

"Thank you, Warren," said Emily.

"I'd rather you not thank me. I'm not certain I'm doin' either of you a favor. But at least I know where to look if you go missing.

Chapter 40

The mayor sat behind his desk, too lazy to put a log in the potbelly stove. That was Beatrice's job. He'd had a runny nose and cold hands ever since Martha let her go.

"I'd offer you coffee, but since . . ." The mayor groaned. "Haven't had a cup worth drinking since Beatrice left."

"Ain't here for coffee, sir. It's my hat," complained the sheriff.

Weston stood next to the sheriff, paying little attention.

Confused, the mayor asked, "Your hat? What about it?" He looked to Weston, who seemed just as baffled. "Do you know what the sheriff is getting on about?"

"His hat, sir?" said Weston.

The sheriff stepped forward. "I have the teacher and Frenchman behind bars."

"Mr. Parrish?"

"Yeah, he and the Frenchman had it."

"Who's the Frenchman?"

Weston answered for the sheriff. "Mr. LeFevre, sir."

"Oh, him," said the mayor. "And they had your hat?"

"Yeah," said the sheriff. "I found it during our search."

"Did they steal it?"

"No," answered Sheriff Weasley.

The mayor leaned back, his arms draped over his ample belly. "Well, you can't arrest a man for having a hat he didn't steal."

"But I lost it in the gorge," said the sheriff. "It was in the *gorge*! And he's injured."

"Who's injured?"

Weston answered for the sheriff. "The Frenchman, sir."

"Hmm," said the mayor. "You're saying Mr. Parrish and LeFevre could only have your hat if they found it in the gorge. And LeFevre is injured as if he came across something he didn't expect while there... like Wallace's monster?"

"It's what I'm sayin', sir. You were lookin' for who went after the monster."

"Yes, I was," said the mayor. "Now we must decide how to handle it. First, we must agree on the details and never deviate. So, when you and Shear's boy went to verify the Wallace story about the monster, you got attacked and dropped your hat, barely escaping—right?"

"That's right!"

"And they, Parrish and Frenchie, found your hat while attempting to kill Wallace's monster."

"Yep," said the sheriff. "They broke the law."

"Umm-hmm," agreed the mayor, "further agitating the monster, and that poor teacher died. It's perfect." The corners of the mayor's mouth turned up in a grin. "We'll make an example of them. No one will dare attempt to hunt the monster after that."

Turning his attention to Weston, he said, "I need you to build me a gallows. I'll give you two days. Can it be done? Can you do it?"

"Ya, but—"

"Build the gallows to hang three at once. That way, if we hang two, everyone will see there's room for one more. Build it across the street, in the park. Two days. Get to it."

"You're not going to hang 'em, are you, sir? Mr. Parrish was my teacher, and people in town may feel that finding a hat may not warrant the noose."

"Let me worry about that. Don't forget, Weston, we're doing this for the people. Mr. Parrish nearly brought this town to its knees. Everyone would have gone hungry had I not been mayor. This way, he can never hurt anyone, not anymore. Weston, you're dismissed, and I want to hear hammers pounding within the hour."

Weston hurried out the door while the mayor turned to the sheriff. "You and I are going to your office—find out who else is up to no good."

The sheriff held the door for the mayor to enter first. Bronson and LeFevre sat in the back, where little light reached the chilly stone walls of the small holding cell. It could accommodate little more than one person at a time comfortably. It functioned as overnight lodging for anyone who staggered out of Ernie's Tavern too late to find their way to their bed. "Get the lantern and keep the door open," ordered the mayor. "Smells like death in here."

The sheriff struck a sulfur match and lit the wick. He carried the lantern to the back, where the mayor had already pulled up a chair and was speaking to the men on the other side of the iron bars.

"Well, what have we here?" asked the mayor, seeming pleased. "I can't express how nice it is to see you both."

"Pleasure's all yours," said LeFevre.

"Yes, it is. It certainly is," the mayor chuckled. "Has the sheriff been treating you well? Are either of you hungry? Thirsty?" Bronson and LeFevre only stared. "Shame on you, Sheriff. Get these men something to drink."

"I could use the toilet," LeFevre complained. "Unless ya want to clean the floor."

"How about you, Mr. Parrish? Do you require the same?"

"Afraid so. I can run home and come back later."

"Let's talk first," said the mayor. "Can you hold it?"

Just then, Weston rushed in holding a bundle of torn campaign posters. "Mayor, you may want to see this."

"What is it, Weston? Can't you see I'm busy?"

"Pardon me, sir. I can come back if . . ."

"No, no, tell me now. What is it?"

"I was out all night," said Weston. "I walked up and down Main Street a dozen times. That's where your posters were, and I don't recall who you assigned to take them down after the election, but it wasn't me. And I swear I didn't see a soul past curfew. So you can imagine how surprised I was when I found these this morning." He handed the mayor several torn and vandalized posters.

One such poster had words painted in red, all over the mayor's face. "Heed God's voice and none other! What does that even mean?" asked the mayor. He glanced angrily at Bronson and LeFevre. "Weston? How many?"

"How many what, sir?"

"How many did they vandalize?"

"All of them, sir."

"All of them?"

"Yes, sir. What would you have me do?"

"Elections are over, so get rid of them. I won't need them anymore, and why don't I hear hammering? I gave you two days is all!"

"Sorry, but I've been up all night."

"Then have Ernie and Hyrum assist you, but get it done."

Weston excused himself and hurried out the door.

"Now, gentleman, where were we?" asked the mayor. He held up the poster so Bronson and LeFevre could see it. "Know anything about this?"

"Wasn't us," said Bronson. LeFevre agreed.

"No, I believe you, Mr. Parrish, and especially you, Mr. LeFevre. I don't see either of you as churchgoers. This lawlessness has the earmark of one of the parson's parishioners. I've been informed as to what he is preaching, and see here? The consequence."

Bronson leaned forward, unafraid. "Or perhaps it is the consequence of losing the people's trust."

"And how have I done that?"

"Take guns away and people stop trusting. They'll wonder if taking away elections is next. Then what? Their food? No telling the control you'd have over the town leveraging the food they need to survive."

"Always thinking the worst, aren't you?"

The sheriff stepped forward with two pairs of handcuffs. "Turn around, both of you." Reaching through the bars, he cuffed both men. The keys rattled on an iron ring as he unlocked the cell door. "This way, Frenchman."

A shackled Lefevre hobbled out of the jail cell, wincing from the pain of his broken ribs. The sheriff gripped the cuffs behind him, shoving while enjoying each moan elicited from the injured man.

"Now that we're alone, Mr. Parrish, I wish to offer my sympathies. Losing an election can't be easy, though I've never lost one, so I am left only to imagine how bitter you must feel."

"No, I can handle losing. It's the corruption, stealing the election—"

"Give it a rest. There's never been a more fair election. Your problem is you were foolish enough to believe you could win. You have yourself to blame for that."

Bronson looked away while turning his back to the mayor.

"I suppose you've nothing to say, Mr. Parrish? No witty remarks? Hmm?"

LeFevre came shuffling through the back door with the sheriff close behind.

"Your turn, teacher," said the sheriff, pushing LeFevre into the cell, then yanking Bronson out by the arm. "Come with me." He then led Bronson out the back door.

The mayor leaned back in his chair and crossed his legs. "So, Mr. LeFevre. Why are you even here? You have a minor offense I could easily erase. You could walk out of here presently. Mr. Parrish is the troublemaker, not you. I don't believe you had anything to do with his scheming, and, quite frankly, I don't care if you did. All I want are the names of the others you've recruited. Mr. Parrish can't pull off an insurrection by himself. Who else is there? Start with who defaced my posters."

The mayor walked to the sheriff's desk and rummaged through a mess of papers. Finally, he found what he sought—a blank sheet of paper, a feathered pen, and an inkwell. He returned and handed them to LeFevre through the bars. "Make a list, and let's get you out of here. Right now. I'm going to be honest with you. You can't help Mr. Parrish, but you can help yourself. If you have any brains, you'll start writing."

The mayor hadn't even finished his sentence, and LeFevre, wet pen in hand, was hard at work. He stopped, thought, and then wrote some more. As he did so, the mayor leaned in, trying to figure out how many names he wrote. LeFevre finally stopped and handed the paper back to the mayor, who held it close to the lamp to read it.

"Hmm," said the mayor. "I see you remembered my mother's name. And you also had a few nice things to say about her. You didn't spare me either, did you? Lots of flattery." The mayor took a deep breath. "You're a stupid man, Frenchie." He scrunched the paper and then dropped it onto the floor.

"And you're a tyrant," said LeFevre.

"Well, now," said the mayor. "You just talked yourself onto the end of a rope."

No time passed before the door opened and Bronson staggered in with the sheriff close behind. "Are we interruptin', sir?"

"No, we're done here. We'll give these men a few days to think. Make sure they have water rather than bruises. We'll need them to look pretty if they don't start talking."

Chapter 41

The stars twinkled above New Harmony, but not a soul enjoyed them. Instead, all were shut away in their homes with curtains drawn. Curfew was in effect, and the streets lay abandoned but for Weston, who rode through the night, enforcing the law.

Meanwhile, Emily and Marco hid away in a dimly lit dilapidated house in what was once Emily's childhood bedroom. She sat on the same wooden board where Bronson sat several nights earlier, Marco on the floor opposite her. They'd only brought one lantern, which they kept partially covered to shield its glow. "If you find the source of the voices, how do you intend to stop them?"

Marco shrugged. "I have my gun. I hope to run them off, whatever they are."

"I hope that's enough," Emily said. "People are being led as if with nose rings and don't even know it. But Parson Burroughs knows. He's the one who told me not to listen." Emily leaned in close. "Are you certain you wish to do this alone? I can come with you."

"Emmy, you know why."

"I know. I'll be here when you come back. Just come back no matter what."

"And if I don't, you know what to do. If I disappear, there will be questions."

"Yes, I know. I know what I must do."

Emily followed Marco to the back of the house, where the horses waited. Marco untied Rosso and was about to climb on when he felt a hand on his arm. He turned to face Emily, and she wrapped her arms around him, her head against his chest. Marco drew her close, and they embraced for a pleasant moment. Then the moment passed and they separated, reluctant to infringe on the memory of someone they both dearly loved.

Marco grabbed the saddle horn and cantle and pulled himself up, sitting tall astride Rosso. "I'm leaving the lantern with you," he said. "There's plenty of moonlight for me to see my way. You can't sit in the dark all night. Do try to sleep while I'm away."

Emily looked up at him. "Please be careful," she said. "I'll be waiting here."

He pulled on the reins and clucked his tongue. Rosso turned as Emily backed away, watching Marco ride into the night.

Reluctantly, she went back into the house. Alone with her thoughts, she remembered days long past. Into the kitchen, or what once was a kitchen, Emily walked. She remembered sitting at the table as a young girl and asking her mother when her father would be home. She looked out the back door to where Tippy once ran in the backyard. The memory of voices long ago returned to her, her mother calling her to supper while Papa told her that freckles were kisses from the sun. She'd never liked her freckles as a girl.

"Mama," she said, swept away with emotion as she spoke to the ghosts of the past. "I'm sorry for what happened to you. I would've done anything to save you. I rang the bell for you, Mama. Did you hear it?"

Then, suddenly, the cold, dark night conjured memories of the tool cabinet where her father had hidden her the day he disappeared. "And you, Papa," she called out to the emptiness. "Where did you go? I waited like you told me to. And where are you now? But don't you worry. I'll find you and the men who murdered you. I'll make them pay."

She felt a surge of adrenaline brought on by a purpose she could no longer ignore. "I can't find you, Papa, if I do nothing but wait around here!"

At that, Emily tore through the house to where Rooster waited. There was something she could do, something she wouldn't share with

Marco, knowing he'd never allow it. As far as Emily was concerned, their last embrace was more of a farewell. She had already weighed her decision and felt it was worth the risk, even if she might not see the morning.

Emily waited for a time after Marco left before also heading north. She regretted that she might not be waiting when he returned and that she might never return, but merely watching others risk their lives was unacceptable, and she was determined to do more than wait. Skirting the town on farm roads, Emily carried only the unlit lantern. She traveled past fields and pastures until finally stopping short of the crossroads, where several paths converged with the main road that led north out of town. Emily stared into the dark. Up ahead, she saw something that startled her. Someone waited. She couldn't skirt around them. Did Marco suspect she'd follow him? Did he wait to make her go back?

She rode slowly toward whoever stood in her way. Her heart sank when she recognized Weston, who seemed just as startled to see her riding toward him. He pointed his gun in her direction. "Emmy?"

"Weston, is that you?" Emily pulled back on the reins and came to a stop.

"What are you doing out here? You know it's forbidden." He holstered his gun. "You can't be here!"

"Weston, you're understandably upset."

"Of course I am! I've got to take you to the sheriff now."

"Please, listen to me. I'm truly sorry, but—"

"Sorry for what?" he interrupted. "What are you doing out here?"

Emily tried to think of an excuse, but nothing came. She wasn't any good at deception, and she had no time. "I can't tell you," she admitted. "But I must go. And, Weston, nobody can know what I'm doing, please. If you ever cared for me as a friend—"

"What makes you think I cared for you?"

"You once brought me flowers," she said, desperate to convince him to let her go.

"I never brought you flowers. What are you talking about?"

"Before Christian died, he told me you left them for me when we were younger. He should have apologized to you rather than me. I never had the chance to thank you. I'm sorry. It was sweet of you, and I would have liked the opportunity to thank you."

"So what? What matters is why you're here, breaking curfew."

"I'm sorry, but I can't tell you. You don't know, but—"

"Stop saying you're sorry. You don't know what I risk not turning you in."

"Please listen," she pleaded. "The monster didn't kill Christian or Ms. Madison. Trust me, I beg you, even though I can't tell you how I know. Not yet, anyway, but I will soon enough."

"Then who did? Who killed them?"

"I'm going to get proof. That's what I'm doing, but it wasn't the monster. Please, I won't tell anyone you saw me. When you learn the truth, as will everyone, on which side would you rather be—the side of truth or the side of a murderer?"

"Me, protecting a murderer? That's what you believe? So, let me understand. You're suggesting the mayor—"

"I don't have time for this conversation. I've only a little time to prove what I know. Haven't you suspected as well?"

"Emmy. I can't allow this. There are things you don't understand. I have no choice but to turn you in." Weston pulled his gun. "And now I'm the one who's sorry. You're coming with me."

"All right, then," said Emily. "You'll have to kill me, and when the truth is known and everyone realizes you killed an innocent woman to protect murderers, you can tell them you're sorry. And by the way, you're not the only one whose father disappeared." Emily motioned for Rooster to go. She closed her eyes, anticipating the shot from Weston's gun.

Instead, the horse moved unimpeded past him, and she without injury, but she heard shouting behind her. "Don't you tell anyone or else!"

A little farther, she came to where the road leading up the mountain branched off, where Marco had turned. Emily had no intention of following him, however. Instead, she turned left toward the gorge. When the canyon walls began to close in on either side, she stopped and lit the lantern. Then, with the clomping of horse hooves echoing through the canyon, she prayed. "Please, God, let me not be afraid!"

Chapter 42

"Wake up! They're coming for you, and they have guns. Get up now or sleep forever!" the voice called out, stirring the beast awake. A growl filled the cave. Claws shot out from the pads of his paws, and he bolted out and into the meadow. He crouched low, hunting, the dark hours belonging to him. *Are they foolish enough to try this at night?* he wondered. *I see and smell everything.* While sniffing the breeze, the beast turned his ears forward. Something sour hovered in the air. *Sweat*, he thought. *Human sweat. Invaders.*

"You hesitate this time, you die," said a voice. "Take the kill or else . . ."

Hardly making a sound, he disappeared into the tall grass. As he waited, he thought, *I'll need the element of surprise, depending on their numbers.*

He heard the voice again. "How dare they come for you, innocent as you are, wrongfully accused! You've done nothing to deserve this! Rip them apart! Teach them to never come after you again. Make them pay."

The beast saw lantern light moving toward him through the grass. He crouched lower and held his breath. *Almost*, he thought. *Let them come closer.* Then came the neighing of a horse, along with the sound of footsteps.

The minutes seemed to stretch on forever. Then the beast heard what sounded like someone moving through the grass, and the smell of sweat grew more potent as the light drew close. *Wait*, thought the monster. *Wait.*

Now! As the beast sprang from where he hid, a voice screamed inside his head. "Jonathan, no!" His claws retracted just in time, but his momentum sent him crashing into a woman, both tumbling through the grassy meadow, the lantern flying out of her hand. Fortunately, the flame extinguished before it lit the meadow on fire and plunged them into a fiery inferno. But, now, everything was black. Jonathan's vision quickly adjusted, but the woman appeared blind. He circled her, looking for a gun, but found nothing. He sniffed the air, capturing her scent. What he smelled, he owned, and she was known to him.

"Forgive me," said the woman, her voice shaky. "I beg you to forgive me, but I had to come."

Jonathan moved back and cursed the voices. *You nearly had me kill a woman. Liars! Why do I listen to you? You knew she meant no harm.*

On the ground in front of him lay the woman he'd encountered when he'd taken the hat south. She rose to her knees and scooted away as far as she could. In the dim light, he could see that she trembled, jumping whenever Jonathan moved. He retrieved the lantern, the handle in his mouth, and slowly approached. She recoiled as he drew near. The glass in the tin frame of the lantern rattled as Jonathan set it in front of her. He watched until her hands finally found what she sought. She set the lantern in front of her and pulled a phosphorus match from the pocket of her sweater.

As the match sprang to life and the wick took hold of the flame, terror filled the woman's eyes.

How gruesome I must look, Jonathan thought. *I am a monster.*

His coal-black, deep-set eyes stared back at her. A grizzly jaw with shiny canine teeth extended downward, overlapping his black lips and gums. He could hear her heart thumping in her chest and watched as she struggled to breathe. Finally, she managed to speak.

"Can you understand me?" the woman asked.

Jonathan nodded.

"You really can? You understand what I'm saying?"

Jonathan nodded.

"My name is Emily," she said. "And you brought us a hat. Did the man who wore that hat kill Christian? Did you see him do it?"

Jonathan tilted his head, listening. *How do I answer?* he wondered, but then the woman asked another question.

"Did an older man who wore the hat kill a younger man?"

Jonathan nodded.

"You saw him do it?

Another nod.

"We were to be married, the murdered man and me. I believe the same person who killed him also killed my father. The person responsible is an evil man, and he blames you."

Jonathan growled, and the woman trembled.

Realizing he'd frightened her, he quieted, moved back, and bowed his head. Slowly raising his eyes, he watched her closely, noting the tears running down her face, and felt her sorrow. Yet, somehow, the anguish accompanying his curse felt soothed by her presence. Jonathan felt the comforting nature of the woman, her soft voice and graceful movements causing him to yearn and feel.

Taking a deep breath, she asked, "Is there anything else I need to know?"

Jonathan was silent, not knowing how to answer. Eventually, he nodded.

"Yes?" she asked, and he repeated the gesture. Then he watched and waited. After a pause, she asked, "So you had nothing to do with the murder?"

Jonathan shook his head forcefully. This time, the woman stayed calm, watching him.

"Was anyone else with the man who owns the hat?"

A nod.

"That's a yes," said the woman. "Another young man?"

Jonathan shook his head.

"Then, no," said the woman. "An older man?"

A nod.

"All right," said Emily. "An older man. Was he tall, short, fat, or skinny?"

Jonathan just stared.

"Sorry," she said. Let's try again. Was he tall?"

Jonathan shook his head.

"Skinny?"

Jonathan shook his head again.

"So he was short and fat, like the mayor."

Jonathan felt unsure who the mayor was, but he nodded.

"Thank you," she said. "That's all I need to know. You're very kind. You could have torn me to pieces, I know."

Jonathan swung his head forcefully, the thought of hurting her abhorrent to him.

In apparent understanding, she said, "You're right. I don't for a moment believe you are a killer."

Jonathan sensed a deep sorrow in her.

"It's just that these men . . ." she said. "Evil men, they killed the man I loved, the man I intended to share my life with. Of course, they blame you, but I see through their lies. I wouldn't doubt they've murdered others, including my father and mother."

Jonathan's heart constricted as her tears flowed. He scooted closer and watched as she moved closer as well.

"They're bad men," she continued, "but I don't know how to stop them. But that's not your concern. God willing, I'll find my father and bring justice to these evil men."

Jonathan extended a paw, his head down, his eyes closed. Emily took it in her hand, then lifted it and pressed it against her cheek, and for a moment, Jonathan felt something stir within him—a distant memory he desperately sought to recall. Then, in the blink of an eye, he was gone, leaving the woman alone in the lamplight, surrounded by the meadow.

Chapter 43

TEMPUS FUGIT—time is fleeting.
Been another attempt, the monster to kill.
Alliance at risk. Awake or perish.
They or you will burn at the landfill!

Despite the ranch house being chilly, the ashes in the bedroom fireplace having gone cold, Robert awoke in a pool of sweat. The voices inside his head called to him, but he could not answer without fear of waking Martha. So he pulled off his blanket and quietly crept from the room.

The sitting-room fireplace was as cold as the floor under his bare feet. Rubbing the sleep from his eyes, he answered their warning, keeping his voice soft so as not to be overheard. "Who? Tell me. No one dares harm the monster. I closed the gorge. It's strictly forbidden."

A deep, raspy voice filled his head. "Is that accusation in your tone? You assume we are lying?"

"No, not at all. I would never—"

"And yet, another attempt, and this one very close. The monster may be dying even now, dear Robert, which would be awful for you. Nevertheless, you hesitate to seize control and risk losing everything. This warning is but a courtesy."

Still only half awake, the mayor peered out his window. He expected blackbirds but saw only a darkened sky. "Please tell me again," he whispered, "why exactly should I care? I understand the beast is useful. I want it to live as much as anyone, but, honestly, I learned there was such a thing as a monster merely days ago."

The voice hissed. "Penitence. The monster does penitence for a debt not yet satisfied!"

"All right, then, tell me who dared to defy my order. They will hang, and you will witness how I intend to honor our arrangement."

"It does not matter who. Always another, always, always. Until you are feared, your control is incomplete, your possessions insecure. Once all fear you, only then will none dare come against you. But, poor Robert, no one respects you, and you have more reason to worry than you know."

"Who is against me? Who now threatens me?" The mayor began to feel the same fear he wished to inflict upon others, his insecurity amplifying his discomfort.

"Those closest to you will be your undoing. Unless—"

"Unless what?" the mayor demanded, but the room had gone still. Suddenly, flames leaped onto a partially spent log in the fireplace, and the room grew warm, the newly kindled firelight reflected in his eyes.

Robert suddenly felt abandoned, as if his world burned around him, the voices having abandoned him. *They're no longer here*, he sensed. *The fire no longer fears their presence, and though I can't frighten fire, I can frighten people. Soon New Harmony will fear my presence. Now is my turn, and New Harmony will fear me.*

He stared into the fire, imagining Bronson and LeFevre with nooses around their necks. "I will show no mercy until I am properly respected!"

Chapter 14

The sheriff slept in his office chair the night following the mayor's orders. The next morning, he rubbed at the stiffness in his neck and stretched his aching back, his discomfort adding to his sour mood. He couldn't risk any unknown coconspirators freeing his prisoners. And coconspirators there were. The vandalism of the posters proved it. By the time the mayor walked in early that morning, the sheriff was groggy and ill-tempered.

Forgoing a greeting, the mayor got right to the point. "Any luck? Coming to their senses, are they, Weasley?

"Not as of yet, sir. The Frenchman kept me up all night, askin' if I was comfortable, rude as rats nibblin' at my heels."

The mayor drew the curtains as sunlight streamed through the front window, "Sheriff's Office" painted on the glass. "Get Mr. Parrish over here. And, Weasley . . ."

"Yes, sir?"

"As soon as Weston finishes his project, have him paint the word *Interrogations* right here under 'Sheriff's Office.'" The mayor tapped the window to show exactly where he wanted it. The idea brought a smile to the sheriff's face. He led a shackled Bronson to where the mayor stood looking out the front window, grinning.

"Take a gander, Mr. Parrish. I've something you ought to see. It's certain to add to Mr. LeFevre's comfort since he's so concerned with such things." The mayor stepped aside so Bronson could look out the window at the park across the street. "So, why don't you describe to Mr. LeFevre what you see?"

"Hey, LeFev!" Bronson yelled.

"Ya?"

"About the hammering . . ."

"What is it?"

"I owe you a dollar."

"Gallows, huh? Can't say I didn't tell ya."

"You certainly did. I'm looking at it."

"Hey, Mayor?" called LeFevre from the back. "You're rich. Would ya loan Bronson a dollar? I don't figure he's got his wallet on his person."

The smile left the mayor's face. "You are mistaken, gentleman, if you believe I had that built to frighten you. I intend—"

"No, sir," said Bronson, cutting the mayor short. "I don't presume to believe you built it to frighten LeFev and me, oh no! You built it to frighten everyone in New Harmony. What's more? You have every intention of murdering the two of us to accomplish that. But I suppose we're the fortunate ones, aren't we?"

"Fortunate? You're many things, Mr. Parrish, but fortunate isn't one of them."

"No? But at least LeFev and I won't simply disappear. People will know what happened to us and who is responsible."

Scoffing, the mayor said, "You think you're so knowledgeable, but here's where you're wrong. I intend to use it, but only if you force my hand. You mean nothing to me, Mr. Parrish, and the Frenchman even less. I'm more interested in anyone else who threatens my town. The truth is, you lost the election. Nobody wanted you. I'll give you a horse, and you leave New Harmony for good. You have my word, your freedom for the names of your accomplices."

"Hmm," said Bronson, still peering out the window at the gallows. "If nobody wanted me, why cheat? No, I'm most certainly a threat. I'm not going anywhere other than across the street. And I'm pleased you're not about trying to frighten LeFev and me. It won't work."

Frustrated, the mayor struck Bronson in the stomach with all his might, leaving him hunched over and gasping for air.

"You fool!" said the mayor. "You assume to know it all—how I stole the election and how I've made people disappear. It turns out it doesn't matter what you know or even what I know or do. It only matters what people think they know."

The mayor grabbed Bronson by the chin and lifted his head. "Before I take you across the street, you'll tell me who is trying to kill the monster other than you two."

The mayor delivered another punch and waited for a response, but Bronson remained silent. Then, finally, the mayor yelled to the sheriff, "Put him back and bring me the Frenchman!"

The sheriff shoved a shackled Lefevre through the office to the front window, then yanked Bronson back to the jail.

"See for yourself, Mr. LeFevre," said the mayor. "No more hammering, the rope at the ready. But you have my word as mayor—I'll set you free, but only you, and only if you give me names."

LeFevre stared out the window. "Ya give your word as mayor, do ya?"

"I do."

"But you're not the mayor. You're a loser who stole an election. Bronson, the legitimate mayor, and I are already dead, and we're not taking anyone with us."

"Both of you are fools! Don't you see? You and Mr. Parrish will only be the first. After that, I'll hang as many as it takes, even if that means hanging every last person in New Harmony. So before I put a rope around your neck, why not save the innocent people who will die just because I suspect them of treason?"

With that, the mayor gave LeFevre a parting blow to the gut. LeFevre began coughing up blood as the mayor turned and left, leaving them to their fate.

Chapter 45

When the bell above the school rang, people rightly assumed it meant another town meeting. The entirety of New Harmony hungered for news. Council members rode through the streets, calling for people to attend. "Everyone to the town center!" Crowds converged on the center of New Harmony. As they arrived, those unaware of the gallows' construction were only mildly surprised. It had sprung up practically overnight. There had never been a hanging in New Harmony, but no one questioned it, so conditioned were they to the mayor's whims.

After returning from her encounter in the meadow, Emily waited in the ruins of what was once her home. Suddenly, she heard the bell ringing. Oh no! Where was Marco? He should have been back by now. She closed her eyes and prayed he was safe. She looked north, hoping to see him, but he wasn't there. She began to pace back and forth to calm her nerves, closed her eyes again, and prayed some more. "Please, God, let me see him coming!" Emily opened her eyes and stared into the distance. The sun's brilliant light bathed the valley, but she saw no one coming. And then she thought she saw something move in the contrast of light and shadow. She waited, staring.

Wasting no time, she mounted LeFevre's horse and rode out.

"Marco, you're alive!" she called, awash in relief as she rode up beside him.

"What happened to you, Emmy? Your dress is soiled and torn, and you've bruises. Who did this to you?"

"I'm fine. Please believe me. I'm more concerned about you. What happened up there? Did you see anything?"

"It pains me to report that I failed you again. I saw nothing. It was no different than when I was a boy, when Christian and I climbed the mountain, but for the taunting voices asking me what I looked for. When I said, 'you,' they told me I arrived at the wrong time."

"The wrong time?"

"It's what they said, in my head. I'm not certain what happened after that. I found myself riding here with no recollection of leaving."

"Perhaps it's just as well," said Emily.

"There is one other thing," said Marco.

"What?"

"Though I saw nothing, I did feel something. They're up there, on the mountain, and they are evil, unlike anything I've yet experienced. But enough of my report. What happened to you?"

"We haven't time now. I can explain later," said Emily as she pulled on the reins. "You heard the bell ring?"

"I did."

"We must hurry."

People filled the streets as they rode into town. They stopped at Emily's for a quick change of clothing, Marco tending to the horses as Emily quickly ran inside, finding the house empty, her uncle and aunt having already left. She reemerged with a clean dress and shawl that covered her bruises, and together they mingled with the people headed to the center of town.

When they arrived, the mayor stood at the podium with the sheriff, pulling up his pants and preparing to speak. They found a place in the park across the street, next to the gallows. Seeing the hanging device was an unwelcome surprise, especially knowing Bronson and LeFevre sat behind bars.

Emily whispered to Marco, "They intend to hang them. We're too late!"

There was no need for the sheriff to silence the crowd. He moved to the base of the steps in front of his office, long gun in hand. As if under a spell, the people watched in quiet anticipation. The mayor gripped the podium and looked over the entirety of New Harmony. Even the children had come to watch. Emily looked over to see her neighbor, Barbara Folsom. She held her son, Porter, only a year old, on her hip, her other five children gathered around her.

The mayor grinned as if pleased with the attendance, wishing everyone to witness what would unfold. He looked across the street at the gallows and stared.

Emily followed his gaze, looking to see what had grabbed his attention. Three blackbirds watched the proceedings. They sat on the crossbeam where the ropes dangled. Puzzled, she thought, *Didn't Constance say the mayor talks with birds?* Emily turned her attention back to the podium when she heard the mayor speak.

"Good people of New Harmony. As your esteemed mayor, I humbly stand before you, happy to report that the crops continue to grow as promised."

A cheer rose, and the mayor waited for the exuberance to subside.

"The harvest will be sufficient come fall due to the prudence toward the collective good I shall administer. We may yet emerge from the coming winter without the tragedy of starvation. I can assure you, with new regulation, an equal portion of our bountiful harvest."

The cheering persisted, though several farmers seemed alarmed at the thought of sharing their crops rather than selling them.

The mayor continued. "I wish that were all I had to report. Unfortunately, it's come to my attention that certain miscreants took it upon themselves to rid the town of the beast. But, as I predicted, they failed, and with the most dire consequences—the beast's retribution on that poor, innocent teacher. So, you see, I had good reason for enacting a law forbidding the hunting of the beast. And now you will all witness the consequences of jeopardizing our safety."

Emily could hardly comprehend what she heard. To Marco, she whispered, "Can you believe it?"

"Sadly, yes."

"All lies. How do they get away with this?"

"I don't know."

"We must stop this!"

Emily watched as the mayor signaled to the sheriff, who disappeared inside his office, emerging a moment later with Bronson and LeFevre gagged and cuffed in iron chains. A murmur rippled through the crowd, and people gasped when they saw who the traitors were.

Marco stood stunned as Emily whispered, "This can't be happening." She closed her eyes and prayed, though she knew her prayer would go unanswered.

The sheriff pushed Bronson and LeFevre from behind, forcing them to climb the steps to where the mayor continued speaking. "As I said before, I wish it weren't so, but hard things become necessary. If not, all must suffer the consequences of the misbehavior of the few, and we, the innocent, perish."

At those words, the blackbirds took flight. Emily watched as they circled above, unnoticed by the townspeople, while everyone heard the same chant weave through their minds.

> *String them up and hang them high.*
> *To hell with their rotten souls.*
> *For exciting the beast to mangle and kill,*
> *Let them dangle from the gallows pole.*
>
> *Drop a lead coin for the guilty.*
> *Pay the ferryman's toll.*
> *For the good of all who are innocent*
> *Drop them on the gallows pole.*

The crowd began to behave like a mob. Screams of "Hang them!" rang out.

The mayor looked over at Bronson and LeFevre and shrugged. "Appears they really didn't want you after all." The mayor turned to the sheriff. "Weasley, you know what to do. Take them away." A cheer rose from the crowd as the sheriff pushed the two men from behind. With broken ribs and fractured arm, LeFevre stumbled down the steps.

"Step aside, people!" hollered the sheriff while forcing his prisoners through the mob.

Bronson averted his gaze from those jeering at them.

Ms. Schumer, an older widow, lurched forward, landing a sharp slap behind his ear. "The teacher's blood is on your hands!" she screamed.

As the convicted crossed the street, the mayor continued. "I fear more attacks and more death, thanks to these traitors. We must make another appeasement offering soon. Moreover, I need you all to listen carefully. I'm aware that some do not comply with my orders, the same orders that keep the beast at bay and the innocent safe. Have any of you seen anyone not willfully complying with the law? Tell me now. Have you overheard anyone speaking treasonously or rebelliously?"

"The Burroughs!" screamed Abigail. "The parson and Hannah! They say not to listen. And I heard the parson deny that you, Mayor, caused the sun to shine. Useless prayers did it, not you!"

Susannah cried, "I heard it myself!"

"Weston?" The mayor looked over his shoulder at the council. "Where's Weston?"

"I'm behind you, sir."

The mayor turned around as Weston stepped forward.

"Oh, there you are. Take the Burroughs to the sheriff's office. Wait for me there."

"But, sir!"

"Do as I say!" ordered the mayor. "Go get them!"

Weston peered into the mob. Over the commotion, someone hollered, "They're over here!"

Hesitantly, Weston entered the crowd and moved toward the parson and his wife. Everyone backed away from the Burroughs as he approached.

The mayor called out, "Anyone else?" The crowd hushed as the blackbirds returned to the gallows pole. Yet unnoticed, they squawked and flapped their wings excitedly.

"All right, then," said the mayor. "These traitors leave us no choice." He looked across the street to where the sheriff prepared Bronson and LeFevre to drop, pulled a parchment from his coat pocket, and began to read.

OFFICIAL PROCLAMATION

Let it be known that having been found guilty of treason, one Bronson Parrish and one Lamont LeFevre, per (laws against treason), are hereby sentenced to death. Born witness on this day, September 30, 1860, that they shall hang by the rope until dead for the crime of treason. God have mercy on their souls!

Such crimes as heretofore listed were committed during times of emergency orders by duly elected Mayor Robert Owen II, mayor of New Harmony Township in the county of Posey

Signed, Robert Owen II

As the mayor folded the parchment and returned it to his pocket, a voice called his name.

"Robert!"

He paused, scanning the crowd. "Robert!"

"Beatrice, that you?" In the crowd, the mayor found the tiny woman, his secretary until Martha had released her from her duties.

When their eyes met, she said, "Please don't do this!"

"But I've no choice."

"It's not lawful, Robert. You need the council, all of them."

Emily noticed that some seemed to question his authority. For the briefest moment, he hesitated, staring into Beatrice's pleading eyes, but then he raised his voice.

"I have the council's vote. Under the circumstances, emergency orders! The execution is legally warranted. I'm sorry, Beatrice. I take no pleasure in this."

Her expression turned to one of sadness as she retreated into the crowd.

Across the street, standing near the gallows, Emily and Marco watched. Shackled, Bronson and LeFevre stood with hangman's knots dangling in their faces, ready to slip over their heads and cinch around their necks. Tears streaming down her face, Emily locked eyes with Bronson.

Marco whispered, "I should be up there, me alone. Mr. Parrish didn't leave the house, and Mr. LeFevre wouldn't have gone had I not convinced him to."

"None of us are guilty," said Emily. "The mayor and the rest bear the guilt. They should be up there facing the noose. I was north of the gorge only last night. Am I condemned? I am not, nor are you, nor are they! We are innocent." Emily struggled not to look away, holding Bronson's gaze. She mouthed the words *I'm sorry*.

Bronson closed his eyes and nodded again.

The crowd now circled the gallows. Mrs. Hopkins tapped Emily's shoulder. "Excuse me," she said. Her little ones moved past Emily and Marco to see the execution more closely, their mother following. "These are bad men," she told her children.

"No, they're not!" said Emily. "They're not bad."

Mrs. Hopkins scowled. "Don't say that! They're only children!"

The chanting grew wild as their voices rang out from the center of town. "Hang them! Hang them! Hang them!"

The sheriff slipped a hood over LeFevre's head and secured the noose. The chanting stopped, replaced with murmuring, as he attended to Bronson, placing a hood over his head and slipping the noose around his neck. Then a hush settled over the crowd as the sheriff gripped the lever. He looked at the mayor, who raised a hand, then quickly lowered it. The sheriff pulled the lever and the floor fell away. Two valiant men dropped, their heads snapping to one side, their bodies bouncing lightly as the rope went taut.

The blackbirds perched on the crossbeam took flight, beating their wings and cawing as they disappeared into the northern sky. The dangling bodies twitched for a minute and then went still. Emily watched it all, unwilling to turn away, determined to remember this evil until the judgment bar of God if need be.

Once the trap door opened and their perverse desires were satisfied, the crowd dispersed, their bloodlust mollified.

Marco put a hand on Emily's back. "It's time we go. Nothing more we can do."

"They won't get away with this! Swear to me, Marco! We won't let any of them get away with this!"

"They won't! I swear it!"

Once the street in front of the park emptied, Weston attended to the grisly business of the gallows. Of course, no family members would retrieve the corpses, but it wouldn't have mattered. Neither Marco nor Emily dared claim the bodies for fear of the implications.

The mayor crossed Main Street to where bodies hung. He pulled a dollar from his wallet and stuffed it in Bronson's front pocket. "This is for Mr. LeFevre there. I believe you owe him. He was correct, after all, Mr. Parrish."

"Mayor, sir? What would you have me do here?" Weston said, but the mayor either ignored him or failed to notice.

"Mayor?"

"Oh, forgive me, Weston. I was lost in thought. What are you asking?"

"What should I do with them? Should I make them coffins, and is it a suitable expenditure for reimbursement?"

Reluctantly, the mayor said, "You can burden me with the expense personally. See to it that they are buried." Then, turning to leave, he hesitated and looked back. "On second thought, haul them to the landfill and burn them. No suitable expenditure for traitors, even if I pay myself." As the mayor headed to his office, he mumbled, "Burn them on the pyre."

Chapter 46

The sheriff bounded up the town-hall steps, "Mayor?"

The mayor paused and held the door. "What is it?"

"The Burroughs—I have them in my holding cell. What now?"

"Do you recall the word I requested to have painted on the window under where it says, 'Sheriff's Office'?"

"*Interrogation*?"

"Yes, correct. So what do you suppose we should do?"

"Interrogate," said the sheriff.

"But do you understand the purpose of such?"

"Um, sure?"

"We need names, Weasley. There's more requesting the services of the gallows. We need only to know who they are. Make another list."

"I'll have the parson's wife singin' like a canary."

"Do that! Make a list. We need names."

The sheriff exited the building as the mayor entered his office and closed the door.

"Hello, Father."

The mayor spun around. "Eugene! You startled me, son. But I'm glad to see you."

Eugene sat on a chair in the corner by the stove. "I wish it were true."

"Why? It's been too long, which makes me grateful for whatever reason you've come. So, what brings you?"

"Fine, then, I'll get right to it. Why, Father? Why kill those men, Mr. Parrish and Mr. LeFevre? What crimes did they commit?"

"You heard the proclamation, didn't you? They endangered the entire town. That innocent young girl, the new teacher at the school, she's dead because of them."

"You don't believe that!"

"Why? Don't you? Or perhaps your hatred of me has blinded you."

"Father, Mr. Bronson came to me; he knew you stole the election, as do I. I saw you leave the building that night. And what about those who've disappeared and those the monster supposedly killed? Father, I'm begging you to stop. Consider what you're doing. The parson is a man of God, and Hannah's a saint. They've done more to help people than anyone here. For heaven's sake! Don't you worry about your soul?"

"I would if I were responsible for them. What they've done, they've done to themselves. There's the law to consider."

"No, Father, you've taken the law upon yourself, believing you are the law. That's not how it's supposed to work.

"Eugene, my son. You presume far too much. Everything I do is for the good of New Harmony. I didn't cause the sun to dim, but I sure as hell got the damned thing to shine! Besides, I've made this town what it is. People owe me!"

"What, are you god now? Is that why you locked up the parson? You want the people to worship you?"

"I don't care what you think, you know. I do what's right for our family, the family you've somehow forgotten. And what makes you think you can talk to me like this? You may be my son, but your deliberate withdrawal from the family has consequences. One is any right to speak to me the way you do. Do I make myself clear?"

As the mayor spoke, he heard a voice whisper. "Those closest. They will be your undoing. Unless—"

"I want nothing to do with you, Father!" Eugene shouted. He leaned over his father's desk. "I warn you. Stay away from my family! You have no son, no grandson. Do I make myself clear?"

It took all the restraint the mayor had not to lash out as the voice in his head grew louder. Instead, he watched as Eugene stormed out, yelling as he left, "Stay away from my family!"

The mayor waited to be sure his son was long gone before leaving the building, locking the doors as he went. He walked down the front steps and peeked into the window of the sheriff's office. Seeing the glow of lamplight, he walked inside. The sheriff sat in his chair, feet perched on his desk, eyes closed.

Startled awake, Weasley said, "Oh, Mayor, It's you!" He quickly put his feet on the floor and sat up.

"Come with me, Weasley. We need to talk."

The sheriff followed the mayor outside and shut the door so the Burroughs couldn't hear.

Once they were alone, the mayor said, "Let the Burroughs go, but keep an eye on them, and don't let them leave town. We'll arrest them when we're ready and send them straight to the gallows. Right now, we need the cell for someone else.

"Who's that, sir?"

"I don't dare say it."

"Tell me who, and I'll have 'em locked away before curfew."

The mayor's gaze lowered, and he put his hands in his pant pockets. A moment passed until, finally, he said it. "My son."

Part 3

Mount Erebus Goes Silent

Chapter 47

Coot's claws tapped the wooden floorboards, his wet nose sniffing out the unfamiliar scent of his new surroundings as he wandered about the Hampshire home. The sound of Marjorie filling his water bowl brought him trotting into the kitchen.

"Are you sure this is all right, Auntie?"

"He's no bother. Coot's welcome here." Marjorie scooted the bowl closer to the back door with her foot. "It's you we're concerned about, dear. Sneakin' out past curfew—people gonna get the wrong idea, and if someone reports you . . . Well, then what?"

"I'll be careful."

"Not a matter of bein' careful, Emmy. There's the monster . . ." She looked at the bruising on Emily's face and arms. "And what's this?"

Albert walked in from the bedroom. Before he could sit, Marjorie got his attention. "Al, would ya look at our dear one here? She's got scratches and . . ." She touched Emily's cheek and gently nudged her head to one side so Albert could see.

He leaned forward. "Oh my. What happened?"

"Don't make a fuss. I'm fine," said Emily.

"But you're not fine," said Albert. "Look at you!"

Emily sighed and pulled out a chair. "Can't we please just sit down?"

"We will," said Albert, "but first, tell us what happened."

"Both of you, listen carefully. It's not important. There are more pressing matters."

"None more important than what happened to you," said Marjorie.

"Believe me, there are much more important things. Are you prepared to listen?"

"But, of course," said Albert.

Emily hesitated, pondering how to say what must be said. *How do I tell them they must leave New Harmony? Will they believe me? Or will they blame me, assume it is my fault—something I did?*

Her heart ached, but she knew what must come next. She excused herself only to return a moment later with an envelope. "Here, I need you to see this." She handed it to Albert. "It's all arranged," she said. "After sundown, both of you are leaving with Marco to Bloomington, and that's that." It wasn't exactly how she planned on telling them, but she couldn't think of a less troubling way to get them to leave.

Holding the deed and banknote, Albert asked, "What is this? What's happening here?"

"Papa, listen, Mr. Parrish knew who the real monster in New Harmony was, and because of it, he and Mr. LeFevre paid with their lives. Mr. Parrish left us that. He knew the mayor would come for Marco and me next. Neither of you are safe."

Marjorie held out her hand. "Let me see!" she demanded. Albert handed her the envelope. Then, while looking at the papers, she said, "Emmy dear, we can't leave here. This is our home! All of our friends are here, and . . ." Marjorie looked up, visibly upset, but Emily wasn't there. They heard her in their room, packing their belongings. "What does she think she's doin'? We're not leaving!"

Emily called out to them from their bedroom. "You can and will! You've no choice. The mayor had Parson Burroughs and Hannah arrested for no reason. Do you suppose either is a threat? As if they would harm anyone!"

"I imagine not," Albert called out to her.

"Course not," said Emily. "They're good as dead unless I can save them. But I can't do anything unless I know you're safe." She returned to the kitchen, dragging a travel chest behind her. "And it's not safe here anymore. The Burroughs are next, and then comes the purging. And I remind you, Mrs. Owen isn't wildly fond of me and has no reason to be. I assume she suspects me of knowing things I shouldn't, and she's right."

"If what's yer sayin' is true, we're not leaving without you," Marjorie insisted.

"I can't leave, not yet, but . . ."

"Then neither are we," said Albert. "We'll face whatever happens together."

"I'm not staying on a whim or because . . . I heard the sheriff released the Burroughs, but they're still in danger. I must convince them to join us in Bloomington, or I fear they will share the same fate as Mr. Parrish and Mr. LeFevre. I intend to meet you there, with the Burroughs, all safe."

Albert grew restless, worry creasing his forehead. "You go with Margie. I'll convince the parson and Hannah to join us."

"Albert, I'm not gonna leave here unless we all do," said Marjorie.

In frustration, Emily conceded, "We haven't time to argue. We'll all leave together. Agreed?"

Marjorie nodded, but Albert had second thoughts. "But what about the Burroughs?"

"Start packing the rest," said Emily. "I'll figure it out."

Chapter 48

"Ugly business today," Martha said as she removed the pillow between them, cuddling the man she fell in love with so many years ago. "Town's much better off without Parrish and that repulsive Frenchman, Mr. Le-whatever. I never liked him. Vulgar, vulgar man."

"Martha?"

"Yes, Robert." She pushed herself up, propped herself on more pillows, and looked at him. "What is it, dear? You seem distracted."

"I fear telling you."

"Telling me what?"

"Hmm, well . . . I had Weasley arrest Eugene this afternoon."

"But . . . but why? Why do that?"

"Eugene was in my office, waiting for me, after the hanging."

"What does that matter? He's our son."

"I know, Martha, but our son aligned himself with Parrish. They were working together. They planned to destroy me, us. Eugene said as much. Didn't hide it nor deny it."

"I don't believe you. Eugene wouldn't dare. Our son is more intelligent than that. He may be insolent, but never . . ."

"I wish it weren't so. Unfortunately, accusations flew from Eugene's mouth like bees from a hive. He accused me of nearly everything save assassinating the president, not that I wouldn't want to. Someone ought to rid the union of that Mr. Lincoln."

"Did he accuse you of saving the harvest, keeping food on our plates?"

"No, dear. Eugene left that out. But he did mention the election, saying I meddled. He even suggested that the monster was innocent of killing anyone. He implied I was responsible."

"It doesn't matter. Who would believe such nonsense? I want to know why our son sits behind bars."

"He's been sticking his nose where it doesn't belong. He dared to tell Parrish I stole the election. What more might he have told him? What would you have me do?"

Martha moved away from Robert. He watched as she studied his expressions, weighing his intentions, his choice of words.

It's time, Robert thought, *time to come clean. She needs to know the whole truth, and there's no reason not to trust her. She would never permit anyone to take what's rightfully ours.* "Martha?" he said. "I made a deal to save New Harmony, a deal with . . ."

"With what?" she asked. "What deal? Can you be any more vague?" He'd opened his mouth to answer when she said, "Never mind, whatever it was you were about to say. What does it have to do with our son?"

"Have you asked yourself how I knew the sun would shine? Or, as many suppose, that I caused it to shine?"

"I only care that you did. You take care of us. Now, what about our son?"

"Allow me to explain," said Robert, "from the beginning. Just stop talking and listen."

"I'm not talking, so go on . . ."

Pent-up words spilled out of his mouth: his encounter with the otherworldly beings, the arrangement, everything. They shared a rare moment as Martha sat speechless. When he finished, she finally spoke. "So what are they? Solve the mystery and tell me."

"They call themselves the sisters or something. But I suspect they are more."

"More than what?"

"Not certain how to explain."

"Well, try harder."

"They're ancient. They speak of history, Rome, and Greece as if it were yesterday. They toy with time."

"What do they look like?"

"Witches, hags, not similar to the young girls in Salem but much like those found in the pages of William Shakespeare. Although, they can transform themselves."

"You could have said they were witches from the beginning."

"And I would have, Martha. But they are not."

"Robert, you're giving me a headache. Then what are they?"

"I don't know—the source of our myths? That's how they describe themselves. They are the sisters—and they offer no further explanation. But I do know they are our benefactors, the purveyors of our fate. With this alliance, all things are possible. Our dreams can extend far beyond the boundaries of New Harmony. My political ambitions are limitless."

"And what do you suppose they want . . . in return?" Martha asked. "What are they to gain? Surely something . . ."

"Yes, of course. I must deliver them food and drink. The creatures call it sustenance. That's the appeasement I gather for the beast but not really for the beast. Up there, on the mountain, I give them half of what we gather and keep the rest for us. That's the sum of the deal save for one stipulation."

Martha looked at him curiously, then asked, "And that is?"

"For whatever reason, I must ensure no harm befalls the monster. And, as mentioned, provide them sustenance—delicious food and drink. How can I not be satisfied with the terms of our agreement?"

Wrinkles formed on Martha's forehead. "Too good to be true, maybe."

"Maybe," said Robert. "I can't shake the thought that the sustenance is nothing more than a distraction. There must be more they want, things I'm not privy to."

"So, what do *you* suppose they really want?"

"If there's more, I don't know."

"I don't know either, Robert. Making a deal with whatever they are may be more dangerous than we imagine. I pray it's not your soul they're after."

"If it is, they can have it. What use have I of it if we lose everything? Besides, I had no choice. As it was, I lost the election, and not by a little. Had I not swapped ballots, it would have been our demise. Only a matter of time before Parrish ended our plans. But now? Imagine the possibilities."

"Oh, my dear. You did the right thing. How many men would have gone to the lengths you have for their families? That's worth enough to redeem your soul if that's what they're after!"

"If it means making strange alliances, I don't care," agreed Robert. "They delivered Parrish into our hands, saving us from hunger and poverty. But, unfortunately, dear, it was they who warned me about our son. If not for them, Eugene's hatred would ruin us."

"A bitter pill, dear. I admit it. But you did nothing wrong, though the burden of our son is heavy and we walk on thin ice. People here in New Harmony seem good from the outside, but inside, they rot with envy. They'd love nothing more than to see us living in squalor. They hate us under their smiles. I feel it. They are no different than the greedy blackbirds and starlings that rob us of our grain. But our own son, Robert, delivering us into their hands and watching us fall to ruin?" Tears welled up in Martha's eyes. She wiped them with the handkerchief she kept on the nightstand and lay back on her pillows, turning her back to Robert.

He looked at her mournfully and spoke softly. "I'm grateful you understand. Eugene and Bronson were scheming among themselves to butcher us. I fear our son is behind it. And, sorry to say, but he's no longer our son. He renounced us while demanding we stay away, and his insistence included Alexander."

Without turning her head, Martha said, "Let me talk to him, Robert, perhaps talk some sense into him. Just on the off chance."

"Yes, dear," he said. "Anything is worth a try, but don't expect much."

"I won't, but promise me, Robert, we salvage our grandson whatever the outcome."

"No question."

A grateful Martha rolled over and hugged the man she loved. "I only wish I knew where we went wrong as parents."

Chapter 49

"Good evening, Mrs. Owen." Weston extended a hand to help her down from the carriage.

She refused his offer and handed him a lantern instead. Weston graciously took the lantern while she grabbed her handbag from the seat beside her.

"And my handbag." She held it out and waited.

"Oh, sorry. Weston took the handbag and stepped back. Without further assistance, she stepped down.

"Where's the sheriff?"

"I'm on duty tonight, ma'am. It's curfew. I'm sorry. I don't know."

"All right, then, Mr. Weston Riley. You have a key to the sheriff's office, don't you? I need to visit with my son."

"Yes, ma'am." Weston fished the key from his pocket. "Oh, Nellie stopped by, wanted to see Eugene. If she returns, what do I tell her?"

"What did the sheriff say?"

"No one other than you and the mayor." The smile on her face answered his question. He handed her the lantern and her handbag and proceeded to unlock the door. "Forgive me, Mrs. Owen, but I've responsibilities. I'm to enforce curfew this evening, or I'd stay."

"Enforcing curfew can wait. Stay here, outside, until I'm done. And do make sure we're not disturbed. You can lock up once I leave, but stay close. Eugene is to talk to no one other than Robert, Weasley, and me, no matter the hour. Is that clear?"

"It is, ma'am." He held the door, then closed it behind her.

The light of Martha's lantern penetrated deep into the office. She peered into the back, seeing the figure of a man behind bars. "I should have realized the sheriff wouldn't have a lantern for you. He has a dark side, that man." She set the lantern on the sheriff's desk and lit a candle, which she affixed to a holder, then walked to the dank cell at the rear of the office. "Rather drafty in here. My goodness. Have you a blanket?"

Martha stopped to take in the sight of her son as he sat on a cot, his back against the cold, hard wall, his head turned away from her. There was no blanket, no water, only a bucket in the corner. She shivered, rubbed the goose bumps on her arms, then pulled up a chair and sat down. "I'm at a loss, son. What heartache you're causing your father and me. Where do I even begin?"

"Hello, Mother," Eugene said coldly, not turning to meet her gaze.

"Now, son, why the disdain? It's not as though I can't hear it. You assume yourself the victim." She placed the candle on the floor between them, just outside the bars. "This is not at all what your father and I want for you."

"You didn't happen to bring the key to the jail with you?"

"I don't carry a key. That's what the sheriff is for, but if I—"

He cut her off. "I didn't think so. But, of course, you know it's in his desk drawer over there. That tells me everything I need to know."

"What you need to know, son, is your father is only trying to scare some sense into you. I can't simply release you. That would only make things worse. But I am here to help. Do you understand how serious things are? You're facing the hangman's rope! Is that what you want?"

Eugene finally turned to look at her. He leaned forward. "What do you want me to say? Finally, now, you want me to talk and not simply listen?"

"No, you listen!" Martha said sternly. "I hate to see you like this, but you brought it on yourself! Give me a reason to get you out of here. Tell me you'll stop your insolence, your accusations."

Eugene turned away, showing no interest in hearing more.

Martha scowled. "So, you have nothing to say? Not even an apology? Oh, I know what you're thinking. You feel entitled to judge your father and me. How dare you! Nothing comes easy in this world. Nothing comes without sweat and blood."

"Blood, Mother? Interesting choice of words."

"Your father and I do what it takes. We fight, we win, and we give you everything without you having earned it! You want for nothing, and what do we get for our troubles? You choose to be our enemy! What about honoring your father and mother? Don't you understand?"

Offering no defense, Eugene sat in silence.

"Say something!"

Still, he kept his mouth closed. The candlelight gently swayed on the stone walls as silence engulfed the space. Finally, Martha grew tired of waiting.

"Your father," said Martha, "he's resolved. He's finished with you. But we're family. I know he'll release you on my account if I vouch for you, but I must be certain. I must know you will stop defying us and remember who you are. You're an Owen, damn it!"

Eugene opened his mouth to respond, hesitated, and then said nothing.

"What?" Martha shook her head in disgust.

"Doesn't matter," said Eugene. He leaned against the cold stone wall.

"Fine! What is it you want to say?" She craned her neck and looked away, staring at the front window.

"Whatever I say, you can be relied on to turn your head, much like you're doing now."

"Don't give me that! I birthed you, boy!"

"Yes, you did, and I'm sorry if you regret it. But can you look me in the eye and tell me Father had nothing to do with the Stewart's disappearance? And what about the rest?"

Martha yelled, "The rest of what?"

"The rest of everything you know and everything you don't know. There are things about Father, your husband, I can't begin to tell you."

"You can stop right there! There's nothing about your father I don't know."

"Oh, I bet there is."

"Nothing," Marth insisted.

"What about his indiscretions?"

"What's that supposed to mean? Is that what this is about?" Martha looked perplexed. "So what? You have a half-brother. I would've entirely rid ourselves of the mess if it had been up to me. But it wasn't."

Eugene was shocked. "How can you sleep at night? If you know everything, as you say, how can you live with the guilt? The Stewarts, the teacher, the Shear's boy? You're as guilty as your husband!"

"May I remind you that my husband, as you call him, is your father. You shall address him as such. And to assuage your concerns, I live with it just fine. You're the one who knows nothing! Nothing of defending our family or getting ahead. Your father has gone to great lengths to build everything we enjoy, which means nothing to you. So I ask you the same. How do you live with that?"

"I can't! I can't continue knowing my parents are murderers. So here's what I propose. The key is in the desk drawer over there. Set me free, and I'll take my family and leave, change my name, and you'll never hear from us again."

"And never see my grandson? No, thank you!"

"Ignoring murder is one thing, Martha, but can you live with yourself after murdering your son when everything I say is true—and you know it? Yet you're willing to have me dead rather than admit it. Let me out of here, and you'll never hear from me again. You and your husband can rot in your lies, but at least you won't have your son's murder on your conscience!"

"Oh, now you're our son?" Without another word, Martha extinguished the candle and stood, picking up the lantern on her way out and leaving Eugene in the dark.

Chapter 50

"We haven't much time, Papa." Marco rushed about, shoving clothes into a traveling trunk.

Tommaso waded through memories as he walked through the house. First, he stopped to look at the bed he'd shared with Caterina. Then, mournfully turning away, he glanced at Christian's room. The door was closed. Tommaso walked over and touched the doorknob but didn't open it. Then, so only he could hear, he whispered, "Goodbye, my boy."

"Ready, Papa? Marco called out. "Our time is spent."

"Coming," said Tommaso. He turned and joined Marco in the kitchen.

Marco closed the trunk and fastened the buckles. "Help me with this, would you?"

"Ya put your mama's hairpin in the trunk, the ruby red one she wore on Sundays?"

"I did, Papa, and the letters you wrote each other. I have them all here. Now, please help me. We mustn't keep the Hampshires waiting."

Marco locked the back door, and then he and Tommaso hefted the trunk onto the wagon. They rode quickly through the night. To their relief, no lights appeared in the windows they rode past.

Outside the Hampshire home, Albert, Marjorie, and Emily anxiously waited, their trunks ready to be loaded. They heard a window open across the street and a voice call after them, "You better hurry!" Walter's silhouette filled the window.

Several neighbors peered through curtains, surely shocked by such blatant defiance. Emily was certain they would have immediately reported the violation had it not required breaking curfew. Within a short time, the wagon was headed east toward Bloomington.

"We need to get as far away as possible before sunrise," said Marco. He kept his gun close, wondering what he would do if caught with it.

Emily crawled onto the seat next to Marco as they rode through the fields and pastures. "Not much farther," she said, sighing with relief. "Once we're clear of Harmony, we should be safe."

Marco asked, "How are they doing in back?"

"Cramped, no doubt, but good." Emily looked at the sky above them. "We're blessed with a full moon. I believe it'll be safe to light the lantern soon. Marco, have you a gun?"

"I do." Marco pulled back his coat. The steel of the handle glistened in the moonlight.

"May I see it?"

Marco pulled it from its holster and handed it to her. "The ammo's beneath the seat, just in case."

"It's not loaded?"

"No. We were rushed. I didn't think of it."

They soon passed the Carver place, the farthest farm east of town. "Another mile and we can relax," said Marco.

"Stop for a moment, would you?"

"Is it important? I'm sorry if you forgot something, Emmy, but it's too late."

"It is important, please. Just for a moment."

Marco pulled on the reins and noticed the ammo pouch in Emily's lap.

"What are you doing?" She lowered herself from the wagon, the pistol held firmly in her hand. "Emmy, get back in the wagon."

"I'm sorry. I can't leave without the parson and Hannah. We'll be right behind you. Just go!"

Marco set the brake and jumped down. "We're not going anywhere! We leave together. We agreed." The anger in his voice surprised Emily.

"I know we agreed," she said. "But you see why I can't. They'll hang the Burroughs as they did Mr. Parrish and Mr. LeFevre. I can save them."

"But they're in jail. What are you thinking?"

"No, they're not. The sheriff let them go, but they're not out of danger."

Marco gripped her arms tightly and looked hard into her eyes. "I see what you're doing, but Emmy . . ."

"I'm sorry!" she pleaded as she pulled away, which left Marco with no choice but to let go. "Bronson put me in charge of keeping everyone safe, and that includes the Burroughs. So go!" She turned and ran back toward New Harmony.

Sitting in the wagon bed, Marjorie, Albert, and Tommaso watched, growing more concerned with every second.

"Where's she goin'?" Marjorie asked.

"She's going to get the Burroughs." Marco pulled himself up onto the wagon and grabbed the reins.

"Go get her!" Marjorie tugged on Albert's arm. "Albert, we gotta turn around."

"She's trying to save the parson and Hannah. I can't stop her."

Marjorie panicked. "But they'll arrest her. We can't just leave."

Marco turned to face them. "We can't go after her, Miss Hampshire. People saw us leave. They'll catch us for sure. She stands a better chance without us. I'm sorry."

Marco released the brake and whipped the reins.

In the silvery light of the moon, Emily paused. Tears burned her eyes as she watched those she loved so dearly move away. It was then that the seriousness of what she'd done became clear. She felt like crying. What if she never saw them again?

I can't go home, she thought. *They'll find me there. I'll have to make contact with the Burroughs in the morning. But first, I must devise a way to get them out of New Harmony without anyone noticing.*

On the ride out, it had surprised her how many windows had been boarded, how dark and abandoned everything looked. She realized there was no one she could ask for help without placing her life or theirs in danger.

She bowed her head, closed her eyes, and offered a silent prayer. When she opened her eyes again, she saw one dim light still shining in the window of a small house just off the road, tucked in the trees. *Moses Carver! Of all people—he's the one! Thank you, Lord!*

Chapter 51

Hearing the bedroom door creak open, Robert sat up in bed as Martha entered. "Back so soon?"

"He's hard-nosed, Robert. I wasn't there but a minute before the insults started flying. I can endure only so much." Martha put down her sweater and pulled a nightgown from the armoire. "His irrationality feeds his anger. Both run deep."

"As I feared," said Robert. "Couldn't spare his own mother, could he?"

"His mind's twisted. It is we who are evil if he is to be believed. I'm grateful your father isn't alive to see it."

"My son, the end of the Owen legacy. He wouldn't have believed it. Hardly believe it myself."

"Utter betrayal." Martha began to prepare herself for bed. Her dress dropped to the floor. She stepped over it, leaving it for the housemaids to pick up in the morning. "We see how the disciples regarded Judas, don't we, dear?"

"Judas at least had the decency to hang himself."

"I don't want to hear any talk of hanging. Eugene is our son, and I, his mother. Our son is redeemable, so promise me you'll find a way to save him. I cannot bear to see him hang."

"Even if it be our undoing, letting him go? We risk everything. It's what the sisters foretold."

"Oh yes, the sisters. Forgot about them. Robert, what if we declare Nellie unfit? What if we raise Alexander as our own?" Martha slipped into her nightgown.

Robert got out of bed and put another log in the fireplace. "Dear, you still haven't answered what to do about Eugene."

"No, I haven't. I suppose we can't keep him locked away indefinitely. And although it pains me to say it, you must break him."

Robert pulled down the sheets. "Are you saying what I believe you're saying?"

"Perhaps. Doesn't the Holy Bible state that *fear* brings forth wisdom?"

"Hmm, *fear*. One can accomplish much with fear. Comforting to know it's in the Bible," said Robert as he climbed between the freshly laundered sheets.

"Well, it is. You'll find it in the first chapter of Proverbs."

"It's decided, then."

"Agreed. I'm counting on you to save our son."

Martha snored into the night while Robert tossed and turned, haunted by night terrors. Sleep finally overtook him just as the last log on the fire stopped popping, went dark, and the temperature dropped. Then came a tapping at the window. It was six past three in the morning. The moon's soft light streamed in, glistening off the imported lacquer floors. Robert stirred awake and craned his neck to see something move past the window. A scraping noise came from under his bed. He held still. More scraping. A mouse?

Just then, he heard more tapping at the window. The noise persisted until, finally, Robert could take no more. "All right! I'm awake!" he whispered so as not to wake Martha. He rose from his bed, put on a robe, and put on his wool slippers. Then, quietly, he sneaked out of the room, walked through the front parlor, past the rear sitting room and kitchen, and onto the back porch. In the ample moonlight, he surveyed his vast property, then looked skyward. An elaborate array of stars shone brightly above, and he scanned the horizon for blackbirds but saw none. Then, just as he was about to turn around and return to the bed, he heard a voice or, rather, a hissing sound.

"Sssustenance. We are waiting!"

"You'll get more sustenance, as agreed, and soon." Robert stared into the night, still looking for a blackbird or two.

"Sssoon?"

"Yes, very," Robert said. "These things take time! Why the hissing?"

"Hisssing?"

"Yes, hissing. Never mind. After tomorrow, my position will be secure, as I hope it will be when I run for governor. I expect your help."

"Governor? Yesss. We can help, but firssst you must sssubdue your enemiesss."

"Subdue? I will. After tomorrow, I may do as I wish. I have a plan no one dares oppose."

"There isss one!"

"If you're referring to my son, Eugene, he's no longer a concern. I have him locked away at the moment. However, I do require assistance in the matter. Tomorrow, I need the town to fear me. I must make an example of those who oppose me, and my son must know I am not to be trifled with. Most of all, he must fear me! Can you assist me with that?"

"Asssissst? You have our asssistance already. Yet, ssstill, you musssst do sssomething worthy of fear, though fear isss our ssspecialty."

"Good," said Robert.

Suddenly, whether a trick of the moonlight or something more nefarious, Robert's eyes turned obsidian black for the briefest moment. "Tomorrow," he said, "the blood of my enemies will turn cold as their hearts stop."

"Yesss, they will. Now you may sssleep, dear Robert. Sssleep comfortably."

With that, the mayor felt a wave of drowsiness. He turned and walked back into the house. When the door closed behind him, three black snakes slithered off the porch and into the tall grass.

"Perhapsss we should've sssaid there isss another who may ssstop him."

A chorus of hisses answered. "Sssoon enough. Sssoon enough!"

Chapter 52

The door creaked open, the smell of cooked beans and sawdust wafting into the open air. Emily felt the warmth of the fire and stared at the silhouette of the large man in the doorway. He stood there for a moment that seemed to stretch uncomfortably forever.

"Sorry to disturb you, Mr. Carver. I know how late it is, and . . . well, my name is Emily, Emily Hampshire. I don't believe we've spoken." Emily offered her hand, then quickly withdrew it.

"I knows who ya are—Jed's daughter. Whatcha doin' here?"

"I'm afraid I've nowhere else I can go. And although I'm not sure exactly how to say it, I felt impressed to knock on your door, and I'm aware of how strange that sounds."

"Hmm, ya don't mind da curfew?"

"The explanation is rather complicated."

"Best come in, then." Moses moved from the doorway, making room for Emily to enter. The inside looked as it appeared from the outside, logs cut with an ax and handsaw. A bench seat and table, also fashioned from cut logs, took up the space beside the fireplace.

Emily rubbed the goose bumps on her arms. "Your hospitality is greatly appreciated."

Moses placed another split log on the fire, then moved the small bench next to her so she could sit.

"Much obliged, Mr. Carver."

Emily looked about the meager surroundings: the unpainted walls, the wooden box holding a single plate, bowl, knife, and spoon. She noticed clothes hanging from nails and above them a roof that served as a shelter from the rain. Nodding, she said, "Very comfortable."

"It is. Your pa helped me build this place. Don't get no visitors, though. Wasn't expectin' nobody neither."

"I hope I'm no imposition."

"Nope," said Mr. Carver while averting his eyes. "Don't think me rude. I ain't much fer words."

"It's all right, Mr. Carver. I'm more than pleased to sit here without conversation, although I'm curious to know how you knew my father."

"Yes, ma'am. I knew 'im."

"You knew him how?"

Mr. Carver scooped cornbread, collard greens, and beans sweetened with molasses from his cast-iron oven, portioning them evenly on a plate and in a bowl with a wooden spoon. He handed the plate and spoon to Emily. She sat on the bench while Mr. Carver sat on the floor, his back against the wall. He tipped his bowl to his mouth and began to eat, barely looking up at her.

"It smells delicious. Thank you, Mr. Carver."

Mr. Carver nodded and kept eating.

Once she finished, she set the plate down. Mr. Carver's bowl sat empty beside him. Head turned, he stared into a corner of the room.

"Mr. Carver?"

"Hmm?"

"Would it be too forward of me to ask how well you knew my father? I was very young when . . . Well, when . . ." Emily stopped.

After a lull, Mr. Carver nodded. "Sad day."

"Oh, yes, the worst. It's just that . . . there is so much I don't know about him."

"Hmm."

"It would mean so much to learn what you knew of him. What was he like?"

"Yer papa, he was a Godly man. He don't care what color a man is. When I first come here, I couldn't buy nothin'. Not when I first come, could I. Mr. Hyrum say the mayor don't allow for it, don't want me puttin' down roots. Soon, others like me comin'. He don't want that.

So yer pa, he made purchases fer me an' got me what I was needin'. Gave me a job at the mine till the mayor found out. By then, I had crops. So . . ."

"You knew him, Mr. Carver. Can you tell me what happened to my father? Do you know who is responsible?"

"Maybe."

"You suspect someone?"

Mr. Carver nodded. "Never shoulda run fer mayor, yer pa. Tried warnin' 'im like I did yer boy."

Surprised, Emily asked, "My boy?"

"Yer young man," said Mr. Carver. "I told yer boy ta stay away from the mayor."

"My young man? Are you referring to Christian?"

"Think so."

"When?"

"While back. He was walkin' in the rain, if I recall. Gave 'im a ride. He was goin' to the Owen Ranch. I warn him ta stay away."

The news of Christian struck a painful chord in Emily. "Thank you for trying."

"Did my best."

"I'm certain you did. Mr. Carver, my father trusted you, did he not?"

"Yes, ma'am."

"He must have. And I believe it isn't by chance that I have found my way here. I intend to find justice for my father, but first, there is something I must do. May I stay until morning?"

"Stay long as ya need, Miss Hampshire."

In the warm light of the fire, Emily studied the man's face. What hard times must have etched such deep lines, and what amount of loneliness could have tempered his eyes and softened him from the pain of such hard times?

"Mr. Carver?"

"Hmm?"

I regret not having known your acquaintance with my father earlier. I would have visited you. Would you have wanted that?"

Mr. Carver nodded. "Yeah."

"Thank you, Mr. Carver."

Together, they sat in the warm glow of the fire. Outside, the wind kicked up and whistled through the gap in the doorframe. Emily's world was falling apart, but for the moment, she felt warm and safe.

Above the crackling of the fire, Emily heard Mr. Carver whisper, "Miss Hampshire?"

"Yes, Mr. Carver?"

"Call me Moses."

"All right, Moses."

"What ya doin' here? I needs ta know."

Moses Carver listened as Emily's story unfolded, from how she'd waited in the tool shed for her father to how she'd jumped from the wagon, fleeing to Bloomington to save Parson Burroughs and Hannah. And how, her entire life, she wanted to find her father and see justice done to the men she heard while hiding in the tool shed.

"How ya gonna do that—find yer pa?"

"I've considered that question most of my life, and I know of one way and one only," said Emily. "The mayor or the sheriff will show me where they put him. Then, I need only one to confess his murder in front of the town."

"That what that's for?" asked Mr. Carver. Emily followed his gaze to the ammo pouch at her side, the heel of the gun poking out.

Emily nodded. "It is."

"Gonna get yerself killed is what yer gonna do. Listen here. Come mornin', I get the parson and Mrs. Parson, bring 'em back here. Meantime, ya stay here. They be lookin' for ya. After that, ya let it be. Ya get away from here. Take them with ya ta Bloomin'ton."

Emily's eyes began to water. "Moses. I'm most grateful, and I'll stay and wait until the Burroughs are safe, but after that, I will find a way to see justice done. No one will be safe in New Harmony until someone does. That's what my father meant to do, willing to give his life for it. Now, so am I. I intend to finish what he started, or . . ."

"Or I help," said Mr. Carver.

"I was about to say something else."

"I know. But ya come here, found me fer a reason. What yer pa started, we'll finish together, and don't ya worry 'bout the Burroughs. In the mornin', ya stay here till I get back."

Chapter 53

At 8:19 a.m., the sheriff poked his head into the mayor's office. "Checkin' in, sir. Decide what ya want done with yer boy?"

"Don't stand out there. Come in."

"Yes, sir." The sheriff stepped into the office and sat down.

"Don't make yourself comfortable, Weasley."

The sheriff quickly stood. "Pardon me, sir."

"No, it's fine. Sit. Forgive my irritability, Weasley," he said. "I'm a bit cross this morning. How's my son?"

"He ain't talkin'. Stubborn as a raccoon."

"Yes, I'm afraid it's a family trait. Let him stew awhile. We have something else to discuss."

"That is?"

"Gather the council. Emergency meeting. One hour, in the chamber. Have Weston do it while you arrest the Burroughs. Put them in with Eugene."

"Arrest them now, sir? Ain't ya still worried about the governor gettin' more complaints? I figured that's why ya let 'em go."

"Not anymore, Weasley. Upon further consideration, with the war drawing closer every day, a civil war is what folks are beginning to call it, a bloody conflict is at our doorstep. All eyes are on the South, and, as it turns out, war is a better distraction than even a monster."

The sheriff looked confused. "Then why arrest the Burroughs?"

"Fear, Weasley. It's how men garner power! I'm destined for more, to make history, my name to be on every tongue! And where I'm going, you're coming with me. Our destinies are bonded. The parson is but a small sacrifice. Our fate is to greatness, to save the Union. Understand?"

"I suppose."

"Well then, what are you waiting for?"

The sheriff exited and ran down the hall, bumping into Beatrice Moser. "Now ain't the time, Ms. Moser!" he said. "I wouldn't go in there unless yer bringin' 'im coffee."

Beatrice peered around the sheriff at the mayor's office. "So Robert's in his office, is he?"

"See for yerself." The sheriff continued on his way out of the building and into the street.

The mayor heard a light rapping on his door and looked up. "Beatrice?"

"Hello, Robert."

"Why, Beatrice, I'm pleased to see you. I've missed not having you here."

"That's good," said Beatrice.

The mayor smiled. "Well then, what brings you?"

"Robert, may I be blunt?"

"Of course."

"All right, the . . . what you did to Bronson Parrish and Mr. LeFevre, you can't do that! You must follow the charter subject to the state law. There must be a public hearing for a capital offense. Once you read the charges and after all available evidence is laid bare, the accused can face his accusers and defend himself. Afterward, if a consensus of the people agrees on the verdict of guilt, the sentence can be legally administered. But you must send the evidence to the territorial judge in Bloomington, along with an affidavit of guilt signed and agreed upon by each committee member. Only then will executions be deemed lawful. You can't just render a proclamation like the one you presented. Besides, you can't possibly have proper documentation."

"Why not? You heard the people. They are all witnesses to their own consensus. As for the paperwork—a mere formality."

"I'm aware of the complaints to the capital, to the governor, and if they investigate—then what? Those men were gagged. That is what people witnessed. There was nothing legal about how you did that."

The Mayor stared at her for a while before saying, "Do you intend to report me?"

"Robert, you could be charged. I'm here to help you. I worked for your father and your grandfather before him. Do you think so little of my loyalty? I'm assuming justification that would explain what you did, in which case you have no obstructions in doing things legally."

"Dear Beatrice. Never would I doubt your loyalty. However, you're retired. You needn't concern yourself with these matters."

"But, Robert, I am worried. You never would have done what you did had I still been here. You must follow the law."

"Believe me, I appreciate what you're saying," said the mayor, "but things are different now. You don't understand the threats like I do. I don't blame you. You're not here to be aware of emergencies I'm facing. But everything is fine, absolutely fine."

The mayor grinned, gently spun her around, and led her toward the open door.

On her way out of the building, Beatrice passed Martha, who stood quietly in the hallway with her arms folded, glaring. "What business have you here?"

"It's a public building," Beatrice answered. "I've every right to be here. I came out of concern for our town, but mostly for your husband."

"Well, you're done, so you can leave. Much of what we're dealing with could've been avoided had you done your job."

"I regret you see it that way, Martha, but regardless, I wish you a good morning." Beatrice nodded kindly and excused herself, leaving Martha to glower.

Martha quickly turned and went straight to Robert's office. "Don't tell me. I know what she wanted."

"Yeah, she warned me that I need the council before a hanging," said Robert.

"She knows perfectly well that Weston won't sign. She's just trying to stop us, Robert. You should put her on your list."

"We'll eventually come to her. But right now, I have much on my mind, and I'm about to make an impression on our son, give him a front-row seat."

"I hope you're right, Robert," said Martha. "Just how do you plan on doing that?"

"Weasley's on his way to fetch the Burroughs. They're next."

"Good," said Martha. "That Hannah is the height of pomposity, always so saintly! They're the perfect criminals to set the example. After that, Eugene will think twice and maybe . . ."

"But if it doesn't work, darling?" asked the mayor.

"It must work," Martha insisted, "as soon as he fears you. With fear comes respect. That's what he lacks: the wisdom to know it. Says so in the bible."

"A lesson he'll learn today."

"Sheriff's on board?"

"Of course, Martha. Weasley's always on board."

"All right, then, the Parson and Hannah," she agreed. "I'll draw up the proclamation and make it official." She turned to leave.

"Wait!"

She stopped and looked back. "Yes, dear?"

"Maybe you should draw up a judgment of council," he said, "and have the council members all sign, just in case."

"You know why I can't," she said. "Weston is a thorn in our sides, and had you listened to me initially, we wouldn't have this illegitimate problem."

"You needn't remind me. Why else have we kept him close? But I don't suspect Weston knows anything. And for the most part, he complies. He built the gallows! We can do what we want without him."

"Like I said, Robert, I'll draft the mayoral proclamation, and you'll sign it. That's how we're going to do it."

"Fine," he agreed. But before Martha exited, he said, "One last thing."

"Yes, dear?"

"The hags, the sisters, they warn of another traitor. I assumed they meant Eugene, but their warning might be for someone else. They never give names, no matter how hard I try to wrest it out of them. Can you think of anyone else who may oppose us?"

"Hmm," thought Martha. "Not unless you mean Miss Hampshire."

"Jedediah's daughter? You've kept an eye on her? You suspect something?"

"There's something about her I don't trust. She's smart and never lets on to anything. She was a former student of Mr. Parrish. I noticed how they warmed to each other after her fiancé died—"

"Shear's boy?"

"Yes, dear, you remember."

Robert grinned. "Of course I do."

"Well, now," said Martha, "I fear Miss Hampshire has become unstable—from the trauma. At least I suspect as much, and she may imagine things . . ."

"Say no more. When the sheriff returns with the Burroughs, I'll order her arrest. Start thinking of an offense, one the people can understand and embrace. We've room for three on the gallows."

Martha felt a pinch of conscience. Eugene's accusations lingered somewhere in her mind, but she knew they were best kept suppressed. She fanned her face with her hand, and it soon passed. "I suppose we can't afford to be too careful, can we?"

The mayor grinned again. "Hearing cries for mercy and seeing useless tears, Eugene might think differently."

Martha nodded. "It's a good plan." She turned and left Robert sitting alone.

He watched the clock, counting the minutes before he lit the funeral pyre, and thought, *Weston will have plenty to burn after today!*

Chapter 54

Weston entered the town hall through the front door. Before making his way to the chamber room, someone called to him.

"Weston, is that you?"

"Yes, Mrs. Owen."

"Come here."

Martha was busy preparing documents and didn't look up when Weston entered her office. "When you see the sheriff, tell him to arrest Emily Hampshire—mayor's orders. Put her in with the rest of them."

"Mayor's orders? Shouldn't he be requesting?"

"You need to ask?"

"No. It's just . . . it's gonna get crowded in the cell, ma'am. That's all."

"Why does that matter to you? Besides, they won't be there for long."

"I'll tell him, ma'am," he said as he left her office, head hung low. *Something's not right*, he thought. *Now, what have you done, Emmy?* He exited the building as the sheriff came up the steps. "Mrs. Owen asked that you arrest another."

The sheriff asked, "Who?"

At first, Weston didn't respond.

"Who?" he asked more forcefully. "Not gonna ask again."

"Emily."

"Who?"

"Emily Hampshire, the teacher."

"That so difficult? Be right back." The sheriff headed to where his horse waited. Weston, feeling a sharp pain in the pit of his stomach, looked on as he rode away.

Weston watched as the mayor followed Mrs. Owen into the chamber room. The council members were seated except for the sheriff, who had yet to return.

"Where's Weasley?" asked the mayor.

Weston answered, "He left to arrest Emily Hampshire. He's yet to return."

"We'll wait," said the mayor. "I need Weasley here for this." As they waited, the mayor sat down and began signing documents as fast as Mrs. Owen slid them in front of him.

The chamber door swung open, and the sheriff barged in, beads of sweat dripping from his brow. "The Hampshires are gone! Neighbors watched 'em leave last night durin' curfew. They weren't alone either. Shears and his boy, the doctor boy, left with 'em!"

"What about the teacher? Did they mention seeing her?" asked Mrs. Owen.

"Saw 'em all leave like chickens fleein' the coop," said the sheriff.

The mayor stood, and the room went quiet. "Admission of guilt," he declared. "If any of them return, arrest them immediately. Is that clear?"

After a consensus, the mayor's eyes bore down on the council. "All right, then. Let's get started. As you know, we operate under an alliance that assures our success, but not unless we do our part. The agreement comes at a considerable cost, so I intend to get everything it affords us." He pointed with his chin toward Mount Erebus and said, "Our benefactors up there, although their appearance may be disconcerting, might as well be the holy sisters of mercy. They provide the sun that grows our crops. They will secure our positions in the community and further. And so we must now contend with the terms of that arrangement. If broken, the consequences could be worse than severe for everyone in this room."

As the mayor spoke, Weston thought, *Holy sisters of mercy? Who are they? Are they witches? And why couldn't Ernie tell me? Is he worried about being part of this supposed alliance?* Weston suddenly felt grateful Emily was far away from whatever this was.

The mayor hadn't stopped talking. Weston refocused and listened carefully.

"Our lives hang by a thread. If the monster dies, the arrangement dies with it and our protection. The resulting starvation will be the end of reason and order. It won't take long before mob mentality seizes the town and we must flee or be dragged from our homes, tarred and feathered." The mayor paused, glaring at the frightened faces that stared back at him. "You see now why we have their guns?"

He continued. "Our benefactors, the sisters of mercy, have warned that some in town are scheming, planning our demise. I know it to be true. The parson is not as innocent as some suppose. Witnesses have secretly come forward. Even my own blood, my son, Eugene, is implicated, although it is only an accusation at present. If true, his fate will be no different than the others.

I can only concern myself with our shared fate, even at the cost of my son. Now listen carefully. The terms of the agreement require more than just our compliance. They involve the submission of the entire town. Anyone in New Harmony could break the deal by killing the beast. Therefore, we must preemptively compel others to comply. No action is beyond reason to control our neighbors—for their good and ours."

Weston observed how excited Mrs. Owen appeared to see her husband so engaged. Her eyes glistened, and she smiled as wide as the Mississippi.

"Weasley!" said the mayor. "Go ring the bell. The rest of you ride through the streets. Summon the people. No exceptions! It's going to be a bloody, glorious day!"

The sound of chairs scuffing against the hardwood floor filled the chamber as the council members rushed out the door. The sheriff glared as they exited. Then he followed them out of the chamber room, leaving Martha and Robert alone. She drew him close, an expression of desire in her eyes, and leaned against him, rubbing the smooth surface of his bald head and neck while she whispered, "If only we were home, my darling."

Chapter 55

Gagged and shackled, the Burroughs stood atop the steps of the town hall. The sheriff's rough handling had torn the sleeve of Hannah's modest white cotton gown. Her graying brunette hair, usually twisted in an elegant bun, was now a chaotic mess that hung over her shoulders and face. The parson stood shirtless, chin up, his right cheek swollen. They watched the astonished expressions of neighbors and friends as they gathered. Their parishioners, the same people the Burroughs served and watched over, stood paralyzed in near disbelief. Edward peered through the strands of hair that had fallen into his face at Abigail, Susannah, and Elizabeth, among the first to arrive. Whispering to each other, they stared accusingly at the pitiful sight.

As frightened as Hannah must feel, thought the Parson, *she is not the only one who's afraid.* He wanted to talk to them, reason with them. His tongue pushed against the cloth rag in his mouth.

Hands clasped behind her back, Hannah leaned against her equally helpless husband. With his head down, he touched her forehead with his cheek as his frustration grew at not being able to comfort the woman who was saintlier than any person he knew. A wave of anger rose within him, and he heard a voice inside his head calling after him from a pit of despair.

"Edward, surely you are afraid now, aren't you?" came soothing words that too quickly could be mistaken for words of concern.

How sympathetic you sound, Edward answered in his mind. *No, I'm not frightened. My life here is temporary. There is more than this.*

"Hmm, are you so certain?" came the soft voice, molasses sweet. "You can't possibly know. Faith is not knowing. You do know that, right?"

I'm not listening, and you'll never frighten me.

"But you are listening, even now, aren't you?" As the voice continued, Edward's thoughts drifted elsewhere. "Edward?" it called to him. "The gallows awaits you!"

The parson looked at his wife now, and he groaned. He would welcome the gates of hell rather than witness this cruelty to her. Across the street, the gallows stood under the old oak tree, the ropes hanging loosely from the crossbeam. The crowd's clamor swelled as the mayor exited the building and waved to the anxious people gathered in front of the town hall.

Martha followed after and said something, but the mayor couldn't hear her over the commotion.

"What!" he yelled.

"The council's gathered, dear," Martha said. "We're all ready."

"Excellent," he said. Then, pulling up his expensive wool pants and tightening his suspenders, he stepped forward and grabbed the podium. "Good people of New Harmony," he began.

Before the crowd could settle, the sheriff yelled, "Quiet!"

Once people were calm, the mayor continued. "These are hard times. First, near starvation descended upon us, then came a monster, and now betrayal, even treason, has come to New Harmony. What's worse, the traitors are those we least suspect. I see young children out there. I desire nothing more than to leave them a future worth living in. I will not allow evil to destroy everything we have so earnestly built together. That is if I can help it. And you have my assurance that I will do everything in my power to ensure the security of all."

Nervous applause rose from the crowd.

"My heart, being weighed down, must direct your attention—"

Suddenly, the mayor heard a disturbance. Peering over the heads in the crowd, he saw Moses Carver on horseback, pushing his way forward, voice bellowing. In his hand, Moses held a long gun high above his head. People moved quickly out of his way, giving him a wide berth. Folks were stunned to see him, his dark skin shining in the afternoon sun. He was a loner, having never made a fuss before, barely a peep, and now this!

"Burroughs are comin' with me, Mayor! Ain't gonna be no hangin', not today!" The mayor dropped to the floor, scrambling to take cover behind the podium. "Let 'em go, Sheriff!"

The mayor peeked around the podium to see the sheriff slowly stepping forward with his gun raised.

"Lower yer gun, Mr. Carver. Yer scarin' people!" the sheriff shouted.

The curious onlookers fell silent as the drama unfolded.

"First," said Moses. "Let 'em go."

"How 'bout ya come down off yer horse and give me yer gun? Ya ain't supposed to have a gun."

A defiant Moses answered, "Well, damned good thing I do, cause now they ain't gonna be no hangin'."

The sheriff aimed dead center at Moses's chest. "No more talk. Drop it! Now!"

"Not before ya let 'em go and I says my piece!" Turning to the crowd, Moses hollered, "Listen y'all. The sheriff and y'all's mayor killed my only friend, Jed—Jedediah Hampshire. And he ain't the only one. They's others they killed. Now they gonna kill y'all's parson. Is that what you want?"

Above an agitated crowd, Abigail shouted, "Look at him! He's not one of us. Don't you listen to him!"

Some in the crowd agreed with Abigail, but not all. Voices called out in opposition, demanding the parson and Hannah be released. Suddenly, a shot rang out, and the crowd turned silent. Moses slumped in his saddle. His rifle fell to the ground, and he followed after, hitting the dirt with a thud. The sheriff stood beside the Burroughs at the top of the steps, black smoke rising from the barrel of his gun. Sunlight gleamed off the steel as he held it high, challenging anyone who threatened more violence.

Weston rushed into the crowd, taking control of the large, dapple-gray horse as it panicked from the gunshot after losing its rider. The crowd was in a frenzy. Otto, a bald and lanky barley farmer with a prominent mustache, a man familiar to all, pointed an accusing finger. "Mayor!" he shouted. "The sheriff can't just shoot anyone!"

The people erupted, crying out as they pushed each other.

Breathing heavily and rising from the floor to the podium, the mayor waved his hand and shouted, "Order! I'll have order!" He wiped the sweat from his brow with a sleeve. The sheriff rushed the crowd, pushing people back. "Stand down, Weasley," yelled the mayor. The sheriff stepped back.

"Mayor," cried Otto. "The sheriff shot Moses!"

The mayor stared at Weston, who tended to Moses. Weston looked up and shook his head. The crowd knew that meant Moses was dead.

"It ain't right!" hollered Otto.

Abigail came to the sheriff's defense. "Moses had a gun!" she cried. "We all saw it. If he'd followed the law, he'd be alive. But his kind, they never follow the law."

"Abigail's right," affirmed the mayor. "What you witnessed is the result of disobedience. There are consequences no matter who you are."

"And he was about to kill you, Mayor!" Abigail yelled so all could hear. "We all witnessed what happened. The sheriff was justified!"

"That's right!" agreed the mayor. "Sheriff did right. You all saw it. Nothing further to be done."

But Otto Krause stood defiantly. "What we heard were severe accusations. What if they were the motive for the sheriff to silence him? I was there that night, the night Jedediah went missing. I offered to help search the mine, but the sheriff sent me away. I would like to know why."

"Slanderous!" screamed the mayor. "I'd have you join Mr. Carver, so I'd be careful if I were you!"

Otto ducked into the crowd as people erupted, yelling in both protest and support of the sheriff.

Amongst the commotion, Abigail hollered, "The sheriff did the right thing!"

Another shot rang out, the sheriff aiming at the sky. "Mayor ain't done!" The boom of his voice was as intimidating as his rifle.

The clamor subsided into submissive silence. Still catching his breath, the mayor addressed the crowd. "Mr. Carver intended to kill me. Had he complied with my orders and relinquished his firearm, as Abigail pointed out, he would be alive. Mr. Carver bears full responsibility. And as I said before being interrupted, we have traitors among us, those we least suspect. Even my son, Eugene, now sits behind bars."

The crowd gasped, and people began to murmur as storm clouds darkened the northern sky. A light rain descended as Hyrum fetched a wagon to remove Moses's body.

Rallying the crowd, the mayor shouted, "You see? The heavens weep, for the council has uncovered a small number of disgruntled individuals, unhappy with the otherwise fair election, willing to overturn the people's will. They attack our democracy, which I will not stand for, even if it means losing my son. It's that important! Mr. Carver, I now see, took part in that insurgency, as have Edward and Hannah Burroughs, and now I can only suspect Mr. Otto Krause."

Hannah's eyes grew wide. She struggled to spit out her gag and was hit in the spine with the butt of the sheriff's rifle. She groaned, nearly losing her footing and tumbling down the steps.

A woman called out from the crowd. "Eugene did no such thing! Let him go!"

Martha immediately recognized Nellie's voice and nodded to the sheriff. He pushed his way into the crowd to collect her, a commotion ensuing as he weaved his way through the onlookers.

"Over here!" someone yelled. A moment later, the sheriff dragged Nellie from among those standing around her. Only Nellie resisted.

"My husband is innocent!" she cried. "They all are! You're a murderer, Robert, and a liar!" She kicked and screamed until she disappeared into the sheriff's office.

A momentary fear, a passing breathlessness, seized the mayor. At that moment, he felt a deep insecurity. A reckoning was at hand. Resolved to fight that insecurity with action, he pulled a pair of reading glasses and a piece of folded paper from his suit pocket. He read, "'Edward Burroughs and Hannah Burroughs, having been found guilty of conspiring insurrection, are hereby ordered to be hung by the neck until dead. As signed by—'"

Instead of reading Mayor Robert Owen II as written on the paper, he simply said, "Me!" He smiled to himself before looking up. Suddenly, thunder clapped loudly and threateningly. The mayor peered over his glasses to the north, where menacing clouds towered in the sky and plumes of swollen rage raced toward them. Then he noticed the blackbirds, swirling in the breeze, screeching and squawking as if conjuring the storm.

"Appears time is running short," he said. "Before ordering the sheriff to execute my edict where the Burroughs are concerned, there is one last detail. My first responsibility as your mayor is to keep the town safe. Therefore, until further notice, all businesses are closed. In addition, I'm ordering an immediate appeasement offering to temper the coming storm. Don't be stingy. Bring your generous offerings as before. Do it tomorrow, in the light of day when it is safe. Noncompliance constitutes a capital offense!"

The mayor looked back to the sheriff, who stood close to Edward and Hannah. A quick nod and the sheriff gave each a sharp push from the back. With hands cuffed behind her back, Hannah tumbled forward, her head cracking against the stone steps. Blood gushed from the wound as the sheriff lifted her to her feet, her face smeared in crimson, the blood trickling down her white nightgown. Neighbors, friends, and parishioners parted, allowing them to pass without objection. These were not the people they had come to love.

As they passed through the crowd, Abigail rushed toward them. "This is all your fault!" she screamed. "I told you to keep your mouth shut!" She sneered as she stepped back, allowing them to pass.

While they crossed the street, Edward looked at Hannah, feeling profound sorrow. Hannah cried out in pain and choked on the gag, the blood and sweat dripping into her eyes. Edward drew as close to her as he could, but the sheriff shoved them apart, forcing each to stand under their appointed noose. The sheriff slipped the black wool hood over Hannah's head before placing the noose around her neck. He then lifted her chin and tightened it. Once she was ready, he prepared

Edward with a hood and noose while the blackbirds perched on the crossbeam, watching the sheriff complete his work. When he finished, he and the birds looked back at the mayor.

Mayor Owen stood at the podium and hollered, "Bring out my son!"

The sheriff crossed the street a second time and returned with a gagged and shackled Eugene. With Eugene directly before the gallows, Sheriff Weasley climbed the steps to the platform and stood at the ready. All of New Harmony watched as Edward and Hannah tilted their heads toward heaven. When the mayor sensed all were utterly captivated, he nodded. But before the sheriff grabbed hold of the lever, time slowed, and the parson's mind calmed. He looked and beheld Hannah standing at his side. How it was that he could see her, blinded by the hangman's hood, he did not know. Though gagged, he called to her and she heard him. Their eyes locked as Edward felt the cords that bound his hands loosen and he reached out and took hold of her hand. Only then did the sheriff lean hard against the lever and the trapdoors dropped. Rather than fall, Edward and Hannah were freed from the pull of the earth as they ascended, praising God until everything was awash in white splendor.

Stunned by the gruesome sight, the crowd gasped at the audible sound of their necks snapping. The blackbirds took flight as the bodies spasmed at ropes' end. Hannah's shoes fell off as her legs thrashed about, and many dazed onlookers averted their eyes. It was one thing to see a man hang, but the same brutal treatment of a woman, traitor or not, was quite different.

The mayor shouted, "Please lend me your ears!"

A mostly horrified crowd looked back at him. His small, normally unimposing stature now appeared menacing. A simple nod was all it took—a lesson well learned.

"Go now; there's little time. A storm comes and curfew approaches. Tomorrow, bring your offerings."

A near stampede ensued as the crowd dispersed, the town center abandoned within minutes. It was then the mayor heard someone addressing him from behind.

"Mayor, sir?"

He turned to see Weston. "What is it?"

"I believe some may be concerned with . . . you know . . ."

"With what? Say it!"

"Since it's the parson and Hannah, a woman, people may expect a proper burial. Should I make coffins?"

Without a moment's hesitation, the mayor answered, "Absolutely NOT! Burn them at the landfill as you did Mr. Parrish and Mr. LeFevre. Throw Moses on the pile while you're at it. A funeral could elevate them to martyr status—something we don't want!"

Without objection, Weston headed down the steps. As he descended, someone called to him. He turned to see Mrs. Owen and stopped. "Yes, ma'am."

"Leave the Burroughs be. Let them hang awhile but remove their hoods. Let people see them. It'll serve as a reminder when they bring their offerings tomorrow. You can dispose of them after that. For now, get my grandson and take him to the ranch. Tell him his mother won't be coming home, but say nothing more. Let me handle it."

"Will do, ma'am."

Suddenly, a heavy rain descended from clouds that choked the last of the sun's rays before it sank below the horizon. The few people who lingered hurried away in the twilight. Heavenly tears rained down as people locked their doors and closed their curtains. Dogs curled up underneath porches, and chickens stayed in their coops. And although the sun would shine in New Harmony in the morning, these were dark days.

Chapter 56

Emily nervously paced about the Carver house, afraid to light a lantern or even a small fire for fear of being seen.

Something's happened, she thought.

When they heard the bell ring, Mr. Carver told her to stay put, promising to warn the parson and return immediately. But he didn't return. And now it was dark and wet outside.

I can't wait here any longer, she thought. *If Mr. Carver couldn't warn them, I must do so.*

She noticed Mr. Carver's gray wool coat hanging on a nail beside the fireplace. The course wool scratched as she wrapped it around her and stuffed the pistol in a pocket.

Leaving the house, she walked through the rain, the soles of her leather boots sliding in the mud. Coming into town, she moved in the shadows around bushes and through fences, darting between houses and hunkering down behind hedges. With the rain and the curfew in force, there was little chance of being seen. When she arrived at Main Street, she hesitated. Weston or, worse, the sheriff might enforce curfew despite the rain. She looked for a place to safely cross since the church lay on the other side of the street.

Looking north, Emily saw the lamp in front of the town hall still burning.

Soon, somebody will be along to extinguish it. I best wait for the street to darken.

Emily retreated into the alley next to Hyrum's general store. Hands and feet cold and damp, she waited in the shadows, grateful for Mr. Carver's coat. Emily tucked her hands in the coat pockets and waited until the lamplight no longer seeped into the alley, and then she waited awhile longer. Feeling relatively safe, she crept forward and peeked out. There were no lights or movement, only the breeze gently swaying the tree branches in the drizzling rain.

Now, she thought, and ran across the street, slipping into the bushes on the other side. She could see the park and the giant oak. From her vantage point, she beheld an inexplicable sight, illuminated by a flash of lightning. She wiped the rain from her eyes to see that something rocked back and forth in the wind.

No! It can't be. I won't believe it!

She doubled back across the street and hugged the fence along the houses, running as fast as she dared, closer still, until she stopped at the hedge on the east side of the park. She crouched among the piles of sopping-wet leaves, then crawled to the steps of the platform below the gallows. Mud caked her dress, but she didn't care. To her horror, the parson and Hannah hung before her. The parson's back faced her, but Hannah was in full view. Both their heads leaned to one side, blood streaming from Hannah's wound, her stained nightgown waving in the breeze. The rope around Edward's neck allowed him to twist in the wind, his body slowly turning until Emily could see his face, purple and swollen, his mouth still gagged. She recoiled at the sight.

Without concern for being heard, Emily declared in a strong voice. "I promise you, Parson, and you as well, Hannah, I will bring the light! And with it justice! I will! You have my solemn word!"

A light appeared in the window of a nearby house, and the front door cracked open. Emily ducked behind the platform as a man stepped onto his front porch and peered into the misty rain. He looked up and down the street but saw nothing except for the rain and two innocent people swaying from the gallows.

Chapter 57

A back wheel slipped into a rut, shaking the wagon violently. The recent deluge had damaged the road for the next several miles. Drifts of dirt crossed the path before them, rocks having settled in the wheel tracks. Marco slowed the horses. The last thing they needed was to break down. Traveling for hours at night in a heavily loaded wagon increased the chances of a mishap.

Tommaso climbed onto the seat next to Marco. "Where'd she go?" he asked. "They're worried back there."

"So am I, Papa." Marco's brow furrowed. "I need to go back, talk her out of whatever she thinks she's doing. If she's found now, with us missing, there's no telling what the mayor will do." The wagon kept rolling, bumping them around in the night air.

"We go back," said Tommaso.

"They'll already know we're missing, Papa. We can't all go back."

Tommaso looked down and said nothing more. The sun was rising, the storm subsiding. They'd traveled much of the night, and now the new day's warmth brought welcome relief. Marco did his best to stay alert, though, try as he might, he couldn't tear his thoughts away from Emily. *She has a habit of making sure I'm out of her way, convincing herself it's for my good, but this will get her killed.*

Another bump, and Marco looked over his shoulder. "Everyone all right?" he asked. "If we need to stop, we can. We're far enough now."

"Please," said Albert. "Must attend to private matters."

Marco pulled back on the reins, stopping the wagon and setting the brake. They'd come to a perfect resting place, with plenty of bushes on either side. Marco jumped down and began stretching, letting the blood back into his weakened legs and tingling feet. Finally, he looked for a private spot, retreating behind a bush.

"Someone's coming!" Tommaso called out. Marco quickly put himself in order and came out into the open. Instinctively, he patted his side, searching for his gun, which was no longer there. To his relief, the rider came from the direction they were heading, so it wasn't a matter of being pursued by someone from New Harmony. Squinting, he watched the image of the rider shimmer in the humid air rising between them.

Marco smiled at Tommaso. "What day is it?"

"Thursday," answered Tommaso.

"That's right. It's delivery day," said Marco. His grin widened as Warren rode up next to their wagon, stopping directly in front of Marco, a leather mail bag slung over his left shoulder.

"Where are you goin'?" Warren asked. He looked at Marco and Tommaso and then at the wagon full of trunks and boxes. Just then, Marjorie came out of the brush, followed by Albert. Warren looked over the sight of the fleeing families. The wrinkles forming on his forehead confirmed his confusion.

Said Marco, "No time to explain. I'm afraid Emmy's in danger. Would you happen to have your gun?"

Warren patted the firearm resting in his lap. "Promise you won't turn me in. Why?"

"Warren, please. I require your horse."

"Before I consent, can you tell me why? Where's Emmy? You say she's in danger?"

"Yes, and I need to get her out of New Harmony. If you can deliver our families to Bloomington and return immediately, no one will miss you. I'll leave the mail on Walter's porch."

Hardly a moment passed before Marco was riding Warren's horse back to New Harmony, Warren's gun tucked into his belt, the mailbag secured over his shoulder. He was determined to wait until sundown when the town was locked up tight and the streets lay deserted. Only then could he sneak into town under the cover of night.

Chapter 58

The following day, the panicked townspeople brought whatever they could to appease the dreaded beast, some leaving their cupboards bare. Weston and Ernie immediately began sorting the offerings. They set the perishables apart from the bottled peaches, pears, strawberries, and apricot preserves—those they would store for later consumption. Over half the bottled items, including the spirits, were again secretly divided between the mayor, the sheriff, and the council. Martha's position on the board assured the Owens a double portion.

Robert and Martha stood in his office, peering out the window, delighted as they watched the spectacle.

"It's working perfectly," she admitted.

"And we're just beginning," said Robert. "This time next year, I'll be governor-elect. And if the alliance holds, I'll run for president."

Martha grinned. "It's not unreasonable for another president to come from Indiana. Abe Lincoln came from Pigeon Creek, no less obscure than New Harmony."

"No less," agreed Robert.

Just then, Skinny arrived with their carriage.

"I'll be leaving now, attending to our grandson," Martha said.

"Has he questioned what happened to his parents?"

"He was weeping this morning," said Martha. "I'm very concerned. He's not at the age where he can understand how what we are doing is best for him. This will be difficult."

"It will, but in time, he will understand," said Robert. "Will you visit Eugene and Nellie before leaving for the ranch?"

Martha rolled her eyes. "I'd rather not, especially Nellie. She's bound to make this all our fault. Oh my. What do we do with her?"

"Don't despair," said Robert. "We might even save Nellie. Fear can open minds once they've seen enough of the consequences of rebellion."

"Consequences, indeed," said Martha. "Which reminds me, have you placed Beatrice on your list?"

"She's an old woman. Who would care?"

"I would," said Martha. "This is all her fault. And as for Nellie, the kind thing to do is have her committed as we did Weston's mother. Unfortunately, we can't simply make her disappear."

"Maybe, maybe not," said Robert.

Just then, the sheriff knocked on the door. "Whenever yer ready, sir."

Martha excused herself. The mayor exited the building a moment later, followed by the sheriff. Outside in the street, the council members waited. The mayor hooked his thumbs through his suspenders and grinned. "Are we ready?"

"Ready, sir," said Hyrum.

"Almost," said Ernie. "Weston has a question for you."

The mayor continued smiling. "What is it, Weston?"

"Sir, I'd like to go with you. Ernie agreed to stay and enforce curfew, but I'd like to go."

"Is Ernie deputy sheriff?"

"No, sir," said Weston. "But he is a member of the council."

"He is only a council member and lacks the authority to arrest. We must follow the law, so that is your answer. The rest of you show Weston which pile belongs to you, and while we're away, he will deliver them to your homes. Now, Weston?"

"Yes, sir?"

"Hide our portions in cellars or back porches as best you can. As for the ranch, you can unload Martha's and my shares in the food cellar behind the stable. It should all fit. Now, we have a long journey ahead, with many miles to travel before sunrise. Let's go!"

The orange-red sunset above the pastures and fields of grain to the west signaled that curfew was close at hand. The townspeople were locked inside their homes as the shadows grew long, soon to flood the town in darkness. The secret offering weighed heavy on the wagon. As they pulled out, the sheriff hollered, "Weston, keep an eye out! Anyone comes near the office, arrest them."

Only after the wagon and men on horses disappeared into the night did Weston realize the sheriff had neglected to leave the key to the door. *How will I arrest someone if he doesn't trust me with the key?*

Before delivering the shares of food, Weston attended to the gallows, the bodies still damp from the rain. He first lowered Hannah, her body collapsing onto the platform. He felt the urge to vomit. *Why? Why the parson and Hannah?* he thought. He felt like a Roman soldier lowering Jesus from the cross as he lowered the parson. *The parson was a holy man, undeserving of this.* Then his conscience stirred, and he mumbled, "Are my hands clean?" He wiped his hands together, reminding him of the Roman governor Pontius Pilate.

He loaded his share in the wagon first, and then the bodies. The extra wagon with the councils' portions could wait. He would first take the bodies to the landfill, light them on fire, and deliver his share to his farm close by. He would come back and deliver the council's portions after.

En route, he stopped, the landfill coming into view. His stomach churned. *I can't burn them unless my soul be burned along with them*, he thought. *I may never be forgiven. I don't care what the mayor says.*

He continued past the landfill and to his farm, where he drove his wagon straight to the woodshop, unloaded the bodies, and spread a cloth tarp over them.

I'll make them coffins in the morning, he thought, *do it properly. No one need know.*

Upon hiding the bodies, he resumed the rest of his chores, delivering portions to the council members' houses and patrolling the town for curfew violators.

On his final delivery, he heard the bell ring while stacking the food on Ernie's back porch. *There it is again.* Bong, bong, bong. *It can't be! Who could be doing that?*

Chapter 59

The overburdened horses lunged forward before stopping as the path turned upward.

"Hyrum!" shouted the mayor, "get a run on them horses! Push 'em hard. Otherwise, we're going nowhere!"

"Yah!" Hyrum hollered loudly and cracked his whip.

The draft horses pulled the wagon, breathing hard as they climbed the steepest part near the mountain base. Hyrum had just cracked the whip again to prevent their momentum from dwindling when the school bell sounded in the valley below. Everyone ignored the ringing as Hyrum continued to yell and whip the horses. The task at hand demanded their full attention and a combined effort. Ahead lay a respite, where the road leveled and Hyrum could set the brake. For the moment, all efforts went to the task at hand.

The sheriff yelled to Ernie and Jonas, "Get off and push!"

They all jumped off their horses and pushed as the horses pulled. Slowly, the wagon crept over a bump, leveled out, and traveled another twenty yards. Hyrum pulled back on the brake, and they paused to catch their breath. Then bong, bong, bong, the bell rang out from New Harmony again. They craned their necks and looked down at the twinkling lights of the valley.

"Weasley!" shouted the mayor. "You best go back, check on Weston—see why he's ringing the bell. Delivering this is too important, or I would go with you. You can come back if there's time."

"I'll be comin' back, sir." The sheriff mounted his horse, pulled hard on the reins, and headed back to town.

Chapter 60

Emily trembled, her heart pounding as she gripped the rope. Pulling down hard, she felt the bell's weight tilt as it swung until the clapper struck the lip. Three times it rang, rending the stillness of the night air. She waited, then repeated the sequence as if calling the army of heaven to battle. Finally, she let go and the bell fell silent. Dark thoughts closed in around her, but there was no turning back.

I'm counting on you, Weston. You helped me once, and I need your help again. Please be the man I believe you are.

Only now did she light her lantern, no longer needing to sneak about, hugging the shadows. Leaving the schoolyard, she turned toward the center of town. Windows began to glow with flickering candlelight. She quickened her pace, needing to arrive first.

Fear of a grisly beast ravishing the countryside bled into the nightmares of some, while others dreamed of falling through trap doors and having their necks snapped. The people of New Harmony tossed and turned in their sleep, while the cursed voices serenaded them with a song that heightened their terror. Jarring them from their nightmare, the bell rang, strangely enough, hours after curfew. With dutiful trepidation, they left their homes, lanterns in hand, and made their way to the center of town.

The closer Emily got to the town hall, the more frightened and doubtful she became. *What am I doing, trusting the very people who stood idly by and watched as the mayor hung my friends? Will they allow me to say what should be obvious—that they've been deceived?* Emily sighed and shook her head. *It will be a miracle if I see the sunrise.*

Emily climbed the steps alone. Facing the street, she saw the light from a multitude of lanterns glimmering against the night, all flowing toward her. A small number of townsfolk began to pool at the bottom of the steps, with more arriving by the minute. *So this is it,* she thought, *what the parson knew would happen, what he foretold.*

"Parson Burroughs, can you see them coming? I'm bringing the light, just like you said." As the words left her mouth, they filled her with confidence, the light chasing the darkness from her mind.

Her heart pounded, and her breathing quickened when she heard a sickening voice call to her. *Oh no!* thought Emily, *not the scandalmongers!*

"What is this!" Abigail screamed, charging up the steps, Elizabeth a few paces behind her.

They stopped just short of Emily, and Abigail turned and faced the arriving crowd. "It's curfew! Go home, all of you! This assembly is clearly unlawful! And I happen to know that Miss Hampshire is wanted and the mayor and sheriff will see her arrested as soon as they return. Now get home!" With her hands, she spitefully shooed them away.

Emily watched as people ignored the woman, their curiosity overshadowing Abigail's self-appointed authority. Instead, they stared inquisitively at Emily, waiting to hear what emergency had brought them out of their homes.

Abigail surveyed the gathering. Her eyes widened when she saw Weston pushing through, and she screamed anew. "Deputy Weston's here! Let him pass!"

Emily's heart beat more rapidly. She closed her eyes and spoke a silent prayer. *"Dear God, be with me now. Deliver me or . . ."* She paused before opening her eyes and whispering, "Whatever comes next, just help me not to fear."

Smug satisfaction filled the faces of Abigail and Elizabeth. "Arrest her!" Abigail pointed to Emily. "It was she who rang the bell!"

"I'll handle this, Abigail," Weston said calmly. He brushed past her and approached Emily.

Not willing to be ignored, Abigail yelled, "But she is causing us all to break the law, to violate curfew. Deputy Weston, you must arrest her. I happen to know the mayor has already called for her arrest."

Weston turned to face her. "Who is violating curfew, Abigail? Are you? I happen to know the mayor wants ALL violators arrested. Now, that includes you. And where do you suggest I put everyone?" Before she could argue, Weston stopped her. "I suggest you step back and remain quiet before you spend the rest of the night in jail."

Abigail huffed. "The sheriff will think differently," she murmured as she retreated down the steps, Elizabeth in tow.

Weston turned back to Emily and spoke quietly. "What are you doing here? Why have you returned?"

In the lamplight, Emily saw genuine worry on his face.

"Please tell me, what do you not understand? The mayor intends on seeing you hung. Do you realize the position you've put me in?" He peered over his shoulder to see Susannah join Abigail and Elizabeth, the three town provocateurs now in full force, aligned against Emily and Weston.

Abigail cried out, "The mayor called for her arrest. We assembled demand it! Miss Hampshire threatens us all!"

Elizabeth and Susannah screamed their support.

Weston hollered, "Not another word, or—" He turned back to Emily with tear-filled eyes. "Emmy, I'm sorry, but they're right. I've no choice."

"We always have a choice, Weston," Emily pleaded. "I know your heart. I know you are a good man or I wouldn't be placing my life in your hands. I knew you would come. I counted on it. And right now, I need your help."

"I'm so sorry, but . . ."

Before Weston could make a move, Emily drew Tommaso's pistol. Shocked, he backed down the steps.

"She's got a gun!" Susannah screamed, and a commotion rose among the gathering crowd.

Weston shouted, "Quiet, everyone!" Then, turning his attention to Emily, he said, "Please put it down, Emmy. You won't shoot me or anyone else. It's not who you are."

All eyes watched her, waiting to see what she would do. Some cried out in support, while others, fearful of the implications, demanded her immediate arrest. Theirs were the loudest voices. Gathering strength, Emily took a deep breath and addressed the people.

"Arrest me if you will, but first you must listen! All of you! I left New Harmony, never to return. But as you see, I stand here, risking my life for your welfare so you may know the truth. I appeal to your kind nature and sense of justice to hold your judgment and hear me out. In return, I will bring proof of murder!"

Walter, her neighbor from across the street, pushed his way to the front of the crowd. He held his lantern high, and Emily could see the worried look in his eyes. "Please, Emmy. Watch what you say. They can use it against you."

"Thank you, Mr. Buchanan, but I've waited my whole life, too afraid to say what I know. It's time these people hear the truth." She gripped the gun tightly in front of her, her hands shaking. "I pray you all listen!" she shouted.

"Don't listen to her!" screamed Abigail.

"Shut it, Abigail!" yelled Walter.

Just then, Emily heard a familiar voice and peered into the crowd. *Ms. Woolhauser?*

Sure enough, Ms. Woolhauser barged through the crowd, coming to her defense.

"Yes, shut it, Abigail!" she shouted. "You are a nuisance. I've long waited to say it, and I dare say others would agree."

Abigail shrieked, disappearing into the crowd as Ms. Woolhauser continued. "We all need to listen to what Miss Hampshire has to say. We all need to stop being afraid. So arrest me, too, Weston, if you must. Having one of my students put me in jail would be interesting. You must not have learned a thing in my class." Ms. Woolhauser turned to Emily. "We're listening, dear. Little Weston here can't put us all in jail, so go on."

"Yeah, go on!" yelled Annette St. Clair. Followed by her husband, Stu, she came up alongside Ms. Woolhauser, where the three stood in solidarity.

Surprised at seeing Annette, Emily thought, *The little mouse found her voice. I'm not alone!* "Thank you," Emily mouthed.

Ms. Woolhauser and the St. Clairs smiled back at her.

With renewed hope, Emily addressed the people. "Most of you have known me my entire life. I've taught some of your children. I see the faces of many who comforted me when I lost my mother and when my father went missing. So I stand before you, that same Emily, risking her life with only a prayer that you will hear me."

As Emily spoke, the three blackbirds circled high overhead, then landed on the crossbeam of the gallows. They quietly observed from across the street.

"She's not to be trusted!" screamed Abigail anew. "Look at her. She has a gun. She's a nuisance, a troublemaker. She partnered with Mr. Parrish, the parson, the Frenchman, and the rest. Have you all so quickly forgotten? She can only offer lies!"

An uproar ensued as quarreling broke out, and with people so divided, a resolution seemed impossible, especially with the loudest voices continuing to be in opposition.

"Let her speak!" Old Man Taylor hollered as the pushing and shoving began turning the crowd into a mob.

Weston finally spoke. "It's all right, everyone! Calm down! We can give her audience, and then . . ." Abigail was about to protest when Weston looked at her sternly.

The crowd quieted enough for Emily to continue. "I've come to know with certainty that the mayor had my father murdered. The sheriff was there when my father went missing, coincidentally on the very day my father entered the mayoral race. And wasn't that Mr. Parrish's crime? Running against the mayor?"

The people were stunned into silence. Emily had spoken forbidden words, and there wasn't a soul in New Harmony that didn't know it. Emily saw the pleading in Weston's eyes.

"That's enough, Emmy! There are sufficient people here to dig your grave without you doing it for them!"

Emily had gone this far and would not back down. "Allow me to go free and I will return with proof of murder," she said. "I know where to find it, and I will. If I come back with nothing, arrest me, hang me. I don't care. I'm doing this for all of us! My only request is that each of you, as neighbors and friends, demand that the mayor allow me to present the evidence upon my return. Bronson Parrish gave you a chance by challenging the mayor, a chance to free yourselves from tyranny. It cost him his life. I now offer you a second chance. In so doing, my fate lies in your hands. You, friends and neighbors, are my only hope! The mayor can silence me only if you consent with cowardice or complacency; if you do, my death will rest upon your heads. And it is with certainty that I will be allowed to speak at your judgment in front of God and the angels!"

Astonished, the town knew not what to make of the accusation.

"Furthermore," Emily continued, "I must share with you a detail I have since learned. The monster you fear is not what you've been told or believe. It was I who traveled north of the gorge. I confronted the beast and discovered that—"

The crowd gasped. More forbidden words, and now even some who'd shouted in support were left speechless.

Abigail, Elizabeth, and Susannah cut her short, screaming for her blood so loudly none could hear Emily. Pushing and shoving commenced as the mob mentality returned.

"She endangers us all!" screamed Abigail.

"She cares nothing for us! She'd have us all torn to pieces!" Elizabeth hollered.

"To the gallows with her!" cried Susannah.

Boom! A gun discharged. People stopped and ducked. Everyone turned to see Marco walking up the steps, his old flint rifle spent, his finger still on the trigger.

"Emmy, keep my father's gun on them while I reload. If anyone comes within ten feet, shoot Abigail in the chest. The bullet won't find her heart. She hasn't got one. But shoot her there regardless, and don't feel remorse. Remember, she'd see you hang."

The startled crowd backed away as Marco filled the gun with powder.

He had more to say as he reloaded. "Everything she's told you is true! I was there when the monster first confronted us. Yes, there is a monster, but it didn't attack anyone!"

"The mayor wants to divide and frighten us so he can force us to surrender our guns and harvest, even making us afraid to say what we know to be true. He's using our fear of the monster to control us so we are incapable of anything more than being subservient fools. He's manipulating us for his purposes, power, greed, and all the rest. And he will murder to keep us from knowing the truth."

"Do something!" Susannah yelled to Weston. "You're the deputy. This is wrong!"

"Quiet, Susannah," Abigail protested, Emily's long gun still pointed at her. "You want me dead?"

Abigail fled into the crowd as the blackbirds perched on the gallows. They didn't squawk, nor did they take flight, their presence unnoticed.

The more vocal of the townspeople, the ones operating out of fear, chanted their demands. "Seize them! Hang them!"

Though sensing the injustice, others remained quiet, while a few willing to drop from the gallows alongside the righteous cried for mercy.

Amid the storm of fiery words, threats, and pleas, Emily watched as Weston wavered. *Weston must realize Marco and I are dead either way*, she thought, *especially now, after everything we've admitted to. So what choice has he but to arrest us?*

Weston looked at her, his expression angry. "You are not solely risking your life but mine, and for what?" He scolded her while trying to keep his voice down. Then, before Marco could finish reloading, Weston raised his gun. "Put your gun down, Emmy!" he demanded. "Do it now!"

"Don't, Emmy!" Marco said. "I'm nearly finished loading."

Emily looked at Weston. The hurt on his face was devastating. She nodded. "All right, Weston, if you can live with yourself knowing the mayor has murdered people like my parents, the parson, and so many others, if you are no different than they are—very well." She lowered the barrel. "I made a mistake, Weston. I believed you were a good man."

"Emily, no!" cried Marco. Just as he finished reloading, Emily set down her gun. But before he could do anything, Weston had his rifle pointed at him.

A restless mob pushed forward, closing the distance, ready to deliver Emily and Marco to the gallows. They stared at Emily with mad, contorted, snarling expressions that hungered for her death—a frenzy that threatened to tear her and Marco apart.

"Stop!" yelled Weston, swinging his rifle at the mob. "Move back!"

Shocked, they quickly complied, staggering backward.

"Listen to me!" Weston yelled as the crowd hushed. "The mayor, council, and sheriff aren't delivering food to the monster, not so much as a crumb. Instead, they're offering it to the mountain witches. They have an unholy alliance, and that's all I know." He handed his rifle to Marco, walked down the steps, retrieved a crowbar from his wagon, and walked over to the sheriff's office. There, he pried open the door, busting it off its hinges. He disappeared inside, taking a lantern with him.

Emily picked up her gun and joined Marco, keeping the mob at bay. "I know you're all afraid!" she called out. "I know the voices from the mountain tell you to be fearful. I struggle alongside you, but it's a spell of enslavement we must break! I assure you that you can break it. Parson Burroughs told me how, and now I'm telling you. It's simple. Just stop listening. He tried telling all of us, but now he's not here, and you can imagine why!"

Just then, Eugene and Nellie exited the sheriff's office, Weston following close behind. Free of his shackles, Eugene climbed the steps, Nellie staying back with Weston. The crowd was eager to hear what he would say.

"It's time!" Eugene called out. "Time for the truth, and I have much to tell. I was there when Emily's father went missing. It was no accident, no cave-in. My pa had the sheriff murder Emily's father. Then the sheriff hid his body in the old mine. And I was there when the sheriff dropped her mother's body behind Ernie's tavern, knowing that harsh judgment would determine the cause of her death. I was young and powerless, warned not to talk for the good of our family—always for the good of our family. I watched in silence as my father stole your labor and votes and skimmed from your shops and farms, enriching the Owen family at your expense. I saw the intimidation in your faces and heard your conversations hush as I walked past, never blaming any of you for keeping my family at a distance. I'm not so young anymore and no longer powerless—not anymore. It took a while, but I found my voice. You see, I'm standing in front of you. Forgive me for not standing up sooner than now, but here I am. And it's time we all stand!"

While Eugene addressed the crowd, Emily excused herself, quickly making her way to Weston as tears filled her eyes. She hugged him, not wanting to let go.

"Thank you," she cried. "I was right about you. You are good!"

"Then you knew something I didn't," he said. "But we'd better figure something out, or we'll all hang, and I won't be a good man much longer. Do you have a plan, or did you ring the bell on a whim?"

Suddenly, a shriek came from deep within the crowd. "What's this?"

People stepped back as Martha Owen climbed the steps.

"Get back to your homes! Now!"

Weston looked to Eugene.

"Don't look at him!" Martha yelled. "You look at me and put my son and his whore back in their cell. You're the deputy. You're in charge."

Weston nodded and moved to cut her off when she slapped him. He grabbed her wrist and dragged her, screaming, scratching, kicking, and threatening to release hell on anyone involved as they disappeared into the darkness of the sheriff's office. Emily followed with a lantern.

The astonished crowd looked back at Eugene, who stood at the top of the steps. "Everyone, please return to your homes. We've all been through enough. No more curfew. You're free to do as you will, but I ask that you please go home."

The people of New Harmony were in disarray, finding it difficult to overcome the fear that had defined them ever since the eclipse. Barbara Folsom looked to Eugene with grave concern. "Shouldn't we believe your father? He is mayor, after all, and, I mean, he did cause the sun to shine, didn't he?"

"And the monster attacked and killed. We all know that," said Boyd Kensington.

"I want to see proof," hollered Amelia Taylor, "and so does everyone else, and I believe Emily will provide it if given a chance!"

Ms. Woolhauser charged up the steps and addressed the people. "I believe Miss Hampshire as well. I taught her as a child and worked with her when she became a teacher. I can tell you I've never heard her utter an untruth. If she finds her father, it proves what Eugene is saying. If it was an accident, her father would be buried deep in the mountain forever. But for now, Miss Hampshire is risking her life. As she said, she was safely away from here but returned for our welfare.

She risks everything, and what do we risk by allowing her a chance to prove her allegations?"

Eugene quickly added, "All we risk is our innocence, but we are decent people. We cannot continue without knowing the truth. If anyone here is against knowing the truth, speak up!"

People looked at one another. And since no one wanted to admit they lacked moral virtue, no one objected.

"It's decided. It's time the truth set us free."

Across the street, the three blackbirds on the gallows took flight. They rose silently through the air, unnoticed, circling high overhead until a southerly breeze carried them toward Mount Erebus.

CHAPTER 61

Martha frothed at the mouth like a rabid dog. "When Robert returns, he'll see you dead! You hear me? You'll hang with the rest of the rubbish in this godforsaken town." She snarled at Emily, who held the lantern while Weston turned the key. They heard a clank as the lock engaged on the cold iron bars.

"You may be right. Only time will tell," said Weston. "For now, you're staying right here."

"May I remind you, boy, that you swore an oath. There still may be time. These people, they're using you, lying to you!"

"Murder? You presume I swore an oath to protect a murderer?" asked Weston. "Your own son is the accuser."

"And you, Miss Hampshire, I look at you and see a Jezebel, a dead woman," Martha said, then began to plead. "Weston, they are all lies. You don't want to hang with her, and you won't! I give you my word."

Weston shook his head. "No," he said. "I've seen enough. I believe your son. I believe he's telling the truth. Somehow, we will eventually all know the truth. Then we'll see who hangs."

Weston and Emily left Martha alone in the cold, dark jail cell. Her shrieking and vile threats persisted until they exited through the broken door of the sheriff's office.

Once outside, Weston took Emily to where they could speak privately. Assured of not being overheard, he said, "This is far from over. How do you intend to find your father? He's been missing for what, fifteen or twenty years? If you don't find him, and the odds are against it, what does that mean for those who stand by you? Mrs. Owen is right. What we're doing could go very badly. I hope you've thought this through. I hope you knew what you were doing when you rang the bell."

"I have a plan, Weston."

"What is it?"

"You wonder why I rang the bell. I did it to find you. I didn't have time to search for you all night."

"But in doing so, you brought the entire town. That was risky. You're fortunate to be alive. Did you think of that?"

"That's what the gun was for. Them, not you."

"But how did you know I would help?"

"Faith."

"Oh yeah. Faith in God. I should have guessed."

"And you."

"Well, you had a gun. I suppose that helped." Weston laughed.

"It did, and I'm sorry I pointed it at you."

"Would you have shot me?"

She shook her head. "Never."

"Well, to be fair," said Weston, "I pointed a gun at you."

"Could you have . . ." she asked.

"I didn't."

"No, you didn't. And now I intend to get us out of this mess," said Emily. "But that requires one last favor, the reason I rang the bell, the reason I need you."

"What for? What can I do?"

"When the mayor and sheriff return in the morning, don't let on to anything. When they arrive, people will be shut away in their homes. They won't know of your involvement, not for a while. Hopefully, we'll have enough time for my plan to work."

"And how is that to be done?"

"Tell them, the sheriff in particular, that I'm responsible for all this and that you tried stopping me."

"The town knows differently, but I'll take my chances."

"You should be all right. First chance, tell them you overheard where I might be hiding, that you overheard the mention of the old coal mine where my father worked. I want the sheriff to come looking for me there."

"You're certain you want that?" Weston's eyebrows rose. "Is that where you'll be?"

"Yes. And if you accompany the sheriff to the mine, we can force him to show us where to find my father. I'm certain that's where he will be found, in the mine."

"Hmm." Weston nodded. "All right. Anything else?"

"There is. For my plan to work, Eugene, Nellie, and Marco can't be here when they come down from the mountain. And you can't allow the sheriff to enter his office, or Mrs. Owen will ruin everything."

"Oh yeah," said Weston. "So what do I tell them? How am I to keep him for looking in the office?"

"Tell him someone broke his door and freed Eugene and we're all hiding at the mine. But have your gun and horse at the ready. If it goes badly, they'll be tired from the trip up the mountain, and with a fresh horse, you can outrun them. You can find my family in Bloomington. Find Mr. Carver and take him with you if you can."

"You don't know?"

"Know what?"

"Emmy, the sheriff killed him."

Emily staggered back. "When? Why?"

"Moses tried to stop the hanging of the parson and Hannah."

Emily's eyes narrowed, and her fists clenched at her sides. Trembling with rage, she said, "You make damned certain the sheriff comes looking for me. I'll be waiting! Don't tell anyone but the sheriff where to find me, especially not Marco or anyone else. Only the sheriff, and come with him if you can. But if not, I'll deal with him myself."

Chapter 62

As the townspeople returned to their homes, Nellie climbed the steps to where Eugene and Marco stood talking to one another. Emily and Weston soon joined them. Weston tossed the keys to the jail to Eugene. "Here," he said. "Your mother's your responsibility now."

"I'll see it from here, Weston," said Eugene.

An anxious Nellie asked, "Weston, where's Alexander? Is he at the ranch?"

"He's there, ma'am. I delivered him there myself."

"What about the guns, Weston?" asked Eugene. "Where are the guns?"

"Also at the ranch, in the rear cellar, behind the stable."

"Good," said Eugene. "I'll take Nellie, and we'll head there now. Marco, you're the only one who's armed. Will you make sure my mother stays put?"

Marco nodded.

"I'll send reinforcements as soon as possible. If a retreat is necessary, rally with us at the ranch."

"All right," said Marco.

Eugene turned to Weston. "And you, Weston, gather whoever you trust to come to help us. Start with the farmers north of town. They're more likely to support us. Have them meet at the ranch, where they can retrieve their guns. If we must make a stand, that's as good a place as any. Emily, come with Nellie and me. You're unsafe otherwise, but we must hurry . . ."

"Excuse me, Eugene," Weston interjected, "perhaps I should stay here and guard the sheriff's office. I'm armed and better suited to handle the mayor and sheriff if that's what it comes to."

Eugene agreed. "All right, then Marco will recruit as many as possible, so long as we can trust them. We may have to shoot our way out of this." Everyone agreed. "But we must hurry. There's much to do before my father returns."

As they quickly dispersed, Emily pulled Marco aside. "What are you doing here? Where's Auntie and Albert? And your father?"

"They're safe," he said. "They're with Warren in Bloomington by now. I rode his horse here. We passed each other along the way."

"I can never thank you enough," she said. "I might be hanging across the street now if it weren't for you. But now you're in as much danger as I am."

"Pardon me if I still feel the sting of your abandoning me on the road. I've not yet forgiven you, and I don't care that you are only trying to protect me. It was wrong for you to do that."

"Please, Marco, will you forgive me?" She could hardly bear seeing the hurt in his eyes. "I'm trying to make things right, to make the town safe for everyone."

"Eugene and the rest can handle it from here. Let's go. You've done enough. Anything more, and you are certain not to survive. I'll recruit some farmers, people who will join Eugene at the ranch, and then . . ."

Emily looked deep into his eyes and saw his concern for her. She knew he would stay and help if only she would leave. He was only trying to save her, but Emily couldn't leave. "I'm sorry," she said, "but there's something I must do, something I've intended to do my entire life. I can't turn away from it now."

"No. There's nothing more for you to do. You're leaving here tonight. Mr. Parrish and Mr. LeFevre ensured we had everything required to start over."

"Marco, you're not listening."

"Why can't you turn away? Is it proof you're after? Don't you understand? These people, the Owens and the sheriff, will never be held accountable. They just won't. You can have all the proof in the world, and it won't matter, not even if the town can't dispute it. These people are stubborn. If we don't leave New Harmony, we will die here. And we will die only a few hours from now. Can't you see that?"

"I don't care."

"You don't care?"

"No, Marco. Leave if you must, but I'm staying to finish this, or it will haunt me forever. And more people will be hurt, or much worse, while I'm safely away."

"But these people, they're not thinking right. They're under a spell, Emmy. How can I convince you? I climbed Erebus and although I saw nothing, there is evil there. And there's no way to stop it. Even if we could, these people, they'll watch like the sheep they are while we hang."

"Marco, they're not the mayor's sheep. The parson would be the first to tell you that, and they're worth saving. That's what he'd say. That's what my father believed."

"Little good that did either of them," said Marco. "And now you're being just as stubborn as everyone else here. I only returned because I'm unwilling to lose another person I . . ." Marco fell silent.

The pleading in his voice tugged at her heart.

"I've caused you too much pain, Marco. You should leave here for good. I want you to be safe. God willing, I'll follow."

"I would, but you heard Eugene. I must acquire recruits and arm the town. I'm unsure what we'll do when the state militia is alerted. But I won't run now. I'm not a coward."

"I know you're not. And there are others here who are not cowards. You can find them and put guns in their hands. But to stand any reasonable chance, I must have proof, and I believe I know exactly where to find it. May I use Warren's horse?"

"If you won't reconsider I suppose you may, Emmy. I'm certain to find another."

"You'd better hurry. Gather those you can. And, Marco . . ."

"Yes, Emmy?"

"Thank you, and please, never lose faith, not even in me."

"You just watch yourself," said Marco reluctantly.

"I will," Emily assured him. She mounted Warren's horse, but before leaving for the mine, she noticed Weston sitting on the steps, waiting. She thought, *Weston will face the fire when the mayor and council return. God, please be with us now!*

Chapter 63

The sheriff took his time riding into town, happy not to be headed up the mountain with the council. He preferred to never see the witches, or whatever they were, again, not if he could help it. Up ahead in the dark, he saw no fire raging from town, or else the sky would be awash in yellow light. He assumed that the reason for the bell ringing couldn't be too serious, nothing he couldn't handle. He'd cleaned up his share of messes and had no problem cleaning up more—the first of which awaited him up ahead.

In the dark, three women waited on the side of the road. *Now, what is this?* he wondered. *Who'd be defying curfew? I need to convince the mayor we need a larger jail.* He tapped the wood stock of his rifle, a habit he had acquired since becoming sheriff. *I ought to shoot 'em now.* But then he thought some more. *And miss the pleasure of pullin' the lever? Nah.*

"Hey, you up there!" he shouted. "It's well past curfew. What do ya think yer doin'?"

"It's us, Sheriff. Eliza, Susannah, and me, Abigail."

"Didn't ask who you were, just what yer doin'."

"Believe me, Sheriff, we're on your side," said Abigail. The other two enthusiastically agreed. "There's been an incident. That Emily Hampshire rang the bell and coaxed everybody out after curfew. She's the lawbreaker, not us. People thought it was official, but that's not the worst."

The sheriff sighed. "I'm listenin'," he said. "What's the worst?"

"Miss Hampshire told everyone that you and Mayor Owen murdered her parents. She said she could prove it. She and that Shear's boy, the doctor one, not the one the monster killed—"

The sheriff interrupted. "Yeah, Marco, the doctor. Go on."

"The two of them, they broke Eugene out."

"Wait!" said the sheriff. "Who let Eugene out?"

"They did," said Susannah. "The teacher and—"

Abigail interrupted. "Emily Hampshire and Marco, the doctor."

"Where was Weston Riley?"

"He helped them," Abigail said. "Sheriff, aren't you listening? Weston let them out."

"What!" After all the threats, the sheriff could hardly believe what he heard. *Never suspected Weston as a traitor.*

"That Weston, he pointed his gun at me," said Abigail. "I was petrified, and I don't mind saying that we," she waved her arms to indicate all three of them, "tried stopping them."

Susannah and Elizabeth nodded wildly, punctuating that they were, in fact, heroes.

"I'm sure ya did," said the sheriff. "Best run along. Lock your doors. I'm gonna have an unpleasant conversation with Mr. Weston Riley, and he ain't gonna like it."

Chapter 64

Weston sat alone in the dark on the stone steps in front of the town hall, waiting. Shadows moved in the flickering light of the gas lantern at the bottom of the steps. As he looked around, something to the north, down Main Street, caught his attention. There, a lone rider approached at a leisurely pace. He stood and squinted. A lean, hatless man with white sleeves and a black vest rode on a black horse. *The sheriff!* Weston hadn't expected to see him so early. *But where are the others?*

As the sheriff drew closer, he shook his head at Weston. Then, with a look of utter dismay, he took in his office with the busted door barely hanging from its lower hinge. He stopped just short of Weston, not having to get any closer to survey the damage.

"All right, Weston," he said. "What happened?"

But before Weston could answer, the sheriff climbed off his horse, rifle at his side. Weston began to wring his hands but quickly stopped so as not to look suspicious.

"Hard to say," Weston said. "It was unbelievable, everyone breaking curfew—nothing I could do. I couldn't arrest them all, and some had guns. I suppose we didn't gather them all."

"No, suppose not," said the sheriff. "Do go on."

"Even you presumed Emily Hampshire fled from here. I can assure you she did not. She was here. She rang the bell. Emily is responsible for the whole thing! I was forced to go along with it. There was nothing for me to do. There were far too many guns."

The sheriff only stared. "And the door to my office? What about that?"

"Well," said Weston. "Emily Hampshire and Marco Salvatori—you know the ones I'm speaking of?"

"Yeah, I know 'em."

"Well, they let Eugene and Nellie go free. So what could I do? They were armed. I did mention they were armed?"

"Ya, you did," said the sheriff. "But weren't you armed, or am I mistaken?"

"Armed but outnumbered," Weston confirmed nervously. "I had to play along."

The sheriff looked over at the door to his office. "Any idea where I can find 'em?" he asked. "Where do ya think the teacher and the doc went?"

"I overheard something about a mine. Not the eastside mine but the other mine, the one no longer in operation."

"The mine, huh? That is convenient."

"Huh?" Weston stood briefly, then quickly sat back down, unconsciously wringing his hands again. "I can't tell you more than that, but I'd like to go with you. I need to make things right."

"Oh yeah. You come along," said the sheriff, "make things right." He walked over and stood in front of Weston. "But first, I need you to stand up."

Startled by the request, Weston looked at the sheriff. "You want me to stand?"

"It's what I said," said the sheriff.

"Oh, all right." Weston cautiously stood and waited.

"Now turn around."

"Sheriff, please listen to me. I tried to stop them! I did! It was one against a dozen guns. I ordered them to stop," he said as convincingly as possible. "At least I did that, being alone and all, outnumbered." Weston's right hand began to twitch.

"Oh, I'm sure ya did," said the sheriff, nodding. "I'm sure ya did," he repeated. "Now turn around!"

Chapter 65

In the lamplight, under a waning moon, Emily stood in the old yard, staring at the boards that blocked the entrance. She hadn't been to the coal mine since her eighth birthday when her father went missing. After a supposed search failed to recover his body, the mayor declared it unsafe. Then, soon after reacquiring the mine, he'd closed it for good.

Why didn't I think of this? she thought. *There are no tools here to remove the boards. I should have realized the mayor wouldn't want anyone snooping around.*

Removing the boards would take too much time, time she didn't have. Undeterred, however, she went about her plan. *I'll figure it out.*

It was then she had a hopeful thought. *There may be a tool in the old shed.* But as she approached it, she noticed the door was missing, and she realized she likely wouldn't find anything.

Still, she slowly stepped inside, fearful of disturbing the ghosts that occupied her memories, the memories the shed conjured. Her eyes instantly found the tool cabinet, the sight briefly stealing her breath. She set down the lantern and looked inside. It was old, broken, and empty but for the dust.

So small, she pondered. *I remember it being bigger.*

She stood at the very spot where she last saw her father kneeling, trying to comfort her on that fateful day. She heard his voice as clear as the breeze whistling in from the outside.

"I need you to stay here until I come to get you. Don't make a sound," he'd warned.

A murky shadow fell over Emily as the cabinet door from her memory closed.

I haven't time for this, she thought as she shook herself loose from the bitterness of the past. Thoughts of her current situation flooded her consciousness as she stepped away. *The cabinet will no longer hold me. I've grown, Papa, and I'm not hiding anymore. I'm going to find you.*

Emily went about her plan, finding a way to get a drop on the sheriff, hoping Weston and the sheriff arrived together. Unsure how long she would have to wait, Emily knew only that she must be ready when they came. She tied her horse to the post by the shed, hoping the sheriff looked there first, the more obvious place to find her. She planned to hide on the other side of the yard and catch him off guard once he had his back to her.

Emily searched the far side of the work area, looking for a suitable place to wait undetected. Finally, she spotted a small, collapsed structure. *Huh. This must have been the original shed before Papa owned the mine.* Among the rubble was the perfect spot to lie in wait. Before extinguishing the lantern, Emily loaded her gun. Alone in the darkness, she reminisced about her father, and for the first time, felt hopeful for the closure she desired. *If I can prove that Father is not buried under rock and dirt as was reported and force a confession from the sheriff, I'll have the proof I need and, hopefully, justice.* She smiled at the thought. An hour ticked by, then another, until she doubted the sheriff would ever come. *No,* she reassured herself. *He'll come.*

Just then, she heard the distant sound of a horse and wagon approaching from town. *So this is it. Please, Weston, be with the sheriff,* she silently pleaded as her heart pounded against her chest. She wiped her brow with her sleeve and took a deep breath, telling herself not to be scared.

I am not afraid. Faith over fear. She repeated it until her heartbeat slowed and her breathing calmed. *Stay alert,* she thought, tightening her grip on her gun.

Emily peeked out from the shadows as the wagon pulled up to the fence that encircled the yard, not entering it, as she had hoped. A moment later, she heard the same boorish voice she heard so many years ago, the shout of a demon without conscience. "Hey, teacher, come out here now!"

Not yet, Emily thought as she huddled in silence, closing her eyes while concentrating on her breathing. Patiently she waited, hoping to hear him walk across the yard and into the shed. Trusting that Weston was with him, she gripped the handle of her gun, her fingertip on the trigger. *Wait,* she told herself. *Not yet.*

"Teacher!" yelled the sheriff. "Hey, teacher, I brought someone to see ya." She listened carefully, unwilling to respond for fear of revealing her position. A scuffling sound came from within the wagon bed, and against her better judgment, she peeked out from her hiding place. A lantern perched on the wagon seat shone brightly. In its light, the sheriff propped someone up, someone who could barely stand on their own. *Weston!*

He was hurt. Her heart ached, and anger rose from deep within her, as did concern for her friend. *He needs medical attention. I must get him to Marco as soon as possible. But how?*

The sheriff held a knife to Weston's neck. His gun was strapped to his hip, loaded for Emily. They stood at the entrance of the yard alongside the wagon. "Hey, teacher! If ya wish young Weston to live, best come out. I know ya care about 'im and he cares about you. Weston here swore an oath, then broke it. Only one reason he'd do that. You're friends or more than that, aren't ya? So come on out. I won't wait all night."

Emily knew how this was going to end. The moment she walked into the yard and dropped her gun, the sheriff would either slash Weston's throat and shoot her or take them into custody for a public hanging. Either way, her plan had failed.

"Come out now, and I'll make it quick, show ya some mercy. There'll be no sufferin', ya have my word." He kept the blade pressed against Weston's neck.

Emily sat in the dark, her back against a pile of boards, the grip on her gun slackening. "Papa," she whispered. "I waited, just as you told me. I waited my entire life, but you didn't come back like you said you would. But I knew I would find you one day. Today was supposed to be that day, but I failed. I don't know if you can hear me, but if you can, I am asking you to please help me. Papa, help!"

When no answer came, she looked at the lonely stars and felt a cool breeze on her neck. If there would be justice, a reckoning for the crimes committed by the mayor and sheriff, she would never know it, as it became more likely by the minute that she wouldn't survive to see it. She focused on her breathing. But it wasn't up to her, only cruel fate. So little was up to her anymore. She looked through watery eyes to where the sheriff waited. Dust swirled around the demonic figure in the lamplight. She was about to stand and show herself when she heard a noise. She cocked her head to one side and squinted into the darkness.

"I'm givin' ya to the count of ten before I slice his throat," yelled the sheriff.

She could wait no longer. She stood, gun in hand. "Over here!" she called out, "just let Weston go. Please! I forced him to help me."

"There ya are. Look at that. You have a gun. Ya do realize that's a violation punishable by hangin'? And you dare point it at me," the sheriff sneered. "You're not very smart, are ya, teacher?"

"I'm pointing a gun at the man who murdered my father. If the law were fair, your crime would be punishable by death."

"How long ago was that? Ya sure can hold a grudge, can't ya? But you're only forestallin' the inevitable. So drop it and get over here."

"What about my mother, Sheriff? Murdered her as well, didn't you." It wasn't a question.

The sheriff pushed Weston forward, trying to keep him from crumbling to the ground, the knife still against his neck. "Yer ma wouldn't shut up. A few drinks and she blabbered. And now yer talkin' nonsense just like her. Put yer gun down and come over here."

Seeing movement out of the corner of her eye, Emily glanced over, but nothing was there. She continued engaging the sheriff. "Why

Christian? Tell me. And Ms. Madison, why? Was it only to cause fear, to blame a monster?"

"Yeah," said the sheriff with a chuckle. "Sorry 'bout yer boyfriend. Wrong place, wrong time. And the teacher—"

"You're the only monster!" she hollered. "You and the mayor! Your day of reckoning will come. If not now, then—"

"Nah," he interrupted. "Least of all now." The sheriff crept closer. "Like I said, I'm not willin' to wait all night, sweetheart." The sheriff took a step closer, but he didn't have to. Emily walked into the light.

"Put it down," ordered the sheriff, placing Weston between them. He motioned to the gun. "Won't do ya no good."

"Going to keep it if that's all right with you," said Emily.

Weston gasped, and a trickle of blood ran down his neck.

"Not all right. I'm starting my count. One, two . . ."

From the darkness came a low growl. A cloud of dust billowed up as a giant silhouette rose against the moon-frosted backdrop of Erebus. The beast stepped into the light, walking upright like a man, and came to stand beside Emily, its eyes never leaving the sheriff. The sheriff's eyes widened, and his grip on the knife went slack. Even with its back hunched, the beast towered over Emily.

"I suggest you drop your knife." Emily released the breath she'd been holding as the sheriff's blade hit the dirt. "And the gun? Slow, or I'll shoot and my friend here will tear your limbs off."

The monster leaned forward, growling at the sheriff, as Emily pointed her gun between the sheriff's eyes. Finally, he let go of Weston, who collapsed to the ground.

"Now, the gun!" Emily ordered.

The sheriff slowly pulled his gun from its holster, dangling it in front of him. And then, in a quick motion, he aimed and fired. With a loud bang, the bullet hit its target. Shoulder jerking back, the monster let out an ear-piercing roar. Before Emily could pull the trigger, the beast leaped through the air, knocking the sheriff off his feet, the gun flying into the dark. Before the sheriff knew what happened, the beast pinned him to the ground, pressing down hard, leaving him crying for mercy and struggling for breath. Blood from the monster's shoulder dripped onto the sheriff's chin and neck. Its coal-black eyes narrowed as it looked into the sheriff's eyes, blasts of its hot, rancid breath filling the sheriff's nostrils.

"Wait!" yelled Emily, but the monster didn't listen. Instead, it snorted and howled wildly. Emily quickly approached, pleading, "Don't kill him. Not yet!"

Baring its teeth, the beast turned and growled at Emily, causing her to stagger backward. Resisting the urge to run, she prayed, "Please, Lord. Help me not be afraid." She watched in horror as its head pivoted and its eyes narrowed in on the sheriff.

Suddenly, the beast looked up, ears straight as if an unseen something or someone spoke to it, stopping the attack. Still groaning from the discomfort of the wound and licking the blood seeping from its shoulder, the beast looked at Emily.

"Please wait," Emily pleaded. "Don't kill him. This man murdered my father, and I believe he hid his body in the mine, but I need him to show me where."

"I can show her," cried the breathless sheriff. "I know where to look. But please don't hurt me!" The sheriff looked at Emily with a fear she had never seen before. "Tell this thing to get off me, and I'll show ya," the sheriff bellowed like a coward, but the beast stayed put.

"Please," said Emily. She grabbed the sheriff's knife from the ground and cut a piece of cloth from the bottom of her skirt. With it, she applied pressure to the beast's wound. Its snarling softened, and it slowly backed away, staring intently at the sheriff, its eyes never leaving him.

"All right, Sheriff," said Emily. "You're going to show me. Let's go." She nodded toward the mine.

"I only follow orders," the sniveling sheriff said as he stood, his pants wet from urine and caked in dirt.

But Emily wasn't listening, too concerned with how she'd remove the boards blocking the entrance. It proved no barrier for the beast, who swiped at the boards, which splintered like so many matchsticks. Emily gently touched the beast's arm. "Would you keep an eye on him? I'll retrieve another lantern. Father never entered the mine without a spare. I remember that."

She moved quickly through the yard to where Weston sat in the dirt. She knelt beside him. "Can you stand with help?"

"I think so," Weston said weakly. "I don't see that I'm bleeding. Took a blow to the head. Brain's scattered is all." He rubbed his head while they slowly walked to the wagon, where he climbed into the bed and lay down. "Emmy?"

"Yes, Weston?"

"Is that what I think it is? Is that the, uh—?"

"It is," said Emily. "We feared the wrong monster, I'm afraid. This one never hurt anyone."

"It didn't?"

"No. Will you be all right alone?"

"Yes. What are you going to do?"

"I'm going to find my father."

Chapter 66

While Vernon kept guard in the front yard, Marco followed Eugene to the back lawn of the ranch house and behind the stable, where the rosebushes grew. Eugene descended the stairs into the cellar, Marco close behind. With a hammer, Eugene broke the lock and opened the door, the musty smell of earth mixed with fresh pinewood wafting into the air. Eugene leaned over and held the lantern high so he and Marco could peer inside. In the light, they saw newly fashioned crates tightly stacked with food, leaving barely enough room for them to walk.

Eugene set the lantern down and picked up a crate. "Here, take this." He handed it to Marco. "Let's take them outside." He hefted one himself, and, then, together they removed enough crates to reach the back, where Weston said they would find the confiscated guns. Eugene set the last of the crates on the pile when one slipped, fell, and broke open.

"Marco, look at this!" He reached in and brought out a glass jar. "Nellie's peach preserves. The ones I brought to the first appeasement. There's no doubt now that Weston told the truth."

And just as Weston promised, they found a small armory at the rear of the cellar. In less than an hour, they'd loaded them all in the wagon. Marco recognized one of the long guns and picked it up. He admired the shiny brass screws, the golden patch box, and the maple stock.

"Eugene," he said, "mind if I take this one? It was LeFevre's. I imagine he would want me to have it."

"It's yours. Promise to put it to good use. That's also what he would want."

Marco nodded. Holding it reminded him of walking through the gorge, LeFevre tightly gripping the gun. Then he remembered feeling Emily close and watching Bronson and LeFevre dangle at the gallows, their lives choked out. "No question," said Marco. "Putting it to good use—that's what he would want."

Eugene patted him on the back. "Best hurry, Marco. It's getting late. It took longer than I thought."

"I'll start with the farmers, like you said," said Marco. "I know the St. Clairs, Morgans, and Thompsons will help us. Care if I take Vern with me? I have another matter I must attend to and I could use his help."

"By all means, take Vern with you. Spread the word and gather as many as possible, then let's meet at the town center park. I'll have the guns there, ready to hand out. Just be sure to get there before sunrise."

Marco gathered Vernon, and together they headed to the stable for their horses.

"Tell them to hurry!" called Eugene. "We haven't much time."

"I will," said Marco as he mounted his horse. Vern sat next to him, ready to ride. *Then I need to find Emmy,* he thought. *She's up to something.*

Chapter 67

The mine went deep into the heart of Erebus's coal beds, a confusing web of tunnels, chambers, loops, and dead ends spreading out in every direction. So perilous was the labor that a miner entering knew the possibility of being swallowed by the dark, never again to see the azure sky or stars at night. For most miners, it took months of working the mine, perhaps years, to feel confident navigating its depths. If Emily's father's body lay here, she might never have hoped to locate it alone. Only someone who knew his whereabouts in the maze of tunnels had a chance of finding him. And that someone was the sheriff, who now led Emily and the monster deep into the void.

As they entered, its abandoned state became apparent. The wooden support beams appeared tired, as if struggling under the weight of the mountain. The air was cold, bone dry, and unmoving, as if dead. Emily rubbed the bumps on her arms and could see her breath in the dim lamplight. With each step, the narrow tunnel devoured the moonlight coming in from the entry. It took just a few steps before the only light came from their lanterns, while all around, the threat of dirt and rock caving in on them threatened to turn the mine into a permanent grave. The inky blackness licked at the flickering light, nearly dousing the flames and abandoning them to the dark.

Approximately every nine feet, depending on the loose grade of the earth and the likelihood of collapse, they passed support beams. Only where the earth turned gravelly were the support beams more closely spaced.

The monster's mass bumped a beam, causing dirt and dust to cascade down. Emily coughed, the stale air and dust drying her throat.

She ran her fingers through her hair, feeling the pebbles embedded there. Turning her head, she spat, then tucked the gun under her arm and pulled her blouse over her nose with one hand while holding the lantern with the other. How had her father endured this day after day?

Emily followed at the rear, keeping the beast between herself and the sheriff, the beast's girth preventing Emily from seeing what lay ahead. She had only to follow. Each time the tunnel led in a different direction, Emily imagined how frightened the sheriff must be while guiding them through the maze of tunnels. She noticed how they slowed each time the tunnel split and the sheriff decided which direction to go. How did he know the way?

Ever deeper they went, and with every step the sheriff took, he did so tentatively, lantern held out in front of him. Each time the path diverged, the sheriff navigated under the hulking figure of the beast who smelled of wet dog and breathed menacingly behind him.

They took a left, then went right twice, then left again. Emily tried to memorize the route, just in case. Then, up ahead, they encountered three separate tunnels. The sheriff didn't hesitate, continuing straight, the monster and Emily following. How would she ever remember the sequence? Then, just before the tunnel split again, she noticed that every time the tunnel split, someone had marked the crossbeams with a subtle white blotch.

The sheriff followed these markings, she realized. He must have marked the tunnels when he hid her father's body. It would be far too easy to get lost or have one's lantern run dry long before finding the way out. Such a mistake could mean certain death if no one knew where to search.

Emily inhaled as deeply as she could through her blouse. It felt like taking a shallow sip. She felt light-headed, her breathing feeling more labored in the thinning air, their lanterns using more oxygen than their share. She hoped it wouldn't be much farther, and as that thought crossed her mind, she noticed they were slowing.

"There!" said the sheriff, pointing. "Looks bottomless, but it's not that far down. I've shown ya where. Now let me go."

Emily didn't reply. Sheriff Weasley wasn't going anywhere. She needed him to confess his guilt in front of the entire town before this was through. She cautiously ventured forward, the monster placing himself between Emily and the sheriff, pinning him against the rock wall. A small tunnel broke off the central passage to the left, the crossbeam above it nearly all white.

"Let me go," he repeated more urgently. "It'll be our secret. I can assure ya the girl will be safe. Or you can come for me in the night if ya wish."

Ignoring the sheriff, Emily entered the tunnel, her lantern revealing little aside from what appeared to be a very dark area.

"What's that smell?" she asked when a putrid odor like that of spoiled meat stung her nostrils—a recent kill.

The sheriff remained quiet, still cowering next to the monster, but he didn't have to answer. Emily knew. She took another step and nearly slipped. *I better be careful,* she thought, realizing the gravel beneath her feet and the slope posed significant danger. She inched her way forward, lantern in one hand, and steadied herself on the rock wall with the other until she came to a shaft that dropped straight down into a bed of coal.

Emily contemplated what it would take to see anything at the bottom, let alone retrieve a body. It was far too deep to climb down. Even if she could descend, it would be impossible to climb out. *Papa, if you're down there,* she thought, *I'll have to come back with men and ropes to get you.* It was then she had a thought. *I can follow the white paint on the beams again.*

Suddenly, something light at the bottom of the shaft caught her eye. She struggled to comprehend when she suddenly realized she was looking at a white shirt.

Emily cried out, "Sheriff, what have you done?" She continued peering into the pit. The longer she stared, the more the dim shapes became apparent and what she saw made sense. Next to the shirt was a child's brown leather shoe, a woman's matted blonde hair, a torn and filthy cotton nightgown practically covered in coal dust, and the back of a hand.

Young Matthew! she realized. *The Stewarts—they're all here! So this is where they've hidden the bodies.* She peered farther into the pit. *Papa, are you down there?* She was unprepared for the rage that built within her. She moved back a bit as the monster approached. She wanted it to see. She wanted the entirety of New Harmony to see the evidence and demand justice. She looked back at Sheriff Weasley, who watched her sheepishly, still holding a lantern. She could see the desperation on his face. Emily imagined he thought of escaping, but that was unlikely. Now that she had the evidence of their crimes, flight would be fatal. They wouldn't need his confession.

Emily held the lantern over the shaft as the monster moved forward. Crouched on its massive haunches, almost motionless, it leaned forward and peered down. Its black lips glistened with foamy moisture, and the sound of its breathing reverberated throughout the quiet tunnel. The beast snarled and bared its teeth.

"Thank you," Emily whispered, "deliverer of justice." Her appreciation for the beast grew by the minute. She tenderly put a hand on its massive head, resisting the fear conjured by its grotesque face and powerful jaw.

Then Emily heard a thud, and the monster toppled forward, the ground beneath it crumbling under its weight. Emily watched as it fell into the shaft. Stunned, she turned to see the sheriff picking himself up, having thrown all his weight at the beast. Emily dropped her lantern and reached for the gun tucked under her arm. She heard the breaking of glass as the flame extinguished. In that moment of confusion, the sheriff shoved her into the pit.

In the faint glow of the sheriff's lantern, she could see that the monster held her in its arms, having cushioned her fall. As it set her down, she teetered on the bodies under her feet, the stench overwhelming her. Her stomach convulsed violently, and she vomited, throwing her farther off balance. Regaining her equilibrium, she covered her nose with her blouse again and looked up. High above her stood the sheriff.

"Ya wanted to find yer pa, didn't ya? There he is. Say hello!"

The beast growled.

Overcome with the horror of her situation, Emily cried out, "People are on to you, Sheriff! Everyone knows you're a murderer! You're not getting away with this!"

He burst into uncontrollable laughter. "Stupid girl, I already have. It's time we collapse this mine. What do ya think? Some dynamite? For public safety, of course. Wouldn't want anyone else goin' missin' in here."

Emily screamed, "Get us out of here!"

The sound of Sheriff Weasley's laughter faded down the tunnel, the light of his lantern eventually disappearing and leaving them in pitch-blackness.

When all fell silent but for the beast's breathing, a tearful Emily said, "I am not afraid. Faith over fear. Your hands, Father—if it be Thy will. I'm not afraid," she repeated. "Faith over fear. Your hands, Father, but only if it be Thy will." But the words were not enough to keep her from sobbing.

After what seemed like hours, Emily felt the beast's fur against her as it softly huffed and growled.

"It's all my fault," she whispered in despair. Thoughts of her father drifted up from the heap of discarded bones and tattered clothing soon to be her final resting place.

"Papa," she whispered and felt the monster move beside her. She didn't care if it heard her. "I found you, Papa," she said. "At least I did that. I can die knowing where you are. There's comfort in knowing we'll be together soon." Tears running down her cheeks, she wondered how long she would have to wait for death to retrieve her.

Chapter 68

"Wait here!" hollered the mayor.

Hyrum set the brake and jumped down, nearly toppling over with the shifting of time and place. Mount Erebus played its tricks again, and though silent, the earth under his feet oscillated as if an earthquake vibrated the mountain. He steadied himself by leaning against the wagon and looked at the mayor.

"Get all this unloaded," the mayor ordered as he dismounted and knocked on the outpost door. Then, stepping back, he waited.

What I've come to ask for, thought the mayor, *is unpleasant. How to even ask? My own son—a treasonous thorn. Martha would have it fester, unwilling to do the hard thing.*

As it had before, the door creaked open by unseen hands, the fireplace within suddenly springing to life. The mayor leaned inside and spoke into the darkness.

"We have it, the sustenance. And plenty of it."

A gravelly voice came from inside. "Shepherd's pie?"

"I believe so. Not certain, but likely." The mayor looked to where broken crates and shattered bottles from their last visit lay scattered. The dark figures slithered out the door and moved cautiously to the wagon, keeping their eyes on the mayor. Hyrum unloaded the offering while Ernie unpacked the wine bottles. Jonas watched without lifting so much as a finger. Baking several loaves of cornmeal bread and a raspberry tart, which was enough work as far as he was concerned, gave him an excuse to sit and watch. Once everything lay on the ground and the crates had been opened, the old hags sat down to eat. They ate as slowly as thick tar poured from a bucket. With each chew of their protruding jaws, they peered over their pointy noses at the mayor as if waiting for something more.

The mayor tapped his foot nervously. "Please excuse any abruptness on my part. It's just that, well, can we possibly hurry this along?"

But the creatures ignored him, slowly pinching a little food here and reaching to sample another bite there. They selected what most suited them and brought it to their gaping mouths. They chewed like vultures, bit by bit, never taking their eyes off the mayor.

Though the mayor grew impatient, he knew better than to push his luck, not with these foul creatures.

Taking their time, they nibbled and stared, stared and nibbled, waiting for something, or so it seemed. Without the mayor knowing, the alliance teetered in the balance. But the nasty vermin, slowly chewing on sustenance, they knew.

Chapter 69

In the pitch-black, Emily leaned against the beast, listening to the rhythm of his breathing as it rocked her gently back and forth. How frightened she once was, but not anymore. The motion calmed her, and she prayed.

"Dear Father, which art in heaven. Hear me pray." She stopped and listened. The massive beast shifted beside her. She started again. "Dear Father, which art in heaven. Hear *us* pray. We give thanks for bringing me to my father and finding the others so cruelly murdered. And we are not afraid. We put our trust in Thee. And if this is our appointed time and we are to see the morning light on the other side of this life, then so be it. We accept Thy will. But we ask and pray that there is more You would have us do. If there is, let us see the light of day. Deliver us from this darkness. We pray and trust that Thy will be done." Emily sat in silence, still listening to the breathing of the giant beside her.

When the beast shifted again, Emily asked, "What are you doing?" More shifting. "What do you want me to do?" Something lifted her arm. It came to rest over what felt like a broad, furry shoulder. "You want me to hold on to you? Is that it?"

The beast grunted, then lifted her hand and pressed it against its head. Emily suddenly realized it nodded. "You want me to hold on?" Another nod. "Yes," she said, "you're saying yes!"

She stretched an arm over its other shoulder, the side injured by the sheriff's bullet. The beast winced. "I'm sorry. I'll be careful." Another nod. She could feel the fur, wet and sticky from the warm blood seeping from the wound. She clasped her hands tightly together.

The beast's furry bulk quickly shifted, and its claws extended. Emily felt its muscles rippling under its fur coat and realized she was being lifted. Then came a jarring heave, and the muscley mass of hair shifted again. Another twist and dirt, coal, and small rocks fell past her. Emily could feel her feet dangling above the void.

Time slowed as each shift in weight moved her from side to side, moving ever upward. Emily clung more tightly to the beast, who grunted as its claws dug into the coal bed. Again, she felt a push upward as they slowly moved into invisible space.

Suddenly, Emily recalled the light shining through the church's colorful stained-glass window and the depiction of a frightened Peter lifted from turbulent waters. "Lord," she whispered. The beast paused. "Save us," she said.

With those words, the beast appeared to gather strength, moving more deliberately upward. Emily's strength, however, began to wane, her grip weakening. She was about to let go when the beast set her down on the hard ground. She felt around on her hands and knees, sensing they were out of the pit, her exhilaration quickly replaced by the stark realization that they would never find their way out without a lantern.

The monster let out a growl so loud Emily had to cover her ears. Did it also realize they were doomed?

She threw her arms around the beast. "I'm sorry. Truly, I am," she whispered. She buried her head in its fur and felt comforted by its warmth. And then her father's last words came to her through the darkness. "When it's time, I'll come get you. Don't be afraid!" She remembered her conversation with the parson and repeated his words aloud. "Let not your heart be troubled, neither let it be afraid."

She put her hands on the beast's head and said, "I wish I knew your name. You have a name, don't you?" She felt it nod. "May I call you friend? For you certainly are." She heard another snort, and there came another nod.

"I don't know how it will happen, my friend, but we will see the light of day. The parson told me I'd be imprisoned in the dark, just as he once was, and only then would I see the light. Well, I see the light, my friend. We're getting out of here. I don't know how. I only know that we are. That's how it works."

Emily heard what sounded like sniffing. Then she felt a gentle push at her back, and the beast lifted her to her feet and propelled her forward. She held her hands above her head to avoid bumping it on the ceiling or walking into a support beam. As the beast sniffed and they continued to move forward, Emily suddenly realized it followed a scent—the sheriff's.

Emily took hold of the monster's fur, no longer pushed along but led through the dark. They made slow progress in quick but short steps. She knew they would reach the entrance eventually. Her concern was for Weston. Would they arrive in time?

Chapter 70

Somewhere ahead of Emily and the beast, the sheriff hobbled through the tunnels, following the white marks in the light of his lantern. He could hardly believe his good fortune, having barely escaped the monster. If it hadn't been for his quick thinking, he might already be dead. Adding to his exuberance, up ahead, a moonbeam streamed through the entrance. He'd almost freed himself from the bowels of Erebus when he heard a roar from deep within the mountain. *No,* he thought. *It can't be!*

He stumbled out of the tunnel and into the yard, searching for his gun and knife. Seeing a glint of steel in the dirt, he tossed Emily's gun aside and retrieved his own. Then he headed straight for the wagon. His first order of business was to take care of the traitor. Heading to the back, he peered into the bed, only to find it empty.

Worse, Emily's horse was missing. Somehow, Weston had recovered enough to ride back into town. Behind the sheriff, a loud growl echoed from the mine.

The beast is comin'! I gotta hurry! What kinda sick person befriends a monster? he wondered. *An abomination is what she is. The teacher deserves a miserable death.*

As the growling intensified, the sheriff quickly hobbled back to the entrance. He pressed his back against the cold, hard rock where he'd be hidden when the creature emerged. There, he waited, gun primed and ready, his hand shaking. It wouldn't be long before sunrise, and he was determined to put the beast down before then. After that, he'd drag Emily back to town and hang her and Weston together. He grinned at the thought of pulling the lever.

As it emerged from the mine, the beast turned its head toward the sheriff, ready to spring, but not in time. There was a loud bang before it could attack, followed by a scream from within the mine.

The sheriff began reloading, never taking his eyes from the heap of monstrous flesh lying in the dirt. He cautiously approached with powder charge and ball ready, lightly kicked the beast, and stepped back. When he got no response, he did it again with the same result. Satisfied, he turned his attention to the teacher. Holding his lantern high, he peered into the mine. Staring back at him was Emily, caught in his light, crouched down and hugging a support beam.

"Thought I'd take ya to the mayor, but no! I'll have no more trouble from ya. Be no hangin' either. Nah, I'm gonna take ya back so ya can be with yer pa, just like ya asked me to."

The eastern horizon began to glow with the coming sun. Emily retreated farther into the darkness of the mine. His lust for revenge demanded he kill her now. Holstering his pistol, he searched for his knife. Shooting her wouldn't do. Too easy. A knife was more personal. He wanted to enjoy this. His eyes locked on his blade as the first beams of morning light illuminated the area. He pulled it from the powdery dirt and stared back into the mine, eager to pursue his prey, when suddenly he stopped and turned around. Behind him, the beast stirred. Then, to his horror, its massive body rose from the dirt. It narrowed its black eyes and bared its glistening white teeth.

Startled, the sheriff dropped the knife and reached for his pistol, but it slipped out of his hand before his trembling finger could find the trigger. He dropped to his knees, sifting through the dirt, looking for it. Panicked, he looked back over his shoulder. The roar that came from the monster chilled the sheriff to the bone and caused him to shake uncontrollably. He gasped, let out a whine, and went for his knife, but it was too late. A single leap and bite to the neck tore his carotid artery and collapsed his windpipe. Blood gushed from the wound as the beast stood, its jaws still around the sheriff's neck, and whipped him about like a doll before tossing him to the dirt, severing his head entirely from his body.

The monster slumped on all four paws before tumbling to the ground. Emily ran out of the mine and into the yard, kneeling at its side. "Please, please don't die! Breathe! You must breathe!" She watched its chest rise and fall more and more slowly. Its eyes, barely open, stared back at her. Emily cradled its head in her lap and gently touched its face. She was once terrified to look at it, but this was no monster.

She watched as the beasts' gaze grew distant, staring at something she couldn't see.

Chapter 71

"This is not what we agreed on! Not at all what I wanted." Jonathan was both pleading and adamant.

"Alliance sealed!" hissed the ancient and shadowy figures. "You requested; we provided—simple as that."

"No, no, that's not what happened. I didn't intend to kill anyone, least of all the woman and her children. I never agreed to that! Only, the land—the land he took was rightfully mine. I'd already filed the paperwork and—"

"Our alliance is a contract, young Jonathan, a contract you signed with your blood. Why else would it require you pay with blood? Would you rather pay our fee with your blood or the blood of your enemies?"

"He was not an enemy, least of all his wife and children. I didn't want what happened. I only wanted what was mine. I swear you tricked me."

"Tricked you? And how do you suppose we did that, hmm? We offered you what belonged to him, and you felt entitled to take it, all of it. Burning his house voided his claim to the land. Without the requirement of building his home, his deed was void."

"I had my reasons, my justifications, but I am not a murderer."

"Oh yes, you are," said a sickly voice. "You made your choice, young Jonathan. But it is never too late. Every contract comes with an escape clause," the voice wheezed. "If you sacrifice your blood, our contract becomes void and your soul is redeemed. But for now, since you signed the agreement, you must live with the terms. Only one death can set you free, so be careful not to die needlessly."

"But I didn't fully understand the arrangement. I never would have agreed had I known!" said Jonathan. "You made me a murderer!"

"Who lit the fire? The Southern gentleman's wife and children perished at whose hand? And all for something you desired—to claim their land as yours. Isn't that what you asked for?"

"I don't care, nor will I deliver your sustenance or whatever nonsense. Only wanted blood, and that wasn't the deal we made." Jonathan held back the rage behind the tears streaming down his face. The sight of the children's corpses burned, the barrel empty of accelerant in his hands, was more than he could bear.

Then came the voices he could never hope to escape. "Offer penitence or pay the price."

"But how? Tell me how."

The more ancient one finished the riddle. "A payment in blood. Only your blood will suffice—nothing short of a fair trade. Blood for blood, the proper sacrifice."

Another voice echoed within his skull. "You cannot run. We'll find you and settle your debt."

The trio of loathsome voices chanted. "What matters to us are your sins, not your concerns or regrets. They matter nothing to us. However, your soul? Oh yes! Oh yes!"

Their ancient black garb suddenly transformed into feathers, and three blackbirds took flight, leaving Jonathan with his thoughts.

What have I done? he contemplated as fear washed over him. There would be hell to pay. *My wife,* he thought. *Will they exact revenge on my wife? Does her blood factor into the contract?*

He was a day's ride from home. He took strips of meat from his pouch and ate as he rode through the wooded hills, stopping only once to drink at a stream and rest his horse. It would be nightfall before he arrived, and his wife would be worried. She had taken ill and required his help for even her most basic needs. He loved her, and she loved and needed him. He'd made the deal for her, for their future together, with the resources in land and crops they needed. The sisters had promised prosperity, enough for Jonathan to properly care for his ailing wife, but they'd failed to mention the price.

Not much farther, he thought as he rode. *Soon I'll be in her arms. Dare I pray as much?*

In the distance, above the trees, he saw a yellow haze. The pungent odor of burning wood and debris hung thick in the air. He spurred his horse to a full gallop as he exited the woods into the clearing that skirted his home. Men on horseback watched the inferno in front of them. He saw the Southerner, the man whose house he'd burned and whose family he'd killed. Others with rifles and torches circled the smoldering ruins. Suddenly, a bloodcurdling scream issued from within the burning structure.

"Jonathan! Jonathan! Help me!"

For Jonathan, it was more than a memory of that dreadful day. It was as if he were there, witnessing the horror, hearing his love cry out to him. *I was too frightened, too worried about myself. I didn't even try to save her!* He wept in self-condemnation, his sorrow as deep as an ocean of tears. *I should have rushed into the fire, picked her up from her sickbed, or died with her. But what did I do?* He struggled to remember. Then, to his horror, everything came rushing back, his memory restored. He'd run into the woods as fast and as far as his horse could take him. He'd looked back at the fiery nightmare. *The fire was meant for me, but I abandoned my wife and lost my soul. Fleeing into the wilderness, I lost my humanity and became a monster.*

The beast peered out through mournful eyes, his fate realized and owned. *I understand now why I ran and from what. The memory brings unbearable pain!* Hot tears ran down Jonathan's face. *I remember my wife. Yes, her. It was her voice, the one who called after me. I even remember her name—Grace. My dear Grace!*

Jonathan's thoughts drifted back further in time. He remembered his first meeting with Grace as she wrapped potatoes in her apron at the market. He remembered their walks and lying next to her at the day's end. He remembered watching her garden, holding her hand as she suffered from the illness, calling for the doctor, and praying she would not suffer. In his mind, he stared longingly into her eyes and felt her hands gently holding his face. He relished her touch and her voice.

"Breathe! You can't die." He heard these words, felt her so close, reaching beyond time and touching him, urging him to take another breath. But, instead, he stared blankly as his vision went dark even though his eyes remained wide open.

The lantern dimmed as the earth rotated toward the sun, emerging from the shadows. Emily kept her vigil, the beast's head cradled in her lap. She touched its cheek and felt not fur but a smoothness. She looked down to see its jaw shrink, its entire body changing. It happened so gently, as if she watched something natural, something entirely expected. There was no shock to it, no surprise, only wonder. Locks of long brown hair cascaded over her hands and into her lap. When the transformation was complete, she held not a beast but a man.

"Please don't die," Emily pleaded. "Breathe! You must breathe!"

The man's eyes drifted back to Emily, an expression of recognition in them. When his lips moved in an attempt to speak, Emily put her ear to his mouth and heard a faint whisper. "My name is Jonathan."

No sooner had he spoken than his eyes focused on something just above them. "My dear Grace, have you come for me?"

Emily watched as tears pooled at the corners of his eyes.

"Forgive me," he said. "My love, please forgive me!"

Jonathan looked at Emily once again, and although he may have seemed confused about who was at his side, whether Emily or someone else, it didn't matter. What mattered was that he, Jonathan, was not alone in his final moments, either in this world or the next.

He stretched his arms up as if reaching for someone, then brought his hands close to his face. "My hands," he said quietly. "These are my hands."

As Jonathan slipped from this world into the next, his eyes remained fixed on whatever lay beyond. As the last breath of air escaped his lungs, Emily gently closed them.

Chapter 72

"What are they doing?" Ernie whispered as they watched the witches nibbling at the food and peering back at them.

"The way they stare at us," Hyrum whispered, "it's unsettling. What do they wait for?"

"Haven't any idea," said the mayor. "Ernie, is there anything we've overlooked? Everything's unloaded?"

"Of course, sir. It's all there. They're just staring at it."

The mayor excused himself and approached the hags as they sampled the substantial offering. He tried again to say something to the unresponsive audience as they chewed and stared. "Excuse my impertinence. May I speak?"

They continued staring as if the mayor hadn't said a word. The sun was near rising, and the mayor grew impatient. Finally, he went to where Hyrum and Ernie waited.

Ernie was most concerned. "What do we do?" he asked.

"We wait," said the mayor. "We can't leave yet. I've urgent business I must discuss with them, a way to get rid of my son without Martha blaming me."

Suddenly, the creatures screamed, "Our monster is dead!" Then, turning away from the offering, their black, hooded eyes stared hard at the mayor, who stumbled backward as if punched.

"What's wrong?" he pleaded. "I've done everything you asked. Look, the sustenance," he pointed at the offering. "It's here, just as you asked!" The mayor's desperation caused the others to quiver in fear.

"Alliance broken! Penitence is paid by one, and now penitence is owed by another!" They pointed bony fingers at the mayor, who fell to the ground, terrified.

Startled, Hyrum, Jonas, and Ernie fled, leaving the mayor in the dirt. They ran as fast as their legs would move before being picked up by some unknown force and thrown backward. Suddenly, the wagon spun in the air, along with the crates, food, bottles of wine, and even the horses—all of it caught in some kind of tornado, tumbling about as the mist churned, digesting them whole. As they watched everything spinning and spinning, they heard a loud bang and felt a forceful impact, like a cannon blasting a ball into their guts. Then everything disappeared into nothingness.

Chapter 73

From the north came a lone rider, slumped over his horse, slowly carried into town. Weston held on, trying hard to keep from losing consciousness and falling to the ground. *Gotta get help for Emmy,* he thought, *if I'm not too late.*

Not far from the town, Weston felt a change come over him—a sensation akin to his sinuses draining and his head clearing. He entertained new thoughts, thoughts previously considered forbidden. He even had ideas that now made perfect sense, ideas that previously seemed unreasonable.

For a moment, he felt naked and vulnerable. How strange to operate entirely under his own will, without fear, without the reasoning of a lunatic. The spell that had once bound him and the town dissipated into thin air, but not before he heard these departing words:

Your mayor had you fooled.
But you were willfully misled,
The monster that you feared,
For you, its blood was shed.

Your compliance is what matters,
It fed your mayor's delight.
He did not cause the sun to shine.
He lied to you in spite.

With Apate's charms, he spoke to you,
She, the goddess of deceit.
By such means, he grew in power,
To murder, steal, and cheat.

> *Foolish to listen and follow a foe,*
> *Now his fate for you to seal.*
> *Your mayor has no power here.*
> *Do with him as you will.*

Weston struggled with a new reality. *There is no need for a curfew,* he realized. *There is no need for the appeasement offering, nor do we depend on the mayor to save the town.* And then he marveled. *What I thought was my own reasoning seems so foreign to me now.*

Weston turned his thoughts to Emily's welfare. He remembered lying on the ground, hearing the sheriff calling for her to come out into the open. Then came a scuffle and the howling of a beast. *Did the sheriff kill Emmy? Did the monster harm her?* Weston was as determined as he was injured. He rode past the town center park, heading directly for the ranch. When he rode through the gate, the sun was already up.

"Help!" he hollered. "Emily needs help!"

The stable doors swung open, and Eugene and Marco ran into the yard, followed by several other men, all armed and ready.

"Get him down," Eugene insisted. He and Marco caught him as he slid off the saddle and into their arms. He struggled to speak as they laid him on the manicured grass.

"Someone needs to help her! Emily—she needs help!"

Marco examined Weston's head wound. "Where is she?" he asked. "Tell me! Quickly!"

"The old mine north of town."

Marco turned to Eugene. "Get him inside. I'll see to Emily."

"Be careful," said Weston. "The sheriff's with her. She may already be . . ."

"Take Stu with you," said Eugene. "Go quickly!"

Marco rode north as fast as he could, rifle in hand. Stuart St. Clair ran to the stable to retrieve his horse, unwilling to let Marco face the sheriff alone.

"Eugene?" said Weston.

"I'm still here."

"Did you hear the voices, the rhyme about your father?"

"We all heard it."

"I'm sorry," he said. "I know he's your father."

"No need," said Eugene. "You were right about him. The time of pretending and looking the other way is over. What that means for the future is uncertain."

"Your father will be returning soon. I'll need a gun."

"Your fight is over, Mr. Riley. You've done enough."

Nellie came running from the house. "Eugene, bring him inside." He and several of his parents' ranch hands, including Skinny, carried Weston to the front door. Nellie held it open, but they stopped before entering.

"Ma'am, we're not allowed in," said Skinny.

"You are from now on. Now bring him inside!"

"Yes, ma'am," said Skinny, and they carried Weston into the house.

Chapter 74

Once the whirling and tumbling slowed and the mist evaporated, Hyrum found himself sitting on the wagon, the brake set and reins gripped tightly in his hands. He looked back to see the mayor, Jonas, and Ernie on horseback, their mounts neighing and stomping about nervously.

"What just happened?" Hyrum asked. The others stared at him blankly. "Was it night and now it's day in the blink of an eye?"

As they all struggled to comprehend their strange circumstances, the mayor asked, "Where's the wall?"

Ernie shook his head. "What wall?"

"The wall!" the mayor hollered. "The misty wall. Where is it? It was right there!" The mayor pointed to the trail in front of them.

Hyrum dropped the reins, holding his head, feeling dizzy and scared. Ernie and Jonas still contended with their frightened animals. All they remembered was arriving at the effervescent gate. They'd stopped before passing through it when, suddenly, night turned to day. Each man felt a sense of déjà vu, like he had done this only hours earlier. But it was only a feeling.

"Get moving!" shouted the mayor.

Hyrum looked behind him expecting to see an empty wagon bed, but instead, it was full of food and unopened crates.

"Hyrum, what did I tell you?" The mayor looked at the others, addressing them all. "We're dealing with tricksters, so keep your wits about you. I don't care if the mountain crumbles beneath us. That appeasement must be delivered. Now move!"

Hyrum went to release the brake when he heard a melody play in his head. The expressions on the faces of the others told him they, too, heard it. The sultry voices that once held their emotions captive now only delivered a notice, as if someone read a letter. "Your mayor had you fooled," said the voices. "But you were willfully misled, the monster that you feared, for you, its blood was shed," and so on. Finally, it ended with, "Your mayor has no power here. Do with him as you will." Then came a deep silence, as if the mountain had fallen into slumber.

Frightened, the mayor looked at each man. They all stared back, their expressions saying it all. Everything had changed.

"No, no, no. It can't be!" Spittle flew from the mayor's mouth as he raged. "How dare they!"

A nervous Hyrum looked away. Ernie's eyes widened, and Jonas looked off to the side, too frightened to meet the mayor's gaze and unable to grasp the implications of what he had just heard.

"We have an agreement!" the mayor screamed. "Their sustenance is right here! Each of you, listen to me. I will deliver it! The agreement holds. I'll see to it like I always do!" The mayor dismounted Buck and hurried to where Hyrum sat on the wagon. "Get down from there! I'll deliver it myself. You three, get back to town, find the sheriff. Make sure everyone is locked down. Shoot anyone who gets in your way. We don't need them up there. We can handle this ourselves. Now get moving!"

The mayor climbed onto the wagon and took the reins while the others turned their horses and headed toward New Harmony. Without the dark powers magically smoothing their way, the trail was much more precarious, requiring more time to descend. Strangely, as they descended, they felt a clearing of their heads, and each questioned the wisdom of aligning themselves with strange beings, though they kept those thoughts to themselves.

Chapter 75

As the sunlight warmed the eastern fields, people emerged from their houses, set free from the spell.

A wagon loaded with unclaimed guns pulled up to the town hall.

"Keep an eye on these," said Eugene. "I'll be back shortly." He climbed down and handed a rifle to Old Man Taylor, who sat in the wagon beside him. He headed to the sheriff's office and walked through the broken door, his keys jingling in his pocket.

"Good morning, Mother."

"Not at all," said Martha. "I sincerely hope you've come to your senses." She moved uncomfortably, her hand on the small of her back.

"I certainly have. I've come to my senses, so thank you."

"Sarcasm is not becoming of you. I taught you better than that. I'm your mother. Have you forgotten? And where is your father?"

"Knowing you are my mother only adds to my heartache. And we both know where he is. He's on the mountain, scheming with the devil."

"You've lost your grip, son. You are delusional. You know that, don't you? This won't end well for you, though there may still be time."

"Who knows how it will turn out?" said Eugene. He took hold of the shackles that hung on an iron nail. "I need you to wear these."

"What for?"

"Letting you out." Eugene opened the door and walked inside the cell. "Hands. Let's see them."

"No!" she yelled and kept her hands held rigidly at her sides. "I'm not some common criminal. I'm your mother."

"So you've said. Hands, Mother. Now!"

"We did everything—everything for you! My only crime was having you!"

"Or saving grace. That'd be my take on it. But I'm done trying to reason with you."

"Bah, we both know what you are. Ungrateful. Disrespectful. A horrible son. I should have drowned you the moment I pushed you out."

"Sorry you feel that way. Interesting how the tides of fortune rise and fall. Only recently, you were threatening me. I suppose I shouldn't take it personally, though, should I? You and Papa killed how many innocent people? So hands out! Now!"

"I didn't hug you enough. That it?"

"Now, Mother. You know who raised me; your servants did that. I failed to understand their coldness toward me until I was older. Then, one day, it occurred to me. I was your son, and you mistreated them. It all made perfect sense."

"You know, I stopped your father once from ridding you of the life I gave you. But I won't stop him this time. When he returns, and he will, you'll hang! And I, your mother, won't shed a tear."

"We'll see." Eugene looked over his shoulder and yelled, "Mr. Taylor?"

A faint voice answered from outside. "Ya?"

"Give the bell three rings. Call the people. Let's see what they say once they know the truth." He turned to his mother. "Are you as curious as I am?"

"Be right back," they heard from outside.

In the distance, the bell rang loudly. Bong, bong, bong.

Chapter 76

Wagon weighed down with food, the mayor whipped the horses. He couldn't arrive at the old guard post fast enough. He wasn't about to allow the decrepit old crones out of their deal. *They'd better be there!* he thought, growing angrier the closer he got. *Have they forgotten our agreement? They can't abandon me. I won't allow it! I'm doing all the work, gathering their food, bringing it up this godforsaken mountain, hanging people—none of it easy. They should be grateful. If they wish to renegotiate the terms, I'm willing, but they are not breaking the deal. I'm the mayor. I can run them off!*

Time moved forward, unencumbered, as it would on any typical day. The sun shone brightly overhead when the mayor arrived at the old fort. He pulled back on the reins and stopped.

Everything was as it should be. The mayor struggled to grasp a reality that no longer existed. *No mist? No shifting time?* "Where are you?" he called out. Walls no longer held up the roof. It lay collapsed and decayed. The tree out front where he had tied Buck was nothing more than a stump. There wasn't even a door, broken crates, or shattered bottles, only the buzzing of the typical fly.

"We must talk!" he shouted. "I know you can hear me! I'll sit here all day if need be. I demand you come out!" He sat on the stump and waited. He looked up, hoping to see the blackbirds circling overhead, but he saw nothing but the azure sky. Beads of sweat stung his eyes, and he wiped his sleeve across his brow.

He heard something move behind him and quickly turned around. But it was only a mouse weaving through sticks and leaves until it disappeared into a small hole. It was then he heard a sound from the valley below. He stood to listen, then walked through the pines to the edge of the ridge, where he peered down. He heard it again—the school bell, calling people to gather at the town center.

Chapter 77

Marco rode as fast as he could on the same dirt road Emily had walked so many years ago on her eighth birthday, the last time she'd seen her father alive. The closer he got, the more forcefully the wind blew. Marco noticed a wagon parked just outside as he rode through the wooden gate into the yard. Squinting through a cloud of dust, he dismounted with his rifle. Someone knelt on the ground. He approached carefully. "Emmy?" he whispered.

Not far from where she knelt, a man's body lay motionless, the ground around him blood-soaked. Marco approached Emily, the barrel of his gun at the ready. In Emily's lap lay another man, lifeless and naked. His bare feet and hands were calloused, his body dirty. Emily leaned over him, her hands gently cradling his head.

"Emmy?" When she remained silent, Marco knelt beside her. "Are you all right?"

Quietly, she answered, "Yes, Marco."

He looked over again at the body a short distance away. "The sheriff?"

"Yes."

"And this one?"

Emily looked up. Through tears, she stared into Marco's eyes. "This is Jonathan. He brought us the sheriff's hat." She looked down and cried. "I don't have anything to cover him with," she said through her tears. "He deserves his dignity. Will you help me?"

"I'll be right back," said Marco. He pulled the saddle off the horse and grabbed the blanket underneath, then returned and placed it over Jonathan.

"Thank you, Marco."

"Are you certain? This is a man. We both know who brought us the hat."

"I was here, right here, when he changed, Marco."

"Changed?"

"Yes, changed, and he saved my life."

"I . . ." Marco was at a loss for words.

"I don't intend for you to understand, not now, but . . ."

"All right, later, then. Let's get back to town."

Together, they lifted Jonathan and placed him in the wagon, leaving the sheriff's body where it lay.

"I'm afraid we must hurry," urged Marco. "It would be best to arrive before the mayor returns. Or we can head to Bloomington. There will be enough people to confront the mayor, plenty of guns aimed in his direction."

"I would, Marco, but I promised to return with evidence. If they allow it, and I don't find myself at the end of a rope, I've plenty for them."

"To New Harmony, then."

Chapter 78

Hyrum hesitated at the edge of New Harmony. Main Street stretched before him, filled with people. Ernie rode up alongside him. They both stared.

"Somethin's wrong," said Hyrum. "You heard the voices, everythin' the voices said underminin' the mayor. That happened before the bell rang."

"I heard it," said Ernie, "but did they?"

"Yeah, did they?" Hyrum pointed to the people filling the street. "I'm worried."

"Either way, we'd best go see. I've never seen the mayor so angry."

They waited for Jonas, who was only now catching up to them. "What do ya make of it?" he asked, rubbing his eyes and yawning.

Ignoring Jonas, Hyrum, and Ernie stared.

"Weston or the sheriff would've rung the bell. No one else," said Ernie. "More likely the sheriff's got it taken care of, whatever the emergency."

Jonas yawned again. "I'm tired. Leave it to the sheriff."

They continued into town when Ernie noticed someone with a gun in his hands up ahead. "Is that Vernon? And is that what I think it is, in plain sight?" He then noticed others with guns in hand. "Who's handing them out?"

"Yeah, and why would the sheriff allow that?" asked Hyrum.

"He wouldn't," said Ernie.

"Now I'm more worried," said Hyrum. "Like I said, somethin' ain't right."

The closer they got to the town center, the more rattled they became.

Ernie pulled back on the reins and stopped. "Look over there, in front of the town hall." He pointed to where people surrounded a wagon full of guns. "Someone's handing them out, and I don't see Weston or the sheriff."

"No! It's Old Man Taylor, that's who," said Hyrum. "What the hell's he doin'?"

Ernie kicked his horse and rode closer to the crowd, shouting, "Stop what you're doin' and put those back!" People turned to see him riding toward them, Hyrum and Jonas following behind. "Put them back now, I said. That's an order!"

A moment later, all three men found themselves looking down a half dozen barrels. Frantic, Ernie looked toward the town hall, expecting to see the sheriff. But instead, Eugene stood at the top of the steps. Behind him stood Eugene's mother—in shackles.

"Where's the sheriff?" Ernie yelled.

"Bring them here," Eugene called out, then turned to Vernon. "We'll be needing a few more shackles. Vernon excused himself and headed to the sheriff's office.

In no time, Ernie, Jonas, and Hyrum stood beside Martha, all shackled. Nellie stood beside Beatrice Moser while Vernon brought the podium out of the building and set it in front of Eugene. Once everyone recovered their rifles, pistols, and even a few old-style muskets, Eugene cleared his throat and called out to those gathered. "Please, everyone! Listen! I don't have the flowery words of my father; what I have is the truth."

It took awhile for the crowd to settle enough that everyone could hear.

Eugene waited patiently before continuing. "I was a young man, barely acquainted with the world, when Jedediah Hampshire, Emily's father, went missing. That's what you heard, but I knew differently. He didn't just go missing. I was older, fifteen years, when my father had me go with Sheriff Weasley. I watched as he stopped Emily's mother from breathing and left her behind the tavern. I was scared. When I asked the sheriff why, he said she died of an enlarged mouth. My father assumed you'd all say she died at the bottom of a bottle rather than at the hands of the sheriff. My father was right. That's what you did. But I knew otherwise. I knew the truth. My parents did all they could to ensure I'd never tell anyone while justifying the Hampshires' deaths on the altar of their comforts."

"Rubbish!" Martha screamed. "Don't believe him! My son's a liar! He doesn't know anything! My son aligned himself with Mr. Parrish in a treasonous plot. He's not to be trusted. You all knew he was in jail. Do you think we would put our son in jail for no reason?"

Eugene turned and addressed her so all could hear. "Mother, hold your peace. You'll have your turn once I've finished. Or I can have you gagged like those my father executed. They didn't get their say, did they?"

"Beatrice?" Eugene motioned for Beatrice Moser to step forward. She came up alongside him, and he introduced her to the crowd. "You all know Ms. Moser. She served our town and my family for many years before my birth. She knows the law, and we must follow it. There can be no vigilantism, or we are not better. So how must we proceed?"

Beatrice looked into the faces of those gathered, the ones who stood idly by as innocent people hung unlawfully, even chanting for their deaths. Quietly, so only Eugene could hear, she said, "It's of utmost importance you follow the law. Never deviate!"

Eugene answered so all could hear. "She insists we follow the law. All right, then. How?"

"Well . . ."

"Go on, Ms. Moser," said Eugene. "We're listening. Tell us how to proceed without losing the moral high ground."

"Hmm," said Beatrice. "With the mayor's office and the council compromised, I see only one way forward."

"And that is? Tell us."

"Very well. You must send all the accused to the district magistrate judge in Bloomington. But first you must read the charges, allow for the collection of evidence, and list all witnesses."

"Hear that, Mother? You're headed to Bloomington. I'll not have the consequences of your crimes on my conscience."

Martha screamed at the people, ignoring her son. "My son is sick! He needs help!"

Then the sound of Abigail's voice pierced the crowd. "This is not justice! It's an uprising is what! It's unlawful, an outrage, and you are all participants if you listen further! I suggest you all go home! Right now!"

Susannah and Elizabeth shouted for the people to disband and leave.

But the people became unruly, shouting and pointing fingers rather than disbanding, several raising their guns. Shouts of treason against the mayor were met with calls for clemency for the man who made the sun shine. New Harmony was divided while the more levelheaded called for calm. Eventually, the crowd settled down.

Eugene yelled as loud as his lungs allowed. "We are not a mob! We uphold the law! Anyone considering any other course of action—leave now! The truth serves the law, and the law serves the people. We are the people. Without the truth, the law subverts. Hear me then, and judge for yourselves."

Again, he waited for the crowd to settle before continuing. "Bronson Parrish came to my house just before my father had him executed. Mr. Parrish knew my father stole the election, as did I. I saw him do it. There was no other reason to hang Mr. Parrish but to keep the truth from you, and what was Mr. Parrish's crime? Knowing the truth and not keeping his mouth shut. And I knew if I were to say anything, my own family, like the Stewarts, would go missing and none would be the wiser. You'd all believe a lie, just as you always have. I regret not helping Mr. Parrish. I should have stood up to my father then, but I feared what he would do to my family. After what I saw my father do to Mr. Parrish and Mr. LeFevre, however, I could no longer hold my tongue. I was guilty by my silence. We are all guilty!"

Eugene's eyes searched the crowd. "Where's Old Man Taylor?"

Nellie whispered in his ear. "He went to get Weston at the ranch. He's due back soon."

"Thank you, dear," said Eugene, returning to the crowd. "I'm unable to prove any of this now, but I have reason to believe the monster's victims were no such . . ." Eugene stopped speaking, distracted by the sound of an approaching wagon. He looked north, his eyes widening. "Here comes Emily Hampshire now!"

Emily drove the wagon while Marco and Stu rode alongside. As the wagon and riders approached, the townspeople parted, allowing them to pass through.

Emily stopped short of the steps and called out, "Someone, please, I need a proper blanket. Anyone?"

Mrs. Lovell, who lived nearby, spoke up. "I'll go get one." She hurried away.

Everyone patiently waited for her to return. After a few minutes, she reemerged with a wool blanket held tightly in her arms. She handed it to Emily.

"Thank you, Mrs. Lovell. Would you please help me?"

Emily stepped over the seat and into the wagon bed. Mrs. Lovell stood on the other side of the bed, and together they spread the blanket over someone in the back. Emily lowered herself and then climbed the steps to where Eugene waited.

Scratched and bruised, her dress torn, gritty, and covered in coal dust, her face red from salty tears, Emily stood before the town. People were stunned at the sight of her, disheveled and bloodied. She stared out, looking at those gathered, not saying a word.

"Are you all right?" asked Eugene.

Emily nodded, then slowly approached the podium while gathering her thoughts. Marco climbed the steps and stood beside her. She took a deep breath and spoke clearly. "I have the evidence!"

The crowd gasped.

Boyd shouted, "Tell us! What have you?"

"I discovered where the mayor hides the bodies: in my father's mine, the one the mayor closed. You have only to follow the white marks on the crossbeams to find them. I found my father, the Stewarts, and others I can't say." Faces awash in shock and sympathy stared back at her. "Even the Stewart boy, young Matthew's body, lay discarded like trash in a coal shaft."

Several women cried, hardly believing their ears. In the solemn moment of remorse, the people heard the sound of an approaching wagon. Distracted, Emily looked south and recognized Weston, battered and beaten, his head bandaged. Still, he came.

"He's alive!" Heart full of gratitude, Emily stepped away from the podium.

Before she could run to him, Marco stopped her. "Don't concern yourself with Weston now," he told her. He's fine. I'll bring him here, but you must keep talking." Reluctantly, she returned to the podium as Marco assisted Weston up the steps.

"I must tell you things that are difficult to comprehend, but you must hear them. The creature we feared, that saw us locked away in our homes, was not as we supposed. Though I don't deny the physical form of a beast, he was anything but a monster. He even had a name. What the mayor claimed to be a monster now lies dead over there!" She pointed to the wagon with the body. "See for yourselves. He is no monster and never was, only in appearance."

Phillip Wallace's voice carried above the crowd. "But it was a monster! Attacked me and my boy!"

"I know what you saw, Mr. Wallace. I'm not saying you're lying. But tell me, tell everyone here what you saw. Could it have easily killed you?"

"Why, yes," admitted Wallace.

"Were you hurt?" asked Emily. "Did it so much as leave a single scratch to your skin? Can you show us any injuries?"

Wallace hesitated before answering. "No."

"And your son? What about him? Surely your boy can show us some evidence of injury?"

"No, but the teacher. It killed that teacher," said Wallace.

Emily shook her head. "Is there anyone here who saw the teacher murdered by the monster? Anyone?"

When no one spoke, Emily continued. "Mrs. Owen lured Constance Madison from the school, telling her lies to get her to come out. That's how they took her—the real monsters, the ones who murdered her, the mayor and the sheriff. And Mrs. Owen, she played her part."

Martha cried, "Lies! All lies! She speaks with the devil's tongue!"

Again, the crowd erupted at the accusation.

Eugene urged calm so Emily could continue. "Tell them what happened to you at the mine," said Marco. "That's what they need to hear."

Once the commotion subsided, Emily continued. "As I left here, promising to return with proof, the sheriff came and nearly took my life. But the stranger, the same who lies dead in the wagon, sacrificed his life to save me. Without his help, I would be dead, the promise I made to uncover the truth buried forever." She stared hard at the people, wiping away her tears. When we recover the bodies, you'll have your proof. Then what? Will you come to terms with the deaths of those many of you wished to see executed? Will you demand justice to ensure these crimes never harm the innocent again?"

Emily felt a tap on her shoulder and turned to see Weston. "May I?" She stepped aside and let Weston have the podium.

"The mayor," he said, "made a deal, admitted as much in front of the council. I was there. The appeasement offering, all your food, was divided between the council and witches."

Martha screamed at Weston. "What deal? There was no deal! This is all so ridiculous. Witches? No such thing." She turned and appealed to the people. "Surely you cannot believe this rubbish!"

"Not finished," said Weston. "Look no further for your offerings than in the homes and cellars of the council. You'll find the sheriff's share of your property in his cellar. What is missing was sacrificed to the witches on the mountain." Weston looked back at Eugene. "I'm done."

Eugene looked to Beatrice Moser. "What now?"

She pointed at the council and Martha. "Their turn to explain, offer a defense."

"Very well," said Eugene. "What of it? Any of you care to defend yourselves?"

Hyrum looked down and said nothing. Ernie shook his head, while Jonas shrugged and said, "I didn't want the food. I had enough."

Martha's eyes narrowed on her son. "So what? Believe what you want. They are not witches. Your father put them to the test."

"Then what, Mother? What are they?"

"Deceivers—deceivers of men. And we, the council, were just as deceived as the rest of you. We are all victims! If your father hadn't made a deal, the crops would've died and the entire town would have gone hungry. Would that have pleased any of you? You would've starved. Is that what you wanted? Do you want the truth? The truth is that each of you owes my husband, your mayor, and me—every single one of you. My husband did the hard things. He caused the sun to shine and the crops to grow. Or have you all forgotten?"

"So, Mother, was part of the arrangement to murder innocent people, people who threatened you or got in your way?"

"So what if it was? What difference does it make? Do the math, son. How many would have died from hunger? Besides, we were just as deceived as any of you. All of you begged for us to hang those people. If we are guilty, then so are you, every one of you." Martha turned her attention to Eugene. "You as well, son. You knew all along and did nothing. But if you consider it, since we're all accomplices, we're all innocent since we were all fooled."

"Was father misled when he killed Emily's parents? That was before the eclipse and the voices."

"Ach, the Hampshires. Insufferable, simpleminded fools. I had nothing to do with that. But you listen to me. Your father and I run this town. Without us, there is no New Harmony."

"Very good. Everyone, you've heard my mother." Eugene turned to Martha. "Have you anything more to say?"

Martha stared into the shocked faces staring back at her and lost her words. But no matter, she knew there was nothing left unsaid. Fate had turned against her, and her head hung low.

Eugene then addressed the crowd. "What are the demands of justice? As to the matter of my mother—Martha Owen—what say the people? Have you heard enough to send her shackled to Bloomington, to the judge there? You have each heard the evidence as would a proper court. What say you?"

This time, no voices sounded in their heads. Instead, their thoughts belonged to them and them alone, their judgments made from a place where evidence was based upon truth.

"Send her away," said Walter Buchanan. "Let her be tried for her crimes there." His wife agreed.

"To Bloomington," hollered Ms. Woolhauser.

Chants of "Bloomington!" rose up, loud and clear.

Eugene looked out and saw Abigail, Susannah, and Elizabeth. "Speak now, after hearing the evidence, if anyone believes my parents are innocent." The silence was deafening. "Ms. Moser?" She came alongside Eugene. "What now? What are the demands of the law?"

"That's it," said Beatrice. "Your parents will be tried fairly and dealt with according to the law."

"All right." Turning to the council members, he asked, "Where's my father?" None were anxious to answer. "Hyrum, you tell me. Where is he?"

"We left him on the mountain. He'll be coming soon."

Eugene looked to Ernie, who nodded, as did Jonas.

"Vern, please see to my mother. Have her climb the stairs to the gallows and wait for my father there. Perhaps then she will understand how Hannah Burroughs felt."

As Vern led her away, she swore at the council. "You swine! You all swore an oath of loyalty, God help you. You are all liars, and fire and brimstone will see to your souls."

"Calm yourself, Mother. We're not going to hang you today, and unlike those you condemned, you'll receive a fair trial. After that . . . Well, I'm sorry, Mother. I truly am. You may see a noose regardless."

But Martha wasn't finished. She screamed to the crowd. "Can't you all see the jealousy within yourselves? None here can stand to see others who have more, who earned and deserve much more than themselves. Your covetousness blinds you, and that goes for the council as well. They will say anything to save themselves. They are all weak men."

Hyrum stepped forward, voice raised, "Your husband leveraged our livelihoods. It was between following his orders, not to mention the sheriff's threats, or losing everything we worked for. What did you expect us to do? It was not jealousy, Mrs. Owen. It was survival."

"That's enough," said Eugene calmly. "We've all said our piece. Now we wait for my father. He'll be along soon."

Chapter 79

The apparition hoped for on Mount Erebus never materialized. Not a trace of the sisters of fate remained. The mayor finally gave up and headed down. Forced to abandon the wagon and sustenance, the trail no longer suitable for wagon travel, he rode bareback. Tired and beaten, he determined to head to the ranch house, slip under his blankets, and close his eyes. As he rode into New Harmony, he couldn't help but notice the commotion ahead. *What now?* he wondered as he heard the roar of the crowd gathered at the center of town.

I can't deal with anything more, he thought as he struggled to keep his eyes open. *The sheriff can handle whatever it is. Or it can wait until tomorrow.*

He thought of skirting the gathering, but he was too tired to think of an alternate route, and Buck trotted along. The closer he came, the harder it was to comprehend the drama in front of him. *There's someone on the gallows, but who? The sheriff must be plenty busy.*

He cocked his head and stared, the blood draining from his face. He felt like he would pass out. It couldn't be! The mayor screamed at the top of his lungs, "Stop! What's going on here?" Enraged, he rode toward the crowd gathered around the gallows. The people turned, as did the woman who stood under the crossbeam.

"Robert!" Martha screamed. "Help me!"

"Martha!" he hollered back. His horse stopped, and the mayor looked into her swollen eyes.

"Robert!" Again she screamed. Several men on horses weaved through the crowd and headed toward him, rifles in their hands.

In sheer terror, he turned Buck around and spurred him to a full gallop.

As he rode, he looked back to see the men in pursuit, riding as fast as they could. *I stand a chance if I reach the gorge—just a little farther!* Alongside fields of corn, wheat, and barley, he rode as swiftly as Buck could take him. Behind him lay everything he possessed, the accumulation of generations now stripped from him, the entirety of his life blotted out. The severity of the moment had turned the value of things upside down. Only survival mattered now.

Up ahead, he saw the gorge. *Almost there,* he thought. *If I can make it to the wilderness beyond, no one will find me.* He craned his neck and looked back as Buck slowed. He'd put some distance between him and his pursuers when Buck stumbled. Robert whipped the poor animal, but instead of carrying his rider farther away, Buck collapsed.

Over the horse's head he flew, arms and hands outstretched to break his fall as he tumbled end over end, impacting the gravel road and rolling to a stop. The mayor looked back at Buck as the animal struggled to gain his footing. He tried calling his horse, hoping to remount to further his escape. But once on his feet, Buck fled as if chased by a bear. The mayor looked up at the men pursuing him. How quickly they closed the distance!

He turned and looked in the direction of the gorge and then back at the men on horses. He'd never make it. Only then did he feel the darkness that surrounded him. He looked down at his aching hands, expecting to see bloodied palms. "What's this?" he cried. Startled, he stared hard at what should have been arms, hands, and fingers. *Where are my hands? What are these strange things, moving as I will them to move? These hairy things are not my fingers!*

For a moment, he was distracted from the men fast approaching. Then, hearing the thundering of horses, he looked to the gorge.

He urged himself up off the ground and raced forward. The men on horses kept coming, but he was faster, faster than men on horseback with no time to question why. He got to the gorge and dove into the brush but didn't stop there. He ran the rest of the day until he felt an odd sensation inside his head. He stopped and slumped down among the shrubs that grew along the creek.

Now what? He pressed his paws to his head.

Something or someone had painted his memories black, his remembrances of New Harmony fading into the recesses of a mind locked away. He peered into the heavens and cursed his Creator for whatever this was. Then, high above him, he saw the blackbirds circling. He growled and snorted. For some reason incomprehensible to him, he loathed the creatures. He screamed, but echoing through the mountain pass was the cry of a wounded animal. He stole into the woods, never to see New Harmony again.

Chapter 80

Coot ran ahead as Marco and Tommaso walked east down Parrish Lane. Further on, they could see the tall oaks and willows that bordered the New Harmony cemetery, casting long shadows into the neighboring fields in the early morning sunlight. Above the mature trees, the starlings soared in waves, scattering and smoothly coming together as if sweeping the sky above, whisking away the hovering spirits of the newly departed. Tommaso was grateful to be back in New Harmony. Everything felt different, more peaceful.

"You say they're already there?" asked Tommaso.

"Yes, Papa. Emily sent word that she'd be waiting for us at the gate. She appears to be up ahead."

"And Albert and Marjorie?"

"They too," said Marco. "Now they have more than just a marker for Emily's father. It's certain to bring them comfort. He lies next to her mother. But not only him. Emily requested that Mr. Carver be buried nearby. He lies next to her father."

"Moses?"

"Yes, Moses. According to Emily, he and her father were friends. She took the news of his death very hard, almost as if she were responsible."

"From what I hear," said Tommaso, "the sheriff bears the full weight."

"He does," agreed Marco. "But let's not speak of it in front of her."

"Course not," said Tommaso. They walked along the path that followed the slatted green fence lining the cemetery. Up ahead, Emily waited among the yellowish-brown leaves that fluttered in the crisp fall breeze, some tumbling like gentle rain.

As they walked, Marco grinned. "Look there. She sees us coming."

"Hello, young Emmy!" Tommaso hollered.

"Hello, Mr. Salvatori! Marco!"

Tommaso beamed. "We're coming."

"I see you are, Mr. Salvatori."

"Your aunt and uncle, are they here?"

"They are, sir. Auntie has laid yellow roses on the Burroughs' graves already. She has plenty for Christian and Mrs. Salvatori. They're waiting for us where Weston placed markers for Mr. Parrish and Mr. LeFevre. Sadly, they are only markers."

"Very good," said Tommaso as they greeted each other with hugs.

Emily and Marco passed through the gate, side by side, when they noticed Tommaso had fallen behind. They looked back to see him gazing into the sky, lost in contemplation, as the flock of starlings soared high above them. The starlings moved, bound together in life, swirling about, nearly brushing the ground, then rising high above the earth while banking off the breeze from the east. It was an unpredictable ballet, a display of wonder.

Tommaso's eyes widened, and he quietly mumbled, more to himself than anyone else. "The fall and redemption, ever the same."

Marco called to him. "Papa?"

"Hmm?"

"Papa, what did you say?"

"The birds, son."

Marco and Emily gazed into the azure sky. "What about them, Papa?"

With a small sigh, Tommaso quietly said, "They bring a memory."

"They are beautiful, Mr. Salvatori," exclaimed Emily, a hand over her heart when she heard a melody coming from trees lining the cemetery. "Is that what I think it is—what I'm hearing?"

Marco asked, "What is it you hear?"

"Can it be a whippoorwill this late in the morning? Especially when they are so rarely heard at all but never at this time of day? Usually, they sing only after sunset and sometimes before the sun rises."

Marco listened more attentively. "I believe it is a whippoorwill."

"Yes," said Tommaso, "it don't seem to mind the time. Sings all the same."

Under her breath, Emily whispered, "Mama? Can you hear the whippoorwill? Can you see the starlings?"

Marco turned a curious eye to Emily. "Pardon me?"

Lost in memory, Emily paused before answering. "Just that my auntie told me about how, when I was born, a whippoorwill appeared on the windowsill just before the coming dawn. It is said that they gather souls and deliver them safely to heaven."

"Yes, I've heard it rumored," said Marco. "Not scientifically proven, but . . ."

"No, Marco," admitted Emily, "I suppose not. It's only something people say."

Marco raised an eyebrow. "There are, however, things unprovable yet real."

"Miracles," said Emily.

"Miracles all around us," said Tommaso, clearing his throat. "Consider the starlings, how they fly, all together as if one"

They each gazed skyward. "That is something," said Marco. "How is it accomplished? How do they know when to soar upward, or downward, or to turn with such elegant synchronicity? How do they not collide and tumble from the sky?"

Tommaso raised his hands and, standing amid the living and the dead, said, "Life! Life is in full display. Are we so different? What we do, others have done before. They've experienced the same pain, the same joy, the same love. All the same. It's one eternal round. The starlings, what they're doing up there, where did it start? Where does it end? One dies and another takes its place. Forever."

"No, Papa. We aren't," said Marco, captivated by the starlings whirling high above them.

Then, without a word, the three moved together, following Coot as he sniffed the grass, exploring his new surroundings. They came to where Caterina and Christian lay beneath a sheet of winter grass, a yellow flower already placed for each. Tommaso knelt and touched Christian's wooden marker, examining the handiwork. "Weston made a new marker. It's good."

"He did, Papa. Weston is a good man."

"He took good care, I see."

"Yes, Papa. I believe he hurts badly. I think this new marker is Weston making amends."

Tommaso next visited Caterina's grave. He kissed his fingers and gently touched her marker. "Amore mio," he said.

"I'll give you some privacy," said Emily, excusing herself. She joined her aunt and uncle at Mr. Parrish's and Mr. LeFevre's markers, which Weston had placed beside Theodore, Suzanne, and young Matthew Stewart's graves. And next to the Stewarts lay the parson and Hannah, their placement meant to remind people of the tyranny that had wreaked havoc on New Harmony.

Once she'd placed a flower on each of their graves, Emily took the last yellow rose and walked to the far corner of the cemetery in the shade of a solitary cottonwood tree. She knelt at a lone grave that held a stranger to everyone in New Harmony but her, someone believed to be a monster. And yet, only weeks before, his casket had led the procession, delivered to the cemetery in the glossy black funerary wagon pulled by a shiny black stallion. Behind the funerary wagon, the others, the victims of the evil that plagued New Harmony, arrived in wagons adorned with gardenias, lilies, and roses. It was Jonathan's and the other's final earthly journey, and the bell above the school rang the entire way.

Emily knelt at Jonathan's marker and ran her fingers over the words carved in the wood: "Jonathan 1860," and below his name, "Our friend." In the quiet, she whispered, "Thank you, Jonathan. You were no monster, not to me. I will always be grateful, and you will always live in my thoughts and heart." She placed the flower on his grave and stood.

Marco cautiously approached, not wanting to interrupt. "Forgive me, Emmy, but are you ready to leave? Your Aunt Margie asked that I remind you she has supper waiting."

"All right, Marco, but I've one last thing to do." She stood and walked to Christian's grave. Marco came up alongside her. "Marco, please, would you give me a moment with your brother?"

"Certainly, and don't feel rushed. You've all the time you need." He nodded before heading to the front gate, where the others waited.

Alone, Emily knelt in the grass beside Christian's marker. Hoping her words somehow found their way over as many mountains, valleys, or oceans as were required to reach his ears, she softly said, "I never got to say goodbye. I want you to know the sheriff paid with his life for what he did to you, though it doesn't make it hurt any less. You're still not here by my side, my love, and I don't know how to move on, to stop loving you. If I brought you any peace in this life, please help me now." She wiped the tears from her face and slowly rose to her feet. She saw everyone waiting and started walking toward them before turning and whispering, "Goodbye. I'll always love you."

Chapter 81

Black smoke from a trash fire floated high above New Harmony. No bell rang to put it out. No bell rang to show respect. Instead, wooden planks and boards burned at the landfill, along with the crossbeam used to hang the innocent. In the end, the fire didn't spare the innocent or the guilty. Weston stared into the red-hot flames as they consumed the lifeless body of Sheriff Weasley. He offered no words of comfort, tears, farewells, or goodbyes.

On his way home, he drove the empty wagon down the road that passed the Owen ranch. Pulling back on the reins, he stopped in front of the house. He'd promised Eugene he would visit when he could. *I suppose now is as good a time as any*, he thought, *though no more of my apologies can lessen my guilt.*

As he sat and lamented his past, he heard a voice.

"Weston! Over here!"

He suddenly regretted having stopped.

"Weston!" Eugene called from the ranch house beyond the now sparse poplar trees that partially hid the Owen property. "I've something to discuss with you," he hollered. "Can we speak?"

Weston pulled onto the road that led to the ranch and through the open gate. As he approached, he noticed Eugene sat in the rocking chair on the porch, grinning.

Perhaps this will be a pleasant visit.

"So good to see you, my friend," said Eugene. "I've been waiting for you."

"Oh! You have?"

"I have."

"Well, I took care of . . . you know . . . at the landfill. Won't be seeing the sheriff around."

"An unpleasant task. I'm grateful you took care of it. We won't see my mother either."

"Heard. Are you all right?"

"I'm not sure. While she was my mother, I find tears are a mystery to me . . . or I should say the lack of tears. Nellie tells me that a mother's work and sacrifices are what bonds a mother to her child and a child to its mother. She sees no mystery in my lack of tears, not when my mother relegated her parental responsibilities to the servants. When I read the letter from the judge in Bloomington saying they found her dead in her holding cell, I could only conclude that she couldn't live with her conscience. I'd like to believe that, somewhere inside, she had one."

"Her choice may be a mercy to you."

Eugene looked curiously at Weston. "How so?"

"Well," said Weston, "she saved Nellie and you the hardship of a trial."

"Hmm. I believe you're being far too generous. I can imagine how bitter she felt when my father ran away like a coward, leaving her with the burden. It's truly tragic. Either way, she's in God's hands now."

Weston's shoulders drooped, and he spoke quietly. "Eugene, I wanted to say how sorry I am."

"What for?" asked Eugene.

"I was party to all of it, not just your mother. For that, I—"

"Oh, never mind all that. Please, won't you come inside?" Eugene opened the front door wide. "Why, if it weren't for you, things would be far different, far worse."

Eugene led him into the ranch house. Weston had never seen the inside. His eyes widened. "That such a beautiful place is found in New Harmony, it's—"

"Embarrassing?"

"No," said Weston. "It's magnificent!" He stared at the wood floors.

Eugene noticed and said, "Yes, the wood shines like glass. Nellie loves the lacquer."

"What's lacquer?"

Eugene grinned. "Something new from Italy. Weston, much of what you see belongs to you."

"I'm confused. What are you saying?"

Eugene's expression became solemn. "I believe you do know, brother."

The wrinkles in Weston's forehead grew long. "I don't understand."

"What I'm saying," said Eugene, "is that we are half brothers, you and me. It no longer needs to be a secret. Half of all this is yours. Tell me you did not suspect it all along."

Weston nodded. "I did, but I don't want any of it." With his coat sleeve, he quickly wiped at the tear that rolled down his cheek. "I only had one father, Wayne Riley, and he disappeared. There's no more to it than that. No offense."

"None taken. But you understand that that doesn't mean half of all this can't be yours."

"No! No, Eugene. I would dishonor my father to accept your offer. All this is yours. I could never . . ."

"It's not all mine, not all of it. And I'm removing my father's name from all the deeds and businesses in New Harmony. Because the ranch belonged to my grandfather, an honest man, I'll keep it. But it wasn't enough for my father, who had his fingers in everyone's pockets. Whatever he took, I'll return. As for your interest, please forgive me, Weston, but I had to offer."

"And you did. But now, can we keep the secret, if for nothing else . . ."

"Well, yes, but I had to tell Nellie, though she is unique among women. No one will ever know. We will both honor your wishes."

Sniffling, Weston said, "I've brought enough dishonor to my family. I deserve worse, but not my father, so thank you."

"Think nothing of it. And since we're speaking of your father, I heard Marco and Vernon found him in the mine with the others."

"They did. I began to worry until he and Emily's father, Jedediah, were found at last. I buried him next to my mother on the hill that overlooks the house."

"Finally having him home, Weston, must be comforting."

Weston nodded. "Nothing short of a blessing."

Eugene smiled broadly. "Well and good. You found your father, and as fate would have it, I now am the son of a missing father. If only I had tears. But I've only regrets that things were not different."

"I've plenty, too many, of my own regrets," said Weston. "And now, is there anything more? I should be leaving."

"There is. I have something to ask of you."

"Who me?" asked Weston.

"Yes, you."

"All right, I'm listening."

"Well, you heard I'm filling in as mayor until November when the town has an election. I agreed because, as I said, I wanted to remove my family's interests from all the deeds and businesses my father finagled. It'll only be for a short time, and I won't run to replace my father. But I know who will or, at least, who ought to."

"Not me!" said Weston. "Haven't I done enough harm? People will never trust me again, nor should they."

"Don't be so hard on yourself," said Eugene. "Think about it. Would you? You do have experience on the council."

Weston looked sternly at Eugene. "There's no need for me to think about it. Yeah, I was there on the council, followed your father, did what he said. I built the gallows." Weston stared at his hands. "Those were my nails and my hammer. My hands! I watched innocent people hang and did nothing. And when the parson and Mrs. Burroughs hung, I saw something . . . something that made me know I was condemned. There is no coming back for me."

"I was there, Weston. I was forced to witness what happened. I saw it all. What more could you have seen than I did?"

"Did you see them leave this world before the sheriff pulled the lever?"

"What? No."

"I did. I saw them . . . delivered from evil, delivered from the gallows I built. It was God's own mercy. The town may not hold me responsible, but I will never forgive myself. I am condemned forever. But you, you can do something. You can restore honor to your family's name. That's something you should do."

"If what you are suggesting is politics, well, Weston, the Owen family is tarnished in that regard, and for good reason."

"Yes, but you can do something about it," said Weston. "Look, I'm not certain how to say this, but I'll say it just the same. I'm the one in need of forgiveness, not you. Your guilt is only by association. Right now, New Harmony needs a Mayor Owen but one with a good heart who loves the people. We serve in the way God intends, and the people will decide. Hold a fair election, and if the people choose as I suspect they will, you'll be mayor. Then, generations from now, there'll be a Mayor Owen regarded with fondness. Redeem your family name; there's honor in that, and at least you can find peace there. But what can I do? I can never make amends for my bad deeds."

"Now, now, Weston. You concern me, my friend," said Eugene. "Surely you can do something as well."

"Very well, tell me what."

"I don't know. Perhaps remain on the council. That's where you might start."

"No. What I need I could never find there."

"Tell me," said Eugene. "What is it you need?"

"Forgiveness. I need forgiveness. Even if others forgive me, I can never forgive myself. And so I may never find it. I've nowhere to even look."

Eugene nodded understandingly and patted Weston on the back. "I can't imagine what would have happened if it hadn't been for you, my friend. I shudder to think about it. Listen, I feared my father my entire life. I spent hours struggling with how to stand up to him, always falling short. He considered me weak, lacking the determination to elevate my status at any cost. I tried. I tried to make him proud. But the more effort I put into it, the worse I felt about myself. Even so, I did what I had to. In some regard, I believe our histories run parallel. Although we may both be plagued with sleepless nights, wondering what took us so long, we eventually stood up to him. Perhaps we can find solace in that, and in the end, what choice is there but to live with it?"

"Well, isn't that the hard part?" asked Weston. "The living-with-it part?"

"Yes, something my mother wasn't capable of doing, unfortunately. But you and I were accomplices. Finding forgiveness and forgiving ourselves will take time. Meanwhile, be kind to yourself, Weston. You're a good man. I'm thankful to have you as a brother, though it will remain our secret."

"Well then, thank you, brother. Our secret."

Chapter 82

Emily traversed the short path through the pink and yellow rose bushes, noting the empty trough. There was no one to refill it. Upon arriving at the church's front doors, she was overcome with sorrow, seeing the broken hinges and splintered wood. She imagined how horrible it must have been for the parson and Hannah to hear who she suspected was the sheriff breaching the sanctuary. She shook her head in disgust. *They would have opened the doors had he knocked.* Swinging the heavy wooden doors open, she peered inside and smiled.

Rays of light shining through the stained-glass window above the pulpit banished the shadows of the empty interior. The darkness that once enveloped New Harmony was gone, and the colors from the window filled the chapel with a hopeful brilliance. She looked at the window as if seeing it for the first time.

Careful not to disturb the peace, she quietly moved forward, passing the rows of seats as she walked down the aisle, her eyes never straying from the colorful depiction etched in the window. She stopped just before the front row of seats and sat down, reverently bowing her head. From somewhere behind her in the stillness, she heard a faint sound. Realizing she wasn't alone, she turned to see Weston sitting in the back corner, his head down. He seemed unaware of her presence.

"Weston?" she called to him.

"Yeah?"

"What are you doing here?" Weston sat motionless.

"I suppose the same thing you're doing here," he said as if speaking to the floorboards.

"Don't!" said Emily.

"Don't what?" Weston finally looked up. "Don't what?" he repeated.

"Don't think you could have done it any differently."

"And you are referring to what, exactly?"

Emily walked back to where Weston sat. His shoulders drooped with the weight of shame. She sat down quietly, waiting for inspiration, praying for the right words. She looked up at the window and saw something she hadn't noticed before. Finding the inspiration she'd hoped for, she reached out, placing her hands over his clenched fists. "How many times have you seen that window?"

"Why? I mean, I don't know."

"Well, look again," she urged. "Please, Weston, just do it."

He looked at her. "In my defense, I'm not usually like this," he said, his eyes red and swollen.

"There's no shame in having feelings."

His fists relaxed, and he looked at the window. Together, they stared at the light beaming brilliantly through the stained glass.

"Can you see it?" Emily asked.

"See what? Emmy, please. Don't take me for being rude, but I've seen the window more times than I can count."

"So you see it? Or am I alone in having not noticed it before?"

Weston let out a sigh. "What is it I'm supposed to see?"

"Something I hadn't seen before," said Emily. "But now I see it in a new light."

"I'm listening. Go on."

"Peter's hair."

"What about it?"

"It's wet," she said, "nearly covering his face."

Eyebrows raised, Weston looked at her as if she'd lost her mind. "So what if his hair is wet?"

"Exactly! So what if Peter went under the water? We all go underwater."

"And what does that mean?"

"You still don't understand?"

"Suppose not."

"Look. Peter's not sinking as everyone supposes. He's rising. Maybe going under the water is the point." Emily could tell by Weston's expression that he began to understand. "Look, I was in the church with the parson when the town was under a shadow. The window with Peter and the Savior was dark, as if underwater. I couldn't see it then, but look at the light streaming in now. It shines, the window; it's shining, and Peter is rising, do you see? But only after being submerged and not having the necessary faith. Weston, we, too, are rising. So, what if going under the water is the point of all this? It is the struggle for the soul, as the parson taught. So what if our hair is wet? So what if we went under the waves? It isn't what matters, is it?"

Emily stood, walked to the front of the chapel, and entered the parson's office. She took the Bible from his desk and returned, handing it to Weston. "This is yours. Tomorrow's Sunday. I'm going to ring the bell in the morning at nine o'clock. Have a sermon prepared. Tell them Peter denied Christ three times and the rooster crowed. Tell them we've all made mistakes. We must all find forgiveness. In this very church, the parson once told me to bring the light. Now I'm telling you. You now have a calling. Understand?" Emily smiled and headed to the door.

"Emmy?"

"Yes, Weston."

"Remember the flowers?"

"Of course."

"They were from me."

"I know."

"Emmy?"

"Yes, Weston."

"I'll be ready in the morning."

"Good, very good," she said. "Things are as they're meant to be. You help people find forgiveness, and you'll find it for yourself."

"Very well, Emmy. But will you do something for me?"

Emily nodded. "All right, what would that be?"

"Would you pay a visit to Ms. Abigail Williams, and, um . . . Ms. Boyer and Ms. Howe?"

"For you, I will, but why?"

"Invite them to Sunday service. They have the same need I do."

"Hmm . . ." said Emily. "Whatever doubts I might have had no longer remain. I am left only with the calm assurance of your calling. Your heart yearns for the redemption of all, and that's what New Harmony needs. And you, Weston, are meant for this. I suspect Hannah and the parson look down on you now, pleased as can be."

"Thank you, Emmy. Perhaps I'll believe it myself—in time."

"In time." Emily nodded, then slowly turned and walked out of the church without another word, leaving him in good company.

Chapter 83

One Year Later

Large paws dug into the moldering log by the creek, unleashing the rancid smell of decay. Drawn by the odor, the beast foraged through the rotten wood underneath, sniffing for termites, red ants, and whatever juicy morsels it could find. Having had its fill, the beast strolled to the creek, wetting its tongue, lapping up the fresh water, then splashing about to cool off. As it lumbered about, its head swayed from side to side, its eyes peeled for the next meal. Little concerned the beast outside of food, not even the blackbirds circling high overhead.

In the heat of the afternoon sun, the beast sought the shade of a nearby cottonwood tree. It scratched at the chiggers and fleas as it leaned against an earthen mound of rock and dirt.

From above, the blackbirds screeched, causing the beast to freeze. Suddenly, with eyes wide and ears at full attention, it heard eerie sounds penetrate its mind. Quickly, it raised off its belly and began shuffling about, clawing at the dirt. Violently thrashing its head, it could not quiet the words, though incomprehensible, that reverberated through its skull.

"How satisfying seeing you thus!" said an ancient voice.

"And how effortlessly you've surrendered," said another. "Quite satisfying."

"Yes, quite," came a third voice.

"We can practically taste your bitterness even though you've no recollection of whence it came. Such bitterness. How exquisite!" came the trio of voices.

The beast met each exclamation of satisfaction with snorting and growling.

"I'm afraid the beast doesn't understand. How quickly our monster has lost its words."

The beast bolted through the tall Indian grass and into a grove of elms to escape the frightening noise, then cowered under a hedge of black chokeberry and butterfly weed, but the voices were unrelenting.

Said the high-pitched voice with delight, "Much rather have this one than the other."

"I agree, sisters," said the most ancient of the three. "This one is much more deserving. The more deserving, the more delightful."

Then, two sisters begged the older, "Can we take him down now?"

"Patience, dear sisters," said the more ancient one. "To every soul we weave a yarn, the length of which is measured in minutes, days, and years. Speak not of today but of tomorrow when I take the scissors in hand and sever the yarn."

"And that is why you, more than we, are feared by some and welcomed by others."

"Yes, at the next eclipse, I will take my scissors, meting out justice, yet, curiously, we will still hear the sound of heaven weeping."

Epilogue

A calm, eastwardly breeze rolled across the tall grass in waves, and the leaves on the trees quivered above the trickling brook. Under the warmth of the sun, a flurry of exotic flowers opened into lovely blooms transcending anything Emily had ever seen. She inhaled the perfumed air and looked up into the blissfully blue sky. Cottony white clouds drifted aimlessly by as if lost on the breeze. A familiar barking distracted her. She looked over her shoulder to see Tippy running down a grassy green hill, coming toward her.

Tippy, I haven't seen you in years! Why, I was just a little girl. It's been so long.

His tail, black as coal but for the white tip, wagged as he moved back and forth through the emerald-green grass. She noticed Christian and Marco headed toward her down the same hill in an unbroken bond of brotherhood.

Christian picked flowers as he went along. He hesitated, wanting to choose only the finest, but they were all perfect. Marco did the same, gathering all manner of perennials. Finally, they came to a place where they both stopped. Tippy ran to them, his tail wagging excitedly. Christian handed Marco the flowers he'd picked as the shadow of a cloud passed overhead. A moment later, it moved off, leaving the green hill bathed in sunlight once again. Marco added the flowers he'd gathered to those Christian handed him, the bouquet now a collection of both.

Christian knelt, and Tippy snuggled into his side.

Tippy loves Christian as I do, Emily thought.

Christian brushed his long black bangs aside as he always did, the smile that followed sending tremors through her.

It was then Emily noticed that only Marco came toward her, with Christian and Tippy looking on from farther up the hill.

Can't they come down? she worried.

Her concern dissipated as she watched a smiling Marco approach with the flowers he and his brother had gathered, a bouquet rich in color and variety. Their splendor defied description, so vibrant as to suggest she'd somehow gotten lost in a dream.

Marco handed her the bouquet, and she gently touched the petals. *Am I still in Indiana? Are roses here this red, sunflowers this yellow, lilacs so purple, and lilies as white as if their petals dropped from heaven? Are they to be found so vibrant and perfect in New Harmony?* She inhaled the sweet, delicate scent of the lavender and pink cherry blossoms. Her eyes found Marco, and in his face, she saw gentleness and a depth of feeling she hadn't previously noticed. She saw a good man, a man she suspected loved her. There was evidence of it in his eyes. A sense of peace flooded her.

Hugging her pillow more tightly, Emily dreamed on, feelings of contentment and gratitude bringing a smile to her face. She'd brought the light and finally felt at peace. And now, deep within, she heard a new song, her heart beating in harmony with that of another.

In the morning, she woke with a craving. But before she did anything about it, she responded to another letter from a Union soldier, a doctor who faithfully wrote her every week. Loyal to his commander and his president, whom he referred to as Father Abraham, he believed he was making a difference in the world.

Long after the neighbor's rooster announced the new day, Emily had asked Aunt Marjorie for a favor. Together, they'd bustled about the kitchen, mixing ingredients and filling the house with the scent of something divine, a scent that no longer triggered the pain and discomfort of all she'd lost. She smiled as she pulled the cider cake from the oven, thinking of how it now reminded her of her mother's love.

Old-Fashioned Cider Cake Recipe

Ingredients

    1 cup vegetable oil
    1½ cups sugar
    1 tsp vanilla
    2 eggs
    1 cup fresh, local apple cider
    2½ cup flour
    1½ tsp baking powder
    1 tsp baking soda
    1 tsp salt
    1 tsp cinnamon
    ½ tsp ground cloves
    ¼ tsp allspice

Yield: two 8" round cakes, or one 9" × 13" pan

Directions

Using a mixer (or by hand), blend the oil and sugar until well mixed.

Add the vanilla and eggs and blend thoroughly.

Combine the dry ingredients and add to the bowl—mix in slowly while adding the apple cider—just until everything is smooth and incorporated.

Pour batter into greased cake pans and bake at 350° for approx. 30–35 minutes, or just until center is done when tested with a toothpick.

Allow cake to cool and turn out of pans if desired.

Dust with confectioner's sugar to serve.

Enjoy!

Courtesy of Mann Orchards (Since 1877 Methuen, MA)

To the Reader

Did you enjoy this book? I'd love to hear what you thought about it. Please leave a review wherever you bought this book or wherever fine books are sold. It would mean so much to me as reviews are a book's lifeblood

To contact me, learn more about me and Groundswell Books, receive bonus content, or subscribe to my mailing list and be notified of future events and publications, please visit StevenLRirie.com.

About the Author

Steven L Ririe is the founder and chairman of the Silent Heroes of the Cold War National Memorial Committee. In 1998, he uncovered the details of a top-secret plane crash near the peak of Mount Charleston, Nevada. USAF 9068 was en route to Area 51 when it crashed into the mountain on November 17, 1955. Due to the classified nature of the mission, the families of the fourteen men who perished were kept in the dark as to the fate of their loved ones. Thanks to Steve's efforts, these families were notified, their loved ones recognized, and a memorial built in their honor.

The fate of Flight 9068 and Steve's quest to bring closure to the victims' families was featured on the Travel Channel's *Mysteries at the Museum,* in the Russian edition of *Newsweek,* and in the *Smithsonian Air and Space Magazine.*

Steve has been a Las Vegas, Nevada, resident since 1961 and is a member of the Association of Former Intelligence Officers. In June

2002, Steve testified before Congress on preserving Cold War historical sights and artifacts while recognizing the Silent Heroes of the Cold War National Memorial with a Congressional designation. Both memorials were dedicated in May 2015.

In addition, for nearly two decades, Steve has volunteered in a ministry at the Southern Desert Correctional Center, overseeing the spiritual needs of the inmates there. He lives with his wife, Marianna, has four adult daughters, and is a proud grandfather. Learn more about the 1955 top-secret plane crash on the Facebook page *Silent Heroes of the Cold War.*

To learn more about Steve and his books, check out StevenLRirie.com.

About the Series
As the Starlings Fly

The setting is the mid-1800s, just before the American Civil War, a period that closely mirrors our world today. Today, citizens of the United States are divided, just as in the mid-1800s. This was when Robert Owen founded a utopian socialist experiment in New Harmony, Indiana. To Steve's knowledge, Owen pioneered socialism. Steve believes that while Owen's intentions were noble, he created the poison apple that is communism, granting far too much power to the government at the expense of the people.

Now, some may read the series only for the story. Others will come away with an understanding of the spiritual implications and hidden meanings found in the intricate workings of humanity that either bring freedom and prosperity or authoritarianism and poverty. Steve hopes his series finds its way into the hands of a new generation that is unaware of the nuclear threat they face at every moment, day and night. He hopes his words will help them know they can be the light that outshines those who would plant fear and rob them of freedom and the pursuit of happiness.

www.ingramcontent.com/pod-product-compliance
Lightning Source LLC
LaVergne TN
LVHW091532070526
838199LV00001B/28